$25.95

The Crimson Palace

The Crimson Palace

Jacqueline Briskin

G.K. Hall & Co. • **Chivers Press**
Thorndike, Maine USA   Bath, Avon, England

This Large Print edition is published by G.K. Hall & Co., USA
and by Chivers Press, England.

Published in 1996 in the U.S. by arrangement
with Bert Briskin.

Published in 1997 in the U.K. by arrangement with the author.

U.S. Hardcover 0-7838-1929-3   (Core Collection edition)
U.K. Hardcover 0-7451-5403-4   (Windsor Large Print)
U.K. Softcover 0-7451-3858-6   (Paragon Large Print)

The text of this Large Print edition is unabridged.
Other aspects of the book may vary from the original edition.

Set in 16 pt. Bookman Old Style.

Printed in the United States on permanent paper.

British Library Cataloguing in Publication Data available

Library of Congress Cataloging in Publication Data

Briskin, Jacqueline.
   The crimson palace / Jacqueline Briskin.
     p.   cm.
   ISBN 0-7838-1929-3 (lg. print : hc)
   1. Soviet Union — History — Revolution, 1917–1921 —
Fiction. 2. Large type books. I. Title.
[PS3552.R49C75 1996]
813'.54—dc20   96-29261

Prologue

Long before the Crimson Palace was built, the nomadic fisherfolk who eked out a living in the inhospitable northern swampland believed that this one particular bank of the Neva was sacred: on summer nights, when opalescence never left the sky, the curve in the broad river gave off a strange pink glow. Here at the hallowed midnight hour, priestesses would gather to cast their runes and perform the other secret rituals that ensured a good catch.

After Peter the Great had thrust a borrowed bayonet into the sodden earth, the first excavation for St Petersburg, his magnificent new capital, the thousands of unequipped serfs forced to dredge the swamp and construct the city lived in hovels along the once sacred bank. Many decades later their descendants were evicted by Catherine the Great: the tsarina had decided on this site to erect a palace for her young Paskevich favourite, a monument of sorts to his virility. Sensitive to the roseate quality in the pale summer nights, the empress chose crimson walls to complement the immense Italian marble pediment that depicted her and her lover cavorting with gods and goddesses. In winter, the snow and the frozen river refracted sunlight with such dazzling intensity that the contrast between vivid red paint and white marble hurt the eye.

Later generations of Paskeviches would dot the endless Russian horizon with mansions and villas, but the Crimson Palace remained the place to which they brought their most cherished treasures, amongst which was an American girl, my grandmother, Marya Alexiev.

In my memory she lives on as a tiny old lady not much taller than I, who applied cosmetics with movie-star abandon, wore her curly white hair short like a halo, and favoured trouser suits — at the time, considered indescribably daring in San Francisco. To me she was a tremendous figure. When I visited her we shared a ritual of being ceremoniously served Blum's coffee crunch cake, a sinfully rich concoction, and hot chocolate topped with a melting snowcap of whipped cream. If I stayed the night, she let me stay up to watch the *Dinah Shore Show.* But these sybaritic pleasures weren't the real attraction of the immense apartment on Nob Hill. I hungered for the magical tales of her ten-year sojourn in Russia — memories she usually kept locked away like the jewellery in the wall safe behind her mink and sable coats. I can remember sitting on her thick white carpet with my scabby knees drawn up to my chin, asking a question about her life in that vanished world; then holding my breath, waiting, hoping, praying that those oddly pale, mascaraed eyes would take on a faraway glaze which meant she would begin to talk. The gypsy fortune-tellers, the great barbaric gems, the armies of servants, the seventeen silk evening gowns, the champagne suppers, the extravagances that were hers during her tenure as a mistress. Later, she had given herself utterly to love. She'd survived tragedies, been witness to monumental events of the Revolution, seen horrors that would haunt her sleep for ever. In the Civil War she had assassinated one of Lenin's right-hand men.

Because I loved, admired and, to a certain extent, feared my perfumed little grandmother, it wasn't until long after her death that it crossed my mind that her memories might have been fingered so often that they were moulded into legend. After all, she was of a romantic temperament and quite old. And yet she never played to the gallery; in fact she generally was oblivious to her audience — me. If she hadn't been, she would have censored many of the details in what I've come to call her Crimson Palace years.

1909

The unlimited and supreme Autocratic power belongs to the Emperor of All the Russias. God Himself commands that he be obeyed.

Article of law dating from the reign of Peter the Great

Russia is under a regime of reinforced surveillance . . . The army of regular and secret police grows continually. The prisons and places of deportation are filled with those sentenced for political reasons . . .

Excerpts from a letter of protest written by Leo Tolstoy to Tsar Nicholas II

Chapter One

Marya Alexiev gripped the forward rail of the Channel steamer. In weather like this, the French coastline would remain invisible for several hours, but she gazed eagerly towards the grey-blurred horizon. This would be her first sight of continental Europe. The unpleasant easterly and occasional spits of rain had sent passengers below, none of the crew was in sight, and Marya was unaware of the tall, hatless young man who had stood at the bow facing back towards England. As the dark, mottled clouds swallowed up the chalk cliffs he began to walk along the port side, adjusting his easy stride to the roll of the deck.

Believing herself alone, Marya had done nothing to prevent her coat — a peculiar anachronism with full bustle-like gathers — from blowing up to reveal her slender calves and the long darn in her white lisle stocking. Her hat, far newer, was large-brimmed and difficult to control in the wind. She pulled it off, squashing the buckram-stiffened velvet under her arm. Released, her thick red curls flew back like a pennon.

At a sharper gust, the steamer wallowed sideways. The slant of deck took her by surprise. Her small boots slipped perilously on the varnished wet planks. She gyrated wildly, her arms windmilling. The hat skimmed into a roiling grey hill of water. Gripping hard on the sea-wet rail, she managed to keep her balance.

Then, abruptly, the prow dived downwards.

Her cry was swept away by the wind. Her feet slithered under the metal bar into space. Dangling by her gloved hands from the rail, she resembled one of those clockwork tin dolls that swing from side to side on acrobatic bars.

Her thoughts remained astonishingly lucid. *I can't hang on much longer. I'll never survive in this sea. Isn't this the time for my life to pass in front of me? Shouldn't I be thinking of San Francisco, poor Father, Boris, Aunt Chatty — and, yes, of Paskevich?*

The shadowy sea-weed embedded in the rising purplish grey wave seemed like a drowned body beckoning her to dance.

She felt the thwacking tremor through her palms. Someone — probably a sailor — had hit the rail beside her.

As sea-water swept over the bow, a strong heavy arm clamped around her waist.

She was hauled on to her feet. The hand gripped her firmly. As the deck became horizontal and she could grab on to the rail again, she took several long, shuddering breaths.

'Thank you,' she gasped.

Her rescuer, she now saw, was not a crewman but a passenger. Her first confused impression was of height, dark hair falling in wet strands.

Shifting his grip from her waist to her elbow, he stared down at her as if in surprise.

Men often did a double take like this on confronting Marya. Her nose, forehead and chin were without distinction, yet few forgot her. Even sea-wet and pale from her near-brush with death, the face was memorable. Her eyes were unusual, an odd silvery grey rescued from colourlessness by near-black rims around the iris. Her upper lip, full and soft, was raised up like a pretty beak from the even white teeth: a flaw maybe, but one that was highly expressive — she could appear seductive, alluring, innocent, impulsive or delighted by pleasure.

As they gazed at each other, a drop of sea-water trembled on her thick lashes and fell on her cheek. She blinked. 'You saved my life,' she whispered breathily. 'I was on the brink of drowning.'

'In mid-Channel the squalls can get strong.'

'Oh! You're bleeding. Below your left eye.'

He touched the line of blood oozing down his high-boned cheek. 'I must have slammed into the rail harder than I thought,' he said.

'You could have gone overboard, too.' Her voice trembled.

'It was nothing,' he interrupted.

'But you're *bleeding.*'

'A little cut.' He fished under his overcoat

for a handkerchief. He wadded the linen against the wound. 'I'll survive.'

She was breathing more evenly. 'How can I ever thank you?'

'By not saying another word. What you need is a hot drink and to get out of your wet coat.' Gripping her arm, he led her along the rolling deck towards the main hatch.

They halted in the shelter provided by the overhanging quarterdeck.

'If you hadn't been here . . .' Her voice faded into the wind. *If he hadn't been on deck, if he hadn't risked his own skin, I would have drowned, I'd be dead by now . . .* Her knees went rubbery. Gripping the polished brass rail, she leaned against the long bin where the deckchairs were stowed.

'Are you all right?' he asked.

'I guess I do need something hot.' Continuing to grip the rail, she forced liveliness into her voice. 'And my brother'll be delighted to stand you to a sherry.'

'That's very kind.' He looked at the white caps. The wind had quietened a little. 'But I'll stay on deck.'

'Please? How else can he repay you for saving his only sister from a watery grave? Besides, you need patching up.'

'A little pressure'll stop the bleeding.'

Until now, his long, angular face and deep-set blue eyes had made him — or so it had flashed through Marya's mind — a mature brooding Heathcliff. As he returned her smile, she thought: *Why, he's not much older than I am. Maybe twenty or so.*

'If you want to know the awful truth,' he said, 'I get sea-sick below, and I don't on deck.'

She smiled. 'Lucky for me.'

'And, besides, the main lounge is off limits to Second Class passengers.'

'Oh, all these classes! What stuff!'

'You're American, aren't you?'

'Right. And you're Russian.'

He blinked with surprise. He had lived the past two years in London, where accent counted as everything, and had been near-universally accepted as English.

'How do you know that?'

'Ah, my crystal ball . . .' She lowered her lashes with a mysterious little smile before adding: 'You have the tiniest hint of a *g* when you say your aitches.'

He said formally: 'Permit me to introduce myself. Stephan Strakhov at your service.'

'I'm Marya Fedorovna Alexiev.'

'*You're* Russian? But you just said —'

'It's true, I *am* American.' Now she was speaking Russian. 'Mother was a Californian. Boris —'

'Your brother?'

'Yes. Boris and I were born in San Francisco, which makes us Americans. But Father registered us at the Imperial Consulate. And that means we're Russian. Hybrids. What part of Russia are you from?'

The ship's horn blasted. Marya jumped,

15

and then took a cautious step to lean against the bulkhead.

'You really do look a bit shaky,' he said. 'And your coat's soaked through. I mustn't keep you.'

Just above the choppy waves, a gull was struggling against the wind. Watching the almost stationary bird, Marya said: 'I get sea-sick, too.' It wasn't exactly a lie; the flat smell inside ships did put her off, but only a little. 'Are you on the way home?'

Instead of responding to her question, he asked: 'What about you? Where are you heading?'

'Paris. We're staying at the Crillon, then it's St Petersburg.'

'You're with your family?'

'Father's dead,' she said in a flat unreconciled tone. 'Mother died when we were young. There's only Boris and me and Aunt Chatty — Miss Charlotte Dunning. She's not exactly an aunt; she's a cousin of Mother's.' Her voice regained its vivacity. 'Have you been up at Oxford? Cambridge? Or were you on vacation?'

Stephan was returning to Russia illegally, having served only two years of a three-year exile. 'I was working.'

Marya heard the curtness as a door closing politely but firmly between them. She held on to the rail with both hands and looked out at the rough sea.

After a few seconds he said apologetically, 'Is this your first trip?'

'Yes, our first. What's Russia like?'

'Didn't your father tell you?'

'Poor Father, he never stopped telling us. He'd go on and on about the magnificent palaces, the cathedrals with glittering domes, the long, lazy summers in the family dacha, the Easter celebrations — he was given dozens and dozens of rich Easter loaves by the peasants who worked the family's estates. The peasants were always singing, or so Father said. Simple, honest, pious folk, who put their trust in God, revered the tsar as their Little Father, and took joy in obeying their landlords or masters.'

'You don't sound convinced.'

'I've always adored fairy-stories.'

The deck pitched. Stephan braced his long legs, planting a protective hand next to hers on the bulkhead rail. 'Russia's huge, with thick pine forests, broad rivers, big country houses that nestle in the snow. There's the Crimea with its flowers and villas. St Petersburg floats like a dream on canals and rivers.' His voice went low and sombre. 'I don't deny that it can be the finest place on earth . . .'

'But those peasants weren't as happy as Father said?'

'There are no schools for their children. Brutal landlords take over their fields. They're taxed. Their sons are conscripted without a hope of becoming officers. In the city, workers earn the lowest wages in

17

Europe. In good years they go hungry, in bad years they starve. And the Government never gives them a chance. It's so repressive that the censors black out *revolution* and *constitution* in our dictionaries —' He stopped mid-sentence. The blood had soaked through his handkerchief and he took out a fresh one, folding it into a wad. 'But I'll spare you my politics.'

Again Marya heard finality in his tone. 'In London,' she said, 'we went to the Tate Gallery. The way the sea just melts into the sky and there's no horizon reminds me of the Turners there. I don't mean the landscapes; I mean the water and mist paintings hidden away in the basement —'

'My favourites,' he interrupted.

They exchanged awed looks as if they had uncovered a long-lost treasure. Marya forgot Stephan's brief curtness, the unpleasant wetness inside her coat, she forgot her recent brush with death. They discussed the Turners, then they discovered that they both had committed to memory certain passages in the novels of Jane Austen and Count Tolstoy. Stephan admitted with a flush that he 'tried to write poetry'. His wound stopped bleeding, and a bruise darkened his eye-socket. The sea grew calm, the sun pierced the clouds to gleam on a low dark crust of land.

'France,' she cried. 'France!'

A few passengers ventured on deck. Then a bow-legged petty officer was moving around to advise the voyagers that they must go below to fill in documents for the French officials.

'By now poor Auntie will be positive I actually was swept overboard. How can I ever thank you?'

He waved a hand, dismissing her gratitude. 'Thank you, Miss Alexiev, for making the crossing enjoyable.' The polite meaningless formality seemed a treachery to him, and evidently also to Marya Fedorovna Alexiev. Her silvery eyes shone too brightly as she said goodbye.

In Berlin, Stephan stayed with Eugene Yakir, a Georgian engineering student who had been an early recruit to the Democratic Reform Party, which Stephan had founded at St Petersburg University. Like Stephan, he had been arrested by the Okhrana, the tsarist secret political police, and sentenced to three years' exile.

The two young men had come out of a freezing rain to the beer-permeated shelter of the corner bar, the *kneipe*, where they were the only patrons not wearing work-clothes.

Yakir had very dark eyes and a face so round that it seemed a caricature. 'I have German financing for a magazine,' he said. His voice had the changing resonance of a cello. 'Nothing grand, of course. It'll be like the old days in Petersburg. I'll edit and set type, you'll write.'

'Thanks for the offer, but I'm going back to Russia.'

'So am I, the minute the sentence is up.'

'On tomorrow's train,' Stephan said.

'Tomorrow? Are you mad? Our sentence isn't up for a year.'

'The Democratic Reform Party is falling apart.'

'Where are your brains? The Okhrana's everywhere. It'll give them the greatest pleasure to pounce on you like wolves on a bear cub. And this time, my friend, should you be lucky enough to survive the interrogation it won't be exile. Oh no, nothing that pleasant. You'll moulder in some dank prison cell.' He paused to gulp down the last of his sausage. 'The border police have nerves in their noses that sniff out a false passport.'

'I'm using my own.'

'Your own papers?' Yakir tapped his round skull to indicate insanity. 'Honest revolutionaries don't last in this world, Strakhov.'

'There are several pieces I did in London.' Stephan pulled a small notebook from his pocket. 'Take any you want. Or the entire collection. I call it "My Sister, Liberty".'

'As lyrical as it sounds?'

'Probably disgustingly so.' Stephan drained his stein and wiped the foam from his mouth. He had spent much time polishing the articles, all the while visualizing that full, soft upper lip, the play of emotions in those huge opal eyes, the marvellous skin which glowed as if hundreds of candles blazed within her. How could a girl, by her own admission poor, wearing an ancient coat, be travelling First Class? And how could she and her family afford to travel to St Petersburg, much less stay at the Savoy and the Crillon? He was overwhelmed by the need to say something, anything, about Marya Alexiev. 'I met an American girl on the boat.' Picking up his refilled stein, he leaned a hip against the bar. 'Her father was Russian, and she was on the way to St Petersburg, her first visit.'

'A girl?'

'It's not what you're thinking.'

'Strakhov, Strakhov, we've been friends a long time. I'm supremely aware that, unlike me, you're not the type for a quick tumble. Ergo this is true romance in bud.'

A carter shoved in beside them, shouting for more wurst.

Stephan touched the scar on his cheek.

'What a nasty bruise. Is it a memento from her Russian father?' Laughing and clapping him between the shoulder-blades, Yakir picked up the notebook. 'Well, don't look so glum. I'm sure these are excellent. We Georgians have an old adage that says nothing sweetens the poet's pen like a dash of unconsummated passion.'

I cannot know if my words inspire love,

Or if love, my love, inspires poetry,
For love and poetry both flourish amid
The mysteries of those wilder shores.

Chapter Two

Thick snowflakes clung briefly to the glass before oozing in wet horizontal lines across the dark, fogged carriage window. In the walnut-veneered private compartment the radiator gave off hooting whistles and too much heat. Miss Chatty Dunning fanned herself with a tattered *Saturday Evening Post*, Boris Alexiev sat in his waistcoat and shirt sleeves, Marya had undone the stayed collar of her blouse.

They were still in eastern Germany, yet Marya gazed intently at the window as if these snowflakes blowing out of the night were envoys of Imperial Russia. Her thoughts kept circling back to *the* Russian, the man who had saved her from sliding into the rough waves.

Stephan, she thought. How could she think of him as Mr Strakhov? Stephan had revealed no personal details about himself, yet she knew a great deal about him. Most important, of course, that he was the chivalrous sort who would risk his life for a stranger. His coat was shabby, but his gloves were finely sewn ostrich leather; and well-made gloves, or so her father had gravely informed his two children, were the ultimate proof that a Russian was a gentleman. Stephan was a poet. Like her, he had stood in those empty basement galleries bemused by the misty Turners.

Why hadn't he asked if he could write to her? See her? Marya had enough trust in herself to know that the attraction was mutual, and so had let slip that they were staying at the Crillon. No letters had come to her there. Her sigh lightened the cloud on the window.

Touching her bared throat, she trembled beneath her clothing; then, glancing up, she saw her dreamy reflection in the etched mirror above the opposite banquette. Flushing, she dropped her hand.

She forced herself to listen to the conversation. Boris and Aunt Chatty were evidently once more sparring on ground that had become boringly familiar.

'. . . children were born in the United States, so you're American citizens,' Miss Dunning was saying anxiously. The way her thick grey hair curled in bangs, her round eyes, her long, flattish nose and small chin gave her an unfortunate resemblance to a kindly sheep. 'What a terrible mistake it would be to give that up.'

'Come on, Aunt Chatty, brighten up,' Boris retorted. 'We're on vacation.'

'Then, why did we pack up every last belonging and bring it along?'

'We didn't have any place to store our things. Remember?' He smiled at Marya. 'Auntie takes first prize in worrying, doesn't she?'

Boris was nineteen to Marya's eighteen,

but people often mistook them for twins. Brother and sister shared the same fine bone structure and lack of height, and a similar delicacy of features. His eyes, however, were brown rather than her unique grey, his pomaded hair a far less vibrant shade of red. He had none of her compelling energy, and this lack showed in his slouch as he leaned back into the starched linen antimacassar. Brother and sister had both inherited the Alexiev hedonism. Marya, however, enjoyed things pleasurable with a vibrant expression; while Boris's mouth loosened in a self-indulgent way, as if gratification were his due.

Although Boris was by far the more pragmatic sibling, it was he, not Marya, who had believed their father's overblown tales of the family's Russian splendour. His heart told him that he didn't belong in their meagre wooden terrace house on Van Ness Street. He was a hereditary noble. His birthright was luxury, high-stake card games, midnight champagne with naked women, opulent house-parties on the Alexiev estate. To be fair to Boris, his father had neglected to describe either Cherepovits, a muddy village of 307 souls a long day's train ride from Moscow, or the Alexiev 'estate'. The musty odours in the house had caused full-blown hay fever; while dry rot and worms had eaten the wood until the upper floors were too dangerous to use. The surrounding fields had been sold to provide

capital for a meagre income.

Fedor Alexiev had also stretched the truth when he told his children he had married on his Grand Tour. He had, indeed, been on a Grand Tour — but as a tutor. Neglecting his young charges in San Francisco to seduce a Harvey Girl, he had been dismissed. He'd married the pretty young redhead a scant two months before Boris's premature birth.

Whatever Boris suspected of the truth in no way interfered with his playing the role of Russian princeling to the hilt. During the single term that family finances permitted him to enrol at Stanford, he had utilized this role to con his room-mates into ignoring his gambling debts. Boris's carnal experiences went no further than episodes with two elderly prostitutes in the tenderloin district; but Marya, hearing bowdlerized versions of her brother's exploits with women and at the card-table, felt he had admitted her to a larger, more sophisticated world.

Boris was her only remaining close relative; if anything happened to him, she would be dashed against the rocks.

Miss Dunning was saying: 'What bothers me, though, is why we never got our return tickets.'

'A simple oversight,' Boris said.

'But shouldn't we have settled the problem before we left?'

'The Cook's agent didn't hand Boris the itinerary until we were on board the *Lusi-*

tania.' Marya jumped in to defend her brother.

'Dear, I'm not *blaming* Boris — never in the world.' Miss Dunning held a hand to the soft, sagging, vanilla-scented bosom on which brother and sister had been comforted when they were small. 'It's my fault; I'm responsible now that your dear parents are gone.'

Charlotte Dunning, a destitute unworldly spinster of around sixty, got palpitations of her warm heart whenever she considered the numerous dangers that threatened her young charges. They had bestowed on her the affectionately foreshortened nickname 'Chatty' for her endless supply of unmalicious gossip, garnered for the most part from the *San Francisco Chronicle*'s Society page.

'Look at it this way, Auntie,' Boris said with forced airiness. 'It's probably the sole vacation we'll ever have, if the family has to rely on me to support them.'

Miss Dunning's expression became tender. 'I'm sure your Stanford friends would have rushed to give you the sort of job that you deserve if only you'd let them know —'

'A gentleman', he interrupted stiffly, 'couldn't possibly make that kind of request. I tried every employment agency in the Bay area.'

'My poor Boris, of course you did.' It was now Miss Dunning's turn to soothe. 'And then there's your health . . .'

'Auntie, the truth is it might be best if Count Paskevich does ask us to stay. The Alexiev name means something in Russia.'

'You're American!'

'Father registered us for dual citizenship, so I'm a Russski, too.'

'How could you joke like this? Russia's full of anarchists and the revolutionaries —'

Boris was laughing. 'Oh, Auntie, don't you know the *Chron* headlines that sort of rot to increase circulation?'

'But, dear, what about all the assassinations? Why, Tsar Nicholas's own grandfather was killed by a terrorist bomb. And what about that terrible uprising four years ago in St Petersburg? A revolution, they called it. Why, I remember as clearly as yesterday the way your dear father stayed in the house for days, doing nothing but read every paper he could lay his hands on, and how grateful he was when the Army crushed the riffraff. We *never* have that kind of godless violence back home.'

'That's because God's emigrated and is living in America . . .' Boris's arch tone faded. He hunched over, his meagre body racked by dry repetitive coughs.

Marya swiftly reached for Boris's specially prescribed codeine lozenges. Boris sucked, impeded by the coughing. Miss Dunning and Marya leaned forward, watching him anxiously.

Boris had spent the first weeks of his life in a nest of blankets and hot-water bottles,

28

a swaddling that continued in its psychological form. When winter fogs embraced the
San Francisco hills, he would develop a
low-grade fever. Given Mrs Alexiev's fatal
TB, it was no wonder that the Alexiev household revolved around Boris's weak chest.

When the coughs subsided, Miss Dunning
said in a resolutely cheerful tone: 'Aren't I
the silly one to make such a fuss? What
could be more thrilling than Count
Paskevich's invitation?'

At the illustrious name Marya gave a little
shudder.

Count Ivan Arkadievich Paskevich. The
Alexievs were a remote collateral kin to the
legendary count. Marya and Boris privately
called him 'Ivan the Terrible'.

On his three trips to the western coast of
the United States, Paskevich had summoned the family to the Presidential Suite
at the Palace Hotel. He was several years
older than Fedor Alexiev, yet infinitely more
vigorous. He strode about the sitting-room
with the rapid assurance of youth; he spoke
decisively and authoritatively on an immense number of subjects. A fringe of virile
black hairs edged his bald pate. His thick
shoulders and barrel chest topped dispro-
portionately spindly legs — a physique rescued partially by magnificent tailoring. He
exuded the odour of Cologne, brandy, tobacco and power. The Alexiev children had
given him the secret nickname because of
his stinging wit. His small dark eyes glit-

tered as brightly as the diamonds that studded his watch-cover as he turned from one Alexiev to another, as if they were amusing zoo animals. And certainly in his presence the little family, normally warm and loving, showed its worst pretensions. The carefully coached children sat side-by-side, either silent or letting loose some private matter like unpaid electricity bills or Father's staying in bed until lunch. Mrs Alexiev, extending her little finger parallel to her teacup, strewed euphemisms for every natural function. Mr Alexiev's self-deceptions blossomed as he held forth on the 'concerns' that temporarily prevented him from returning 'home'.

In 1903, the Alexievs' luck had turned truly bad. Galloping tuberculosis swept away Mrs Alexiev. In 1906 the earthquake and ensuing fires destroyed block after block of the city, including their wooden terrace house, which was uninsured. In 1908, the railroad in which Mr Alexiev had invested his entire meagre inheritance declared bankruptcy. A few days after this disaster, during a heavy fog, the widower blundered — either purposefully or not — onto the cable-car tracks.

Paskevich, on his most recent visit this autumn, had invited the orphans to dine with him. Marya's loyal impulse was to refuse this ugly arrogant patrician who had mocked their parents. Boris, though, brown eyes shining, had informed his sister that the Fairmont served the finest food in the city. Hearsay, of course: restaurants were well beyond the Alexiev budget, especially now when they had only the two hundred or so inherited dollars to tide them over until, as Miss Dunning put it, 'Boris found his feet'. Marya couldn't deny that she would like to sample the dining pleasures. She sent off a polite acceptance-note. Her dinner gown, hastily borrowed from a younger guest at the boarding-house, cut for a fuller figure, had a deeply scooped bodice. Marya, unused to displaying her pretty white bosom, surreptitiously tugged at the lace *décolletage* during the meal. Each course — *escargots,* poached salmon, quail *en croûte,* a tantalizing veal dish made with wild mushrooms, delicate raspberry *bombe* — came with a different French wine. Paskevich's clever little onyx eyes followed Marya's efforts with the factory lace. He responded to her badinage, chuckled at her sallies and showed her how to manage the snail shells. His interest spurred her on. Heady stuff, admiration from this powerful aristocrat who knew the celebrated beauties of Europe and decadent St Petersburg . . .

The following morning, headachy, Marya accepted that drinking all those wonderful wines and her coquettish ways had been a mistake. Still, Boris talked her into accepting a second dinner invitation, this time to the Stanford Court. Paskevich also booked a box at the opera — Madame Melba was in town. On the morning of Paskevich's departure, he appeared at the lodging-house in the Embarcadero, where they had taken rooms after the fire. Jauntily pacing around the Axminster rug whose cabbage roses were worn to the woof, he informed the astonished trio that this autumn they would visit the Crimson Palace, his residence in St Petersburg.

'That's incredibly kind of you, sir,' Boris said.

At the same moment Marya demurred: 'We can't accept such a generous offer.'

Throwing back his bald head, Paskevich laughed.

A few hours later a messenger delivered a Gump's jewel-case to Marya. Nestled in the grooved black velvet lay a wide gold bangle embellished with seed-pearls. 'Stop fretting about your Russian adventure, my pet. I have strictly honourable intentions.' She had torn the card into particles. Instead of telling Boris about the message, she had stormed around their rooms shouting that she was returning the bangle and Alexievs didn't take charity.

The next morning Boris came down with a fever. Marya stayed at his bedside sponging his neck and forehead, giving him sips of lemonade when he woke coughing. Before dawn she had gone to her room to take out the Gump's box. Fingering the seed-pearl bangle, she had recalled her father's tales of barbarically splendid Russian gems.

Paskevich doubtless had sent this bracelet in the same spirit in which he had previously sent bonbons. And, as for his note, what else could it have been beyond another example of his indecipherable wit?

A proper vacation will put Boris right, she had thought.

So here they were, speeding towards Russia. Marya leaned deeper into the plush velvet of the seat, her stomach tensing. Every rotation of the wheels was bringing her closer to St Petersburg — closer to Ivan the Terrible.

She realized that the wheels were turning slower and slower.

'What's happening?' Miss Dunning quavered.

'We're at the border,' Boris said.

'This is an express; it doesn't stop,' Miss Dunning panted. 'We've been attacked by anarchists!'

Marya stood to rub at the glass, making a patch of visibility. 'Look, Aunt Chatty. Boris is right. We're in Eydkhunin.' She was pulling her mother's horrible old winter coat from its hook. 'European trains always stop at every little border.'

'What are you doing?' Miss Dunning asked.

'Auntie, I'm stifling in here.'

'You never look before you leap! I refuse to let you leave this compartment. It's snowing, it's pitch-black —'

'Other passengers are catching a breath of

air,' Marya said.

'Who knows what sort of people they are?'

'I'll find out and tell you,' Marya said with a droll glance at Boris as he slid open the door for her.

Chapter Three

After the overheated compartment, the icy air exhilarated Marya. Descending the narrow iron steps, she let the blizzard seize her and dance her across the rock-salted platform to the shelter with the German sign: *Eydkhunin*. A few bundled-up male passengers had braved the storm to parade vigorously below the gas-lamps. A porter with steaming breath trundled a high-piled wagon towards the First Class baggage compartment. A stout peasant woman bent her shawled head into the wind as she ploughed towards the Third Class carriages, which were barely visible through the slanting snow. Blown snow was already mounded against the train wheels.

Marya's experience with snow was limited to rare flurries of petulant flakes that turned to slush immediately they landed on the San Francisco streets. Clasping her hands to her chest, she imagined herself entering a new-born planet, a lovely, pristine, white planet. The painfully invigorating air cut deeper into her lungs, and she exhaled with a breathy laugh.

The tall man near her turned.

With a start, she saw that he was Stephan Strakhov.

He recognized her at the same instant.

'So you *are* going back to Russia!' she

said. 'And on *our* train!'

Raising his grey astrakhan hat in greeting, he smiled. 'The happiest coincidence.'

'Isn't it?' She laughed again. 'How's your cut?'

'I'd completely forgotten it. How did you like Paris?'

'*Incroyable! Magnifique!* And Berlin was *wunderbar.*' Paskevich's itinerary included three nights in a cavernous suite at the Adlon Hotel before they boarded this train.

'So you have a favourable impression of our Old World.' Stephan smiled. The snow-flakes on his hair and eyebrows empha-sized their blackness. 'Is your brother with you?'

'He has a cough; he stayed in the compart-ment.'

'And your aunt?'

'Come out in this storm? Catch her death? Never, never, never. Besides, Aunt Chatty's a born worrier. We're on the Russian border, and the world knows that Russians throw bombs instead of baseballs.'

A yet stronger blast of wind shook the gas-lamps, flickering the light across Stephan's somewhat angular features. 'An astute lady.'

Marya laughed. 'Aunt Chatty's a darling, but that's the first time anyone ever de-scribed her as astute.'

A German official, black leather coat blow-ing around his ankles, stamped through billows of steam, trumpeting through his hands that they must return to the train for passport inspection. As they moved from the protection of the station shed, a mighty gust tore at the platform. Marya staggered. Stephan put his arm around her waist.

'Are you rescuing me again?'

'Preventative measures this time. Arctic blizzards have been known to blow horses over.'

Through the heavy layers of clothing, she felt his warmth and strength. He climbed the iron steps behind her, sheltering her from the wind. She fretted briefly that he would return along the platform to a Second Class car, offering up an inner prayer of gratitude as he followed her to the compartment.

A bulky crimson-faced German border official was squinting at Boris's passport.

'Oh, thank heaven! You're back,' Miss Dunning cried. 'Marya dear, you must promise me to stop being so rash. What if you'd missed the train? You'd have been stranded without any documents. And how would you have managed alone, without a passport or a visa, and no money or ticket — ?' She broke off; peering short-sightedly at Stephan.

'Remember?' Marya glanced in the mirror, attempting to tug her red curls into a semblance of order. 'I told you about a Russian gentleman I met on the Channel steamer?'

'So you're the famous stranger.' Boris's brown eyes twinkled. 'The hero who rescued my daredevil sister from a watery grave. I can't thank you enough. Your ears must have been burning this past couple of weeks; she's never stopped singing your praises.'

Marya's face was pink and glowing from more than the cold as she made the introductions.

'Mr Strakhov,' Miss Dunning said. 'What a pleasure to meet a Russian who speaks English.'

'Auntie's convinced that Russia's nearly as civilized as Timbuktu,' Boris teased.

The German official, rubbing his weathered jaw, was slowly turning the pages of Marya's passport. Peering from her to her photograph then back, he enquired in execrable Russian: 'Fräulein Alexiev, why are you departing Germany?'

'I already explained,' Boris said. 'We only came to *Germany* because we're *en route* to Russia.'

'I am questioning Miss Alexiev, please.'

She replied: 'We're on holiday.' Were they? How would they pay their return passage? Worrisome questions that Marya let slide away as Stephan pulled off his well-made gloves and took off his coat. He was staying. In the light she could see that the cut on his cheek had left a narrow scar.

The locomotive whistle sounded above the wind. The German rapidly stamped her papers, then turned to Stephan. Casually and without haste, Stephan fished under his jacket to his waistcoat pocket, extracting a black passport with the Imperial double-headed eagle embossed in gold. By now the train whistle was drawn out. There was no time for perusal. The German official jammed down his stamp and hurried from the compartment.

'Travelling with anyone, Strakhov?' Boris asked.

'No, I'm alone.'

'Then, as a personal favour to me, stay. I'm starved for a bit of male company.'

'If the ladies don't mind, it'd be a pleasure.' With a clang, the train lurched forward: Stephan kept his balance. His tall body had an easy grace that gave the lie to his cheap grey-striped lounge suit. 'It'll only be a few minutes anyway. At Verballen we'll all be getting off.'

'In this weather?' Miss Dunning asked. 'We'll all catch pneumonia!'

'Now, Auntie,' Boris soothed.

'I can't for the life of me understand why they'd make us change.'

'There's no choice, Miss Dunning,' Stephan said. 'The Russian rails are a narrower gauge.'

'They are?' Miss Dunning asked. 'Wouldn't it make more sense to use the same kind of track as the rest of Europe?'

'This is the Russian way. We're different from everybody else in the world. And different from each other. We have fifty different races, a hundred dialects, a million different opinions.'

'All sorts come to America and blend in,' retorted Miss Dunning. 'That's what makes us such a great country.'

At this innocent chauvinism, Marya and Boris exchanged smiles.

Stephan responded gravely: 'You've penetrated the truth about Russia, Miss Dunning. We're not one country. We're sixteen countries under one flag.'

'So the tsar rules an empire. That makes him the same as the king of England, doesn't it?'

'Unfortunately, no; not the same at all.' Stephan fingered back his hair. 'The British have a parliament; it's a constitutional monarchy. In Russia all power rests in one man. Nicholas the Second. The Empire's his personal possession.'

'Shh, Auntie, be careful.' Boris raised a finger to his lips, whispering: 'Right here in our own compartment, one of the bomb-hurling revolutionaries.'

'Stephan's a writer,' Marya interjected.

'Aren't the two synonymous in Russia?' Boris asked.

The banter moved as lightly as a shuttlecock. Marya made conversation, barely conscious of what she said. Her attention was riveted on Stephan. She took a proprietary interest in the scar. Stephan made far fewer jokes than she and Boris, and smiled rather than laughed. When he did laugh, he had an edgy, tremendously attractive way of running his fingers through his thick black hair.

Too soon lights were blurring beyond the windows. Air-brakes hissed. At some point during the lively conversation they had entered the tsar's domain. As the train ground to a halt, Marya and Boris turned to each other.

'Russia . . .' they both murmured.

Russia, the land of Fedor Alexiev's endless epiphanies. Russia, to them until this second as mythological as Atlantis, Cockaigne, Valhalla, Paradise, Avalon or the Isles of the Blessed. Russia . . .

Into the compartment barged three short, stocky Mongol porters. Snow clumped on their fur hats and clung to the baggy trousers tucked into boots; ice beaded the long, sparse strands of their moustaches. As the trio slung the assortment of antiquated valises from the polished brass racks, Miss Dunning fluttered behind them, begging them in English to be careful. Boris wound his scarf several times around his susceptible throat before shrugging into his overcoat.

Stephan said goodbye and edged into the crowded corridor. Marya took a few steps after him.

'You didn't mention where you're going,' she said, looking up at him.

'I'm not sure myself,' he said uneasily. 'But if you'd give me your address —'

'Miss Alexiev?' boomed a man's voice. A railway official with much gold braid on his dark blue uniform was shoving his way through the tumult. 'Marya Fedorovna Alexiev?'

Marya turned in surprise that anyone knew her name. 'Yes?'

With a deep bow he introduced himself as the Verballen station master. 'I am at your service. Count Paskevich requested that I meet your party and make you comfortable.'

Stephan flinched as if a raw nerve had been jabbed. Turning to Marya, he asked: 'Count Paskevich?'

'We're related — a bit. Through Father's mother's family,' Marya explained. 'I told you we were going to St Petersburg? We're staying with him. It's a complete shock that he has friends here in Verballen.'

'His Excellency telegraphed,' said the station master. 'I didn't mean to give the impression that I was a personal acquaintance.'

'Everywhere in Russia the name Paskevich carries weight.' Stephan spoke without intonation. 'And now I need to see to my luggage, so if you'll excuse me . . .'

'Our address will be the Crimson Palace —'

But Stephan, coat flung over one shoulder like a hussar's cape, was already jumping down the steps into the storm.

The brightly lit hall was filling up with passengers. Thrusting her disappointment to the back of her mind, Marya took in the crowd. Dirtier and shabbier than her father's descriptions, yet immensely more exotic. A group of turbaned Muslims with veiled women. A young peasant girl padded out by at least ten petticoats. Oriental children in long, straight gowns staring at the Americans with great flat-set eyes. Jewish men in long black coats and wide hats from which hair flowed. A bejewelled gypsy flirted castanets at a pair of grubbily uniformed soldiers. A bearded priest chewed a bun, scattering crumbs down his black robe and across his immense silver pectoral cross. The low barrier demarcated the Second Class buffet, where people wore European clothes. Frosted glass screened patrons of the First Class dining-room from sight. Mr Alexiev had described the smells of pine forests, incense, spring flowers; but the odours that Marya inhaled were unique to Russia, a blend of stale sunflower-seed oil, cabbage, garlic sausage, sour beet soup and aged sheepskin coats.

Guiding them through the hall, the station master explained that he was taking them to the Imperial Waiting-rooms which were opened only for royalty, foreign dignitaries and members of Russia's most august families. His voice showed none of his speculative surprise that these three shabby Americans could be related to the influential, immensely wealthy Count Paskevich.

They were nearing the tall doors topped by the gilded Romanov eagle when shouts erupted in the far corner of the hall. A short hollow-cheeked man wearing a thin shabby suit was being grappled by two assailants; in their fur hats and coats they appeared double their captive's size.

Marya heard frightened whispers: 'Okhrana,' 'Secret Police.'

Then a nightmare silence fell on the crowd. Each sound of the struggle reverberated through the hall. One of the burly agents slammed the wooden butt of his pistol against his panting captive's skull, a hollow crack. The man fell. There were whimpers, grunts and muted thuds as the pair aimed their hobnailed boots at the curled defenceless body.

'Stop that!' For a fractional moment Marya didn't recognize the high shaking voice as her own. 'Why doesn't somebody stop them?'

'Leave him be!' A tall man had stepped forward, eyes narrowed, fists clenched.

Stephan.

The two men turned on him. Horrified that he might be their next victim, Marya darted around a family picnicking on the floor, toppling their flask. She grabbed Stephan's arm, holding on to him tightly.

'They have clubs and guns,' she hissed.

He didn't seem to hear her. Taking another step, he unsuccessfully attempted to shake off her restraining hand. Instead, he dragged her forward.

The police were hauling up their prisoner. Drops of blood splattered and his shoes turned inwards as he feebly attempted to make steps as they dragged him to the vestibule. The double doors opened. Cold air blasted in. The moment the doors swung shut, the hall sprang back to life.

Stephan remained tense. 'God, I've been away a long time,' he muttered. 'I'd forgotten what brutes they are.'

Worrying that he might follow the three men, she said hastily: 'Why don't you have dinner with us?'

He shook his head, as if clearing it. She repeated the invitation.

He blinked. 'I'd enjoy that.'

They followed the station master into the Imperial Waiting-room. A tinted photograph of Nicholas II gazed benevolently down at a long table covered with *zakouska* — hors-d'oeuvres. Tiny glasses surrounded bottles of vodka. Miss Dunning, normally a teetotaller, accepted a drink. Nobody but the station master took the mushrooms bubbling in hot cream, the small sausages so hot that the skins had burst, the titbits of smoked fish from the Volga.

A round table was set for dinner. A waiter in a grubby apron rushed about serving them numerous courses. Boris and Miss Dunning recovered, eating heartily as they discussed how much the tsar resembled his cousin, George, heir to the British throne. Marya barely touched the huge meal. Stephan, too, picked. There was no mention of the beating until they had moved to easy-

45

chairs and were sipping glasses of sweet hot tea.

'I can't apologize enough for the unfortunate incident,' the station master said with a cough. 'These assassins with their explosives! Thank God for the Security Police.'

'Violence is always wrong,' Stephan said.

Ignoring the double-edged remark, the station master leaned towards Boris. 'Mr Alexiev, if you will be so kind as to pass on a message from a humble railway official, beg Count Paskevich to return to the ministry. Russia has need of his Excellency's firmness with these wild animals. And now, if you'll be so good as to give me your papers, I'll see to everything.'

Stephan casually tossed his Russian passport in with the American passports. In less than five minutes the station master returned them with the correct stamps. 'Your train has been held because of the weather.' He tugged angrily at an earlobe. 'A blessing in disguise. With this type of rabble around there might be bombs on the track. But don't worry, Miss Alexiev,' he added hastily. 'Our political police will ferret any trouble of that sort out of him.'

'What is it?' Miss Dunning cried. 'What's he telling you?'

'It's the storm, Aunt Chatty,' Boris replied in English. 'Our train won't be leaving tonight.'

'Those damn revolutionary bastards!' the station master muttered.

'You know him, don't you?' Marya said. 'The man they were beating.'

She and Stephan sat by the stove. The lights had been turned down, and they were alone in the shadowy sitting-room. The door to the Imperial Bedroom was open to show Miss Dunning sleeping fully clothed on one of the beds, her head resting on her large well-worn handbag. Boris had closed the door to the smaller room.

'Not exactly . . . I've met him once.'

'Are you connected to his organization?'

'He belongs to the Bolshevik Party. They rely on violence. I don't believe in violence.'

'Yet you went to his rescue.'

'I do believe in fairness.'

'Are you in a political party?'

Stephan turned away. 'Please, Marya, no more questions.'

His reticence seemed proof of his lack of trust in her, reminding her of several things she had pushed to the back of her mind.

'You come to our compartment so your papers are barely scanned,' she burst out. 'You come in here with us so your passport gets stamped with ours. We're your ticket into Russia, aren't we? I shouldn't be angry. It's not much of a payment for saving my life, but . . .' Her voice trailed away as Miss Dunning gave a soft snore.

After a moment or two he said in a subdued tone: 'I was never so happy in my life as when I saw you at Eydkhunin station.'

Her anger evaporated as swiftly as it had arisen. 'Truly?' she murmured.

'You seemed to be waltzing with the wind. I wanted to be the wind.'

She smiled. 'Will it be all right to ask one more thing? Is Stephan Strakhov your true name?'

'Absolutely. And this' — he tapped his jacket — 'is my real passport.'

'Good,' she said softly and smiled at him.

'Marya.'

'What?'

'I enjoy saying it. Marya, Marya, Marya . . .' He tilted his head towards the heavily curtained, rattling, double-glazed windows. 'That storm, the Okhrana — what a welcome you have had to Russia.'

She looked at him, a blush rising from her throat to cover her face. 'I hope the blizzard keeps us here for days.'

Chapter Four

Her wish was granted.

During the following three days, to leave the station building meant risking death: all sense of direction vanished after a few steps in the blinding, whirling snowflakes.

Boris and Miss Dunning never left the Imperial Waiting-rooms. The 'foreigners' in the hall terrified Miss Dunning. Boris disdained the peasants' odours and loud voices — and, besides, in Russia, as a hereditary noble, didn't he belong in rarefied digs?

Marya, however, spent most of her waking hours with Stephan in the station hall. At first the important young American lady who occupied the Little Father's own quarters attracted glances and stares, but after the first couple of hours she became part of the enclosed universe.

The First Class and Second Class passengers clustered near their respective dining-places. Third Class families, mostly peasants clad in local costume, staked out temporary homes, munching on food from their baskets, dozing, laughing, arguing vociferously among themselves as though nobody else were around. Children played leapfrog and other boisterous games, babies screamed and were held to the breast. The solitary passengers whiled away their time exchanging life-stories in a babel of languages. Prayers marked the hours. The Orthodox bellowed hymns with a travelling priest; shawled Jewish men grouped together to sway and mutter; shoeless Muslims bowed, kneeled and prostrated themselves in the direction of Mecca.

The diversity absorbed Marya.

'Already I feel I've travelled all over Russia.' She made an encompassing gesture.

Her arm touched Stephan's. Through the layers of their clothing he was aware, as he had been when he pulled her back from the sea, of her fragility. She appeared larger and stronger than she actually was. Maybe that American aura of independence did it. Not moving her arm, she turned her head to look at him. Her thick brown lashes fluttered. Her irises were the silver mist of fine rain. As they gazed at each other, he could feel her arm tremble.

A little boy wearing an embroidered shirt banged against them.

'God alone knows what kind of germs are out there,' Boris said. 'If I were you, I'd wash really well when I came back inside. And I wouldn't wear that good bangle. Come to think of it, if I were you, I'd stay right here.'

'I've never seen so many fascinating people.'

'People?' he asked with a grin. 'Or person?'

By the third day there was no food left in

the Second Class buffet. In return for the raisin buns and sweet cheese pastries Stephan had been buying her, Marya invited him to dinner again.

There were no shortages in the Imperial Suite. After the enormous meal, Miss Dunning, rubbing her eyes, excused herself.

Marya and Stephan played double patience while Boris watched. After a few minutes, he yawned elaborately. 'I keep dropping off. I hope you two won't be insulted if I turn in.' With a wink at Marya, he closed the bedroom door after himself.

Finishing the game, Marya played badly; and Stephan did, too. Once their fingers touched, and they both blushed.

'Listen,' he said.

'I don't hear a thing,' Marya said.

'That's just it. The wind's let up.'

'Father always told us winter turned Russia into Wonderland.'

'Shall we take a look?'

The clouds had parted to show a blanched three-quarter moon. The station, on the outskirts of Verballen, stood on slightly higher ground than the rest of the little town. Below them, the mounds that were houses and shops, then the flat open countryside a-glitter with bluish lights like one vast diamond. The station platform and this portion of the track had been dug out, and Marya could see the gleam of iron spikes in the march of trestles.

'Ahh,' she sighed. 'Did you ever see a night this exquisite?'

'Never. Everything is fresh and new. I feel as if the world can be painted with every shade of joy imaginable.'

'That sounds like a poet.'

'Pretentious?'

'Not at all. It describes how I feel exactly.'

He guided her down the narrow footpath sunk into the snow of the embankment, and they walked side-by-side along the salt-covered cinders. Their breath steamed. At the soft thumps of snow falling from the high banks on either side of them, Marya gave a little squeak. Stephan took her hand. Her entire being focused on their joined gloved hands. Their faces were grave, and neither of them spoke until they came to a tall building which cast a long black shadow across the tracks. Hoar-frost coated the windows. Moonlight traced the steel bars.

'A police station,' Stephan said.

'Isn't it way too big for a town like Verballen?'

'Not really. Didn't your father explain that Russia has two police departments? We're the only country that does. The Gendarmerie handle all the normal cases — civil and criminal. They protect the ordinary community. The Political Police are a far larger force. Their single duty is to protect the Government. The Autocracy. They have no need to be fair or just — but you saw them in action.' He was staring up at a barred window where the frost had melted in the centre to show a yellowish gleam. 'Every Russian, whether he admits it or not, dreads the Okhrana — the secret police. They pry into everyone's life; they keep files on the high nobility, even members of the Imperial family —'

A shriek silenced him. Even muffled by glass, the cry invoked shuddering terror as it soared to an inhuman bird-like pitch, then sank slowly into silence.

'Do you think it was the man they took in the other night?' Marya asked in a low voice.

'I doubt if he could hold out against Ok-hrana methods this long.'

Without discussion, they turned back. Cloud fingers were covering the moon by the time they reached the station embankment. Stephan halted. Head cocked, frowning slightly, he gazed down at her. She was keenly aware of the smell of soap and masculine sweat; of the warmth of his breath.

Then his mouth came down on hers.

She had been waiting for this kiss, waiting all her life. She had been kissed at parties and on porches. None of those kisses on another continent was remotely like this urgent drowning embrace. Her thighs went weak, her body shook, she felt as out of control as if she had actually been swept overboard and the high seas had engulfed her.

When the kiss ended, he kept his arm around her and they went inside, tiptoeing around the sleepers bundled on the floor.

In the Imperial Waiting-room they took off their outer garments. Marya couldn't look at him. Instead she dropped the hated old coat on the carpet and reached her arms around his waist.

They sank into the small sofa. All her life seemed bound up in his hands on her breasts, the warm breath against her ear-drum. She caressed his shaking arms, kissing his throat, giving herself completely to physical sensation. She forgot that only panelled doors separated them from her brother and the kind, fluttery old woman she called her aunt, forgot the snoring crowd beyond the Imperial Suite. Her past vanished, and so did whatever lay ahead in the Crimson Palace. There was only Stephan kissing the hollow of her throat. Drugged by love, wet in a variety of embarrassing places, she yearned for — She didn't know exactly what she yearned for. Mrs Alexiev had died without giving her a clue; and Miss Dunning, who had fumbled through an explanation of the monthly courses, was a virgin, ignorant of the bedroom rites. Boris, it goes without saying, had reported no specifics of his adventures to his sister. The novels Marya read sometimes referred to wedding nights as 'the great white sacrifice', giving no inkling what that sacrifice entailed.

As Stephan's lips moved on her blouse, her pleasure was so intense that she thought she might faint.

He pulled away. 'Oh God, what am I doing?'

She drew his head down again. 'Stephan.'

'Have you . . . before?'

'I want us to.'

'Have you?'

'No.'

'My God, Marya.'

'Darling . . . ah, darling . . . please . . .'

He groaned and fumbled with his trousers. Suddenly she realized what the sex act involved and momentarily drew away. Then she clasped him as if her life depended on what would happen between them. As he pressed inside her she flinched, gasping at the raw pain, then hugged him tighter. The sofa was too short, and Stephan's position awkward, but neither of them was aware of any discomfort. A faraway workman shouted, a wolf howled, but these and all other sounds were drowned out by their gasping endearments. All at once, involuntary exquisite spasms held her in thrall. He was gasping above her.

They lay entwined for long minutes. Her ears tingled, her fingers and toes were warm and alive.

He shifted to an easier position. 'I love you,' he said.

'And me you,' she said, snuggling her cheek against his shirt.

'Then, you aren't sorry?'

'Stop being foolish. *I* asked *you*.'

'Because you wanted to comfort me.'

She touched the scar on his cheek. 'Because I wanted to belong to you. And you to belong to me.'

'Didn't you guess I was already yours?'

The clock gave three thin chimes.

'The storm's over,' he said. 'Darling, it's time for me to go.'

'Now? But the train —'

'The train'll leave in the morning. I'm not taking it,' he said.

Getting to his feet, he straightened his clothes, reaching inside his waistcoat. Taking her hand, he pressed something warm from his body into her palm.

A ring.

The heavy gold band and the setting had a soft patina that told her the piece was old. From the stone's gleaming pallor, large size and lack of faceting, she decided it was not a precious gem.

'Is it a family heirloom?' she asked. In the past three days she had learned nothing about his family beyond this: they lived in Moscow.

'My sister's. She's dead.'

'How awful for you.'

'I never knew her. She died around the time I was born. She was a lot older.'

'Stephan, I can't take anything this special.'

'It's yours,' he said. 'For ever.'

'For ever?'

'As long as we live.'

Tears filled her eyes as he solemnly

56

touched his lips to her forehead.

He said: 'I'll come back to you as soon as I can. It might be a while.'

'I'll hold my ring and time won't matter,' she said. 'Well, it won't matter as much.'

He kissed her lips lightly. Picking up his coat and the astrakhan hat, he crossed the Imperial Sitting-room and, not looking back, let himself out. For several minutes Marya stayed on the sofa, her thumb rubbing the smooth colourless stone.

Chapter Five

On that misty May morning when Peter the Great used a borrowed bayonet to break sodden ground for his new capital, being a true autocrat he ignored the practical considerations. Stone and timber would have to be imported, as would food. The Neva river and its branches often flooded, submerging the boggy islands. Strange fevers multiplied. Over a hundred thousand unwilling serfs died building St Petersburg: their bones hardened the foundations; their legions of ghosts silently cursed the beauty of the city.

Or so the American visitors were informed by Paskevich's major-domo.

The Crimson Palace, munificent gift of Catherine the Great to the short but heroically endowed Count Grigori Paskevich, included a gilded private theatre, two ballrooms with vividly painted ceilings, innumerable suites of rooms, two miles of corridors, an army of liveried servants. The façade fronting the Great Neva was crowned by a classical pediment adorned with bas-reliefs of the empress and her lover, and the only way Marya could tame her awe of the palace was by having a good chuckle about the stout marble Venus and her beak-nosed Adonis.

Descending the left side of the twin staircases that cupped the main hall for three storeys, Marya slid her hand along the mahogany banister. The intricate tracery of shells had been carved by the same English craftsmen who had come north to lay the great sunburst of rare woods in the hall floor far below her.

She halted on the landing to gaze out of the Palladian window at the broad icebound Neva, a panorama as romantic as any of her father's descriptions. Sheepskin-coated peasants strained to haul enormous burdens heaped on sledges; silver harnesses danced on the sledge-horses; messengers skated in symmetrical curves next to the tracks that had been laid two days earlier, when the ice was judged thick enough to bear the weight of the tram, whose bell she could not hear. On the far side of the river jutted the city's original building, the Fortress of Peter and Paul, whose grim brown bastions now served as a political prison. Above the clumsy enclosure of the old fortress walls soared the Peter and Paul Cathedral. As she gazed, the sun burst out from behind a cloud, and the slender spire became a blazing sword. Marya raised a hand to shield her eyes.

Since her arrival in St Petersburg her time had been so jammed with activity and impressions that the two weeks seemed more like two years. The first evening she had brought up the question of their return tickets: Paskevich had retorted that they hadn't

59

even started their holiday, and they would need to acquire new wardrobes for the coming winter festivities. When Marya had protested that they couldn't accept any further generosity, he had roared with amusement, waving away her objections with his large, strongly tendoned hand. 'My pet, you're not in the American provinces now. Didn't your father explain about Russian families? We provide. We share.' With that he'd ordered Vasilii, his head coachman, to drive Marya and Miss Dunning to Monsieur Bézard, whose *atelier* was on the fashionable Nevsky Prospekt.

So far Marya had seen more of the French couturier than of their host. Twice Paskevich had joined her and Miss Dunning under the immense rock-crystal chandelier of the dining-room, and one night he had escorted them to an Italian production of *La Bohème*. During the arias of Rudolfo, the poet, Marya had thought dreamily of Stephan and wondered when she would see him again. Paskevich, however, had spent a good deal of time with Boris: he had introduced his young relation around the Yacht Club, where titled officers drank, dined and gambled; he had taken him to smoky cabarets where gypsies and naked women danced. Boris had the time of his life learning why St Petersburg was known as the Snowy Babylon. Marya had finally concluded that she had been ridiculously vain to give an anxious moment to the seed-pearl bangle or the accompanying note: 'Stop fretting . . . my pet . . . strictly honourable intentions . . .'

Packing away her worries, she allowed herself to be initiated into that most exacting and fluid art, the couturier wardrobe.

This outfit had been delivered early this morning by Monsieur Bézard's messenger. The teal-blue broadcloth day-suit had a hobble skirt whose narrow hem made walking a near impossibility — the reason she'd held on to the banister. Monsieur Bézard had insisted on the cut; it was the *dernier cri*, he averred, and a certain ultra-chic grand duchess had ordered the identical model. To ensure she got the exact right little spatted boots, the Frenchman had volunteered to take her to the Gostinny Dvor, the huge shopping arcade a few steps along the Nevsky from his *atelier*, guiding her to the city's best cobbler. He had coaxed her into ordering delicate shoes or boots for each of his creations, then had swept her along to the glove-maker and the milliner. He had fussed over Madame Ilona's sheerest, most alarmingly expensive silks and finest webs of Valenciennes lace to be made into lingerie. 'Lucky slim young you,' he had said. 'No need for the corsetière.' Only during these deliciously vain hours did Marya forget Stephan.

Stephan . . .

Underneath her jacket, suspended on a fine chain between her breasts, the antique gold ring was warmed by her flesh. She never took it off and always wore it hidden.

When will I see him again? Are those political police bullies after him? Where is he? Moscow? Tblisi? Kiev? Odessa? When will I see him again? The further he is from here, the safer he is . . . But when, oh, when — ?

She jumped as Boris touched her arm.

'Isn't that view something?' he said.

'I thought you were still sleeping off your big night.'

'Never closed my eyes.' From appearances this was no metaphor: his face appeared coated with ashes, redness veined his eyes.

'You look awful.' Marya's throat tightened. 'You didn't catch cold in that snowstorm, did you?'

'I'm as fit as a fiddle,' he said with a small bitter smile. 'In the pink.'

'Then, what could be so wrong?'

'What a sweet baby you are. If only you knew what a botch I've made of things.'

'Oh, Boris, stop.'

'I'm not exaggerating. You're having such a marvellous time with all those new clothes. Aunt Chatty's in heaven serving tea to those ancient countesses.' Miss Dunning gloried in being taken under the wing of the two impoverished, pouter-pigeon dowagers, distant Paskevich connections who roosted in a corner of the vast palace — the pair spoke passable English. 'And now I've gone and ruined . . .' His voice cracked. 'You won't believe what a vile pig I've been.'

Linking her arm in his, she said: 'Everybody makes mistakes. It can't be all that bad. What's the worst that can happen? We've had a lovely holiday and now we'll go home.'

'You *are* an innocent,' he said. 'We can't leave, not until it's settled.'

'It?'

'A matter of honour.'

Horrified, she pulled her arm from his and stepped back. Incredibly anachronistic as it seemed, Russian aristocrats oiled their pistols and duelled at dawn, sometimes fatally. 'Have you been challenged?'

'I'm not that stupid.'

'Then, what?'

Boris bent his head, mumbling: 'Too much champagne, a lunatic bet on a bridge hand.'

'How lunatic?'

'Five hundred roubles.'

She drew a sharp breath. Monsieur Bézard had proudly informed her that his cutter was the highest-paid in St Petersburg, earning sixty roubles a month.

Boris said: 'I know, gambling that much is despicable, despicable.' As a small boy, he had always repented his mischief at length — a contrition that got him off the hook while Marya, never quite able to eat humble pie, was punished.

One of the liveried footmen was shuffling up the staircase with a large vase of roses and stephanotis: these flowers, like the other blooms that scented the Crimson Palace, arrived from Provence by a special train.

'I have an idea,' Marya said, switching to English. 'Why don't we talk the problem over with Paskevich?'

'He's already baled me out. Twice.'

Marya moved to the other window embrasure, which faced on to Paskevich Square. Shaggy little Siberian horses drew red-painted sleighs, army officers strode along in magnificent overcoats that touched the snow, peasant women round as balls in their grey shawls hawked wooden dolls, squat Tatar tribesmen wore hats that stuck out like pagodas, prim governesses chivvied small charges in fur coats. Then a motor car affixed with small Stars and Stripes, the ambassador's automobile, drove slowly by. A reminder of home that drew Marya back to her role as her brother's keeper.

'My armoires are stuffed to the gills with clothes,' she said crisply. 'I'll never miss a few.'

He blew his nose. 'You know I can't allow that.'

'No arguing. It's settled. Monsieur Bézard's a real friend; he'll help.'

The French couturier was very short, only an inch or so taller than the diminutive Marya. His skin was the tan of parchment, and his warm eyes were a deeper shade of the same hue. He nodded, kind and encouraging, while she bumbled out her urgent need for money.

'But Count Paskevich will help, surely?' Bézard spoke his native French, a language more popular than Russian in St Petersburg society.

'That's impossible. Could you . . . would you sell some of the dresses?'

'Your coat would bring a fortune.'

Paskevich had personally selected the incredibly soft, creamy lynx pelts now draped over the *atelier*'s sofa: he would notice if the coat were missing. 'I couldn't do that.'

Bézard stroked his narrow waxed moustache. 'My dear Miss Alexiev, at your fittings I notice that piece you wear under your clothes. Ladies often borrow on their jewellery.'

Her cheeks grew red. Stephan's ring — the last thing she would part with. 'It wouldn't bring much.'

'The stone's exceptionally large. What is it?'

'An opal, I think.'

'I've never seen any opal with that same fire.' He had taken out a pencil and was scribbling. 'Here's a jeweller just across the Anichkov Bridge. A decent man, most honest.'

'It's only valuable as a keepsake.'

But Bézard was pressing the paper into her palm. Rather than argue, she pushed the address into her needlepoint purse. 'Isn't there any possible way you could sell, say, a ballgown?' She hadn't gone anywhere that required one ballgown, much less three.

He gave her a warm smile. 'But of course I'll try. Let me check with a few clients.'

A sharp wind blew. Vasilii helped her into the open troika, placing the heated bearskin footbag under her boots, wrapping the sable rug around her. Like most Russian carriage-drivers, Vasilii was broad; and his fur-lined blue coat, belted with a gold rope like a dressing-gown, padded him to balloon-like proportions. He wound the reins around his gloved hands and held his arms out straight. The three horses moved into the stream of carriages and delivery-wagons. At the Anichkov Bridge, a gendarme held up his hand to halt the traffic.

Marya, immersed in her financial worries, paid no attention to the other vehicles or the foot traffic.

Then, quite by chance, although later it seemed fated, she looked up.

All her life she would remember the moment: the icy air on her cheeks; the tram-horse urinating in a cloud-surrounded stream; the four bronze stallions that reared at each corner of the bridge; a Chevalier Garde tossing a coin into the bowl of a one-legged beggar; an errand boy lugging a huge brass samovar whose charcoal odours drifted towards her.

Two young men with mufflers wound around their necks and heavy coats strode across the Anichkov Bridge.

The short one wore his blue student's cap tilted towards his nose, and the peak jerked angrily as he spoke. The other pushed at his thick black hair as he responded. Tall, broad-shouldered, hatless . . .

Stephan.

No, she told herself. Impossible. Stephan was in Moscow or Odessa or Tblisi or Kiev. If he were in St Petersburg, he would have contacted her. She was aware that he despised Paskevich, but that wouldn't have stopped him from coming to see her at the Crimson Palace. *For ever*, he had said. *As long as we live.*

Wintry sunlight showed the thin scarline on his left cheek. It was paler now and near-invisible, that scar — *her* scar, as she thought of it.

The two men had passed the troika.

Marya had gone white. After a few seconds a vivid red suffused her pallor. Sitting erect, she opened her purse for the slip of paper.

Tapping the coachman's padded back, she ordered: 'Take me to Sazanov's jewellery shop.'

Wrinkles gouged Sazanov's cheeks, but his hair was crow-black. The scent of his Cologne filled the small, heavily curtained shop.

'Monsieur Bézard said you might have an interest in buying this,' she said in a cold rapid voice.

Sazanov looked down at the ring. The wrinkles around his mouth deepened as his lips drew inwards. 'If you would wait one minute, my dear *gozpozha*.'

He disappeared behind a curtain. When he returned the ring was on a black velvet tray.

'An exceptional piece,' he said. 'A family treasure?'

'A gift.' Her tone remained cold.

'Please, your Excellency —'

'It's Miss Alexiev.'

At this Sazanov bowed respectfully. 'Of course, of course. I should have realized immediately. My friend Bézard has often mentioned the exquisite young American lady staying at the Crimson Palace.' He bowed again. 'If I were you, I'd cherish this diamond —'

'Diamond?'

'But surely you knew? Forty-three carats of diamond.'

Stephan pays well, she thought. *Forty-three carats of diamond for a single night.* Where, though, had a man whose clothes were well worn and who travelled Second Class acquired so valuable a ring? He'd told her he'd inherited it from a dead sister. Marya no longer believed a word he'd told her.

Sazanov put the ring on his little finger, holding his hand out, squinting professionally. 'Completely flawless. The stone was sand-polished. I venture to say in India. The setting, though, is Russian and at least three hundred years old.'

'Is it worth five hundred roubles?'

He smiled. 'Infinitely more.'

'That's how much I need.'

'Miss Alexiev, the diamond's worth isn't altered by your need. Let me advance you the five hundred and keep the piece here as collateral.' He spoke slowly and carefully, as if she were a very young child. 'When you repay me, I'll return it.'

'Good old Bézard, he must have made a bundle selling and buying back your clothes,' Boris said, hugging her joyously. Since she hadn't told him about the ring there was no way she could tell him about the jeweller's loan. 'Here, help me with this, will you?'

Boris had on his new evening clothes. Tonight he had the Paskevich box at the Maryinsky and was repaying the hospitality of his new friends by taking them to see Kchessinskaia dance *The Nutcracker*. Marya fumbled with the white bow-tie.

'Your hands are like ice, Marya.'

'I'm a bit under the weather.'

'The best thing for you is to hop into bed and have a light supper sent up.'

Chapter Six

My dear Marya,

Your absence from the dinner-table worries me. Is it all right if I visit you and make sure you're not failing like poor Mimi?

P

The note was delivered by the wall-eyed messenger-boy who skated on felt slippers through the endless parquet halls and corridors of the palace. Marya, in the silk-panelled boudoir off her bedroom, wished she could say no. Paskevich, however, was of another generation, her host, her benefactor — and furthermore he belonged to a rank that brooked no refusal.

She said: 'Please tell Count Paskevich I'd be delighted to have a little company.'

The weeping had shadowed a delicate lavender below her eyes and puffed out her upper lip. She was dashing cold water on her face when a tap sounded at her door. Startled that Paskevich had appeared so quickly — the messenger-boy had left only a minute earlier — Marya peered at her reflection. Droplets left dark splotches on the white silk of her négligée and caught in the hair tumbling around her shoulders. Wielding her brush, she returned to the little sitting-room. 'Come in,' she called.

He opened the door. 'But, my dear, I would have given you more time if I'd realized you were *en déshabillé.*'

From the amused glint in his eyes, she sensed that he had been completely aware that she wasn't dressed. 'I've known you all my life,' she said. 'Come on in.'

Paskevich, a masculine triangle from the broad shoulders of his magnificently tailored dinner-jacket to his small patent-leather pumps, overpowered the small chinoiserie tables and delicate upholstery. Seating himself in the low slipper-chair, he crossed his short thin legs.

'You don't look ill. In fact, you look charming. But, then, I suppose this is the slight indisposition that ladies suffer once a month.'

Flushing, she stared at the framed pastel scenes of St Petersburg that lined the silken walls. Not even Miss Dunning, after that initial stammered explanation, had referred to her menstrual periods.

'I take back the compliment,' he said. 'Not charming. Exquisite.'

'That's gilding it.' She tried to speak archly, but her mouth was dry. Why had he come here? To seduce her? Thank heavens he thought she had her period. Then she flushed at her vanity. He was teasing her. 'My hair's a rat's nest.'

'Now you're fishing for compliments.' He took out his platinum cigarette-case. As he held it up, the light caught on tiny diamonds that picked out the Paskevich crest. 'Mind?'

'No, of course not.'

He lit one of the yellow cigarettes, inhaling appreciatively. 'This brings back memories,' he said. 'My second wife had these rooms.'

'Wife?' No countess had accompanied him on his American travels; no wife had been mentioned by him or by her father. *Second* wife?

'Don't look so appalled,' he said. 'Everything's been completely renovated.'

'I never knew you were married.'

'Marya, surely you didn't assume me a celibate?'

Her cheeks coloured. In San Francisco she and Boris had discussed Paskevich's intimate life, finally concluding in sophisticated tones that Ivan the Terrible kept a mistress — maybe several.

'My first venture was arranged,' he said. 'I was nineteen, she sixteen. The poor girl died in labour nine months later.'

'How sad. So you have a child?'

'Our son was stillborn.' He took another puff. 'This suite was used by my second wife, formerly a Princess Galatzin. A tall angular lady with a basso profundo voice — I wish I could recall why I married her, but the reason eludes me. Possibly as a favour to her godfather, Alexander III, the present tsar's father — and his polar opposite. Alexander! Now, *there* was a true Romanov! Six foot four, and powerful enough to lift a wagon. Women, he had hundreds of women. What an autocrat! He made every decision as if God in heaven agreed with him. The people adored him because he was totally, narrow-mindedly ruthless. A prime quality in any monarch, ruthlessness.'

'Where is she now, the . . . uh, princess? Your wife?'

'It depends on whether you believe in the hereafter. I don't.'

'She died, too?'

'Yes, of typhus about the time of your father's death.' He lit another cigarette. 'I didn't visit these rooms often. You'd under-stand why if you'd seen her décor. Prune brown, and as many icons as she could cram on the imitation oak panelling. Are you getting the picture of my late wife?'

Consolation being out of the question, Marya couldn't come up with any appropri-ate response.

'Which brings me to my errand.' He stubbed out his barely smoked cigarette in the Sèvres porcelain hand, one of the room's delightful bibelots. 'This is for you.'

Reaching into his dinner-jacket, he handed her a small, royal-blue leather box. The gold tooling of entwined flowers was so fine it must have been done under a magni-fying glass.

She traced the design. 'Thank you. It's beautiful.'

'Spoken with true Californian naïveté,' he laughed. 'Any St Petersburg girl handed a jewel-box immediately opens it.'

Marya pressed a nail to the clasp, and the lid sprang up.

An enormous square emerald radiated green sparks. The diamond setting glittered, the platinum shone. For a moment she saw the gentle patina on the antiquated ring she'd left with Sazanov: the misery showed in her eyes.

'I chose wrongly for Yankee tastes?' Paskevich asked. 'From now on I'll be more restrained.'

'It's magnificent. I can't take it.'

'Why ever not?'

'I think you know.'

'My dear Marya, I confess to being totally baffled.'

'It looks too much like . . . well . . .'

'Like what?'

She flushed. 'An engagement ring.'

Not moving, not blinking, he scrutinized her, and she thought of a sleek black tiger watching a panic-stricken tethered goat. 'That's precisely what it is,' he said.

'But . . .'

'But what? Go on.'

'Oh, all right, I'm American, I'm young, I'm gauche. Now, stop playing games.'

'So much for me as Romeo.'

'You've never said a word — never proposed.'

'That's not true. In San Francisco I sent you a small betrothal gift and explained my intentions. You wear the bangle all the time.'

'I never realized.'

'Didn't you? Not a clue?'

She reddened again. Moving to the love-

74

seat, the furthest point in the small pretty room from his chair, she blurted: 'You haven't spent any time with me.'

'But what do you think I've been doing? I've shown you my home, bought you a trousseau, endeared myself to your family. I've been saying: "This is what my life is like, and this is how you will live the rest of your days." Isn't that better, Marya, than kneeling and declaring my love?' He showed a peculiarly rueful mocking smile. 'I'll do it, of course, if it pleases you; but, believe me, when a man is well past forty the role of impassioned suitor is comical.'

'I know practically nothing about you.' She peered at the glittering green stone as if it were a snake's hypnotic eye. 'I had no idea even that you'd been married.'

'Now you do.' He spoke smoothly. 'Let me see. I have twenty-seven estates, including a hundred miles along the Baltic Sea. This palace and four others, including one in Moscow. Oh, and I just bought some land for a new summer cottage in the Duchy of Finland, not far from Helsinki. I grew up in the country. I saw my parents twice a year, at Easter and at Christmas. I speak seven languages, including Mandarin. I was in the Cheval Gardes, and Tsar Alexander was my general. He appointed me ambassador to the court of Spain. Tsar Nicholas made me a member of his cabinet. By the way, a minister without *chin,* which means not from the bureaucracy, has only been appointed on one other occasion. And today His Imperial Majesty' — as Paskevich said the title, he rose to his feet and made an over-elaborate bow — 'has had the kindness to name me once again to his cabinet, this time as Minister of Finance.'

'Congratulations,' she said flatly.

'I agree. An unenviable position, but how could I refuse? Russia needs me.' As he said this his face drew into mock gravity that increased his simian resemblance. 'Marya, stop equivocating. As my countess you'll be happy — or, if not happy, at least far more comfortable than you were in that hideous boarding-house. That stench of bad cooking! The riff-raff around the San Francisco docks! Besides — be honest — I'm quite an amusing fellow, aren't I?'

'That's not the point.'

Paskevich raised his hands. Strong black hairs sprouted on the back of the knuckles. 'Possibly I should have spoken to your brother?'

Was this a slur? Her apprehension and shock vanished. 'If you mean Boris would sell me —'

He laughed. 'Sell you? Marya, what novels have you been reading? It's more proper for a suitor to apply to her father or brother is what I meant.'

He hadn't meant that at all. He'd been reminding her how rapidly and happily Boris had sunk into Russian opulence. Marya admitted to herself that she, too, had delighted in the sumptuous luxury. Her un-happiness wasn't caused by Paskevich. It was Stephan who had struck the spear into her heart.

'Marya, your beauty has made me forget how young you are, how impulsive. Get into bed and send your girl for a hot-water bottle. By tomorrow you'll see the advantages of the marital state.'

He bent to kiss the top of her head. Marya couldn't control her involuntary shiver.

As soon as the elderly countrywoman, her 'girl', retired to her pallet in the long, win-dowless gallery filled with armoires, Marya's tears started anew. She wept until dawn, drying her eyes when Boris tapped on her door to give her a highly edited version of his night: he described Kchessinskaia's per-formance as 'tremendous', then proceeded to clarify the Imperial scandal concerning the ballerina: Kchessinskaia had been Tsar Nicholas's mistress before he became the most uxorious of husbands, and now the dancer was carrying on with the tsar's young cousin, Grand Duke Andrei. Marya could smell champagne and a woman's per-fumed sweat on Boris's rumpled formal at-tire.

'Boris, let's sell our new clothes. We'll get enough for the Third Class passage to San Francisco.'

'Why do you keep talking about going home? The season's not even begun.'

'We can't keep taking and taking from Paskevich. I feel like a sponger.'

'Sponger?' Boris jumped up from the bed, his face crimson. 'Don't you remember Father telling us how Russians are with family? Didn't Paskevich tell us the same thing? We're his family. I should've let you sleep. You're groggy.'

She stayed in bed all day, mentally going over and over the advantages of becoming the third Countess Paskevich.

The title. The wealth. This palace and four others, the twenty-seven estates, the hundred miles of Baltic seacoast, the new lands near Helsinki. The weight of so much property oppressed her. As Paskevich had reminded her, he was entertaining company. His wit unnerved her. All the time her thoughts kept wandering to Stephan. Even now, knowing that he was in St Petersburg and hadn't contacted her, as she remembered them locked together her body seemed to lose its skeleton. How could she marry an old ugly man whose touch repelled her?

Miss Dunning fluttered in and out every hour or so, allowing herself to be coaxed into attending a soirée with the dowagers.

Boris dropped by on his way to a dinner-party. 'Grand Duke Michael will be there.' His face shone with the anticipated gratification of dining near an important personage.

At seven-thirty, the messenger delivered a note:

It'd be sheer bliss and heaven if you'd dine with me in my study. Ardently and for ever your P.

This atypical effusion, Marya knew, was intended to amuse her. She didn't smile.

She had never been in Paskevich's second-floor study. The maroon velvet draperies were drawn. A round table was pulled cosily near the blazing logs in the porphyry fire-place. The old-fashioned mirror-backed sconces, wired for electricity, cast a sub-dued glow on bulkily comfortable furnish-ings. Huge Chinese vases spilled purple-streaked lilies. On a narrow table stood three large crystal bowls of different caviares: Beluga, Sevruga, Oestra.

What Marya noticed, however, were the miniatures.

A glass-fronted cabinet held a dazzling assortment of diminutive porcelain figu-rines, another cabinet displayed carved ivory figurines, yet another the miniature Egyptian households. Tanagra figurines posed gracefully. A looming display-cabinet was devoted to Chinese goddesses carved in every colour of jade from deep green to delicate mauve; it must have taken a skilled artist a year to carve each one of these exquisite little Kwan Yin.

'What do you think of my collection?' Paskevich asked.

'It bowls me over,' she retorted honestly.

'The pieces log my travels,' he said. 'Those soft paste figures come from all over Europe.' He indicated the various cabinets as he spoke. 'Inca gold from Peru and Colombia. Indian ivory. Netsukes from Japan. The Egyptian figures were buried over five thousand years ago — they're called Ushabti, by the way, and were a humane substitute for the earlier custom of entombing retainers with the deceased. I gathered them on my journey up the Nile to Aswan. And as for the jade . . . well, I told you I was posted to Peking, didn't I?'

Excruciatingly aware of his watchful eyes, she moved to the jade collection. 'They're exquisite. They must be priceless.'

'Everything has a price. The secret of a good collector is to know that price.' He moved to her side.

Marya shifted to the Egyptian cabinet. 'These are finer than the ones in the British Museum. Don't merchants charge accordingly?'

'You rush into things, Marya. Me, I've learned that playing a waiting game brings down the cost considerably.' His teeth showed in a smile that mocked himself rather than her. 'But that's a wonderful dress. Let me look at you.'

Marya circled, uncomfortably aware that the pale-pink shot-silk dinner-gown, in what Bézard called the harem style, had a low *décolletage* while the skirt-slit displayed a lot of leg.

'Yes, my taste is exquisite,' Paskevich said. 'Now, my dear, stop clenching your jaw. I promise not to pop you into a cabinet with the other little treasures.'

She nibbled caviare and sipped the traditional vodka while Paskevich described how he had discovered various pieces. Unlike most collectors, he wasn't a bore: his stories were masterfully told. By the time dinner was served, Marya had relaxed enough to enjoy the food. Paskevich ate aristocratically, taking the heart, the best, of each of the seven delicately prepared courses. Coffee was served with a salver of *tianoushki*, the sticky cream toffees that Marya found addictive.

After the servants had cleared the table and left them alone, Paskevich stood. 'There's something we must discuss,' he said. 'This morning a jeweller I sometimes patronize contacted me. His name's Sazanov.'

Marya's heart began to thud.

Taking a key from his watch-pocket, Paskevich unlocked a desk drawer. 'He believed I might be interested in returning this to you.' He held up the sand-polished diamond. 'I was more than interested. I was fascinated.'

'It's mine.'

'Where did you get it?'

'Oh, I'm a collector, too.' She tried to speak airily.

'Yes, you have two rings, don't you? And,

by the way, I notice you aren't wearing the emerald.'

She didn't respond. Her moist hands were sticky from the toffee.

'Alexiev was on his uppers,' Paskevich said. 'Alexiev never left you anything like this.'

'I didn't steal it.'

'It never entered my head you did.' The keen little eyes were fixed on her. 'Well?'

A log crackled in the fireplace, then silence muffled the room.

'Marya, I've matched wits with the shrewdest minds in the world. So no more games.' Leaning across the desk he held the ring by the band. The smooth diamond seemed to gather all the glowing lights in the study. 'How did you acquire this ring?'

Inwardly quaking, her throat clogged with grief for love betrayed, Marya lifted her chin. 'I don't have to take this badgering.'

'But you do, my pet.' Paskevich slid several pieces of stationery from the open drawer, shaking them open. From across the room she could see Boris's large round signature. 'IOUs. Your brother's. An unlucky man at the card-table. Before you have your morning coffee tomorrow he could be in prison for unpaid debts.'

'You wouldn't.'

'Oh, wouldn't I? He owes me two thousand and forty-seven roubles.'

Marya sank back down into her chair. The fire was warm, she was cold. 'He's never been a heavy gambler.'

'But he's always enjoyed betting. And in St Petersburg, alas, he's fallen in with a group of over-privileged young sports.'

'You arranged it so he'd lose money?'

'Let's say I put opportunity in his path. I plan for contingencies. Have I explained sufficiently why you're obliged to answer my question?'

'A gift. From . . . a friend.'

'Sazanov tells me the goldsmith was Russian. So your "friend" is Russian?'

'Yes.'

Paskevich's gaze was piercing. 'You met him here?'

'On the Channel steamer. It was rough. I almost slid overboard. He saved me.'

'And he gave you a stone like this? You do wreak havoc on us poor males, don't you? Is he why you refused my emerald?'

'No,' she said faintly.

'That doesn't sound too convincing.'

'It's not an engagement ring.' *I just believed it was.*

'Let me think. Why else does a man give a beautiful young woman jewellery?' Paskevich's sarcastic tone grated. Dropping the papers back in the drawer, he returned to stand by the fire, where she sat. 'I intend to find out precisely what happened. And remember this: I despise liars.'

The remark slapped her. She, too, despised liars. 'I refuse to say another word until you stop standing over me like an angry schoolteacher!' she snapped.

The flames jumped, flickering on his face. 'I've got to hand it to you, Marya. Not even Alexander, autocrat *par excellence,* ever used that tone with me, and certainly not our present tsar.' Paskevich returned to his chair and took out his cigarette-case. 'Now, about this man. Was he young?'

She swallowed sharply. 'Do you really want the truth?'

'What else is this about?'

Like a coughing spell, the words rushed out uncontrollably. 'He was young, handsome, probably a revolutionary. As I told you, he saved me from drowning. We met again on the German train.' She paused, squeezing her eyes shut before she went on. 'He stayed in our compartment to avoid passport inspection at the border and stuck with us at Verballen station.'

'Ah yes, your train was held up for several days.'

'The last night there we made love. It was my first time. I guess the ring was to repay me.'

Marya thought of the tenderness, the ecstasy in the Imperial Waiting-room.

Paskevich's large hand tightened on the diamond-crested cigarette-case, denting the platinum. Yet his voice maintained that abrasive amusement. 'Did he by chance mention where he acquired so valuable a trinket?'

'He said it was his dead sister's.'

'The ring's old, made in the days when only the highest nobility could have acquired such a diamond.'

'He had no title; he travelled Second Class.'

Paskevich tossed the dented cigarette-case, and it clattered against the fireplace. 'Let's put this in perspective. You meet some thieving anarchist on the Channel ferry and before you arrive in St Petersburg you've given yourself to him. He pays you off and slides out of your life. Is that an accurate summary?'

He was piling on insults, yet his words barely stung. The wound of Stephan's betrayal was too fresh for her to feel the lesser emotion of humiliation. 'Yes, that's what happened. Now is it clear why I couldn't take your engagement ring?'

'Abundantly clear. Tomorrow I'll meet with my steward to find out which of my buildings has an empty apartment.'

'Apartment? I don't understand.'

'It's not very complicated. As I told you yesterday evening, I'm now Minister of Finance. A great deal of government business — bond flotation and so forth — is conducted with Jews and wealthy merchants. Naturally I can't invite such people here to my home, yet it's often disadvantageous to meet in government offices. So you'll be my hostess. It will be more relaxing if there's female companionship. Boris can introduce you to some of the pretty young ballet girls and milliners he's been taking to bed.'

85

'I'm not a madam,' she snapped, 'and we're going home to California.'

'Yes, my dear, I'm sure you are.'

'There's no need to be sarcastic. I mean it.'

'Tell me, how will you pay for your passage?'

'The ring's valuable.'

'The ring's mine. I bought it from Sazanov. And those IOUs are mine, too. Ergo, so are you. Secondhand goods, but still very lovely.'

'You honestly believe that, if I wouldn't marry you, I'd be your mistress?'

'Marya, you're not a fool, so stop playing one.' He glanced at the desk strewn with Boris's indemnities.

Marya bent her head, biting her lip to hold back tears. 'The way you twist things, you're very clever,' she said.

'The clever also lose,' Paskevich said in a clogged voice.

They were both silent a minute, then he stood. Moving behind her chair, he put his hands on her bared shoulders. His fingers grazed the tops of her breasts.

Nausea rose in her throat.

Twisting from his grasp, she held a hand over her mouth. She caught a glimpse of pain contorting the clever monkey's face. Then she was barging past the cabinets filled with priceless miniatures. The footmen were no longer in the hall. Holding the narrow-hemmed skirt above her knees, she raced up the staircase.

Slamming her door, she ran to the bathroom and vomited the exquisite dinner. After rinsing her mouth, she wove back to the boudoir and stretched out. The pastel scenes of St Petersburg seemed all askew.

Steps echoed down the corridor. A man. Paskevich? Outside her door the footsteps slowed. She held her breath. Was he coming in? She should have turned the key. He'd said he owned her. Then the steps continued, fading into the creaking silence of the palace.

I can't stay here, I can't. Going into the small room where the maid breathed gustily on her pallet, Marya opened the armoire with outerwear, taking her mother's antiquated brown overcoat. Too distraught to bother with a hat or gloves, not even considering putting on felt snowboots, she opened the door and peered up and down the length of dimly lit corridor. Emptiness. She tiptoed past the shadowy niches that held statues, moving cautiously down the staircase. Reaching the hall, she skidded across the huge inlaid sunburst to the vestibule. The night *dvornik,* the doorkeeper, jerked awake, giving her a sullenly surprised look before unbolting the massive front door.

Chapter Seven

A muffled figure glided across the snow in Paskevich Square, going by so silently that Marya recalled those ghostly serfs who supposedly inhabited the city.

She peered at sihouetted domes and spires. Where to go? Where *could* she go? Unlike Boris, whom Paskevich for his own ends had introduced to numerous over-privileged young men, and Miss Dunning, who had attended at-homes and musicales with the dowagers, Marya had met only the palace servants and purveyors of finery. There was no door in St Petersburg that would open to her knock. Once again she felt those fingertips grazing her skin. With a shuddery breath, she began trudging along the cleared quay in the direction of the silhouetted Admiralty spire. Her evening slippers were thin-soled, and the chill penetrated immediately, but she didn't notice the cold. Her mind buzzed with questions, all of them grim. Was Stephan still in St Petersburg? What would Boris do when he came home and discovered she was gone? Would Paskevich toss him into prison? Would Aunt Chatty hold a hand to her long, soft bosom as she got her palpitations?

Several paving stones hadn't been treated with salt. Preoccupied, Marya didn't see the glistening patch of ice. Skidding, she flailed her arms wildly, but she fell. Her chin slammed on to the ice. Her left ankle twisted under her. Sprawled there on the quay in the position of a discarded marionette, she abandoned herself to gasping sobs. Then jangling bells and masculine laughter told her that sleighs were being raced along the frozen river.

Struggling to a sitting position, she attempted to sort out her situation. Two facts jumped out. She couldn't become Paskevich's mistress. She couldn't leave Russia until Boris's mountainous debt was paid and their passage money set aside.

Boris and I will need to find jobs.

Boris has friends; it'll be easier for him.

Where can a woman work in St Petersburg?

Then she thought of Monsieur Bézard. She'd once been in his workroom. A samovar bubbled in the corner where the pressers laboured, seamstresses hunched over whirring Singer sewing machines, and around an immense table women sat hemming or balancing baskets of paillettes that they attached with rapid thrusts of near-invisible needles.

Bézard had told her that he checked the workmanship at night. Which meant he lived on the premises.

It was nearly eleven, the worst of times to apply for a job, but she had no choice.

She limped to the tram-stop and when the tram came she took a seat by a window. Vasilii had never driven her along these mean backstreets. The dilapidated buildings were dark except for joylessly dim drinking-places on the ground floor. A long mound in the snow looked suspiciously like a body. She jumped as the conductor tapped her on the shoulder: the Nevsky Prospekt, he said, pointing, was at the end of that alley.

Hobbling through the darkness as fast as she could, each step shooting pain up her left leg, Marya gave a whimper of relief as the electrical lamp-posts of the Nevsky Prospekt glimmered into view. Bézard's *atelier* window and door were barred. An arrow pointed to the tradesmen's entrance, and she edged down the narrow path, hammering both fists on the wood.

As the door opened, she fell back.

Bézard wore a smoking-jacket: the maroon satin and velvet against his sallow skin gave him the appearance of a Turkish potentate. 'What's all this about?' he demanded. Then he gaped. 'Miss Alexiev? Is that you?'

She must be a sight! Panting, wild-eyed, wearing an antiquated coat, gloveless, hatless, hair dishevelled. 'I'm terribly sorry to disturb you so late,' she said apologetically.

'But you're shivering. I beg you, come inside.'

He led her through the long workroom with its covered sewing machines to a brightly lit room. A couch and two chairs flanked a table where a picked-over chicken carcass and a green bottle up-ended in the wine-cooler gave evidence of a recently consumed meal. Beyond a curtain she glimpsed a bed heaped with tapestry cushions. Bézard's chief assistant, Mishenka, had jumped to his feet. Without his jacket, his collarless shirt open to show his smooth white chest, he epitomized masculine beauty.

'But, my poor Miss Alexiev, you're blue with cold,' Bézard said.

Mishenka shifted a chair to the stove, helping her off with her coat and draping his perfumed serge jacket around her shoulders.

Bézard poured brandy. 'Here. This'll warm you.' Her teeth clinking against the glass, she sipped while the Frenchman continued volubly: 'What a nasty graze on your chin. Those shoes are absolutely ruined. Oh, your poor ankle! Let's see if we need the doctor.' The kindly clucking reminded Marya of Miss Dunning, and she didn't protest when Bézard kneeled to ease off her shoe and ruined white silk stocking.

Boris had sniggered about the couturier's masculinity. Though she had not fully understood her brother's innuendoes, she had known intuitively that Bézard admired her face and body, liked her tremendously, yet never once viewed her as an object of desire. Now she saw that in some unfathomable way he and Mishenka were a married couple.

'You're both so kind,' she said.

'What else is there but kindness?' Bézard dabbed iodine on her chin, and as she flinched he continued in a soothing tone: 'As far as I'm concerned, you can bury Christianity, every branch of it. What does religion offer us? Persecution and wars. If only we each were kind to the other, what a new Jerusalem this earth would be.' He was gently rotating her ankle. 'Does this hurt?'

'Not unbearably.'

'*Bien.* It's probably not broken, then. I'll tape you. Hopefully by tomorrow the swelling will be down a bit.'

After her ankle was tightly bandaged Mishenka gave her a pair of soft grey wool socks that were far too large, but cosy.

'There, that's more like it,' Bézard said. 'You have no more shivering.' He reached for the decanter, shooting the younger man an eloquent glance.

Mishenka excused himself. As the door closed on him, Bézard pulled his chair closer.

'Miss Alexiev, if you wish to tell me your problems, I'll be discreet; but, if you'd rather not, well . . .' He opened his hands and shrugged, a Gallic gesture.

Asking a favour was difficult for Marya. She blurted out: 'I need a job with you.'

Napoleon brandy sloshed in Bézard's glass. 'Miss Alexiev, what are you saying? A lady of your class work?'

'In America we don't have castes. My

mother was a Harvey Girl — she served food at railroad stations.'

Bézard blinked rapidly, then composed himself. 'This is Europe. Russia. And you're related to Count Paskevich.'

'I could learn to sew on a machine, hem, embroider — whatever you need.'

'Miss Alexiev, permit me to be frank. It would take my top seamstress six months to earn the price of the buckles on those sad destroyed shoes.'

She sighed. 'I've been poor.'

'Russian poverty is a thing apart. Let me ask a blunt question. Have you quarrelled with Count Paskevich?'

'I suppose . . .' She sank deeper in the chair. 'Yes.'

'Miss Alexiev —'

'Marya.'

'Marya. Again let me be candid. To be on the count's wrong side is dangerous. I shouldn't speak out like this — he's your relation, after all — but what I say is common knowledge. A few years ago the count believed a Moscow art dealer had cheated him. *Alors,* the Okhrana were investigating the man. And, believe me, the Russian political police can uncover criminal activities in the lives of saints. That dealer is now in Siberia. Last year the newspapers ran a paragraph about an incident at one of the Paskevich estates. There was a charge of embezzlement against his steward. Before the gendarmes could make the arrest, the steward was shot. An accident, or so the paper informed us. Following the Revolution of 1905, in Count Paskevich's bureau those subordinates with liberal leanings — But let's not go into what the Okhrana does to those who go against Count Paskevich's political convictions.' Bézard carefully removed a scrap of thread from his velvet jacket. 'He's a most dangerous enemy.'

'I've always guessed that.'

'Now consider me. Marya, I'm not sure how much of certain matters you comprehend, but you've heard of Oscar Wilde? Yes? Then, you understand a little about Mishenka and me. In St Petersburg there is a certain tolerance, but nevertheless the laws in this country regarding our kind of love are even crueller than those in England. If I hired you against the count's wishes, can you imagine what would lie in store for me — and for Mishenka?'

The warmth of the stove and the brandy had permeated Marya, her ankle no longer throbbed, yet she felt more hopelessly defeated than when she'd sprawled sobbing on the Palace Quay. 'I never should've come here,' she sighed.

'I'm delighted you did. It means you consider me a friend.' Bézard paused. 'Maybe I can come up with a solution if you tell me about the quarrel.'

His eyes were kind. Marya's pride had been vanquished.

She laid out the bare bones of the count's

94

idea of installing her in an apartment.

'That's what he wants?' Bézard said. 'A mistress? From the way he spoke to me I presumed I was designing a trousseau.'

'He did mean that. But . . . well, tonight he learned . . .'

'That you had an adventure? Yes? Good for you. Those who act from the heart, not from the head, are far more trustworthy.'

'Count Paskevich begs to differ.' Marya shivered. 'That jeweller you recommended got in touch with him.'

'Ah, the ring came from the other man? But weren't you absolutely set against disposing of it?'

Fiddling with a long tear in her shot-silk skirt, Marya told the rest of the story.

Bézard gave her hand a compassionate pat, poured her a little more brandy, then leaned forward earnestly.

'Marya, this is not a problem — at least, not a great one,' he said. 'Count Paskevich is witty, cultured, a man of great intelligence, genius even. Powerful. And wealthy beyond Midas's dreams.'

'Money!'

'Don't say it so scornfully. *D'accord*, the count has his bad side. Married to him, you'd have to take the bad with the good. But as his mistress!' He put his fingertips together, kissing them. 'A beautiful little thing like you with a man his age! A story as old as time.'

'All I want is love.'

'Love? You mean the first man? My poor child, where did love get you?'

Tears sprang to her eyes, and she turned away.

After a moment Bézard patted her hand again. 'If that's how it is, dig a hole and bury his memory as deep as possible.'

'What if I can't?'

'Then, remind yourself that Russia is a jewelled paradise for the rich, a frozen abyss for the poor. And, if that's not enough, remind yourself how your handsome revolutionary has behaved.'

Marya's expression hardened. 'There's never really been a choice, has there?' She had considered neither the revulsion she felt for Paskevich, nor the wealth she would have as his mistress. Her decision was reached strictly on IOUs with Boris's scrawled signature. Boris was her entire family. Boris with his weak chest in a Russian prison — Boris in Siberia?

'So you'll return?'

'I must.' She set down her brandy. 'Have you a comb?'

'Leave everything to Mishenka and me.'

Mishenka mended, sponged and ironed her dress while Bézard arranged her hair and powdered her bruised chin. The evening slippers used by clients in the fitting-room were large enough to go over her swollen bandaged foot. Mishenka lined its mate with scraps of silk so that it fitted.

Bézard insisted on escorting her home.

As the droshky halted outside the Crimson Palace, she said: 'There's no way I can thank you.'

'For what? Acting in my own best interest? From now on you'll be my walking advertisement.'

'It's not a business arrangement, and you know it. You're a friend, a generous friend.'

'As your friend, then, I ask one favour.' Bézard glanced towards the pillared entrance. 'Be careful. Count Paskevich is no ordinary protector; you'll never pull any wool over eyes as sharp as his. Be very, very careful.'

Chapter Eight

Silk-shaded sconces threw dim pools of light on to both arms of the staircase. When Marya reached the first landing she saw that Paskevich's study door stood ajar. She had been one of those children who, on being faced with a misdemeanour, had confessed to get the punishment over and done with. She pushed open the door.

Paskevich sat by the fire, his legs crossed, a leather-bound book in his hands. He glanced at her, taking in the mended finery, the old coat in her arms, the bandaged ankle. Without haste he marked his place with an ivory paper-cutter and set down the book. 'Somewhat the worse for wear, but back.'

She managed a careless gesture. 'You knew I went out?'

'Another question like that and I'll have you declared a mental incompetent. This is my home. Grigori' — the night *dvornik* — 'reports to me.'

'I wasn't coming back.'

'Of course not,' he said with amusement. 'You wanted Boris to rot in Siberia and Miss Dunning to freeze.'

'You'd do that?'

'What matters, Marya, is that you believed I would.' He reached under his dinner-coat for an inner pocket, extending folded papers. She took the little sheaf, with one rip tearing the papers in half, dropping them in the fire. They flamed up, curling inwards like petals of a glowing orange flower, blackening and crumpling.

'Wouldn't it have been a good idea to take a look first? Maybe those weren't your brother's IOUs.'

'I trust you.'

'Then, trust me on this, too. Running out of the house when I touch you won't pay off any more of his notes.'

'All right, don't rub it in. You've won. You've made me a whore.'

Until now Paskevich had been smiling. Now his mouth contorted, his brows drew together — an expression of rage and some deeper, less readable emotion. Marya, who had been coaching herself not to show fear, took an involuntary step backwards towards the door. With one stride, Paskevich reached her. Gripping her wrist, he twisted her arm behind her and pulled her towards him. She managed somehow not to cry out at the pain.

'You're terrified,' he said harshly.

'No,' she lied.

'Then, you ought to be.' His mouth clamped down on hers, his teeth bit into her lips, his tongue filled her mouth. She struggled to pull away. The large hands splayed across her buttocks kept her pressed against his erection, the fingers dug through layers of her clothing to part the crack of her buttocks. She made strangled sounds of revulsion and protest, kicking at his legs. His kiss forced her head backwards until it seemed her spine would snap. She could feel the violent pounding of his heart. Abruptly he released her.

The obsidian glitter of his small clever eyes terrified her: she hid her fear under defiance. 'Is this a preview of being your mistress?' she asked.

He slapped her across the cheek, his full strength behind the blow. The cabinet-rows of miniatures spun, tiny eyes of porcelain, clay, jade, gold, ivory stared down as her bandaged ankle gave way and she toppled backwards on to the Isfahan rug. 'Marya, you have no idea,' he said hoarsely.

Crimson brocade stretched over her head. Where was she? Then she saw Paskevich leaning against one of the carved teakwood bedposts as he watched her. His brown velvet dressing-gown was open to the tie-rope, showing a creased throat and a powerful chest thick with black hair. Without his splendid tailoring Paskevich was far uglier yet far less intimidating.

Then, feeling the soreness between her thighs, the raw throbbing all the length of her back, the other, deeper pains, she recalled the narrow leather riding-crop, the punishing fists, the variety of sexual assaults.

How could those obscene tortures be con-

100

sidered the same act as the extravagant pulses, the tender melting — the sheer bliss — that she had experienced with Stephan? Wincing, she pulled the sheet over her bruised breasts and attempted to sit up.

'May I help?' Paskevich asked. His voice was one she'd never heard before. There was none of that patronizing amusement of the past, no hint of last night's savagely degrading insults and commands. He sounded sympathetic, kind even.

'Just don't look at me.'

What had passed between them, his brutality and depravity, should have made her more afraid of him. Yet fear was gone. As was the awe in which she'd held his brilliance, his age, his birth, his position. It seemed to Marya as she struggled to a sitting position that there was nothing left to venerate or to dread in him. Grimacing, she leaned back in the monogrammed pillows.

'You'll have a doctor,' Paskevich said.

'Thank you.'

Springs creaked as he sat on the edge of the bed. 'Marya, what happened last night — I seldom show that side of myself. I've learned to be subtle in the art of vengeance. You see, when I'm hurt, no matter how insignificantly, the itch to strike back possesses me.'

'So I noticed.'

'Let me finish. As I told you, when I was a young child I seldom saw my parents. They left me alone at our estate in Rybinsk with

101

some two hundred house-servants who ignored me, and a brace of tutors who took turns humiliating me and birching me for my pranks — and for any reason they could think up. During those birchings, oh, what a cocky little devil I was. Of course I wept — believe me, I wept — but always in private. Nobody ever got the satisfaction of seeing Ivan Paskevich cry. In families like mine, when the children grow old enough to need lessons no longer, their tutors are kept on in other capacities. I saw to it that mine were discharged without a reference. At the gymnasium I was smaller and younger than the other boys — and considerably quicker-witted. It goes without saying that the others made me suffer. I was tripped, beaten, made the butt of every joke. Again I nursed my hurts in secrecy — thus increasing my schoolmates' efforts. After they pummelled me they would hold my head under the filthy water of a horse-trough. Several times I passed out.'

'Didn't the teachers see it?'

'If they did, they never intervened.'

'Then, why didn't you write to your parents?'

'A Paskevich go snivelling? No, I spent three afternoons a week with the boxing coach. My strength increased with my skill. When two louts in their final year tried ducking me in the horse-trough, I managed to knock out the pair of them. How I savoured the moment! I still do. By the end of the year, the other boys were calling me "a good sort". What they meant was that they feared and respected me. At university it was the same. Then I did my military service with the Gardes. At the time there was trouble along the border in Turkistan. I gave my all, and expected the same of my men. They called me "Fearless Paskevich". I was awarded the cross of Saint George.'

It was Sunday, and the cathedral bells of St Petersburg began chiming. Across the frozen Neva, in the Fortress of Peter and Paul, the carillon chimed out the hourly hymn, 'Praise the Lord in Zion.'

After a few moments she asked apathetically: 'For courage?'

'Yes. But let's call my courage by its rightful name. The desperation of that cornered boy hitting out. Proving to myself, always proving to myself that nobody can take advantage of me.'

In the ensuing silence, Marya recalled Bézard's cautionary tales.

He paused, shrugging. 'Vengeance is neither a virtue nor useful, but for me it's a necessity. I've never been able to forgive a slight or forget a wrong.'

Under normal circumstances Marya would have been deeply touched by the neglected child, the under-sized schoolboy braving filthy water and drowning to cope on his own. Touched, too, that Paskevich was justifying his actions to her — by rank he owed explanations solely to the tsar.

'You hurt me more than I realized,' Paskevich said gruffly. 'Am I forgiven?'

She sighed. 'Usually I don't harbour a grudge.'

'And this time you do?' He reached towards her hand, then let his arm fall. 'Would it help to say you're beautiful, with skin like the richest white silk and hair the rosy bronze of summer dawn, and I could melt in your silver eyes? If that's not flowery enough, how about something fanciful like you're a Botticelli Venus come to life? No, you're too dainty to be Venus. But, as you noticed, I prefer miniatures.' His jocular tone rang too loudly, and he shrugged. 'I'll arrange for the doctor,' he said.

'Thank you.'

'One thing more, and this is a promise. I swear never, never again to raise a hand against you.'

The doctor, accustomed to the secret perversities of the upper class, made no comment as he rebandaged her ankle, pronouncing it unbroken, and rubbed a soothing ointment into her oozing lacerations. For her facial bruises he ordered ice.

She was surrounded by Paskevich's white orchids and holding the ice-bag to her black eye when Boris stuck his head in the door.

'My God! What happened to you?'

She handed her brother the large box of French bonbons that had just been delivered. 'Open this, will you?'

'Marya.'

'You're tearing that lovely satin ribbon!' She snatched back the chocolate-box. 'Paskevich —'

'*He* did this to you?'

'I fell on the ice,' she said.

'Tosh!'

'He's getting us an apartment.'

'An apartment?'

'He needs a hostess.'

'Does that mean what I think?'

'It depends on how dirty your mind is.'

'I'll kill him!'

'There's a brilliant idea. With him dead and you on the gallows, Aunt Chatty and I could starve.'

'Jesus Christ! How can you joke about it?'

'Oh, at first I played the insulted damsel.' There was no need to tell her brother, sitting so dejectedly at her bedside, about the IOUs that would have landed him in jail.

'That's when I charged out and broke my ankle and smashed up my face. Then I decided to see Bézard about a job. He hires skilled seamstresses, not amateurs like me.'

'I'll get work.'

'Bézard says the city's full of unemployed. And the wages are pitiful,' she said. 'Paskevich is giving us the apartment, nice clothes, everything our hedonistic hearts desire. Entertaining the bankers and other such low types that his cabinet post forces

him to slum around with is our sole responsibility.'

'That, and a place in your bed.'

'Stop sounding so priggish.'

'For Christ's sake, you're my sister.'

'Boris, think. Card-parties, musicales,
dancing, endless champagne, gypsies, bala-
laikas.'

'If Father could hear you now.'

'Well, he can't.' Marya reached for the
jewel-box, snapping it open to show the
emerald. 'Behold.'

'He pays promptly,' Boris said with uncharacteristic bitterness.

Marya took what appeared to be a cream,
biting into it. 'The problem is keeping anything sordid from Aunt Chatty's maidenly
eyes and ears.'

'How do you plan to do that?'

'Oh, she goes to bed early.'

Boris bent his head, looking far younger
than nineteen. Like Marya, he was fighting
back tears.

Fourstatskaia 12 was fronted by a row of
tall birches. When the winter sun shone,
bare branches threw shadows as finely
drawn as calligraphy across the yellow
stucco. Marya always climbed the stone
staircase to the second floor with proprieto-
rial gratification. The wages of sin had a
front door with laurel wreaths at the centre
of the upper panels. From the hall flowed a
vista of reception rooms: the dining-room

and drawing-room were as yet unfurnished; however, the music room sported a Bechstein grand piano, a game-table, a black lacquer chinoiserie work-table for Miss Dunning's embroidery, chairs and two deep sofas.

Marya's bedroom particularly delighted her. The wide low bed was covered with a silk Persian rug and heaped with pillows along the wall so that it resembled a Turkish divan. The small tables were crammed with framed photographs: her parents, Boris, Miss Dunning, schoolfriends in San Francisco were all represented, but not Paskevich. Crystal perfume-bottles and a gold dressing-set gleamed on the vanity unit. The bookcase held the latest novels from England and America. The celadon-green wallpaper was imported from China, and delicately brushed oriental cranes swooped around the four walls.

Marya spent her mornings holding one of the novels but gazing at the oriental birds. Her ankle had healed, her bruises had faded, her welts only stung a little when she used her loofah, yet sluggishness continued to entrap her. Miss Dunning fretted, worrying aloud that she was staying up too late — an unhealthy European habit. The good-hearted spinster, who went to bed before ten, praised Paskevich to the skies: she had no idea that their benefactor, who visited three or four nights a week, spent the small hours on Marya's low divan bed.

The young Alexievs celebrated the move to Fourstatskaia 12 with a midnight supper, the first party they had ever given. Boris invited everybody he had met in St Petersburg — the heavy-gambling young officers, the racier young married couples, the prettiest girls from the *corps de ballet.* Marya asked Monsieur Bézard and Mishenka as well as the two pleasant-faced brothers, both lawyers, who lived upstairs. Preparing for the party roused her from her unaccustomed languor. In her stockinged feet she ran around the apartment getting in the caterers' way as she rearranged the bouquets of red carnations, Parma violets, stems of fragrant lilac, huge pink roses that had been delivered with Paskevich's cases of champagne.

Miss Dunning, in her new black dress trimmed with jet beads, managed to stay awake until the guests began arriving from the various balls and dances that preoccupied St Petersburg from Christmas to Lent, then she excused herself. Paskevich and two bankers retired to a corner to discuss a bond issue. Goulenko's renowned gypsy band played, and couples whirled breathlessly through the furnitureless drawing-room.

The gypsies had brought along a fortune-teller. Just before the supper, Boris led his protesting sister through a group that encircled the table where the gypsy was plying her trade. Henna-tinted hair falling in a curtain over her dusky features, she traced Marya's palm with a grubby beringed finger. 'Strange . . . Here's your lifeline. See how it stops, then starts again?'

'You mean she dies young?' enquired a young officer with glittering gold *aiguillettes* swinging from his shoulders.

'Not exactly dies.' The dark fingernail retraced the line. 'See for yourself. She is alive, then dead, then alive again. The line moves to old age.'

'Marya's too gorgeous to grow old,' interjected a tall long-necked ballerina. 'Her lovers — tell us about her lovers.'

'I see many admirers.' The gypsy peered into Marya's eyes. 'You will have two ardent suitors. Both will be from the most exalted circles.'

Marya gave a snort. Stephan was gone from her life, and anyway he was hardly exalted. Oh, eventually, when Paskevich tired of her, she might find another lover — but a husband? Men, even men from lesser circles, didn't marry another's leavings.

'Don't you adore gypsies?' cried the tall ballerina. 'Everybody always marries splendidly.'

'I tell what I see.' The gypsy squeezed Marya's hand so tightly that the emerald cut into her finger. 'Many tears. Great catastrophe. Ah, terrible things . . . But two highborn suitors to choose between.'

There weren't enough chairs, and most of the guests stood balancing supper-plates filled with salads, cold poached sturgeon, asparagus from Paskevich's hothouse.

What surprised Marya was the way Paskevich drew attention. Even now, as he sat on a sofa eating with the middle-aged bankers he'd brought with him, the younger set kept coming over to interrupt his conversation. The prettiest women kept parading hopefully in his vicinity. Younger and more handsome men possessed of great wealth and august titles were here, yet they blended in with everyone else. They lacked Paskevich's unwilled air of authority and energy.

'Congratulate me,' he said with a quirk of his eyebrow. 'I'm to be married on March the seventh.'

The announcement was made quietly, to his bankers. Yet all conversation ceased in the room. Marya's hand jerked, and champagne darkened her lily-of-the-Nile blue satin evening gown. All she could think was what date would the seventh be in California? Russia, mired in the past, kept to the antiquated Julian calendar. America and western Europe used the Gregorian calender: 7 March would be 20 March. Boris, gnawing on his lower lip the way he did when anxious, shot her a sympathetic glance.

Then the voices burst out, demanding the name of the bride.

'Princess Mathilde Mihalovna Stullginsky.'

Later, in the Chinese-wallpapered bedroom, Paskevich turned off all the lights except for one silk-shaded lamp.

'What do you think of my news?' He was undoing the tiny pearl buttons down the back of her dress.

She hoped that it meant his physical demands would be lessened while he continued to support the apartment and visit them. His conversation made her laugh and educated her about art, music, history, politics: though his amusement at her expense infuriated her, she looked forward to seeing him. In bed she was either indifferent or vaguely revulsed. She did her utmost not to compare what happened with him to the night in the Imperial Waiting-room.

'I was surprised,' she said.

'It won't make the least difference to us,' he said.

When she was naked, he kneeled on the carpet, kissing her nipples, kissing her stomach and thighs. He moved one of the slipper-chairs in front of the pier-glass. She looked neither at herself nor at him unbuttoning his trousers. Then he lifted her, sitting her on his lap so that they both faced the mirror. He watched her reflection until the end, when his eyes squeezed shut and he gasped aloud.

Before dawn, he dressed and left.

She hadn't asked him anything about his bride-to-be, Princess Stullginsky, or the wedding.

Chapter Nine

On 7 March an Arctic wind skidded across the frozen canal to rattle the double-glazed windows of Boris's bedroom. The overheated air was filled with odours of tobacco, sweat and menthol. Boris lay in bed, and Marya sat nearby with a book. Though it was barely three, dusk was already falling. As Marya went to switch on the light, Miss Dunning came in. She wore her grey alpaca with a new milliner's confection whose deep crown sprouted ostrich plumes that cast swaying shadows across her long, shyly proud face.

'Auntie, how splendid you look!' Marya exclaimed.

'It's not the thing, don'tcha know,' Boris said, 'to outshine the empress *and* the bride.'

Miss Dunning giggled like a schoolgirl. 'Are you feeling better after your little nap, Boris dear?'

'Fit as a fiddle,' he said with a cough.

'Stuff,' Marya responded. 'You've got a temperature of a hundred and one. Aunt Chatty, he can't possibly take you.'

Miss Dunning's smile faded into disappointment, and she stared down at the creamy card in her hand. Her friends, the dowagers, had somehow arranged it that she received an invitation for the marriage of Princess Mathilde Mihalovna Stullginsky and Count Ivan Arkadievich Paskevich in the Khazan Cathedral. Boris and Marya were delighted not to be on the guest-list. Miss Dunning, however, had cajoled Boris until he reluctantly consented to be her escort.

'I'll bundle up, and come directly home.' With this he gave a barking hack, his spine arched, his face reddened, and he went into a spasm of coughing.

Miss Dunning puffed his pillows while Marya ran for the bottle of red cough-syrup which contained an opiate. After he was breathing normally, they left him to sleep.

In the corridor Miss Dunning caught Marya's arm. 'Marya, dear, Baroness Golytsin and Countess Zotov' — the dowagers — 'are in the wedding party, and they've told me that the tsar isn't just attending the ceremony. He's to give the bride away!' Miss Dunning was guileless in her respectful admiration of nobility and royalty. 'Imagine, Count Paskevich's that close to the Imperial family. A wedding with the tsar and tsarina, the entire Court! You mustn't miss it.'

'I didn't get an invitation.'

'And neither did Boris. Haven't I explained and explained? It's a sheer oversight on the bride's part. Why, *I'm* invited and I'm not even related. And Count Paskevich is so fond of you.'

Marya's face was hot. 'Somebody has to stay with Boris.'

'He'll be asleep. We owe it to the count to make a showing. Nobody could have been kinder.' She paused, saying in a low voice: 'Marya, how can I go alone?'

'I've invited Mishenka and Monsieur Bézard to dinner.'

Miss Dunning's eyes filled with tears, and despite her elegant hat she looked like a mournful grey sheep. Marya thought of the warm-hearted spinster tending them when they were little, comforting them for scraped knees, baking their favourite pies, pretending to ignore their mischievous giggles at her expense, taking them on jaunts to Sausalito on the ferry, stinting on herself to buy them ice-cream sodas and chunks of Giradelli chocolate.

'You're the one who's good.' Marya hugged the soft quaking shoulders. 'I'll send a note around to Monsieur Bézard's.'

Klazkha deposited a silken heap on the chaise in the order in which the silken undergarments would be donned, then she carried the low-cut white gown to the bed, cinching in the waist, returning again with white satin evening slippers that she aligned on the linen towel below. The girl's face, pitted from a bout of smallpox, was pulled into the reverent concentration of a postulant handling sacred vestments.

Klazkha Sobchak alone among the apartment staff, which included two housemaids, a bow-legged butler and a chef, had not previously been employed at the Crimson Palace.

At barely thirteen, she was irregularly young and quite untrained for her position as a personal maid. Work, however, was nothing new to Klazkha. As a toddler, she had already been fetching and carrying for her mother, a widowed laundress employed by the third-floor tenant.

Two weeks after the Alexievs had moved in, the widow Sobchak had slumped over her washboard, dying within minutes. That same day, her employer had hired a new laundress, and Klazkha vanished. A few days later Marya had been going into the fashionable Cubat to meet Boris for dinner when she had spotted the former laundry girl idling along. The bitter wind had whipped Klazkha's brightly cheap shawl around her childish body, and threatened to tear off the wide-brimmed straw hat trimmed with crumpled cherries. The battered whore's hat had brought tears to Marya's eyes. Then and there outside the Cubat, she had offered Klazkha this job. Klazkha had blurted out that she had been arrested. 'They gave me a warning and let me go right away, but now I've got a yellow card.' The yellow card, dreaded prostitute's identification, made other employment virtually unavailable. Marya had hired her regardless. Paskevich, in a coldly majestic fury, had ordered Marya to get rid of the girl — 'No syphilitic, under-age whore works for me, is that understood?' were the words he'd used in front of Klazkha. Marya, ordering Klazkha to stay out of Count Paskevich's way, managed a few roubles each week for the girl from her pin money. Marya had no regrets about her impulsive kindness. That prevalent lassitude hadn't left her, and Klazkha's lack of chatter — abnormal in any Russian domestic and even more so in a personal maid — proved restful. Klazkha ironed beautifully; and, as for the rest of the job, she was learning rapidly. The Crimson Palace servants, who formed a clique of superiority in the building, tyrannized Klazkha for her youth, her complexion, her time on the streets, and mockingly derided her habit of squirrelling away leftovers.

'You chose the perfect dress,' Marya said.

'It's as grand as can be; but what about being white, like the bride?'

With the entire Court in attendance, who would notice her standing with Miss Dunning in the shadowy rear of the great cathedral? 'I'll be wearing my fur over it.'

Klazkha held Marya's discarded underwear against her as yet undeveloped chest. 'Miss Alexiev . . .'

Marya had moved to the pier-glass to knot her hair at the nape of her neck: a lady's maid should be skilled at coiffures, but neither Klazkha nor Marya knew this. 'Mm?' Marya said through a mouthful of hairpins.

'One of them attics is empty,' Klazkha said.

Under the slate roof was a labyrinth of

badly ventilated cubicles. Other landlords rented similar quarters to the poor for a few roubles: Paskevich reserved the cubbyholes for his tenants' staff.

Marya took the hairpins out of her mouth. 'But you don't need to be stuck up there.' Like most personal maids, Klazkha slept in the dressing-room.

'The landlady pushed us out of our place,' Klazkha said, her pitted cheeks crimson.

'Us?'

'We rent a corner in her room, me and my brother.'

'You have a brother?' So that's where the table scraps went. 'How old?'

'Ten — but, I promise you, very quiet. He . . . uh, he don't stamp around. Three summers ago he got this horrible fever that shrivelled up his legs.'

'First thing tomorrow I'll speak to the *dvornik*.' The doorman in this building acted as the concierge. 'You can move in right away.'

Klazkha's seldom-used smile came into play: her face appeared split in two by white teeth.

The droshky horse was covered with blue wool net to prevent the light snow from flying in the cabdriver's face. The hack edged slowly forward, trapped in the great mass of handsome equipages negotiating the turn. The north side of the Cathedral of Our Lady of Khazan, a magnificent curve of Corinthian pillars and biblical statuary, ran along the Nevsky Prospekt. But the entrance, a box-like little affair, stood in the narrow side-street. It was opposite the altar, and in the Russian Orthodox religion the altar must face the east. As the fur-bundled wedding guests hurried up red-carpeted steps, police linked arms against the surging spectators.

The interior of the cathedral, a replica of St Peter's in the Vatican, was lit by thousands of candles. The richly jewelled iconostasis in front of the altar, the sumptuous gold, purple, green and crimson vestments of the priests, the vivid uniforms, the blazing diamond tiaras formed a continent of brilliance amid the black velvet shadows. According to tradition, there were no pews. Marya led Miss Dunning to stand by the nearest pillar.

Miss Dunning, who was short-sighted, took out her spectacles. 'We're miles from the altar,' she demurred.

'Auntie, it's jammed down there. Back here we'll have a way better view.'

A Chevalier Garde, splendid in his gold-braided scarlet Court uniform, escorted a woman in a lustrous sable cloak. Whispers floated like the dust motes. 'Grand Duchess Xenia . . .'

Peering after the illustrious fur, Miss Dunning sighed, whispering: 'The tsar's own sister . . . You're absolutely right, Marya, this is the best spot. We'll see all the guests as they come in.'

A few minutes later cheers rang outside, growing louder and louder. There were nearby shouts of 'Bless us, Little Father! Bless us, Little Mother!' There was a great rustling as the entire congregation turned.

The tsar was trimly bearded, shorter and more compact than Marya had imagined him from his portraits. Drawing a sharp breath, she realized that this was the man who held absolute power over one hundred and fifty million people and a sixth of the earth's land mass. She couldn't control her prickling awe, yet her American side prevented her from sinking into a deep obeisance as others around her were doing.

The tsarina's magnificent diamond tiara trembled, her ropes of huge glowing pearls shook, yet despite this obvious agitation her lovely ravaged face was remote, expressionless.

In the moment that the Imperial pair passed, the tsar turned a worried glance to his wife and Marya saw that his eyes were an intense blue — Romanov Blue, people called the shade. *Stephan has eyes that colour,* she thought, then dug her nails into her palms.

The tsar returned to the entrance vestibule. Patriarch Antiochus, who was to conduct the ceremony, appeared. White-bearded, his white hair falling in curls below his huge jewelled mitre, the old man paced towards

119

the altar. There, Paskevich waited in gold-braided ministerial splendour, orders and medals completely armouring his barrel chest.

The unaccompanied male choir burst into a triumphant hymn. The tsar led the bride from the shadows. Princess Stullginsky's face and bosom were veiled. The lace caught on the diamond *chiffre,* the coveted insignia of a Russian empress's maid of honour, which she wore on the left shoulder of her wedding gown; and as she used her free hand to disentangle herself strands of al-mond-sized diamonds glinted on her thick wrist. A diamond-and-ruby tiara sat squarely atop her head. With her stout, heavily corseted body stuffed into lustrous white satin, the long train fanning out in her wake, she resembled a figurehead on a broad-beamed Viking ship.

'She seems quite old,' Miss Dunning whis-pered doubtfully.

When the tsar reached the altar, the wait-ing Paskevich inclined his head slightly, a nod rather than a bow. The monarch re-leased the bride's arm, moving to the tsar-ina's side. The litany began.

'The Stullginskys are richer than God.' The whisper came from a bent figure to Marya's left. His fringe of grey hair was plastered to his forehead, and he wore old-fashioned satin Court attire with white silk stockings on his spindly bow legs. 'But imagine taking that battleship to bed.'

The companion, another ancient, leaned more heavily on his cane as he chuckled maliciously: 'I'll wager it won't be often. Paskevich has a new mistress, and they say he's quite mad for the little thing.'

'Paskevich? Losing his head over a woman? Tell me another.'

Now the bridal couple were each holding a flower-wreathed candle. The Patriarch's deep tuneful voice echoed through the immense cathedral. 'Vouchsafe unto them love made perfect, peace and help, O Lord, we beseech thee.'

'Amen,' sang the invisible chorus.

'. . . bless now Thy servants, Ivan and Mathilde . . .'

There were more prayers, more psalms sung by basses and soaring tenors. A rose silk carpet was spread for the couple, crowns were held above their heads as they circled the altar. The bride's crown was raised higher than the groom's, for she was the taller of the two.

'Confirm their union in faith and concord and truth and love . . .'

The two old men continued to stare at Marya, then exchanged loud whispers.

Inhaling the scent of beeswax and incense, Marya clasped her hands. They were speaking French, a language of which the dowagers had taught Miss Dunning a few phrases. Thank God she was engrossed by the flower of Russian nobility and the exotically foreign ceremony.

'An exquisite child, isn't she? A daughter of one of the Alexievs. Fedor, I think.'

'Fedor Alexiev? That nobody? The last I heard, he was tutoring the Yeropkins' idiot boys — or was he their major-domo? A servant anyway. Didn't they go to the American Wild West?'

'Exactly. Alexiev died there. Possibly by bow and arrow. Or six-shooter.' Chuckles. 'Anyway, he was a distant connection of Paskevich's mother. When he died, Paskevich shipped the girl over here and installed her on the Fourstatskaia. Oh, he's smitten all right. Even keeps a chaperon; that must be the old grey trout with her. There's a brother.'

Whispers.

'No, nothing like that. The situation's all very well and good as far as the boy's concerned. In fact they say he talked her into it. He's constantly losing at the tables.'

'An unlucky gambler? Sounds as if she might need to expand her clientele to pay his losses. What an exquisitely sensual little creature she is. Always did have a yen for redheads. Might have a go-round with her myself . . .'

To Marya the male whispers resounded, bouncing against the dome, the mighty walls, the arches and naves, reverberating against the gilded icons. Her heart beat at a rapid pace, and she leaned against the pillar.

Aunt Chatty was staring at her. 'Marya?'

122

she said, her voice wavering in and out of the choir.

The velvety shadows were engulfing the entire glittering crowd, and Marya felt herself falling.

The snow was coming down more heavily, but the crowd had not dispersed. The charcoal-braziers that had been set out in the street were surrounded by shabbily bundled people awaiting another glimpse of their Little Father and Little Mother as well as the splendidly noble wedding guests. Everyone turned, peering through misty smoke as Miss Dunning helped Marya from the cathedral.

For Marya the brief loss of consciousness was a chasm. On the far side lay blissful ignorance. On this side, a list of symptoms. Including the latest: passing out. The long, inert hours in her room. The absence of her period — she had never been regular, but when was the last time? While they were staying in London, yes, late November, and this was 20 March on the western calendar.

Their driver was manoeuvring through the mass of waiting vehicles to the cathedral steps. Inside the droshky, Miss Dunning patted Marya's hand.

'I never should have forced you to come tonight,' she said quietly.

'It's all right, Auntie.'

'Marya, I understood some of what those

disgusting men were talking about. What a fool I've been, what a stupid, blind old fool.'

'You're just too good to believe the worst of anyone.'

'It started that night you fell and sprained your ankle, didn't it?'

Marya nodded.

'And I thought he was kind! You're just a child, and he must be nearing fifty. What a degenerate!'

'Auntie, he's not.'

'A relation taking advantage of an innocent little girl? The man's a monster.'

'Do you think we can save anything?' Though Paskevich belonged to a circle that rarely handled money, for inexplicable reasons of his own, it pleased him to dole out coins to the lined-up servants — except, naturally, for Klazkha — then ceremoniously present Miss Dunning with a thick envelope of paper roubles for the household expenses.

'I'll do my best.' Miss Dunning patted her hand again. 'You won't have to . . . *submit* . . . again.'

'Soon he won't want me.'

'Don't be silly. Come to think of it, why didn't I guess? The way he's always looking at you.'

Bells clanged as they clipped past a double-decked tram.

'I'm going to have a baby,' Marya said.

Miss Dunning gave a long, mournful whimper. It took her a while to find her voice.

'We'll invent a dead American husband for you.'

'Oh, Auntie.' Marya squeezed the gloved hand. 'That's the least of our worries.'

Miss Dunning was silent again.

Marya rubbed at the glass with her glove, peering out at the snow. Although Paskevich had explained himself, Marya didn't understand him. He was too much older, he stood at the apex of a brilliant aristocracy, he was immensely wealthy, and furthermore there were the psychological barriers of his boundless intelligence and his mordant wit. One fact, though, she knew for certain about him. He demanded perfection of his belongings. He would never keep a woman with a swollen body.

It followed, then, that her little family would need money. She had never been methodical, but as they rolled through the freezing night she was listing her material assets.

The emerald. She twisted the large stone under her glove. She had no idea what Paskevich had done with Stephan's sand-smoothed diamond, but she did have this ring — given to her, he'd said, without strings. But would he let her keep anything else? Her lynx? She stroked the soft fur. She had no idea what it cost, but probably a fortune. Her clothes. Most women wore larger sizes than she, so they wouldn't bring as good a price. Still, money was money.

Marya tiptoed in to see Boris. His breath

rattled noisily. How would her brother with his delicate chest fare in the cellars and attics inhabited by the poor of this frozen city?

Emerging, she found Miss Dunning. 'You must eat more, Marya. I've fixed you a little bite.'

Marya felt bilious. Rather than argue, though, she spooned up the food that had comforted her childhood: buttered bread soggy with sweetened creamy milk. And all the while questions about survival shot through her head.

Positive she'd lie awake fretting all night, she curled on the divan bed, hugging the bolster against herself. Almost immediately she slept.

Chapter Ten

The light jolted her into wakefulness. Paskevich, kicking the door shut, stamped to her divan bed. Poised over her in his ankle-length reindeer-fur coat, he radiated the night chill and fury. He must have heard she was at the cathedral.

The vital thing, she told herself, *is to keep the things, especially my lynx. No matter what happens, I must stay calm.*

'What's the time?' she asked.

'About three-thirty.' He shrugged off his coat. His wedding splendour had been replaced by a serge business-suit. 'Well?' he demanded.

'Well, what?' Summoning a note of humorous asperity, she reached for the swans-down bed-jacket at the foot of her bed. 'You're the one who just got married.'

'As you're only too aware,' he snapped.

'You saw me?'

'All of St Petersburg saw you. You made yourself excessively visible.'

Those fairy-tale people with their blazing diamonds and flamboyant uniforms in the gilded Khazan Cathedral — the tsar and tsarina, the patriarch in his bejewelled mitre, the grand dukes and grand duchesses, the ministers and high nobility, those two malicious old men, the bride and groom — had they all turned to watch Marya Alexiev sagging against a shadowy pillar?

'Why were you there?' Paskevich asked.

'The dowagers saw to it that Aunt Chatty got an invitation. And she insisted that, since you'd been so wonderfully "kind" to us, I couldn't miss your wedding. With so many important guests I assumed that we'd be inconspicuous.'

'What about Boris? I didn't notice him there.'

'He's ill.'

'Another of his convenient fevers?'

At this slur against her brother, she lost her resolve to keep a mercenary eye on the buck — or, rather, the rouble. 'Did you have to tell the whole world about me?'

'I?'

'Two spiteful creatures, horrible old men, were standing near us. They knew who I was, they knew my name, my father, everything about you and me.' The swansdown trembled. 'They were talking French; and poor Aunt Chatty, she understood enough of it to follow what . . .' Losing her struggle for control, Marya turned weeping to the celadon-green wallpaper.

A chair was dragged to the bed.

'I've never mentioned our relationship to anyone,' Paskevich said quietly. 'But people come to this apartment, and every one of them knows more about life than the excellent Miss Dunning. You're beautiful, lively, and I confess to the crime of glancing in your direction. Why are you taking gossip to heart? This isn't some provincial American hamlet. St Petersburg is sophisticated, tolerant.'

'The one with the cane said he'd give me a go-round,' Marya said in a muffled tone.

'If I knew his name, I'd happily draw and quarter him.'

'Easy for you to be sarcastic.' Marya's throat pulsed. 'You're not the one having a baby.'

At Paskevich's sudden intake of breath, she began to shiver. God, what had she said? Why couldn't she have maintained silence until the truth became self-evident, thus giving Aunt Chatty time to salt away money? Blurting out the truth like that was no way to coax for her wardrobe. A motor car skidded to a halt below, metal doors slammed, and voices called out farewells.

Paskevich's dark glittering gaze never left her face. 'It's mine, then?'

Incredibly, the question had never occurred to her. She had been so wound up in how to provide for them that she hadn't considered the child's paternity. Was the father Stephan, to whom she had given herself in love? Or Paskevich, who had overpowered her in every way? She rested her hand on her flat stomach. In this single protective gesture she accepted the irrelevancy of Paskevich's question. The baby was hers. Hers. If need be, she would walk the streets or commit murder to keep the child safe.

'That night before I made you my mistress,'

he was saying, 'you had your menses.'

'I was . . . depressed, sad. I said I was indisposed.'

'So this could be the absentee radical's responsibility?'

She shook her head. 'Mine.'

He paced across the room. 'What an astonishing creature you are.'

'Make fun of me all you want. Just let me keep my clothes.'

'An odd request for a woman whose dresses soon won't fit.'

'You said the emerald was mine. What about the fur?'

'Secondhand goods are often more valuable than new.'

'Then, we can't keep anything?' Her voice broke.

He moved to a curtained window. 'Marya, I meant it quite sincerely. You have me completely baffled. Why in God's name didn't you simply say the child was mine?'

'It might not be.'

'I needn't have known the ambiguities.'

'Lie?'

'Of course you should have lied.'

'But what would be the point? You couldn't marry me.'

'Marya my pet, men have been known to cherish their bastards.'

As he said bastard she winced. Looking across the luxurious bedroom at him, she was surprised to see her misery reflected on his face.

'I gave you the coat and the clothes as well as the emerald,' he said hoarsely. 'They're yours.'

'How marvellous! Thank you!' She raised her knees, clasping her hands around her nightgowned legs. 'And we can stay here until the first of the month?'

'You keep talking as if I'm about to toss you bodily into the snow.'

'Who can be positive what you'll do? You're so unpredictable.'

'How so?'

'Well, coming here tonight.'

'I've already performed my marital duties.' He pulled a face.

'See? There's a perfect example. Who can understand a man who makes a remark like that on his wedding night?'

'You saw my bride.'

'Nobody forced you to marry her.'

'A fortune like hers is a powerful incentive.'

'Money's the last thing you need.'

'This is what I need.' He pressed a kiss on Marya's mouth. He'd been drinking champagne. The kiss lasted while he stretched out on the bed. His suit buttons pressed through her nightgown and bed-jacket. She flinched. His embrace loosened, and he cupped a hand gently over her breast. 'Sore?'

'A little.'

He sat up, unbuttoning his jacket. 'One advantage of the good Miss Dunning knowing the awful truth — I won't have to leap out of bed.'

'You're staying? Tonight?'

'The Countess Paskevich has her own rooms. And I just told you; my functions have been fulfilled. What else would you like to know? My wife has immense spongy thighs, her nipples reach her navel, her conversation should be bottled to put insomniacs to sleep.'

Marya felt a momentary pity for the stout aristocratic bride. 'That's not very nice.'

'Nice? Me?' He shook with laughter. 'Marya, do you honestly believe a couple of hours in the Khazan Cathedral can work miracles in character transformation? I still have my very sharp, if amusing, tongue. I will never be an uxorious husband. And put your sympathies for my wife to better use. She's a married woman, and the ring is all she wanted. The joys of the table are what make her quiver.'

'You haven't given her a chance.'

In response Paskevich kissed Marya's throat and pulled up her lacy nightgown.

At eight-thirty, Klazkha brought Marya's coffee. Resting the silver tray on her hip, turning the painted porcelain knob, she gave an expert little kick to swing open the bedroom door. Her face drained of blood.

Klazkha, born practical, had never allowed herself daydreams. Still, sometimes, enveloped in the odours of dirty underwear and the steam of the huge, boiling copper pots, her skinny childish arms straining as she rubbed heavy linen sheets against the washboard, she had wistfully considered becoming a lady's maid. These hopes had evaporated when her mother's sudden heart-attack had condemned her to a living hell. Either she was shivering on a streetcorner or being abused in every form of pornographic depravity. To her the male sex had become the enemy. A bestial and alien race. In the presence of most men, she would feel her neck hairs prickle. A few seemed less dangerous. None was entirely trustworthy. (She excluded her brother Josip, dear, sweet, crippled ten-year-old Josip, from this mass condemnation.) Then, like a fairy-tale, she'd been whisked to this palatial apartment where he was never cold, never hungry, and her work was sheer pleasure: ironing the clothes of beautiful generous Miss Marya, running scented baths, straightening this gorgeous room. As in every fairy-tale, however, all would evaporate if she disobeyed one injunction. She must never be seen by the terrifying noble who now slept with his bald head squashing down her employer's naked white breasts.

Paskevich stirred, blinking up at her.

'Marya,' he said loudly, 'wasn't I clear enough about the young whore?'

Marya's head jerked up. 'What? Who?'

'I told you to rid the flat of this diseased little slut.'

Klazkha stood rigid in the doorway, gripping the silver handles. Immobile, her even features drained of blood and expressionless, she might have been a pitted marble statue in a graveyard.

'Klazkha isn't an animal,' Marya hissed. 'She can hear you.'

'Excellent. Now she knows to get off my property.' Paskevich got out of bed with aristocratic indifference to a mere servant seeing his nakedness. His man thing, Klazkha noted, was long, dark and excessively thick. He picked up his silk-and-wool drawers. 'For the charms of your bed I can put up with the fluttering snobbery of Miss Dunning, and I'm willing to pay your hypochondriac brother's gambling debts. I draw the line, though, at supporting syphilitic juvenile strumpets.'

'This is our home until you ask us to leave.' Marya wondered if the thudding of her heart were audible throughout the green bedroom. 'I'll have any personal maid I choose.'

'Get out of my sight!' Paskevich thundered at Klazkha.

She backed away, closing the door with a nudge of her thigh, then scurried down the long corridor.

Paskevich flung on his clothes; he did not attach his collar to his shirt or fasten his cufflinks. Reaching in his pocket, he hurled a banknote on the pillows. 'That's to pay off the diseased creature. See she's gone from my property this morning.'

'If you're referring to Klazkha, I'm keeping her. She's my friend!'

'Exactly the kind of friendship one would expect from an American waitress's daughter.'

'Thank God for America. And no wonder revolutionaries throw bombs here!'

He pulled on his reindeer coat. 'You never learn, do you?'

'I can't imagine why I'm so slow, when I have such an excellent professor in the fine art of revenge.'

His fists clenched until the dark hairs stood out like wires on the large strong hands. What would happen to the baby if he battered her again? She shrank back.

'Stop worrying, my pet.' Paskevich formed a humourless smile. 'I swore never to hit you again.'

After he had stalked from the room, she sank down on the rumpled divan bed. Why, when she was in desperation about her little family's livelihood, had she alienated him?

Klazkha returned with the coffee-tray. Setting it on the bedside table, she mumbled: 'I'll be getting my things together.'

'No, you'll help me dress, then we'll see the door-keeper about your brother's room.'

'Miss Marya, Count Paskevich don't want me here. And he ain't the sort to change his mind.'

'Neither am I.'

The walls of the vacant garret were thin, the roof slanted down sharply, the window was at knee-level.

'It's not much,' Marya said dubiously.

Klazkha bent in the sunlight to peer out of the dust-streaked little window. 'Will you look at that tree? And there's a stove. Oh, Miss Marya, you're an angel. Josip's never had a bed to himself. A warm room. A branch outside the window. Won't he think he's landed in paradise?' Klazkha, normally reticent, hugged her employer.

I could end up being grateful for a dinky attic like this, Marya thought. She went slowly down the steep staircase.

She tapped on Boris's door.

He was sitting up in bed, a woolly white tennis cardigan over his shoulders, a breakfast-tray on his lap.

'You're looking better,' she said.

'Auntie took my temperature. No fever,' he said with his good-natured grin. 'So you've gone against Ivan the Terrible's commands.'

'How did you know?'

Dipping a triangle of toast in his soft-boiled egg, he popped it in his mouth. 'The servants would do the Okhrana proud. No secrets here. The chambermaid told me.' He took a sip of tea. 'Auntie says the wedding was magnificent. Stupendous. Their Imperial Majesties were totally royal.'

'Did Auntie tell you everything?'

'Not right out.' Boris set down his cup,

sighing. 'But I gather my status will soon be uncle?'

'Boris, I'm so ashamed.'

Boris turned to the window. Easy-going, good-natured, in his heart he could cast no blame at his beloved sister; yet at the same time her condition filled him with a sense of dread. He had conned himself into believing that his Russian friends saw the apartment as a generous gift on the part of a fabulously wealthy relative. Soon his companions would know the truth, and then what would they think of him?

'It's not that I don't want the baby,' Marya said. 'The thing is, how will we manage?'

'Look at that sunshine,' Boris said. 'Let's try sledding.'

'Idiot!'

'What's so dumb about sledding?'

'Nothing. Except you're sick and I'm a teeny bit *enceinte!*'

Brother and sister had exchanged the last bit of repartee with brittle voices.

The next three days the weather remained good. In the afternoons, the slow-moving carriages and motor cars of society ladies jammed the Palace Quay. In the Tauride Gardens, Boris and Marya were one of the crimson-cheeked young couples who sledded down the artificial mound called American Hill. Marya, like the other girls, kneeled with her arms clasped around her brother's chest. Activity was a narcotic dulling her fears.

Josip Sobchak, a pale malnourished wisp of a ten-year-old with Klazkha's wide smile, showed Marya his new home, crawling around the small space proudly, his useless withered legs dragging behind him. When Marya went out with Boris that afternoon, she spotted a peasant woman with a pair of hand-carved crutches to sell. Brother and sister helped Josip to learn to balance himself on the whittled pine sticks: by the following afternoon, the boy was capable of manoeuvring himself down the staircase to the back door of the apartment. To celebrate his journey, Marya served him hot chocolate in the music room, then to Boris's accompaniment on the Bechstein she sang a medley from *The Merry Widow.* The boy's translucently white face glowed, and Marya wanted to cry out not to look at them as if they were celestial beings.

Where was Paskevich?

She washed her emerald in warm soapy water, polished the stone with her softest handkerchief and replaced the ring in its tooled box. She examined her coat. Lynx moults: she blew on the soft cream-coloured fur and wondered if the pelt were less luxuriant? She asked Klazkha to press her three afternoon dresses. Klazkha wielded her mother's irons like an artist, her hands speeding lightly across fabric; yet . . . didn't the dresses already look shabby? Marya went into Miss Dunning's room, questioning the expenses until the old lady threw up her hands.

On Friday the weather changed. A blizzard swept down from the Arctic Circle. That evening only a few of Boris's regulars showed up. He and two friends played poker while Marya forced herself to open a book; she wished she could submerge her fears by gambling.

At eleven the door-knocker sounded. Assuming it a late-arriving friend of Boris's, she went to answer.

Paskevich stood there. Snowflakes melted on his sable collar.

'Klazkha's still here,' she said rapidly. 'I took one of the attic rooms for her brother. When the doctor came for Boris, he examined them both. Her brother's got wasted legs from infantile paralysis, but otherwise he's healthy, and so's Klazkha.'

Muffled voices sounded in the music room. The draught coming up the stairwell shivered against the hall curtains.

'Is it necessary', Paskevich asked, 'for us to freeze in the doorway while we discuss your domestic arrangements?' He pushed by her into the little vestibule, slamming the door behind himself. The lights were out, and since neither of them moved to turn the switch they stood in darkness.

'I wasn't going to come here again,' he said quietly.

'Because I'll be fat and ugly?'

'In the ambiguous circumstances, I was decent enough, wasn't I?'

'Yes,' she admitted. 'Then, were you angry about Klazkha?'

'A servant? Affect *my* behaviour?'

'This is your honeymoon week.'

'The Countess Paskevich's new French pastry chef is her one topic of conversation. No, I was proving something to myself.'

'That doesn't sound like you.'

He put his arm around her waist, moving towards the bedroom corridor. 'When a man reaches my age, Marya, his beliefs are firmly ingrained. It was an article of faith with me that in this less than perfect world the truth is so unpleasant that we invent conventions. We build our highest walls of convention around the procreative act. Animals rut, but humankind calls mating by another name.' Reaching her bedroom, they went inside. Klazkha had left one dim lamp burning on the dressing-table. 'Myself, I've always held love to be a blighted and ridiculous myth.'

'Love?'

'Oh, I've been telling myself I lust for that charming little body of yours. But over the past few days, when I should've been paying attention to the pronouncements of our noble tsar or the opinions of those great geniuses, my fellow cabinet members, or reading the latest demands from our great humanistic Duma, I've been a lunatic.'

'I've missed you, too.'

'Is that a compliment?'

'Does it matter?'

'Everything about you matters to me. I'll never forget the way you limped back that night to save your brother, terrified of me, yet so brave. I wanted to be kind, God knows I did, but you told me point-blank that I didn't measure up to your travelling companion, the gentleman who gave you the purloined diamond. And, the next morning, I knew I was still old and ugly in your eyes, and a vicious beast, too. Well, what's the difference? I asked myself. Mistresses are for one thing, and it's not their minds. I'll keep her a while, then *phht.* The trouble was, I did care about your opinion of me.'

Marya held her breath. She heard his footsteps coming closer to her.

'This past week I've been moping around like a superannuated Romeo. During these interminable meetings with the Cabinet, members of the Duma, our monarch, I've been thinking how generous you are. Seeing the way you pull your head back and how those silvery eyes darken when you're angry. I've thought about the way your hair catches fire in the sunlight and given thought to your other, more intimate charms. I've thought about that impulsive unwise candour. I've given consideration to your singing, which is never exactly on key yet entrances your audience. Everyone believed me to be making important notes, but it was your name I wrote. *Marya, Marya, Marya.* Can you believe that? When you and Boris laugh together, I'm jealous. It amuses me when you defy me, yet at the same time I'm furious. The way you wear a new dress, proud yet a bit uncertain, as if you're waiting for the first compliment before you know how lovely you look. I've never been happy the way I'm happy here in this little apartment.'

His recitation had touched her profoundly, yet she couldn't help thinking of Boris's compulsive betting, of Miss Dunning's shamefaced acceptance of the pregnancy, and of the child who might or might not be Paskevich's yet who would be forever branded a bastard.

Stephan . . . he would have married me.

What a ridiculous idea. Stephan had been here in St Petersburg and hadn't tried to see her. He had never once written to her, so why would he have married her?

Paskevich gave a short laugh. 'Older man, pretty girl — banally trite, isn't it?'

'I really did miss you,' she said. It was true. Love was Stephan, love was a deliriously passionate business followed by copious tears. She often disliked Paskevich intensely, and there was always the barrier of that night he had beaten her, raped her, sodomized her, yet his presence invigorated her and with him she was never bored. 'Also . . . well, that last time you were here, in bed, it was . . . I felt quite carried away.'

'Yes?'

'Yes . . .'

He put his arms around her. The cold still permeated the sable. 'It's you I married. You're my wife.' His voice rumbled. The vibrations reached through her nightgown. 'In the Khazan Cathedral, the tsar gave me you as my wife.'

'Hush.'

'I'm your husband, Marya.' He was shaking as if the blizzard that howled down the Fourstatskaia had penetrated the warm bedroom, and she could feel a dampness, like tears, on his face. 'If you ever let any man but me near you, I'll make you long for death.'

1911

Emperor and Autocrat of All Russia, Tsar of Moscow, Kiev, Vladimir, Novgorod, Kazan, Astrakhan, Poland, Siberia, the Tauric Chersonese and Georgia, Lord of Pskov, Grand Duke of Smolensk, Lithuania, Volynia, Podolia and Finland, Prince of Estonia, Livonia, Courland and Semigallia, Belostok, Karelia, Tver, Yugra, Perm, Vyatka, Bulgaria and other lands, Lord and Grand Prince of Nizhny-Novgorod and Chernigove, Ruler of Ryasan Polotsk, Rostov, Yaroslavl, Belo-Ozero, Udoria, Obdoria, Kondia, Vitebsk, Mstislavl and all the Northern Lands, Lord of the Iberian, Kartilinian and Kabardinian Lands and of the Armenian provinces, Hereditary Lord and Suzerain of the Circassian and Highland Princes and others, Lord of Turkistan, Heir to the Throne of Norway, Duke of Schleswig Holstein, Storman, the Dithmarschen and Oldenburg.

Titles of Alexander III

Chapter Eleven

On a warm day in June of 1911, Stephan Strakhov walked along a quiet Moscow street. Lime trees billowed upwards like clouds, casting cool green shade on the pavement. He moved more slowly as he neared the Corinthian pillars that curved on to both streets. This corner building was owned by the Moscow School of Painting whose regulations stipulated that it be occupied only by members of the faculty. Because Professor Strakhov had been so esteemed, an exception was made in the case of his widow: she was permitted to retain their spacious apartment.

Professor Strakhov had died in January of 1910, over a year earlier.

Stephan no longer blamed the Okhrana for the two and a half months it had taken for him to learn of his father's fatal stroke. To be fair, he was to blame. If he hadn't been playing the romantic ass, if he hadn't gone to St Petersburg, where Okhrana tentacles were in every street and agents could spot him on sight, he never would have been arrested. As it was, they'd grabbed him on the way to the Crimson Palace.

In a way he'd been lucky. When the two agents had picked him up on the Nevsky Prospekt that winter afternoon he'd anticipated being hustled over to Okhrana headquarters where the 'interrogation' could go on for months. Instead they had escorted him directly to the railway station, keeping him manacled until they reached Berlin. There, they informed him that he had been placed on the Special File. Stephan was astonished. Few people even knew that the Special File existed, for it was reserved for those crimes the tsar or highest-level bureaucrats wished swept under the carpet. In essence, the Minister of the Interior, under whose jurisdiction the police department lay, was empowered to arrest, judge and sentence, whisking away the accused without a ripple.

Stephan was to complete his three-year exile and a six-month penalty. During this time he was barred from communicating by letter or telegraph with anyone inside Russia. Should he violate his sentence, his nearest family would be sent to Siberia.

His elderly parents wouldn't survive a month in a Siberian prison-camp.

But the Okhrana, all-seeing and all-powerful in Russia, had no authority beyond the borders: Stephan couldn't be prevented from meeting friendly compatriots. They had told him about Professor Strakhov's death. They had told him that Nicholas II was clamping down more heavily on liberal organizations, and consequently that the Democratic Reform Party was faltering. They'd passed on a juicy titbit of Court gossip: the Minister of Finance, Count

Paskevich, had married an ugly heiress and concurrently taken as his mistress a lovely young American relative named Marya Alexiev.

From Russia had come only bad news.

And since his return there had been no let-up. Sighing, Stephan jogged up the black marble stairs.

Madame Strakhov was dozing in the parlour. At every inhalation, her papery white cheeks drew in and her skull showed clearly.

Stephan closed his eyes, attempting to recall his mother as she had been less than two years ago, just prior to his second exile. Though Madame Strakhov had been over sixty then, only a sprinkle of white hair showed at her temples, her round face had glowed, her plump body had moved with the swiftness of youth, her energy had been invincible. Every morning by six, her dress covered by an overall, she had been kneading the bread and the sweet dough for her famous cheese-filled pastries. Her mornings were filled with shopping, helping old Agafia with the house, arranging the studio for the professor's portrait sittings, tending children in the free crèche near the Brest railway line. In the afternoons she had filled the apartment with music: though she had given up a promising career as a concert pianist at her marriage, she continued to practise. She played for friends when they dropped over after dinner — the Strakhovs held perpetual open house — and when the apartment was again quiet and the others slept she would be in her faded blue wrapper pursuing payment for her husband's portrait commissions or corresponding with old friends.

Shortly after the professor's sudden death, Madame had begun suffering from severe biliousness that her doctor had diagnosed as a symptom of grief and of yearning for her exiled son. Agafia, the arthritic old cook who'd been with the Strakhovs in St Petersburg before Stephan was born, loved telling the part where she herself had spoken right out to the doctor, telling him that Madame's problem might well be a growth in the stomach. By then it was too late for surgery.

The sofa creaked. Madame Strakhov twitched, and flung out an arm violently. Pale lips drawing back, she gave a drawn-out whimper. Stephan stroked her hot damp cheek gently. She relaxed and didn't waken. He sat on the piano stool.

The parlour hadn't changed since before he could remember: the same slip-covers made of coarse, country-woven beige linen; the same dented brass samovar; Professor Strakhov's vivid canvases and pastel sketches, many of them unframed, concealing the faded dun-green wallpaper. In that capacious armchair Stephan had sat on his father's lap drowsily listening to the Strakhovs and their guests. He imagined he could hear echoes of long-ago discussions, Tolstoy versus Dostoevsky, Borodin versus Skriabin, Realist painters versus the Wanderersand. The most heated controversies had been reserved for politics. The visitors had all been *intellegenty*, liberals, and Professor Strakhov could have spoken for them all when he asked rhetorically: 'Is this justice, that millions be governed by the whims of one fallible mortal?' Arguments about the means to achieve a more equitable society had been as much a part of the Strakhov flat as the sturdy furniture.

As adolescence had fermented within Stephan, he had embraced justice as the guiding principle of his life.

Madame Strakhov stirred, lifting her head. Her hair, thinning and entirely white now, was piled high with a tall tortoiseshell comb in the Spanish style she had favoured since the first days of marriage. She drew several breaths, as if arming herself against an invasion of red pain.

'Stephan dear,' she murmured. Her once hearty voice had become a whisper. 'How long have you been sitting there?'

'I just got in a minute ago. You seemed to be having a bad dream. Ready for your medicine?'

Wincing, she nodded. 'It's time.'

He wrinkled his nose against the sickly bitter-sweet odour of laudanum as he poured three generous tablespoons. 'Does it help?' he asked.

'Miraculous stuff,' she lied. The increased dosage barely dulled her pain, but plunged her into truncated opium nightmares of her dead daughter and husband. 'How was your morning? Did you see friends?'

'I handed out copies of the new pamphlet. No police in sight. Mamma, the Democratic Reform's really bursting out of its slump. An active membership of five hundred here.'

Madame reached out her thin hand in a congratulatory pat. The wedding ring slid from her finger, and she pushed it back up. Thinking of his sister's ring and how he'd disposed of it, Stephan turned away.

After a pause, she said: 'Lately I've been thinking a lot. Your life would have been far easier if you'd had a more normal upbringing.'

'I don't know about normal, but I can tell you I had the happiest childhood.'

'We never should've kept you up half the night listening to us and our friends jabbering.'

'It made me feel adult, so privileged.'

'You never heard a single voice raised for Holy Russia. Or the Autocracy. Only those fine liberal and revolutionary speeches! They entered into your bloodstream. And you were such a high-minded little boy. No, let me finish. Not one of us put his money, as they say, where his mouth was. We talked, that's all. Talking liberalism, talking reforms — Russian's favourite sport. Talk, talk, talk. You're the only one of us who acted.'

'What about that writer, Behrs, the one who was in Siberia?'

'Oh, maybe there were a few honourable souls who paid more than lip-service.' She sighed. 'You were just a baby. We should have realized we were tempering the finest, purest steel. A bit wild at times, but thoughtful, too. The most honourable of human beings.'

'Hark to a mother's opinion.'

'You *are* pure in your actions,' she said. 'And, as for us, we were too old to raise a child.'

'I couldn't imagine having other parents.'

At this she closed her eyes. After a few moments she asked: 'Stephan, have you ever thought of doing a novel?'

Startled by the abrupt veer in the conversation, he peered at her.

'Why not?' she asked in her new whispery voice. 'You're a fine writer.'

'Do I hear you saying that fiction's a safer occupation than organizing radicals and putting out illegal literature?'

'You've caught me out. But you can't deny that emotion has brought about more change than appeals to reason. Think of Harriet Beecher Stowe. One passionate imperfect novel accomplished more than all the anti-slavery pamphlets and books.'

Stephan moved thoughtfully to the bay window. From the portico outside he'd watched Nicholas II's coronation procession. It was the type of spectacle that got the professor's creative juices flowing, but the Strakhovs had not gone outside. Aged ten, Stephan had considered his parents' avoidance as yet another sign of sincerity. They were true-blue anti-monarchists while he was a softling, incapable of resisting the excitement of cheering crowds, waving flags, bells clanging wildly from Moscow's hundred and one churches, brilliant regiments marching in perfect drill, glittering carriages with members of the Imperial Family — a seemingly endless parade of magnificence winding towards the Cathedral of the Assumption in the Kremlin. When the youthful monarch in his simple army tunic rode solemnly by on his white stallion, Stephan's patriotic fervour reached the uncontrollable stage. Climbing over the marble balustrade, screaming, 'Hooray for Tsar Nicholas! Hooray for our tsar!' he had teetered on the narrow ledge, using both hands to flourish his red, white and blue Russian flag in great reckless circles. Agafia, her breath strong with too much coronation-celebrating, had grabbed his shoulder. 'Are you crazy, risking your life? What a wicked thing to do to your parents! After what happened to your poor sister.'

Sister? What sister?

That night, while fireworks showered stars on Moscow, he had asked his parents. Madame Strakhov had rushed from the room in uncharacteristic sobs. It had been the professor who explained how much it hurt them both to talk about their firstborn. Irena had been eighteen and already one of the Imperial *corps de ballet* when she caught typhoid. 'She died soon after you were born, and she left you a ring of hers. Now that you're ten, you're old enough to have it.'

Stephan again thought bitterly of how he'd disposed of his sister's bequest.

Madame Strakhov was watching him. 'Why the brooding expression?' she asked.

'As a matter of fact,' he said, 'I've jotted down an idea or two for a book.'

'Was there a girl?'

He felt his cheeks grow hot. 'What makes you ask that?'

'First novels', she said, managing a smile, 'often come out of disappointment in matters of the heart.'

As always, he preferred to maintain his emotional seclusion. Yet he was also incapable of shrugging off his beloved dying mother. 'Yes, a girl, and she made the usual promises,' he said as lightly as he could. 'Eternally. For ever. Then she realized I wasn't the answer to a maiden's prayers.'

'Stephan, Stephan, you'll be doomed to disappointment if you expect others to have the same standards as you.'

'You and Father set the example.'

Madame Strakhov shifted her head, wincing. 'That's exactly the sort of thing I mean. Neither of us was a saint. Or even honest.'

'Bosh. And, as far as the little romance

went, I shouldn't have got my hopes up. A moneyless exile with the Okhrana on my tail — I should have realized no sane girl would be serious for more than a few weeks.'

'What was she called?'

'Marya. An American girl from California. Her father was Russian. I met her on the way home two years ago, and the entire romance consisted of an interlude on the Channel steamer and another at the border, in Verballen station.' As he said 'Verballen', he reddened again. 'So much for the past. Now she's kept in grand style by a rich old Monarchist. So you can see how much of a fool I was.'

'My poor Stephan.'

Just then Agafia opened the door. Stephan hurried over to wheel in the cart with their midday meal.

That evening, Madame Strakhov asked Stephan to bring her a coffee in bed.

Taking small sips of the heavily sugared, aromatic Turkish brew, she rested the cup on the sheet. 'Stephan, will you do me a favour?' She glanced towards the tall, old rosewood desk. 'Your father's personal papers, diaries, old letters, are in there. Would you burn them for me?'

'The whole lot?' he asked, surprised.

'Everything. We discussed it several weeks before his stroke. Now it seems almost as if he sensed what was coming.' At a sudden pain, she took deep breaths, gripping the edge of the comforter. 'He asked me, if he died first . . . he said I should empty the drawers in the fire. Not look at anything.'

'Like father, like son,' Stephan said. 'We both treasure our privacy.'

'Maybe the desk is heaped with love-letters from adoring females,' Madame Strakhov jested. 'Coward that I am, I haven't been able to force myself to do a thing.'

'Should I get at it right away?'

'Not tonight.' She gripped the comforter again. When she spoke her voice was a harsh near-inaudible whisper. 'I can count on you?'

'Of course.'

'You'll do just as he asked? Destroy his papers unread?'

'I promise.'

During the night Madame Strakhov lapsed into a coma. She thrashed and cried out but never regained coherence.

After three torment-ridden days she died.

Chapter Twelve

Stephan told old Agafia to take whatever she wanted from the apartment, and the day following Madame Strakhov's funeral he heaped the servant's choices in her brother's wagon.

'There is no kinder, more generous young man in all Russia.' Agafia's rheumatic claws linked behind Stephan's neck. 'May Our Good Lord always shine His countenance on you . . .' She broke off, sobbing.

Stephan's eyes were wet, too. He didn't move from the steps for a long time after the cart had lumbered down the street.

At a quarter to four he went to hear the lawyer read the will — to his mind a depressing and unnecessary formality since he already knew he was heir to the Strakhovs' tiny estate.

Their lawyer lived and practised on the top floor of a building on the Kuznetsky Most, but in his office the traffic was muffled by heavy faded draperies and thick Turkish carpets. An old-fashioned bookcase jammed with thick legal tomes loomed over the immense desk. The big leather chairs were stained and they sagged with much use. Amid the outsize fustiness, the near-midget lawyer resembled a neat grey-haired doll.

Giving Stephan his condolences in a surprisingly resonant baritone, he sat behind his desk to read the brief will and an item-ized list of the inheritance: household ef-fects, the professor's medals, Madame's brooch and rings. The deep voice halted, gathering resonance to boom: 'One eight-room furnished house in Livadia on the Black Sea.'

Stephan, who had been fighting back tears at the dry recitation of his parents' simple treasures, jerked upright so abruptly that his chair groaned.

A furnished house? In Livadia, that most aristocratic Crimean holiday spot? Not only had the Strakhovs never taken a holiday there, but he'd never even heard them men-tion owning a house — they had been out-spokenly averse to private ownership of property.

'What did you say?'

'You're now the proprietor of a furnished villa overlooking a private beach. Evidently quite luxurious from the amount of rent the tenants pay.'

Questions jumped in Stephan's brain. He was about to enquire what else the little lawyer knew about the property, then balled his fists in his pockets. Exposing further ignorance would assuredly brand his par-ents as liberal poseurs. He rose to his feet. 'Thank you, sir, for your time.'

'Do sit down, Mr Strakhov. We haven't finished. There's still the account in the Nevsky Bank to discuss.'

Professor Strakhov had often mentioned

that he put aside a sum annually in order to have a few more retirement comforts than would be granted by the pension from the Moscow School of Painting — savings that must have been heavily dented by medical bills.

'Oh, that,' Stephan said with a shrug. 'It'd slipped my mind.'

The lawyer took off his spectacles. 'I must say you're a cool customer. Not many people forget two million plus.'

Stephan fell back into the leather chair, gaping.

'To be precise,' the lawyer said, replacing his glasses to read, 'two million, one hundred and eighty-seven thousand, two hundred and thirty-nine roubles.'

'But . . . that's a fortune . . .'

'Yes, and drawing three per cent interest. May I offer congratulations? You have a most enviable income.'

A fat fly buzzed and bumped against the dust-streaked window. Stephan stared at it. In his astonished confusion he couldn't tackle how his parents had accumulated so vast a sum — or why. Instead he found himself pondering: *Would two-million, one hundred and eighty-seven thousand, two-hundred and thirty-nine roubles have been enough for Marya Alexiev? If I'd had it then, would she have chosen me over Paskevich?*

'There must be a mistake,' Stephan said thickly.

'Knowing Professor and Madame Strakhov's preference for . . . well, the *frugal* way of life, I, too, was stunned. So I made it my business to check the facts. The Nevsky Bank gave me the exact amount.' The lawyer pushed a bank slip across the worn green felt. 'Here it is in writing.'

Stephan peered blankly at the inked numbers.

'This kind of money needs respectful handling, Mr Strakhov, a great deal of respect. After you've had time to digest the news, we'll discuss investments. If you would be so kind as to arrange a convenient time with my clerk.'

Stephan didn't take the outstretched hand. He didn't pause at the clerk's desk to make another appointment. Leaving the building, he walked dazed through the crowds on Kuznetsky Most.

The apartment felt as if its beating heart had been surgically removed. Stephan's steps echoed as he wandered from room to room. With the exception of the grand piano, the furniture was simple — many of the pieces were made by peasants and brightly painted. The Strakhovs had said ostentation was a social wrong. They had also said that great wealth was a social wrong.

How to connect the high-minded beliefs lived out in this modestly decorated, university-subsidized flat with a luxurious Crimean property and a fortune earning three per cent annually?

161

The two people who could have answered his questions lay in the monastery grave-yard.

Stephan pressed his hands to his head as if to squeeze away the doubts. Because he disliked talking about his dilemmas, he had no real confidant except his journal. He sorted out problems by writing them down. Opening his current brown leather note-book to a clean page, he wrote: 'June 24th, 1911.'

A drop of ink splattered from the nib on to the lined paper. He slammed the journal shut, and the sound reverberated in the silence like the thump of his betrayed, be-wildered heart.

Resuming his aimless pacing, he halted at his parents' bedroom.

The long chest with the painted ark ani-mals, the desk, the pier-glass with its hori-zontal crack, the brass bedstead, now with its stained grey-striped mattress bent over double, had stood in the same places since he could remember. Yet this room, like the rest of the flat, had become *terra incognita*. The dusk-shrouded corners were wadded with ugly black questions.

He sighed, recalling his final promise to his mother.

Unlocking the roll-top desk, he saw her square mahogany jewel-box. Inside were the pearl brooch that she wore on special occasions, her wedding ring, the tiny en-gagement solitaire set in black enamel, and a small grey suede pouch. Unknotting the pouch's silk string, he slid out a flower-engraved gold locket that he'd never seen. He opened the piece, staring at the inset miniature. A sloe-eyed girl with dark hair sleeked back to show her beautifully shaped head. This must be his long-dead sister. Irena . . .

Switching on the bedside light he held up the tiny portrait. The initials *LVS*. His father, who scornfully called miniaturists 'one-haired-brushers', had painted the exquisite likeness. Her neck a long slender curve, her lips full, her dark eyes tilted, Irena had the delicate, highly charged eroticism that he associated with Egypt.

His father had told him all those years ago that to speak about their dead child brought back the anguish of losing her. Stephan, a tactful boy, had never questioned them again, but his filial loyalty was strained by their silence. They seldom spoke of St Petersburg, where they had lived with Irena before the professor had been honoured with an appointment to the Moscow School of Painting. They had never mentioned their daughter to any in their circle, letting even their closest friends believe Stephan was their only offspring, the cherished child of their old age. He bit his lip, staring at the tender portrait. This beauty had for eighteen years been an integral part of their life if not its focus. Never to have mentioned her once? Wasn't that omission a form of deceit?

Replacing the locket in its suede covering, he realized that possibly the answers lay in this desk. Who'd know if he read his father's papers? *I gave my word. I gave my word.*

The top drawer held yellowed stacks of string-tied envelopes addressed to his father in his mother's bold calligraphy. He carried the bundles to the small marble fireplace. His hand shook, and the first match broke. On his second try, the old paper caught. He emptied out the next drawer, hastily ripping pages from old leather diaries to add to the blaze. Crumbling newspaper clippings went up spontaneously. Another drawer held contracts, letters of commendation, documents with official seals. More correspondence. He rushed faster and faster between desk and grate as though fleeing temptation. The fire crackled, flames leaped. In the bottom drawer he found a strew of sketches and photographs. He could see a charming pastel of his sister Irena bending to tie her ballet slipper.

He consigned the pastel, the sketches, the cardboard-backed photographic prints to the flames.

He replaced the firescreen. Not until he was in the dark corridor did he remember the secret drawer hidden in the panelling. He must have been seven or so when his father had demonstrated the place inside the pigeonhole that worked the catch: they both had been solemn, as though he were being inducted into a rite of manhood. The memory brought tears to Stephan's eyes. Blowing his nose, he returned to sit at the desk. The drawer sprang forward.

Inside lay a thick yellowing envelope.

By the reddish glow from the fireplace, he made out childishly round script: 'Stephan Strakhov.'

A bullfrog croaked, a dog barked.

Slowly Stephan lifted the old stationery closer, rereading. Yes, his name.

He wondered briefly if the envelope had been left here on purpose for him to find; then recalled that his father could have had no idea when or if he would return, and furthermore had extracted a promise from his mother to destroy everything.

It's mine. Mine. And it was kept from me.

Brows an angry line, he carried the envelope to the bed. He sat on the bare box springs, he turned on the lamp, he broke the red wax seal. 'My baby son . . .'

Baby son? Stephan stared at the wavery round scrawl. His mother, who had taken penmanship lessons from a retired Court calligrapher, had an exquisite hand.

If you are reading this, Fate has been cruel. I am dead without ever knowing whether you look like me or your illustrious father . . .

The rusty ink blurred. Stephan felt light-headed, as if he might pass out. To keep

165

alert, he read aloud, the way he proofed his manuscripts.

If anything happens to me, Mamma and Papa have promised to raise you, which under the circumstances is very decent of them. They are fine people, but never, never the right parents for a girl like me. And I'll admit I probably haven't been the best of daughters to them. It's not really my fault, or theirs, but our natures. We're totally different. They are content with very little — Papa's painting, Mamma's piano, dreary friends and a lot of puffy talk. Justice, justice, justice. What a waste of time, talking about an idea, something that doesn't exist. Myself, I want what is real. Clothes, jewels, champagne, French furniture. All the lovely things they scorn as bourgois — did I spell it right? I avoided schoolwork — that's another thing that didn't please them.

Ever since I can remember, my dream was to dance. The Imperial Ballet, that was real. Ah, how I longed for the footlights and applause, the admiration — and the pots of money.

And, in all modesty, I was always good. When I was seven my teacher begged my parents to let me audition for the Imperial Ballet School. Mamma was reluctant, but Papa ... well, I could always win Papa over.

I was far the strongest dancer in my class, everybody said so. The teachers whispered about my talent. But even as a little girl I knew talent was just another puffy word. In a career one needs determination and luck. I had the determination to practise eight, ten, fifteen hours a day. And as for luck . . . well, luck smiled on me immediately after the graduation. Like all the graduates, I entered the corps de ballet. *On the evening of the first midnight supper, the ballerina dancing the* pas de deux *in* La Fille mal gardée *fell and injured her ankle. I took her place.*

It chanced that He attended that performance. Like everybody else, I noticed His presence. How could I not?

The Imperial box was practically on the stage.

Stephan's monotone stopped. He stared at the window. The street-lamp cast a misty green brilliance on the still leaves. He could hear his own ragged breathing. No longer able to read aloud, he scanned the juvenile writing.

He presided over the supper. Ah, how He towered over everyone. He boomed in that deep voice which fitted His immense frame: 'Where is the little Strakhov ?'

I had terrible butterflies as I made my way to the head table to make my deepest curtsy.

'Sit here,' He said, indicating the seat beside Him.

Somehow I found the courage to respond. 'Sire, that place is reserved for the pre-mière danseuse.'

'She shall sit there,' He retorted, indicating another chair. 'You shall sit by me.' So gracious, so kind was He, like a great glowing sun drawing me into His warmth.

Before the supper ended I was in love. Head over heels, madly in love. He took me driving in His sleigh, He sent me roses. I thought of nothing except Him and when I'd see Him again. And I walked on air when He made a rendesvous — spelling? — in an elegant house near the Champs de Mars. I still cannot think what happened there was immoral — or, as that stupid Agafia has said, against God's law.

He arranged for me to live in the house. How gorgeous it was — I felt as if I were inside a huge marble jewel-box. Papa and Mamma kept saying that it was evil and unjust that a man nearly three times my age could use his immense power to seduce me. They never even tried to understand. I worshipped him. 'My adorable swan-necked girl,' He called me. He never lied to me. From the beginning I knew nothing was permanent. But what did that matter? I worshipped Him and lived for the moments we were together.

He saw to it that I was given the lead in Tchaikovsky's new ballet. What joy! A triumph!

Then I found out I was to have a child.

The night I told Him, He sat me on His knee and told me there was not a worry in the world for me. He promised a settlement of half a million on me, half a million on our child — you.

Mamma and Papa went half-crazy at my condition. They said your Father, Jesus Christ's anointed One, was evil — they called Him terrible treasonous names. How unfair they were! He changed all our lives for the better. Papa has his full professorship at the Moscow School of Painting. And I have an income for life and this lovely villa in the Crimea.

Mamma has come to be with me during my confinement. Her disappoval hangs like a cloud. Myself, I consider it the greatest honour to bear you, His child.

I have not seen Him since I told Him of my condition; but three days ago He sent you a gift, a diamond worth a fortune set in a ring that has been in the Romanov family for ever.

In the week since your birth I have had a fever. The doctor, a charming man, young and quite smitten, has been coming by at all hours. Having never been ill before, I can't tell how serious it is. But I've been delirious several times, so am writing this letter just in case. Myself, I think my luck will hold. In no time I'll be back at the Maryinsky dancing the première roles.

A few months ago I heard gossip that He had somebody new, this time an actress.

At first it cut my heart to ribbons, I wept and wept, but after a few days I realized that love is a bird that alights, sings its brief, unbearably sweet song, then flies away. Eventually I shall have other admirers. None, of course, will measure up to your Father. Who could? Be proud always, my dear little Stephan, that His blood runs in your veins.

Your mother,
Irena Leonidovna Strakhov

Stephan sat absolutely still on the bare bedsprings of his parents' bed —

No!

They weren't his parents. They were his grandparents. His mother was a frivolous young dancer, and his father was Alexander III.

Alexander III.

The bald narrow-minded giant who had methodically scythed down every reform. A despicable tyrant who had filled prisons and Siberian labour-camps with human misery. Alexander III, promoter of vicious pogroms.

Stephan's heart beat erratically, ponderously. His blood was charged with alien density. It took him a few moments to realize what the heaviness was. Shame. He was weighed down with shame.

He was part of what he loathed most, the Autocracy.

He was a bastard son of a murderous

tyrannical tsar. Half-brother of Nicholas II, also known as Bloody Nicholas.

Screwing Irena's letter into a ball, he hurled it into the fire. As the crushed paper ignited, he rushed to the fireplace. Scrabbling in the flames, he pulled the burning pages on to the marble hearthstone. He beat out the flames with his open hands. Unaware of pain, he crouched there, shoving the scraps he'd rescued into place. He stared at the childishly formed letters as if memorizing ancient spells.

. . . have had a fev . . .
. . . His Imperial Majesty attended . . .
. . . baby son . . .
. . . proud for ever that His blood . . .

The seared skin had come away from his fingers and palms, dangling like fine chiffon. Holding his hands in front of him, he stumbled to the kitchen, yanking open the cabinet where the drink was stored.

He gulped down the leavings of the funeral guests, whatever remained in bottles of vodka, aquavit, Crimean brandy.

Just before he lapsed into a drunken stupor, he saw clearly what he must do with the fortune.

He would use it to rid Russia of its savage inequities. Yes, that's what he would do with Romanov money — he'd spend every rouble and kopek to prise the vast empire from the Romanovs. He would dedicate his poisonous inheritance as well as himself to toppling the Autocracy.

Early that afternoon he was in the building on the Kuznetsky Most, brushing past the clerk and waiting clients.

The startled little lawyer gawked. Stephan's shirt was collarless, his suit wrinkled, handkerchiefs sloppily bandaged his hands, dark hair hung over his forehead, and he hadn't shaved. He didn't, the lawyer decided, look in the least like a man who has unexpectedly found himself a multimillionaire.

'Mr Strakhov, what happened to your hands? You really ought to see —'

'That inheritance,' Stephan interrupted.

'— a doctor.'

'I'm not here to discuss my health,' Stephan barked. 'Everything will go to the Democratic Reform Party.'

'Democratic Reform Party?' The lawyer judiciously clasped his tiny tobacco-stained fingers. 'Is that a political organization?'

'Make out the transfer documents,' Stephan said impatiently. 'I'll sign them.'

'Nothing would please me more than to follow your orders, but —'

'Settle everything today. Now.'

Stephan's peremptory command was a tone the lawyer, whose clients were middle class, never heard in this office.

'Nothing would give me greater pleasure. But there are laws —'

'Laws? What laws?'

'New ones. Regulations that increase su-

172

pervision of political groups. I'm positive that the — what was it? — the Democratic Reform Party has no hand in promoting terrorism or advocating violence. Unfortunately, since the 1905 Revolution the security police lump together liberal groups like yours with the worst assassins. Many people say that the police are far too lenient; they say that, since Russia is an Autocracy, any group advocating change is committing treason by casting doubts on the monarch's judgement.' The lawyer's voice dropped. 'Gifts and endowments to political parties, Mr Strakhov, are tied up in a regular cat's cradle of legislation.'

'Isn't that what you lawyers are paid to do — find loopholes in the law?'

'There are no loopholes. Believe me. Before a bank can transfer funds to any group with a political flavour, the donor must make out a formal request to the Okhrana. You were exiled, weren't you? So that means they'll start a pro forma investigation, which could take years. The Okhrana will be delving into the past, they'll be watching you. Watching me. Watching the Nevsky Bank. And they'll have your Democratic Reform Party under a magnifying glass.'

'Send the income to me, then.'

'By all means.' The lawyer had reached the conclusion that to protect his own skin he must forego professional privacy. He would immediately report this entire conversation to the authorities. 'I shall send your bank drafts to the apartment.'

'Another professor's moving in.'

'Then, where shall I send the money?'

'I'm leaving Moscow tomorrow,' Stephan said.

'You are? Well, the bank drafts can be sent wherever you'll be.'

With a rattling slam, the client stalked out of the office.

Ten days later a cable arrived with a poste restante address in Belgrade.

1912

CHOLERA SEASON
Do not drink unboiled water

Signs posted on St Petersburg lamp-posts
during the summer.

Chapter Thirteen

She swayed on tiptoe, reaching both hands up towards the dangling locket, then abruptly fell on her backside. For a moment her pale grey eyes widened and her mouth opened as if she might cry. Instead she laughed, displaying the gap between her two front milk teeth, a space that enchanted her mother.

'Lally needs,' she said.

Boris dropped the battered gold in the child's lap, and Marya nuzzled a kiss into her daughter's neck which smelled of smoked fish, milk and talcum powder.

Lally squirmed away.

At twenty-one months, 'Lally' was as close as the child could come to saying 'Alexandra'. Her name was Alexandra Alexiev, American style, without the traditional Russian patronymic second name, no *ovna* — 'daughter of' — for Lally.

Her appearance gave no clue to who had fathered her. However often Marya searched Lally's face, she could find no feature that might identify either Paskevich or Stephan. Lally was, as Miss Dunning pronounced, the spitting image of Marya. Bald at birth, the toddler now had an aureole of pale pinky curls. Her face showed the Alexiev delicate bone structure and high rounded fore-head. Her short upper lip curled in a miniature version of Marya's soft mouth when she smiled — and Lally smiled most of the time. Thwarted, though, she would draw her fine eyebrows together and raise her chin: if her demands weren't met, she would hold her breath until her face turned crimson and her lips went a cyanotic blue, then she would emit a series of prolonged howls. These squalls halted the instant she got her way.

The shade of her eyes altered with her moods. Normally the silver of Marya's, her gaze would darken as she concentrated on one of her small games: when she reached the tantrum stage the irises appeared as dark as a thunder-cloud.

She was frowning. Hastily Boris dropped the battered gold locket into her cupped hands. 'Here, poppet.'

He doted on his niece. He sang nursery songs, he pulled her toboggan, he showered down gifts — two huge American teddy-bears and a rag doll bigger than she was. Returning from any trip he bought her a *matryushki*, the nested dolls whose wooden halves she strewed across the floor. He played with her long past her bedtime. Only on the evenings when his friends and bureaucratic superiors were due at Fourstat-skaia 12 did he insist that she be in her cot on time, out of the guests' way.

Miss Dunning didn't share his mortification. Soon after Lally's birth, cuddling the infant to her sagging bosom, the kindly spinster confessed in a low voice: 'Our darling baby's so perfect that it's hard to remember I fretted over . . . well, over anything about her.'

Lally ruled the spacious apartment. The wide-hipped careless cook called her 'Lally-Lally-La' and surreptitiously spooned wild strawberry jam into her mouth. The elderly butler cranked himself down on his rheumatic knees to give her horsie rides on his back. The chambermaids taught her to 'scrub the floor', a game in which Lally soaked herself with great enthusiasm. The boot-boy carved a boat that she sailed in her copper bath.

Paskevich alone didn't succumb to Lally's charms. When she reached up her arms for him to lift her, he handed her one of her dolls. He never bought her toys: his gifts were invariably along the lines of the gem-encrusted gold rattle from Fabergé that he had ordered as a christening present — items too valuable to be anything but a future heirloom. He never held her on his lap; he never broke off a bite of pastry for her. Hurt and aggravated, Marya told herself that, had there been one identifiable feature of his in Lally, he would have behaved differently. *Men have been known to cherish their bastards.* Still, he didn't protest when she breast-fed rather than hiring a wet-nurse, and made surprisingly few caustic remarks when she sacked the over-strict nanny and took over the nursery with

Klazkha's help. Sometimes Marya would rock her baby to sleep, pretending Stephan would be home later.

Lally dropped her battered locket and reached for Boris's gleaming buttons.

As a *chinovnik* — bureaucrat — Boris wore a well-tailored dark-blue uniform with double rows of gold buttons. The fifty-two articles of the Service Regulations, which laid out the benefits, obligations and clothing style of every rank of the bureaucracy, specified the number of buttons as well as the colour of the fabric.

When Paskevich had given Boris this post within his Finance Ministry, he'd wryly told his protégé that the prime duty of a bureaucrat was to kiss the backsides of those above him — advice that Boris took to heart, drinking, gambling and womanizing with those superiors susceptible to such distractions. His assistant, of German descent, one of the limited quota of Lutherans permitted to serve within the bureaucratic ranks, managed the offices with flawless efficiency. Boris dropped by once a week, putting on a stern face as he passed between the stools where low-level *chinovniks* hunched over revenue ledgers of a remote district in Kazakhstan. Despite his attempts to appear mature and commanding, 'our young American', as he was called by his superiors and subordinates alike, inspired fondness rather than respect.

He was leaving for Moscow. In the eighth

rank of bureaucrats, he was entitled to the traditional junket that enabled the echelons with sufficient *chin* to escape the St Petersburg fever season.

Most of the middle and upper classes had already deserted the capital.

The doorbell rang. Boris's taxi had arrived.

'How long will you be gone this time?' Marya asked.

'A month at least.' Lally was pulling at his mouth. Kissing the fingers, he removed each one in turn. 'Marya. Promise not to go on the T-R-A-M.'

'You're joking. Me, keep L-A-L-L-Y from the T-R-A-M?' They spelled out the words because the child's favourite diversion was clambering up the metal steps of the double-decker trams.

'Use a taxi.'

'You sound worried.'

'Only a crazy idiot like you wouldn't be. This summer the hooligans have taken over. All these strikes and demonstrations.'

'Come on, Boris, it's not that bad.'

'Isn't it? And what about this ridiculous scandal about Rasputin and the tsarina? The man's a monk, for God's sake, a holy man, a *starets!* Now, you tell me what gives anyone the right to question the spiritual adviser of their Majesties?' Boris, on being admitted to the bureaucratic service, had been obliged to swear fealty to Nicholas — an oath he took to heart a trifle pompously. 'To spread vile garbage about the Imperial

181

Family! I say Siberia's too good for those rabble-rousers.'

'Have you actually heard something? I mean about violent demonstrations?'

'Who knows what'll set a crowd off? Those damn speechifiers, forever foaming at the mouth against their monarch! And they call themselves reformers!'

As he said this, Marya thought: *Stephan* . . .

She frowned, angry at herself for still mooning over him. 'Caution is my middle name,' she said.

'That'll be the day!' Boris laughed and set down his niece. 'Time to say goodbye.'

Flapping both hands, Lally said: 'Bye-bye, Unca Borie.'

'Have a wonderful time,' Marya said and reached in her pocket, handing him a thick roll of banknotes.

'I can't take that.'

'There wasn't time to shop; it's only what I'd have spent on a farewell gift,' Marya lied. Paskevich had given her the money to buy a gold and platinum minaudière at Sazanov's. Boris's ample salary vanished quickly, and she didn't want him to be indebted to Muscovites, who had a reputation for being rapacious.

Shoving the notes in his pocket, he hugged his sister, kneeled to rub his nose against Lally's little button, and trotted whistling down the staircase.

Marya lifted her daughter to the window. Below waited one of the new American-made black-and-grey Ford taxis patronized by those in St Petersburg's smart set who lacked a carriage or motor car. Boris's trunks were strapped on the back. When he appeared, Lally waved enthusiastically, and so did Marya.

They were still waving when the recently installed telephone sounded. The servants, crossing themselves when this instrument of the devil rang, steadfastly refused to answer. Marya ran to the panelled cubicle reserved for the instrument.

It was Paskevich's fussily correct head secretary. 'Mademoiselle Alexiev,' he said with loud precision. 'His Excellency begs to inform you that he has been summoned by His Imperial Majesty to Tsarskoe Selo. His Excellency has not yet learned how long the cabinet conferences will detain him. He pleads for your understanding.'

Marya smiled at the secretary's formality, which Paskevich mimicked down to the last syllable.

Paskevich.

Her feelings for him veered wildly, refusing to stabilize. His teasing infuriated her, as did his lack of consideration for the servants. She was amused and annoyed at Friday nights, when he led his own guests, the fawning businessmen, to greater heights before subtly popping their pretensions: he would respond elaborately to the admiration of young dancers until they hinted at a private meeting, at which time he would blandly refer to himself as 'a happily married man'. Marya should have felt triumphant, but instead she felt sorry for the girls. (Curiously enough, the mocked guests and bedevilled servants took great pride in their tangential connection to Count Paskevich.) On the credit side, Marya was grateful for this handsome apartment, for the family's comfort and ease. He made her laugh. His honesty pleased her. His intellect awed her: He was knowledgeable in an immense variety of subjects from Cro-Magnon man to American politics, from the latest Parisian fashion to new methods of contraception — she now inserted something called a 'Dutch cap' before they made love. It was on her divan bed that her feelings towards her protector swung like a crazed pendulum. Some nights she clutched his thick shoulders, unable to quieten her orgasmic cries, while at other times his endurance nauseated her.

Hanging up, she sighed. How simple, how sweet life would be with a man her own age, somebody she loved. *Well,* she reminded herself, *that somebody didn't hang around, did he?*

It was time for Lally's eleven o'clock milk and bun. Klazhka was setting out the snack at the nursery table.

Two years had transformed Klazkha. She had grown six inches, and her full breasts strained against the grey-striped uniform while the tightly trim butterfly of her apron bow pointed up the supple slenderness of

184

her waist. When she pushed Lally's perambulator men turned after her, male flattery against which Klazkha tightened her shoulders. Those weeks on the streets had marred her for ever. The other servants continued to ostracize her, an outcast state that on a small scale mirrored Marya's own — St Petersburg forgot its worldly tolerance when it came to public rips in the social fabric like a prostitute's yellow card or an illegitimate child. Accordingly, employer and employee had become friends and confidantes: Klazkha knew Marya's mixed bag of emotions towards Paskevich, Marya admired Klazkha's disciplined saving of every kopek towards a cottage in the country for her and her crippled brother.

Klazkha wasn't a conversationalist. Today, though, she was more than normally silent. As she swept up Lally's crumbs, she said: 'Josip's lost his appetite.'

'Any fever?'

'His head's a bit hot, but he's well enough to keep his nose in his book.' The illiterate Klazkha reported this with a proud little bob of her head.

Marya had taught Josip his letters during her pregnancy, and now supplied the lame child with newspapers, magazines, library books. Other than forays to this apartment, Josip went nowhere: he couldn't have picked up the contagious diseases that stalked through St Petersburg from spring to autumn.

'Probably the weather,' Marya said. 'After I put Lally down for her nap I'll run up with some aspirin for him.'

Klazkha kept Josip's attic room as neat as her own person. Marya's discarded Spanish shawl was folded over the foot of the iron bed, the white rag rug made from the Alexievs' discarded underwear had just been washed, magazine illustrations covered the water stains on the walls. A darned sheet tacked to the slanting roof screened the corner with the chamberpot and washbasin. Josip's crutches were propped against the crude bookshelf. He slept, the birch leaves dappling sunlight on his fever-red face.

Marya deposited the aspirin-bottle and lemonade carefully, but the uneven-legged table rocked.

Josip opened his eyes. Hauling himself up on his elbows, he gave her that embarrassingly adoring smile. 'Miss Marya, will you look at me? Napping like Lally.'

'Klazkha said you're under the weather,' Marya said.

'I'm on the mend,' he said — and slumped back into the goose-down pillow Miss Dunning had given him for Christmas.

Chapter Fourteen

The cabinet meeting at the Imperial Palace in Tsarskoe Selo lasted two days. When Paskevich returned to Fourstatskaia 12, dinner was long over and Marya lounged on the sofa reading *The Portrait of a Lady* while Miss Dunning sat at her embroidery frame. Paskevich flustered the elderly spinster with his penetrating dark eyes, his wit, his overt masculinity — she shuddered whenever she tried to imagine what such a person did to Marya in bed. Redness blotching her long, plain face, she hastily bundled her silks into the work-table, easing from the room just as the sleepy butler staggered in with a tray laden with fresh-baked *piroshki,* a selection of cream cakes and the ornate silver coffee service.

Marya poured. 'How did the meetings go?'

'As usual, they went as usual. The tsar wanted my opinion on how to raise capital without increasing taxes. Bonds, I replied, adding that foreign bankers weren't likely to float our issues if we didn't show progress in domestic problems.'

'Ah, the voice of the great reformer.'

'You should have heard me. Up and down the list I went. A constitution. A parliament with some bite to its requests, not our toothless Duma. Universal franchise, legal equality for Jews and other minorities, et cetera, et cetera.'

'What was the tsar's reaction?'

'Again the usual. He listened with a polite blank expression, then said he'd consider what I'd told him.'

'And?'

'At our next meeting he told me that as Autocrat, anointed by Lord God Almighty, it was his duty to govern Russia. If he caved in to the demands of outsiders and a small group of malcontents within the Empire, he would go directly counter to God's command.'

'He truly said that?'

'He said it and believed it. The tsarina backs him up. The two of them are convinced that, no matter what, they must pass on the divinely ordained Russian Autocracy intact to Baby — that's what they call the poor little Heir.'

'What's really wrong with him?'

'A state secret, my pet. Nicholas and I had a private meeting.'

'Oh? Is this another of your tantalizing mysteries?'

'No further than these walls?'

She raised her right hand as if taking an oath. 'No further.'

'Two of His Imperial Majesty's staff hauled in a trunkful of currency. I'm to place the funds in a numbered account — which means a secret account — in Zurich.'

'Whatever for?'

'The Autocrat of the Russias doesn't explain, he commands. If Nicholas didn't keep to his own bed, if he were like his father, good licentious old Alexander III, I'd say he was pensioning off some mistress who'd given extraordinary service. But Nicholas never strays.' Paskevich held out his cup. 'If you please?' She poured more coffee. 'Only the two of them and their children — and me as trustee, of course — can get at the funds.'

'They own Russia. What on earth do they need with money in Switzerland?'

'Frankly, if I were Nicholas, I'd invest it in guns to shoot down the nihilists, the Mensheviks, the Bolsheviks, the entire contentious lot. Oh, for a whip-cracking tyrant like Peter the Great!'

'What a cynic you are, spouting reforms!'

'My dear, I meant every word. We need reforms in the worst way — not real reforms, mind you, but cosmetic reforms. Rouge and rice-powder reforms that will bamboozle the West. If only other governments could realize that the people will never have a true voice here, Russia's a special case. But they simply refuse to accept that, if the tsar doesn't rule, somebody else will. And far more viciously.' Paskevich finished his coffee. 'It's late, my pet.'

In the celadon-green bedroom he impatiently struggled with the looped buttons that fastened the back of her white summer frock.

She asked: 'Isn't your wife at Tsarskoe

189

Selo?' Paskevich's grandfather had built one of the palatial 'cottages' that lined the avenue between the Tsarskoe Selo railway station and the vast Romanov enclosure.

'Yes, she's there, carrying out her duties as lady-in-waiting. We lunched together once. She ate most of a salmon and an entire cherry torte.'

'Don't you ever exercise your marital rights?'

'Are you joking?' He kissed the back of Marya's neck.

It was one of the good times when she was roused to passion. After, she lay relaxed in Paskevich's arms for a few minutes before rising from the divan bed to pull on what Bézard called a *saut de lit,* a short robe that matched her nightgown.

'Where are you going?' Paskevich asked.

'To look in on Lally.'

'Where's the serving girl of exquisite complexion?'

'Klazkha's with her brother. He's ill.'

He raised himself up on his elbow. 'What's wrong with our crippled scholar?' Paskevich, in his random generosity, had given Josip the complete translations of Robert Louis Stevenson and the exquisitely bound first edition of *Eugene Onegin* from his own library.

'A fever. Oh, and diarrhoea.' The last was a joke. In the Russian summer, everyone from time to time had loose bowels.

Paskevich was out of bed, gripping her

arm. 'Get the doctor on the wire. Now.'

First Marya went to the nursery. Lally, sleeping on her stomach, had thrown off the covers. Marya drew the embroidered sheets into place. Lally thrust up her behind, even in sleep protesting encroachment. Marya touched a finger to damply soft red-pink curls and smiled softly. At this moment her life was a vibrant joyous garden where it seemed the insignificant buzzing of a gnat that she lived in so-called sin with a dominating, infuriating man whom she didn't love.

Holding her loose robe over her nakedness, she went to the telephone room.

The groggy Society doctor, on hearing Paskevich's mistress was summoning him to attend the brother of a servant — no less! — woke his son, who had not yet finished his medical training.

The apprentice physician showed his annoyance at the midnight summons by stamping his feet as he followed Marya up the narrow staircase to the attic. Klazkha answered the door with a wet towel in her hand. A foul brackish odour hung in the room. The burned-down stub of candle showed Josip with the sheet covering him below the waist. He attempted to smile at Marya, then grimaced as his thin semi-nude body twitched.

'I assume you've kept notes of his temperature,' said the medical student to Klazkha.

191

She couldn't write and didn't own a thermometer. 'He's terribly hot,' she replied.

'My dear girl, how d'you expect me to make a diagnosis without proper information?'

'He strains and strains to move his bowels. Now nothing but water or blood comes.'

With a horrified glance at Marya, the young man muttered: 'Cholera.'

The sky over St Petersburg showed a broad stripe of luminous dawn, although it was barely three, as the Daimler zigzagged through the Vyborg District towards the St Petersburg Fever Hospital. Paskevich had decreed that Josip must be taken there, and it had been all that Marya could do to convince him that she and Klazkha must first make the arrangements.

The Vyborg, an industrial section, lay on the other side of the Neva yet could have been a million miles away from the magnificent city Marya knew. Tall chimneys thrust up like brutal fingers from the clenched-fist brick factories. Makeshift huts slumped between dilapidated tenements. Vagrants slept on the wooden footpaths.

Klazkha, who had never before ridden in an automobile, perched uneasily on a jump seat, clutching the soft grey velvet as the chauffeur steered around a corner and under an arched tunnel. They emerged in the courtyard of the St Petersburg Fever Hospital.

Both women drew a sharp breath.

Starting at a door labelled ADMITTANCE, an uneven queue coiled around the yard. Bodies slumped inert in makeshift ambulances of wheelbarrows, a woman bent vomiting on to the bricks, a boy squatted with his ragged pants down. Children wailed, babies thrashed in their mothers' arms. Those healthy enough to retain curiosity turned to look at the mirage-like limousine.

'Miss Marya, could all them folk have got the cholera?'

'The papers would've reported an epidemic,' Marya said. Her certainty wavered as the under-chauffeur helped her out. The courtyard stank with the same brackishly foul odour as Josip's room.

A stout nurse was hurrying towards them. Under her high cap her face was round and sweet. She beamed at Marya: 'You must be Miss Alexiev. I'm the head matron. Count Paskevich telephoned that you are bringing in a servant who's contracted cholera.' She glanced at Klazkha in her dark blue uniform. 'Did I misunderstand? Isn't the case a boy?'

'Josip, yes. This is Miss Sobchak, his sister.' Marya waited until the sweet-faced matron had acknowledged Klazkha with a slight inclination of her tall, pleated cap. 'We decided it would be best to make the arrangements first.'

'How thoughtful. I wish everyone were that considerate.' The matron glanced at the queue. 'Do come in.'

Inside the admitting door, Marya gagged and fought not to vomit. Rows of close-jammed pallets faded into the distance along the broad hallway. A young boy retched. A man screamed in pain. A woman jerked up, whimpering. Lazy flies swarmed, settling like glittering sequins on excrement. Many of the makeshift beds held two patients, the bare feet of one protruding by the other's feverishly red face.

'Ma'am,' a nearby voice called urgently. 'The pot. For God's sake, the pot!'

'Sister will attend to you,' the matron said serenely. The only nurse was at the far end of the corridor. Turning back to Marya, she said: 'They're always fouling themselves, these charity cases.'

'I've got money,' Klazkha said, pulling out a handkerchief. Knotted inside were the silver and copper coins painfully hoarded for her dream of a country cottage. 'I can pay for Josip.'

'Yes, our wards are excellent.' Matron whispered in Marya's ear. 'But crowded, too. Cholera.'

'The papers never mentioned an outbreak.'

'It hasn't been this bad since 1899.' Matron's undertone held a hint of pride, as if the epidemic crowding the hospital enhanced her stature. 'You know what the patients say? If Tsar Nicholas had Blessed the Waters, they wouldn't be ill. Can you believe it, Miss Alexiev? The superstitious fools refuse to drink boiled water. Instead they tell themselves that His Imperial Majesty's endangered them by not saying some prayers over the Neva.'

'Can we see the ward where you'll put Josip?' Marya asked.

'Let's pop in here.'

Three nurses sat talking at a brightly lit desk. In the shadows, a very young student nurse held a basin for a vomiting patient, someone thrashed on the floor, a child wailed hoarsely. Every bed was double-occupied.

A few feet away, a bearded priest was administering the last rites.

'What luck for your servant's brother!' Matron gave Marya her syrupy smile. 'He'll have a whole bed for himself.'

'I'll pay for a private room,' Marya said.

The Matron turned away, coughing. 'The private rooms are reserved.'

'Every single one?'

'Well . . .' She coughed again. 'We have regulations, as you can understand.'

'Are you saying there are private rooms available?'

'Yes, but the hospital doesn't give them to Jews or gypsies or the peasant class.'

'What?'

'We must reserve rooms in case somebody like yourself needs one. But why are we discussing this? I give my word that the lad will have this very bed all to himself.'

Josip, the quiet studious boy who dragged his withered legs on crutches, Josip who smiled at her and Boris with such open adoration. Josip, here?

Taking Klazkha's trembling hand, she said: 'Let's go.'

Chapter Fifteen

'And Josip's not going near that pest-hole,' Marya repeated, ending her tirade against St Petersburg Fever Hospital.

They were at the breakfast table. While Marya spoke, often incoherent with outrage, Miss Dunning hadn't moved. Now she fumbled to decapitate her soft-boiled egg, which was cold. Paskevich, exuding an air of calm indifference, had finished his raspberries and was spooning up a second helping.

'Let me get this correct,' he said. 'Your maid plans to play Florence Nightingale in my attic?'

'I've promised to help her.'

The berry-spoon dropped, clattering under the table. 'Are you insane?' Paskevich demanded.

'Once in a while she'll need a break.'

'You — are — not — to — go — to — the — servants' — quarters.' Paskevich clipped every word. 'You — are — not — to — go — near — that — boy.'

'Why ever not? Cholera comes from drinking unboiled water. It's not contagious.'

'Then, you've seen the records? No? There, I have an advantage over you. The greatest percentage of fatalities occur in the same family.'

'People who don't know enough to wash their hands carefully.'

'Marya,' Paskevich said in a low penetrating tone, 'pick up that bell. Send for your girl. Inform her that a car is waiting to take her brother to the fever hospital. Tell her that he will leave immediately.'

'Count Paskevich couldn't be more right, Marya,' Miss Dunning bleated. 'Poor little Josip belongs where he can be properly cared for.'

'Aunt Chatty, didn't you hear me? The nurses, most of them, do nothing. Everywhere's foul and filthy and reeks. People were dying right and left.'

'A law of nature,' Paskevich said. 'From time to time the poor are winnowed out.'

'My God, you talk as if Josip's an insect!'

'We Russians don't nurse insects. And we don't nurse servants. At least your brother has enough sense to avoid the epidemic.'

'He had a conference in Moscow!'

'Marya,' Miss Dunning interjected in a panting voice, 'think of our sweet baby.'

Lally. What else had Marya been thinking of since she left the hospital? Lally with her cloud of pale red curls, her smile with the gap between white milk teeth. Yet superimposed over her daughter were the contorted bodies, those beseeching whimpers, the supercilious head matron, the inattentive staff — memories that Marya would give anything to prune from her consciousness.

'Yes, what of the child?' Paskevich asked.

'I won't touch her until I've washed,' Marya

spoke with a firm strength that she was far from feeling.

'Much as I admire your rash bravery, during my stint in the Chevalier Garde I learned that useless courage is the cruellest waste there is, and impractical to boot. My dear, you are not a nurse.'

The butler had eased back into the sunny breakfast-room. 'Miss Alexiev, the telephone is ringing.'

Paskevich responded: 'Then, answer!'

'It's the devil's voice —'

'What a household! The servants are either superstitious idiots or diseased whores!' Paskevich stamped from the room, the abjectly cowed butler trailing after him.

'Dear.' Hyperventilating, Miss Dunning held a hand to her heart. 'You really ought to listen to Count Paskevich; he's older and wiser. And Josip will be better off where they understand cholera.'

'Auntie, stop imagining this as a version of the San Francisco hospital. It's straight out of the Dark Ages.' She shuddered. 'A lazaretto.'

'Lally isn't two yet. Small children are especially prone to stomach diseases.'

Unable to bear her own doubts voiced aloud, Marya flung down her napkin. 'Anyone not a babbling idiot knows that!'

Miss Dunning pulled a handkerchief from her sleeve, dabbing at her eyes.

'I'm sorry, Auntie.' Marya got up to pat

Miss Dunning's bent shoulder. 'My nerves are all on edge.'

'The message was for me,' Paskevich said from the door. 'I'm off.'

'Now? Before you finish breakfast?'

'There are some papers that I must get together at the Moika.' The Ministry of Finance faced the Moika Canal. 'My car' — he meant the opulent railway carriage with the Paskevich crest discreetly blazoned on the doors — 'is being hitched to the early train, which goes on to Paris.'

'Paris?'

'It's His Imperial Majesty's wish that I waste no time reopening the bond proposals with Baron de Rothschild.' Paskevich's over-ironic tone proved his anger. 'And have no doubt, ladies, of my success. Three months ago, when we discussed floating a loan, do you know what the French Rothschild told me? As a Jew, he couldn't in clear conscience lend money to a government that oppresses his people.'

'Who can blame him?' Marya said.

Paskevich bowed to Miss Dunning. 'I leave the household in your ever-capable hands.'

Marya went downstairs with him. Ignoring the *dvornik,* passers-by, a beggar and his two chauffeurs standing to attention, Paskevich gripped her shoulders.

'I plan to tell them to return immediately and lug the boy to the fever hospital.'

'You'd do that?'

'Unless you give me your word on this.'

Harsh grooves showed between Paskevich's nostrils and mouth. 'Marya, you must promise me to stay away from the attic until the day after tomorrow.'

'Then, you don't mind my helping Klazkha?' she asked in surprise.

'By then you'll have played with the child and thought about what I've said. You'll have changed your mind.' The small clever eyes were fixed on her so intently that, as he mentally snapped her image, she imagined she saw the puffs of brightness that a photographer makes. He shifted his arms, drawing her into a tight embrace. 'Do you promise me to wait before you go up to the cripple?'

'All right, yes. I'll wait.'

'Good. I'll be gone some time. God alone knows how long Nicholas will detain me there, attempting to accomplish the impossible. So tell me you'll miss me.'

'I always do, Paskevich.'

His brief hard kiss was scented with raspberries and coffee.

The under-chauffeur moved to the front of the bonnet, cranking the motor with powerful circular motions while the head chauffeur handed Paskevich into the car. Undeniably her days and nights would be duller without Paskevich; yet, as always when he left on a journey, she felt as if she had kicked off her too-tight shoes. *It's that arrogant superiority of his,* she thought. Paskevich could be generous to servants, to

201

Ministry subordinates, to the thousands of peasants on his estates; but it was always a lordly munificence, tossed down from on high. He was so far above those like Josip and Klazkha that he couldn't hear their cries or see their pain.

She thought of Stephan's concern for all living creatures and sighed. Stephan, always Stephan. At times she wondered whether it was the ambiguities of Lally's birth that kept him so indelible, but one fact she knew for certain: if it were he who had just left for a lengthy journey, she would be sunk into bleakest depression.

When she returned to the breakfast-table, the high chair had been pulled up and Lally was inexpertly spooning porridge and cream.

Miss Dunning, wiping the small face, reported the latest domestic crises in a high quaking voice. 'The cook slammed the door on Klazkha and shouted that she wasn't about to prepare meals for cripples and . . . uh, bad women . . . She was so loud and crude. Dear, you really must have a talk with her. And Serge' — the bow-legged butler — 'says that all the servants refuse to go up there.'

Serge was bringing in fresh coffee.

'Will you please take Klazkha and Josip a large bowl of this oatmeal?' Marya said.

'Any honest soul who goes near that room's bound to catch the cholera. The likes of that wench bring bad luck.' Serge's mouth puckered as if to spit: it was commonly believed that spittle warded off the Evil Eye. Crossing himself as double insurance, he stalked from the room.

'Oh dear,' Miss Dunning breathed. 'They get quite insolent when the count's not here. Whatever are we going to do?'

'I'll figure out something. In the mean time I'd better take them some breakfast.'

'Go upstairs?'

'What's the choice? They can't starve.'

'Mamma, dat.' Lally pointed her spoon imperiously at Marya's sweet bun.

Marya broke off the end, putting it into her daughter's porridge-covered grasp.

'Fank you,' Lally said with a smile.

Marya had already reached the decision that Paskevich had predicted. She would not help Klazkha with the nursing. She couldn't risk her daughter.

'Auntie, do stop crying,' she said. 'I'll leave the tray in the hall. I swear I won't even touch the door. And I'll take a bath the minute I get back.'

Four days later, on a still morning when low-hanging clouds clutched the city in a hot humid glove, Marya circled the washing-lines by the laundry house. She carried a loaf of white bread tucked under the arm that grasped the heavy iron soup-kettle, while her left hand balanced a pile of clean linen topped with a medicine-phial and two oranges — a special treat that rolled precariously.

The servants remained obdurate in their ban, so Marya had been making this trek several times a day. She had never talked to Klazkha face-to-face. Warped unpainted wood had muffled the medical reports: Josip wasn't so good — diarrhoea, vomiting, bad cramps.

Each time Marya returned to the flat, she filled the claw-footed bath with near-boiling water and soaped thoroughly with a bar of carbolic so harsh that her skin was flaking. She had hired a ragged adolescent boy to lug boiled water up to the attic, to empty the slops and bring down the filth-soaked washing which she paid a laundress quadruple salary to boil.

Boris, still in Moscow, had sent a brief letter informing her that officials were privately admitting that cholera in the capital had reached frightening proportions: he suggested that she take Lally and Miss Dunning to visit Paskevich's new holiday villa by Lake Saimaa in Finland. Paskevich advanced the identical idea in his daily correspondence. The letters from Zurich bore bright stamps that Lally demanded. The envelopes from Paris were unstamped, having been carried to St Petersburg in the diplomatic pouch. As Paskevich had foretold, his conversations with Baron de Rothschild were getting nowhere. 'His Imperial Majesty has ordered me to remain in Paris. He expects a loan to materialize purely because he is God's anointed and as stubborn as a mule.' Her protector seemingly was unconcerned that anything delivered in the leather diplomatic bag might well be seen by the monarch.

Heat blanketed the attic. Setting down the heavy kettle, Marya wiped the sweat from her forehead before she tapped.

There was no response.

Marya tapped again. 'Klazkha,' she called. 'Klazkha?'

'Miss Marya?' Klazkha's voice was faint.

'There's a potful of cold bortsch, and some pills the druggist hoped would stop Josip's stomach cramps.'

No answer.

'Klazkha?'

Rain had started, a muted drumming on the roof over her head. She could hear the excited cries of the laundresses as they raced to take in their washing.

Then she heard a faint rustling murmur. She tilted her head against the warped door. A dog was yapping, and she couldn't be sure if the sound had been imagination.

'Klazkha,' she called. 'Is Josip . . . ?' Her voice faded. She couldn't say *dead.*

Again no answer.

She rested her hand on the doorknob, then jumped back as if she had been burned. *Paskevich's right, and so are Boris and Auntie. I can't risk it. Lally's just a baby. Cholera's even more hideous for the little ones; they dehydrate so quickly.*

Yet Klazkha's voice had been so weak. Klazkha, the only real friend she had. And, to be rational, the disease wasn't spread by airborne germs.

'I won't touch one single thing,' she muttered aloud, reaching for the knob again.

The moist heat had swollen the wood. The door refused to budge until Marya pushed with all her strength, then it swung open so quickly that she toppled forward. Gagging, she involuntarily held her hand over her nose and mouth.

Josip's body barely raised the sheet, which had been neatly drawn up to cover his face. Over the side of the cot dangled an arm. The fingers ballooned at the tips. In the last couple of days Marya had been devouring medical books, and had learned a little about the circulatory system: after the heart ceases to pump, blood sinks to the lowest part of the body.

Klazkha sprawled on the floor. Normally fastidious, she lay with filth oozing from her skirt. Her skin was grey, her flesh lax. Her cheeks moved in and out like a bellows as she gasped to catch her breath. The previous day's food remained on trays. A mouse had gnawed its shape through the loaf of white bread.

'Thirsty . . .'

Marya moved to the stone pitcher, then kneeled to hold the glass to cracked lips. Klazkha drank, retched feebly, and lapsed into incoherent mutterings about cramps in her legs. Marya flung open the window, thrusting her head into the soft clean-smelling rain.

'Get Miss Dunning,' she shouted at the scurrying laundresses. 'Tell her to come into the courtyard!'

When Miss Dunning appeared below, Marya called down that Josip was dead and Klazkha had it now. She anticipated that either the old lady would burst into hysterical sobs or faint.

Instead Miss Dunning lifted her umbrella up higher. 'I'll telephone the doctor.'

'Don't let him send his son. Insist he come himself.'

'There's no doubt it's cholera,' said the frock-coated doctor.

'But she's been drinking boiled water. And the food all comes from our kitchen.'

'Possibly she ate something the brother had touched, or inadvertently used his glass. Maybe she didn't wash her hands properly after tending him.'

'I should've called you sooner.'

'There, there. No blaming yourself. Not another lady in St Petersburg would have been half so kind. Miss Alexiev, when you leave, wash with strong soap. Be doubly thorough. Scrub under your fingernails with lye disinfectant. I'll make arrangements for the girl to enter the fever hospital.'

'Never!'

'It's the only hospital that will accept her.'

'Then, arrange for her to have her own room there. And a nurse.'

'Private care, Miss Alexiev, isn't available for the peasant class.'

'That's what the matron said. It's miserably unfair.'

The doctor's left eye twitched. 'In Russia the terms *fair* and *unfair* have no meaning.'

'I'll look after her.' The words were unpremeditated.

'What?'

'Klazkha's my friend. I'll nurse her.'

'Miss Alexiev. My God! Count Paskevich would never forgive me.'

'It's my decision, not yours. Or his,' Marya said.

The doctor stared at her. After a few moments he said: 'I'll arrange for help.'

Marya tipped a spoonful of red syrup into Klazkha's mouth.

'Miss Marya.' The weak tones rumbled with asthmatic huskiness. 'It ain't right, you being in here.'

'Hush. Let the medicine work.'

'I'm ready to die.'

'No. I won't let you.'

'Let me go to be with Josip —' Klazkha gasped, and jerked up on the bed. 'My leg! My leg's all cramped up!' She lapsed back into delirium.

By now it was late afternoon. No sense of virtue at doing a good deed uplifted Marya as she made the other cot. She felt only staggering guilt. What right did she have to gamble her life?

If she died, what would happen to Lally?

Boris would become his niece's guardian. But, much as Boris loved the baby, her birth shamed him; and, besides, when did he have enough money to look after himself much less a child? There was Miss Dunning, but she was destitute and too old. Paskevich never entered Marya's calculations. Not only was he completely indifferent to Lally, but also the quality of mercy had by-passed him: he would never support a bastard who might well not be his. *He was right: I should have lied, lied through my teeth about her.*

Or she should have tracked down Stephan. *I should've moved heaven and earth to find him. He might not have cared for me, but I could've convinced him Lally was his, and he'd have been too decent not to take responsibility.*

Shivering uncontrollably, Marya stretched out on the springless cot.

The doctor sent a wiry, grey-haired, practical nurse. Born a serf, she had never worked in a hospital and had no formal training. She put on a clean voluminous apron and scrubbed every surface of the attic room with Eusol. She was forever washing the stuporous patient. She added salts to Klazkha's drinking water. When Klazkha screamed with the cramps, she dosed her with an infusion of *oblepikh,* bush oil, to ease the pain.

After three days Klazkha's fever broke. She no longer vomited or strained to pass blood.

'She's on the road to recovery.' The spry little nurse was changing into yet another of her aprons. 'She'll recover.'

Bending over the cot, Marya gripped Klazkha's hand. 'You're going to be fine.'

Klazkha said in a weak voice: 'There ain't no way to thank somebody for what you did. You been good to me, Miss Marya. And you was an angel to Josip. Taking him in when it wasn't made easy by some I could mention. Teaching him to read. Getting him on crutches so he didn't need to crawl like a worm. Keeping him from that hospital.' Klazkha tugged feebly at Marya's hand.

Sensing what she wanted, Marya longed to pull away, yet didn't. Klazkha drew the hand to her mouth, kissing it with chapped lips.

'Klazkha . . . please don't.'

'From now on, whatever you need me for, I'll do it,' Klazkha whispered. 'If you need food, I'll find it. If you want somebody murdered, I'll kill for you. My life is yours.'

Chapter Sixteen

Marya didn't cross the courtyard to the flat. Instead she went to the Egerov public baths. First she used the sauna, ladling water on the coals until steam veiled the naked women who chattered indolently on the benches, flailing herself with the twig brush until her skin turned scarlet. Dizzied by heat, she hosed herself in icy water before tottering to the corridor where attendants stood between the bathroom doors to hand out towels. She scrubbed and shampooed, dressing from the skin up in new clothes that Monsieur Bézard had personally delivered to the baths. Only then did she go home. The cobbles and paving stones, the businessman climbing into a brass-trimmed droshky, the two laughing gendarmes, the young working-class women dawdling along — everything seemed insubstantial, artificial. Tangible reality was the red cholera warning plastered to a lamp-post.

Lally sprawled on the nursery carpet making chugging noises as she pushed a miniature gilded coach drawn by eight horses. Miss Dunning embraced Marya, whispering: 'Count Paskevich sent it to her from Asprey's in London, an exact replica of the coronation coach, and it's stamped eighteen carat. A solid gold toy — imagine that.'

Lally continued her game, eyeing her mother with stubborn obliqueness. When Marya kneeled to put her arm around the pink-sashed stomach, Lally stiffened mutinously.

'No!'

'Just a teeny kiss?' Marya pleaded.

Lally's pale well-defined brows drew together, a signal that she might erupt into one of her small rages. 'No want Mamma!'

When Marya continued holding her, Lally opened her mouth and held her breath, letting out a howl that she accentuated by stamping her buttoned shoes. Released, the child ran to Miss Dunning's chair. She was picked up and patted until her tearless sobs ended.

One of the white stockings was drooping. When Marya moved to draw it up, Lally stiffened yet permitted the service.

'Mamma stay?' she asked.

'I'll never leave you again. Never.' Marya kissed the soft hair, inhaling the French-milled soap and talcum powder. Using willpower, she didn't complete the embrace until Lally put both her arms around Marya's neck; then she drew the child to her, running her hands repeatedly across the firm, healthy little body.

When Marya had moved into the attic room to nurse Klazkha, Miss Dunning had telegraphed Boris in Moscow and Paskevich in London. Her fondest prayer was that one or both men would return to St Petersburg and physically drag Marya down from the attic or, failing that, assert their God-given male dominance by telegraphing their commands that she stop this madness and get back where she belonged. Boris, however, was incommunicado at the summer dacha of his current mistress, Olga Orlovna, a divorced heiress widely known for keeping a *salon* where the highest type of intellectual conversation gave way to a broad variety of carnal activities. As for Paskevich, he'd left his chief secretary in charge at the Savoy Hotel, and the meticulous underling considered any communication below the ministerial level unworthy of relaying to his employer, who was opening delicate preliminary financial discussions at Waddesden, a country estate of the English Rothschild.

Several evenings later, Marya and Miss Dunning were in the drawing-room. Miss Dunning straightened her arm each time she drew a long aquamarine thread through her work. Marya glanced at the evening newspapers. On the back page of the *St Petersburg Gazette* was the headline:
'FIVE RADICAL HOOLIGANS ARRESTED IN KIEV.'
The names were listed in a column. No Strakhov; no Stephan, either. She rested

her head back in the chair.

'Listen,' Miss Dunning was saying. 'There it is again.'

Marya jerked. 'What? Sorry, Aunt Chatty. I must have dropped off.'

'No wonder. You poor dear, you haven't caught up on your sleep. And you're wearing yourself out with Lally. Stay in bed tomorrow and let me take over —' Miss Dunning raised her finger. 'There. Don't you hear it?'

The windows stood open, and the warm night air was filled with male singing accompanied by a balalaika. Marya listened intently. It took her a few moments to isolate the faint whimper.

Rushing from the room, she skidded along the corridor to the night nursery. Before she reached the open door, she could smell that vile brackishness.

The doctor pressed his stethoscope to Lally's tensed, bloated stomach, then sighed.

'Cholera,' he said. 'I'll arrange for properly trained nurses.'

'I want the woman who cured Klazkha.'

'She has no diploma —'

'Get her!'

The doctor turned his professional gaze on the distraught mother. The exquisite face was a powdery white and bone-thin, the compelling moon-coloured eyes shadowed. Complete mental and physical exhaustion, he diagnosed. His most illustrious patient's

214

mistress must be prevented from destroying herself.

'Miss Alexiev,' he admonished firmly, 'this time I cannot let you play nurse.'

Lally gave a feeble sob. Marya swept her up.

'Let me be frank,' the doctor continued. 'This isn't a servant; it's your little daughter. You lack any kind of medical experience.'

'To fill my educational gaps,' Marya said, appropriating Paskevich's withering hauteur, 'you will come to the house three times a day.'

After that the short luminous summer nights blurred with the endless stifling days, and there was only the bewilderment of a tiny girl unused to pain. Lally wailed whenever the doctor appeared. She shrieked whenever the grey-haired nurse touched her. Marya let the kindly old woman fetch and carry, brew the curative herbal potions, but she didn't let her near the cot. Sometimes Lally would be bundled in shawls and shivering in her mother's arms; then the fever would rise abruptly and she'd need to be sponged with iced water. She vomited and her bowels ran until both were the same milky white. Dehydrated, her flesh shrank so rapidly that Marya believed that she could actually see the small limbs shrivelling.

At some point Klazkha's thin but steady hands were there. Lally made no protest.

From then on the two took turns spooning drinks into Lally's mouth, changing her clothes and the bedding, holding her.

This was the pre-dawn hour when illness worsens and death waits in the shadows. Rain had fallen earlier, and the fresh scent of a wet summer night came through the open windows. A safety-pinned linen towel dimmed the lamp to a sepia bubble. In the cot, Lally curled on her side, eyes open, one hand on the gilded coach, the nose of the front horse against her cracked lips. During her illness she'd insisted on keeping the toy with her. Did Lally's attachment to Paskevich's gift indicate that he had fathered her? If Stephan were her father, would he have somehow known and shown up? In Marya's light-headed exhaustion, the two questions made perfect sense.

Lally looked up apathetically. Her eyes were huge tarnished coins in her tiny blanched face. 'Thirsty,' she said with a quavering sign of mournful resignation.

Marya poured orange juice that the cook had boiled, strained and iced. 'Here, darling,' she said, curving her hand behind Lally's back to support her while she sipped from the silver mug. The small bones felt as small and sharp as coral spikes.

The door opened quietly, and Klazkha rustled in. They glanced at each other, and Marya shook her head, whispering: 'No change.'

'The cook stopped ignoring me long enough to say she's cooking you up some blinis.'

'I'm not hungry.'

'Without food you ain't going to keep your strength.'

'How can I leave her?'

'I'll fetch the tray in here.'

Marya sat back in the rocking-chair, instantly dozing. She woke to the smell of blinis and to Klazkha bending over the cot.

'She's burning like a stove,' Klazkha whispered, frightened.

Suddenly the child opened her mouth in high-pitched screams. She bent her elbows. Her desiccated arms fluttered like the wings of a trapped bird.

'Oh my God! Convulsions!' Marya was on her feet, shouting. 'Wake Miss Dunning! Tell her to telephone the doctor! Hurry!'

As Klazkha rushed from the nursery, Marya took Lally from the cot. To hold the wildly flailing body took her full strength. She had no time for atheism: *Please, God, let her live. She has only ten teeth. Please let her cut the rest.*

Then Lally relaxed. 'Mamma,' she whispered, showing those enchanting teeth in a faint smile.

'Mamma's here. Mamma's holding you tight.' Marya kissed her forehead. Cooler. Definitely cooler. Cuddling against Marya's breasts, Lally relaxed and lay still. Marya

217

rocked her, crooning wordlessly.

Klazkha returned. 'Ten minutes, he swore he'd be here in no more than ten minutes.'

'The fever's broken.' Marya and Klazkha exchanged glances, moon-grey and pale-blue eyes shining with the joy that comes only a few times in a lifetime.

Klazkha lowered the side of the cot, rapidly changing the sheets. She came across the room to feel Lally's forehead. Then she laid two fingers to the still chest.

'Oh, Miss Marya.' She kneeled next to the chair. 'Oh, my poor Marya . . .'

Marya's mind blocked the knowledge of what the tremulously spoken words meant. 'Hush,' she whimpered irritably. 'She's sleeping.'

Klazkha's jaw trembled. 'I'd give the world if I was able to wake her.'

'She's better,' Marya said.

'Yes, much better,' Klazkha said, her voice breaking. 'Now, let's you and me pop her back to bed.'

'Not until the doctor comes,' Marya said. She was in a place she had never been before, a timeless place where her blood had frozen and she refused to accept what had happened. She held the knowledge at bay as she gently rocked her daughter.

Closing her eyes, she remembered the midwife holding up a red squirming baby with a funny bald head. That had been twenty-two months ago. Twenty-two months . . . Less than two years. A short time, yet long enough to learn to walk and talk and smile. Long enough to expect jam on the cook's spoon, to expect small gifts to spill like magic from Boris's pockets, yet not long enough to learn that holding up her arms to Paskevich wouldn't tempt him to pick her up.

Paskevich.

He had ordered Marya not to tamper with the immutable law that ruled Russian life: the poor suffer and die, the rich survive. For ignoring this edict, she would never forgive herself.

Miss Dunning, a shawl over her nightgown, tiptoed in. She glanced at Marya, then at Klazkha who shook her head. The elderly woman slumped sobbing against the doorjamb until Klazkha half-carried her back to her room. The doctor came and left. Then a gendarme knocked on the front door, handing the butler a printed form. By law, burial of those who die from cholera must take place within twenty-four hours at specified cemeteries. Services for that day's dead would be held at three in St Nicholas's Church — also known as the Sailors' Church — across from the Vasilievsky Island docks.

Shabbily dressed people grouped around the coffins. Each mourner held a candle: the flickers of light wavered uncertainly across blackened icons and peeling frescoes.

Marya and Klazkha stood alone at the

small white coffin. Miss Dunning, weeping and swathed in heavy black, had fainted as the hearse pulled up. The household staff, despite their genuine love for the child, were kept away by terror of the epidemic. Trepidations shared by the presiding clergy. The deacon waved incense with perfunctory haste; the corpulent priest, tall mitre askew and vast brown cassock bespotted, mumbled the funeral liturgy at breakneck speed.

'It's God's will,' a nearby old woman muttered. 'God's will be done.'

God's will? Dry-eyed, Marya looked down at the wasted little face in the open coffin. *Me. My will. My stubbornness killed you, my baby. My headlong lack of common sense killed you. I killed you.*

As the mourners raised off-key voices in a hymn, Marya whispered to Klazkha: 'She loved glittery things and sunlight. We should be outdoors.'

'Soon enough we will be.' Klazkha blew her nose. She had seen her mother's shrouded corpse drop from the hinged bottom of the rented coffin. Being pragmatic, she accepted that, although Marya had paid good money for Josip's funeral, he, too, had been dumped down with a similar lack of dignity. For this indifference she had been able to blame the callousness of undertakers and priests. Standing over Lally's coffin, however, Klazkha's thin shoulders were bowed. Like Marya, she was weighed down by personal responsibility. She blamed herself for letting her employer, who'd already been a regular guardian angel to her and poor Josip, help her in the attic. If only she'd been firmer and sent Miss Marya packing! She, Klazkha, would be dead, but little Lally would be alive.

Boots shuffled as men stepped forward to hoist the coffins of their loved ones. Marya had hired two of the ragged crowd who loitered around the church entry in the hope of earning a few kopeks as pallbearers — a Tartar father and son with similar doleful faces made yet sadder by their drooping strings of moustache. Gripping the silver handles, they easily hoisted the coffin. To the singing of 'Eternal Memory', the procession leaked out of the church, bearing their dead along the sunlit walk beside gently bobbing vessels. The dirge was briefly drowned out by the clamour of stevedores hauling logs up the embankment.

The small weathered gravestones of the poor had sunk unevenly in the swampy weed-strewn cemetery. A mongrel squatted to do its business by the long, freshly dug trench. The coffins were set down. The fleshy priest made the sign of the cross hastily as he tossed a spray of dirt at each of the still faces. Hammers rang out as lids were nailed down. Shawled women keened and wailed as their bare-headed menfolk lowered the coffins on ropes. The Tartar pallbearers eased down the small coffin, letting it drop the final inches. At the small, evocatively hollow bounce, Marya shuddered.

The mourners sang 'Rest Eternal'. Glossy black ravens stalked to the mass grave, for all the world like landlords surveying property that soon would be theirs. A large bird perched on Lally's coffin.

Someone behind Marya hurled a pebble. It struck the raven. The wing must have broken, for the creature scuttled away unevenly. Marya glanced to see who had aimed so unerringly.

By the cemetery gate stood a bald man too short-legged for his broad shoulders. In his starched white shirt, business suit, a bowler in his left hand, he might have been a stockbroker, a doctor or a lawyer — if it weren't for his posture. That instinctive easy arrogance of body was possessed only by those bred through long generations to wield power.

But Paskevich is meant to be in England, Marya thought. *Auntie must've cabled him that Lally died. But how could he have come so far in a few hours? Anyway, why would he rush to come home for the funeral? To him, Lally was only an encumbrance.*

Paskevich walked around the sorry little gravestones to Marya's side. At the arrival of one so patently high-born, the priest slowed his babbling to a lugubrious solemnity as he intoned: 'The earth is the Lord's and the fullness thereof, the earth and everything that dwells therein.'

Like each of the bereaved men, Paskevich bent for a clod to drop on the coffin. A ritual that marked the end of the funeral. Grave-diggers stubbed out their cigarettes, exchanging cheerful conversation as they raised the shovels. Mourners drifted from the cemetery. Klazkha touched Marya's arm without acknowledging Paskevich, then walked in the direction of the embankment tram-stop. Her freshly ironed uniform hung loosely.

Marya watched the smallest, finest coffin disappear. The diggers' jovial complaints about the heat had no more meaning than the ugly cawing of the ravens. When the long trench was covered, Paskevich took her arm, guiding her to the carriage. Neither of them had spoken.

The horses eased forward. 'Were you any more successful in England?' she asked tonelessly.

'I left before Lord Rothschild got down to any real discussion.'

'Did you have any trouble with the private account?'

'The Swiss bankers are eminently sensible. They made no enquiries; they simply deposited the funds as requested.'

'Did Auntie cable you?'

'Yes, but her message wasn't forwarded. When I went into London my secretary — my *ex*-secretary — gave me her wire. I started home immediately. I wish I'd been here all along.' He paused. 'My dearest, why a mass funeral?'

'The police told us where and when cholera victims must be buried.'

'You're a hereditary noblewoman; that regulation doesn't apply. Boris should have been here to make the arrangements.'

'How could he?' Defending her brother was a dulled reflex. 'He didn't get the telegram in time.'

At home, she went directly to her room. Paskevich followed, shutting the door to stand with her at the window. The previous night's rain had washed dust from the drooping birch leaves. Below on the canal, two husky boys sang as they heaved their poles in unison to propel their barge.

'Would it help,' Paskevich asked, 'if I said she was very dear to me, too?'

A porter with a long, grey beard was humping a steamer trunk down the steps of the next-door building. Watching the old man's struggles, Marya said: 'You never paid attention to her.'

'Marya, by now it should be clear to you that I'm not a man to romp on the floor. I bought her presents instead.'

Unsuitable gifts, as Miss Dunning had said. 'She loved her coronation coach. She kept it with her all the time. I put it in the coffin.'

'She was so like you. Bright, brave, impetuous, lively. But you don't have her temper. Marya, in her worst tantrums that's when she was dearest to me. "Go to it," I'd think. "With a temper like that, who else's daughter could you be?" '

His tone wasn't ironic. He sounded sad and weary.

'At least I knew she was mine.' Marya rested her hands on the window-ledge, noticing without interest that the emerald was loose on her finger. 'Paskevich, I washed so thoroughly, I threw away all my clothes, I was careful, so careful. Just not careful enough.'

He put his hand on her shoulder, turning her to face him. 'Listen to me. You did not give the child cholera. It was impossible for you to give her cholera. It came from some fruit that the cook didn't wash properly. She's always been careless.' His face creased into vindictiveness. 'She's already gone, the bitch. Tell me, is it true what Miss Dunning said: that the servants refused to help you in the attic?'

'They were afraid.'

'They'll be given their notice, too.'

Marya sighed. 'Lally's dead. What's the point?'

'In my father's day they would have been whipped until their backs were in ribbons before being thrown bodily on to the street. I might just follow tradition.'

She gave a shiver.

'It's the Russian way,' he said.

Marya rested her tearless face against the window-pane. 'And I interfered with it.

225

Paskevich, you warned me.'

'You've always cared too much about people,' he said.

' "Impulsively sentimental," you called it.'

'Generous and brave.'

'Pig-headed,' she said bitterly. 'I'm never going to make that mistake again. No more caring. I'm past caring. I'll be flighty. Yes, as giddy as possible. Bézard shall design me a new wardrobe. Nothing black. Black makes me look like those ravens, don't you agree? And I'll play bridge and get my own box at the Maryinsky and at the Alexander Theatre. How do you feel about a banquet at the Hotel Europa? I do so love the Europa's dining-room, so big and with all that lovely stained glass. Or should we take over the Aquarium cabaret for the night?'

'Both.'

'I'll refurnish the apartment. That should be exciting. And invite a larger crowd to Friday nights . . .'

Paskevich held Marya as she rambled on about extravagance and parties. In her misery, it seemed to her that the worst punishment she could inflict upon herself was a remorseless cycle of pleasure.

1913

The celebration of the Tercentenary of our glorious Romanov Dynasty officially opened today with a *Te Deum* in the Cathedral of Our Lady of Khazan. The streets of their Imperial Majesties' route from the Winter Palace were jammed with tumultuously cheering subjects. On the Nevsky Prospekt the crowd briefly broke through the cordon of Don Cossacks to surround their Majesties' carriage with an outpouring of love.

The cathedral was packed with dignitaries and royalty of every foreign nation as well as representatives from near and far corners of the Empire.

May Holy Russia prosper for three thousand years!

May our most noble Monarch long rule over us in health and joy!

Vechernee Vremya, 27 May 1913

Chapter Seventeen

Marya, wearing a lacy chemise and her daring new flesh-coloured silk stockings, stood with her arms raised like an obedient child as Klazkha lowered the emerald and blue chiffon over her head. Studiously fastening the thirty-five faceted lapis lazuli beads that ran down the back of the gown, Klazkha then bore over the large flat jewellery-case with Paskevich's most recent gift: a rope of luminous hazelnut-size pearls that she passed twice over Marya's head, adjusting the first loop high on the throat.

Stepping back, she surveyed her employer critically. Though Klazkha was not yet out of her teens, her face had taken on the permanently sensible expression of a middle-aged schoolteacher. She drew forward a copper tendril in the guilelessly natural Psyche's knot that had taken a full hour with the curling-irons to achieve. 'You'll outshine them all,' she pronounced. It was not a compliment but a statement of fact.

Although other women at the Friday Night might have maids equally skilled, might wear gowns as dazzling, might scour the Gostiny Dvor for the identical unguents, lotions, rice powder and rouge, though they might subtly enhance their eyelashes with kohl and bring a glitter to their pupils with belladonna drops, none would achieve this same incandescence. Marya stared at the radiant corpse reflected in her mirror. To bring herself to this semblance of life she depended on increasingly larger doses of excitement.

She glimpsed a tall dark-haired man, a shadowy figure like the summoned presence in tales of the supernatural. She attempted to convince herself that Stephan was a childish infatuation and she had forgotten him: while it was true that since Lally's death she had thought of him less often, at odd times he would swim into her consciousness. Would he admire this frivolous creature in her jewels and couturier chiffon? She preferred to believe he would not.

'Here.' Klazkha handed Marya the peacock fan whose feathers matched the gown: she was already tidying the room as Marya went out.

The normal Friday Night hullabaloo reigned. On the day of Lally's funeral, Paskevich had fulfilled his threat of throwing out the servants, replacing them with a larger, more skilled — and highly volatile — staff. From the kitchen came the angry bellowings of the Parisian chef. The butler shouted commands at the footman in a grey-striped apron. The round-backed French wine-steward muttered to himself about the exalted vintage of the magnum he was setting in the champagne-bucket.

The little Alexiev — the kindest name that St Petersburg called Marya — was famed for her wild parties. It was whispered that orgies and perversions took place every week. In fact, while the Friday Nights had become larger and more elaborate, the formula remained essentially the same. Charming young things preened in front of Paskevich and his bearded bankers or stout businessmen. Boris and his friends, some from the Finance Ministry, others in a brilliant array of military uniforms, gambled until dawn. Heirs to great titles waltzed with their current mistresses, millionaires' sons sipped the best vintages as they talked of revolution. Men didn't wear dresses, women didn't put on trousers, nobody removed their clothes and no trysts were consummated in the flat. The true scandal of her Friday Nights, Marya often reflected, was not their lasciviousness but their cost.

She had reached the vestibule when there was a knock at the door. Rather than waiting for a footman, she answered.

Bézard, bundled in his mink-lined evening cape, was wiping frost from his narrow moustache.

'Why, Monsieur Bézard, how delightful to see you,' she said. 'But where's Mishenka?'

'Dressing.' The couturier, examining her, collapsed his opera hat under his arm. 'If you'll permit me?' He adjusted the left shoulder of the gown a few millimetres and kissed his fingertips. 'Ravissante! The blue and green would drown out another woman, but against your glowing white skin the colours, they dance!' He tweaked the skirt towards the centre.

Marya laughed. 'Ah, so that's why you've dropped by early? To ensure that I'm up to scratch.'

'I'm here to beg a favour for Baroness Betsy.'

Betsy was not her given name, and she was no baroness. A light-hearted, startlingly pretty blonde, she had begun life as Lyubov, a junior clerk's daughter, taking on her chic English appellation as she emerged from the menial classes by catering to the sexual vagaries of increasingly older and richer lovers, men to whom she was chronically unfaithful. Her feather-brained sense of humour diverted Marya, and the two often joined forces on disastrously extravagant shopping sprees.

'But Betsy should have called me on the telephone. Why send you out on a freezing night?'

'It's a delicate matter. She wants to bring a guest . . .'

Obviously not her creaky official benefactor: Grand Duke Serge, the tsar's uncle, could hardly lower his dignity to attend so raffish a gathering. 'So she has a new flame? But Betsy knows that any friend of hers is welcome.'

Silently, Bézard waited while the footman edged a wine-tub through the hall and into the card room, then he whispered: 'Count Paskevich will disapprove.'

'Are you trying to drive me mad? Who is it?'

He leaned forward to say softly: 'Perhaps you have heard of Iskra?'

Marya dropped her fan. 'Iskra? You can't mean *the* Iskra? The Iskra who wrote *Days of Freedom!*'

Until *Days of Freedom*, Russian radical literature had fallen into two categories: dreary fictional sagas of the lower depths or unreadable manifestoes. *Days of Freedom* was a love-story. A love-story that took place eighty years in the future, at the end of the twentieth century when hunger and religious prejudice had vanished from Russia; when freely elected men and women, too, ruled the happy cities and meadowlands. The novel spoke directly to the heart, yet the details of the future government provided food for the mind. It goes without saying that the censors banned the novel. Repeated police crackdowns couldn't prevent illegal presses from running off fuzzy editions that were passed from hand to hand.

Iskra means 'Spark', an obvious *nom de plume*. Nobody knew the author's true identity, and accordingly rumours multiplied: he was a member of the Imperial Family; he was a political prisoner who had somehow smuggled his manuscript from a Siberian prison-camp; he was a high-ranked bureaucrat, a son of Leo Tolstoy, a mystic, a Jewish exile, a peasant who'd taught himself to read and write. Marya, who had read *Days of Freedom* three times, was certain of one thing. Iskra was young. Who but a young man could have written a novel so permeated with physical love?

Bézard's round eyes glowed with pleasure at Marya's surprise. Retrieving her fan, he turned grave. 'If you'll take my advice, you'll refuse.'

'Refuse?' When excitement was what pumped the blood through her veins, how could she refuse? 'Iskra will be a sensation! So *he's* Betsy's new lover! What a slyboots, not once letting on!'

'Marya, think this through. For Iskra to be here might appear to some that Count Paskevich is agreeing with radical politics.'

'Paskevich doesn't give a hoot about appearances.'

Bézard's expressive face showed a struggle between anticipation of a delicious scandal and his obligations as Marya's friend. 'The count's unpredictable. Who knows how he'll react.'

'We'll find out later.' She tapped his arm with her fan. 'But you're a sweetie pie' — this in English — 'to worry about me.'

As soon as the front door closed on him, Marya ran to crank the telephone. Betsy, at her toilette, was unable to speak, so Marya left a message that the baroness's friend would be most welcome.

As Marya emerged from the telephone

room, her brother was coming down the corridor. Boris wore a tail-coat with an elaborately gold-braided collar. He had developed a round paunch, and his recent step up the bureaucratic ladder to a higher 'desk' gave him a fortuitous excuse to order expanded uniforms. Brother and sister admired one another; then he held a hand over his mouth, coughing.

'What is it?' Marya cried. 'Are you ill?' Since Lally's death, she had become obsessed with Boris's weak chest.

'It's nothing.' He coughed again.

'Boris, you've been overdoing it. Out every single night for weeks.'

'Better to have stayed home, the way Lady Luck's been treating me.'

Marya, trapped in her own frenetic activity, identified with her brother's affinity for the card-tables. 'That bad?' she asked sympathetically.

'It's pretty damn humiliating, telling the fellows above me in the Ministry that they'll be paid on the instalment plan.'

'What you need is an advance. How much?'

'Two thousand roubles.'

'I've nothing like that much,' she said. 'But Paskevich wants to buy me a gift . . .'

'A debt of honour. Otherwise I'd never let you even suggest it. You'll be repaid by the end of the week.'

He took out a tiny silver-covered notepad, scribbling: 'Boris Alexiev owes Marya Al-

235

exiev the sum of two thousand roubles, dated 6 December 1913.'

How many thousands had he borrowed? She couldn't remember. He had never repaid a rouble. She didn't care. She would have far preferred giving him the money outright. This ritual IOU, however, salved his pride. Embarrassed, feeling as if she were colluding in a fraud, Marya folded the slip of paper into the beaded purse that dangled on her arm. She would tear it up later. 'You'll never guess who's escorting Betsy tonight.'

'The Pope? Kaiser Willy?'

'Far more intriguing.' She flicked her fan open, batting her eyelashes before she said: 'Iskra.'

'Iskra? Iskra and Betsy? That pretty little meringue knows Iskra?'

'In the biblical sense, I believe.'

Boris's musical voice deepened as he quoted the most often repeated passage of poetry in the novel: ' "When the whole world is free and the people free, then to the moment will I say, Tarry awhile, so fair thou art." ' Boris's Monarchist loyalties remained, yet being young he felt the tug of Liberalism. 'The famous Iskra at our party. Marya, what a coup for us!'

The warm air smelled of perfumed flesh, newly starched dress-shirts, pomade, savoury hors d'oeuvres, fine tobacco, vodka, champagne and the sweet buttery wines from Paskevich's vineyards in the Crimea. Women's bosoms rose like smooth, tropical white flowers from elaborately draped and beaded *décolletages*. Gems sparkled on throats, slender wrists, fingers, delicately rouged earlobes. Uniforms and orders glittered as men bowed and kissed Marya's hand meaningfully. They didn't stand a chance. Though the hostess indulged in numerous flirtations, she remained faithful.

The major-domo from the Crimson Palace stood at the front door banging his staff on the floor to announce each arrival. Prince Vatsetis, Mr Steinberg, Miss Radzinska, Baron Pulaski — the baron, inheritor of the famed Pulaski racing stable, had begged Marya to accompany him to Longchamps. Pretty shopgirls with young Garde officers in glittering white uniforms. Bézard with Mishenka. The latest *ingénue* from the Alexander Theatre. Half a dozen members of the Imperial *corps de ballet*. A chess champion with his inamorata. The bellowed-out names could scarcely be heard when the evening was in full swing.

Marya's vivid blue-and-green tulle floated amid her guests as she promised a sensation. 'Ah, you'll be electrified. No, I refuse to tell. You'll have to wait and see.'

She kept glancing towards the hall. Betsy was late. Betsy was always late.

A string trio replaced the dance band, the tension grew at the card-tables, champagne-corks shot upwards more frequently, the chafing-dishes of hors d'oeuvres and caviare-bowls were refilled, Paskevich and a Danish bank-owner retired to the study.

It was after eleven when the major-domo rapped his cane on the marble hall-floor.

'Baroness Betsy Pavlovna and Iskra.'

A ripple ran through the reception rooms. Iskra? Iskra? *Iskra?*

Then voices fell silent, the musicians ceased playing. Guests separated to make a path for Marya as she moved towards the hall.

At the low step on to the newly laid marble, she halted. Shock drained the blood from her head. The party sounds behind her melted, the entry-hall disappeared, Betsy's high chattering voice faded.

Marya was conscious only of Iskra.

Instead of shabby clothes he wore a dinner-suit. His dark hair refused to lie sleek, the faint scar (*My scar*, she thought) showed high on his cheek, his deep-set blue eyes appeared nearly black as he gazed at her.

'Stephan . . .' Her whisper was inaudible.

Chapter Eighteen

When Lally had taken her first steps she'd held on to a torn magazine-cover, convinced that the scrap of paper was keeping her upright. Marya clutched the gold handle of her peacock-feather fan for the same reason: if she didn't grip something, she would topple.

'Marya,' Betsy was saying, 'may I present Iskra? What a naughty boy he is. He refuses to tell me his true name. Iskra, this is my dearest, closest chum, Marya Fedorovna Alexiev. She's from the American Wild West . . .'

The lack of pleasantries between hostess and guest went unnoticed amidst Betsy's effusions. Shedding her ermine cloak and smoothing her blonde pompadour in the mirror, she trilled: 'Iskra, darling, do come along. Marya always pops the most divine champagne, and I'm parched, absolutely parched.' Resting a hand on Stephan's sleeve, she swept past envious-eyed women, gaping card-players, aristocratic young army officers, self-made grey-bearded capitalists.

Welcoming the two late arrivals, Boris was aware of standing a full head shorter than Iskra. Wasn't there something familiar about his height, thick black hair, dark straight brows and deep-set, intensely blue eyes? Boris rubbed his tongue reflectively over his teeth. Madame Orlovna's sexually orientated *salon* was the only place he met *intelligentsy*, and his mistress made quite a point of advertising any guest who had a name. As they shook hands, the literary lion made no reference to any earlier acquaintanceship. It didn't strike Boris until the following morning that Iskra was the man about whom he'd teased Marya when they'd first arrived in Russia. Boris gave himself over to the pleasure of swivelling the distinguished guest through the rooms making introductions. Each time a guest spouted praise of *Days of Freedom*, or professed to have quite fallen in love with Osip and Nathalie, the novel's hero and heroine, Boris took it as a personal compliment and beamed. The author responded with a small correct bow.

To Marya, watching from the small gilt couch, each effusion increased Stephan's aura of aloofness. The reserve, like the handsome dinner-suit, was new. There were other changes, too.

Small lines were cut into his forehead, and his cheekbones appeared more prominent. He was a man, an impressive man, self-assured with all these fawning strangers. He had a darker quality now that she couldn't quite put a finger on, and possibly because of this unknown factor was infinitely glamorous.

Watching him, Marya's emotions were so

intense that she could scarcely breathe. A few guests were watching her in the hall. Sitting upright, she forced her mind into rational thought-patterns. *There goes Stephan Strakhov, author and sometime knight errant, hero of your daydreams,* she told herself. *And that's Betsy clinging to his arm. When he goes to sleep tonight, it'll be in her big soft, pink-draped bed. So forget him, the way he's forgotten you.*

Yet, even as Marya harangued herself, her heart felt strange and mushy, as if winter ice were melting inside her ribcage.

The midnight supper was served. Guests crowded elbow-to-elbow at the extended dining-table and the auxiliary round tables. Moving through the hazy smoke that curled from small yellow cigarettes, Marya rested a hand on a shoulder here, laughingly accepted a compliment there. She tapped Paskevich with her peacock feathers, coquetting with his hollow-cheeked Danish banker. Standing over Count Pulaski, she took a nibble of his *rabchick* wing, then dipped a spoon into Prince Vatsetis's dessert, tasting the subtle blend of hothouse fruit, cream and walnuts that had taken her chef twenty-four hours to prepare. Stephan was not in the packed dining-room. She moved through the folded-back double doors to the card-room where Boris and eleven other bridge fanatics were eating a snack as they continued their game: Stephan wasn't in here, either. A few opera *aficionados* lingered in the music room where the soprano was embarking on the 'Letter Aria' from *Eugene Onegin.*

'Marya?' Stephan had come up behind her. 'Might I have a few minutes of your time?'

His formality seemed a rebuke. To pay him back, she rested a finger over her mouth to indicate quiet and tilted her head in a listening attitude. 'Isn't that voice a miracle?' she murmured. 'Yes, when this ends, do let's take a bite of supper together.'

'In private. It won't take long.'

'Oh, very well. This way.' Short train flipping behind her like a brilliant fish-tail, Marya bolted down the corridor to the study. Because of the elegant formality of the front rooms, the family relaxed in here. Magazines and novels, among them *Days of Freedom,* were piled on the sagging ottoman; Boris's fencing mask was propped against his briefcase; Miss Dunning's embroidery frame stood next to the stove. Paskevich and the Danish financier had left their stubbed-out cigars to spread the aroma of stale tobacco. On the desk stood a silver-framed photograph of Lally.

Marya turned her back on the photograph, enquiring: 'Is this secluded enough?'

'I needed to explain why you haven't heard from me. Immediately I got past the border, the Okhrana found me. I was exiled again, a harder sentence. I couldn't send or receive mail.'

'Let's say you had been able to write, how would you have signed? Stephan? Iskra? Or do you have other pseudonyms floating about?'

'Marya, I'm simply trying to clear the air.'

'The great novelist, the man of the hour, making an effort to clear things up — what flattery! My poor head will get quite swollen.'

Stephan's remote air vanished. The small scar showed above his suddenly flushed cheeks. 'Is this what you've become?' he burst out. 'A grand bitch?'

His anger was preferable to his civility yet she felt tears form. Turning away, she glimpsed the blur of the oval picture-frame. *Lally*, she thought. Lally's temper could have been inherited from either Paskevich or Stephan. Rubbing her knuckles across her eyes, she kept her back to him. 'So the police took you into immediate custody? Oh, come on.'

'It's the truth.'

'Right after you left Verballen you were picked up?'

'Yes.'

'So it must've been your double I saw talking with a bearded student as the two of you crossed the Anichkov Bridge right here in St Petersburg.'

Sleigh bells sang in the street, a bubble of applause floated from the drawing-room, the wall clock ticked, a dead chrysanthemum blossom fell with a small papery thud.

'I did come here,' Stephan said in a low

243

voice. 'That's when they got me. On my way to the Crimson Palace. Right after you spotted me, an agent recognized me. No trial. No interrogation. I was quick-marched out of the country.'

She blew her nose. 'Where've you been?'

'All over. Berlin. Paris. Zurich. London mostly. By the time my sentence was up, Father was dead and Mother was dying.'

She murmured her condolences.

'By then I knew about you and Paskevich. And there were other problems.'

'What was wrong?'

'Let's just say a black cloud was tethered above me. So I left the country voluntarily. Before then poetry had been my outlet. I'd been doggedly serious about politics. Occasionally my work ran in *Osvobozhdenie*' — a banned journal, whose name meant 'liberation' — 'but mostly I paid illegal presses to run off my tracts about the theories of Locke and Helvetius. A short book on the Socialist ideal. Essays on the Duma, on the emperor serving as a figurehead. Not counting the Okhrana, I had perhaps a dozen readers. Then my mother, just before her death, hinted that possibly I was just a bit dry. She suggested I turn my pen to fiction. Lo and behold, throughout Russia people stayed up all night sobbing, or so I've been told *ad nauseam*.'

With a glance at the cheaply bound, illegal copy of *Days of Freedom*, Marya said: 'I've cried over it myself. Three times.'

244

'Didn't you recognize yourself?'

'Me?'

'You're Nathalie.'

'Nathalie? I'm not the least like Nathalie. She's generous. Loving. Good.'

'What should I have done?' His anger had returned. 'Thrown in a footnote that she doubled as a cabinet minister's mistress?'

'And who's Betsy's latest lover?'

'There's nothing between us. Nothing. Ask her. Betsy knew from the first that you're the reason I got to know her. She admires you. She sings your praises. She told me you nursed your maid through cholera. And the maid's crippled brother, too. And your little girl died because of it.' Stephan paused, saying with obvious difficulty: 'Marya, the child, she was the right age . . . ?'

'I don't know,' Marya whispered.

Stephan's dark brows formed a straight line. 'So you went straight into his bed? Didn't my ring mean anything to you?'

At the question she winced, reliving the trail of dynamite. That brief glimpse of him, the jeweller's extravagant appraisal, the sand-polished diamond being returned to the Crimson Palace. 'I . . . it's gone.'

'Gone? Where?'

'I knew it was a family keepsake, but I needed money for . . . well, I needed money. Seeing you that day crushed me. On the spur of the moment I sold it. Did you have any idea that the stone was a diamond?'

Colour splotched his cheeks. 'I found out later.'

During this conversation they had drawn closer until she could feel his breath, warm, moist, scented with champagne.

'Stephan, imagine my feelings. There you were, striding along the Nevsky Prospekt as if you'd completely put me out of your mind.'

'It's true, I did forget you. Once I actually went a whole ten minutes without thinking of you.'

Marya's smile trembled.

The door opened. Voices, laughter, a Tchaikovsky song enveloped them.

'Marya my dear,' Paskevich said. 'You're being monopolistic. Your guests are starved for a word with our famous author.' As he spoke, he bowed, smiling. His pupils were dots.

He knows, Marya thought. *He knows I'm alive again.*

'Come, Iskra.' She trilled that false laughter. 'Betsy will be searching for you.'

Marya gazed dreamily into the mirror as Klazkha brushed her hair. The long red waves crackled with electricity. The rhythmic strokes ceased.

'You're a thousand miles away,' Klazkha said.

Marya looked up blankly. 'What?'

'A kopek for your thoughts.'

Marya looked in the mirror, meeting her

confidante's pale blue eyes. 'Iskra is Stephan,' she said softly.

Klazkha sucked in her breath. 'Ain't you told me over and over that romance with him is deader than a doornail?'

'He's thought of me all the time. I'm the model for Nathalie — she's the heroine in *Days of Freedom*.'

The illiterate Klazkha would have perceived this literary compliment as inconsequential if she had not been looking at the reflection of Marya's flushed cheeks and glowing eyes. Leaning closer to the mirror, she said: 'Don't never, never let him come here again.'

'Can't you see I'm alive again? Alive!'

'Oh, I see that. And Count Paskevich ain't blind, neither. Which is why this has got to be nipped in the bud.'

'Paskevich is away a lot.' Across Europe and Asia alliances were being formed, treaties were being signed, and with each political shift Paskevich was summoned to advisory meetings at Tsarskoe Selo or the new Crimean Imperial Palace overlooking the Black Sea, the Imperial Polish Hunting Lodge, the royal yacht *Standart*. 'There are weeks when he's not here.'

Klazkha's fine bosom thrust forward. 'What about servants?' The new staff's resentment of Klazkha was spiced with jealousy of her friendship with the lady of the house. 'Every last one of them a snoop and a tell-tale.'

'Paskevich never listens to kitchen gossip.'

'Don't count on it,' Klazkha said darkly. 'As far as men are concerned, a woman's privates belong to them.'

'Klazkha, you had a bad time when you were young.' Marya sighed. 'Believe me, Paskevich would never stoop to having the servants spy on me.'

Klazkha brushed several strokes in silence. 'Times is harder and harder out there,' she said sombrely. 'More and more people without work. And when folks is homeless and hungry they listen to all sorts of radical and revolutionary talk. The Okhrana has got ears everywhere. This Iskra — this Stephan of yours — don't you think they've got their eagle eye on him? If they spot him all cosy with a cabinet minister's lady-friend, how long would it take them to have him in prison, or worse?'

Marya saw her sudden pallor reflected in the mirror. Klazkha's sensible warnings of personal danger had titillated and excited her. The idea of Stephan endangered chilled her.

A door down the hall opened. Masterful footsteps rang in the hall. During the re-decoration, Lally's nursery had been fitted up as Paskevich's dressing-room. Klazkha hastily swept up the blue-green gown, peacock fan, evening slippers, wispy lingerie, slipping into her cubicle.

Marya remained at the vanity unit.

'You're looking even more exquisite tonight,' Paskevich said, switching off the overhead lamp. He kissed the nape of her neck before he slid his hands under her nightgown. He watched her reflection in the three mirrors. She parted her lips, simulating arousal. Drawing her to her feet, he unbuttoned the nightgown, letting it slide around her feet. He pressed kisses between her breasts and down the central line of her body. She was now facing the pier-glass, and she glimpsed the shadowy reflection of a thick-shouldered bald man in a black velvet robe kneeling as if in worship before a slender white statue. *Stephan,* she thought. *Ah, Stephan, how can I be doing this?*

'What I once felt for you seems mere infatuation in retrospect,' Paskevich said, kissing the coppery triangle.

It was unnecessary for him to mention finding her alone with Stephan; he needed only to remind her of his love, a love whose deviously twisting undercurrents Marya believed she had already plumbed.

Recalling Klazkha's sagacious counsel, she passionately breathed: 'Ah . . . come to bed . . .'

Chapter Nineteen

The following afternoon a red-cheeked Estonian boy delivered one of Betsy's lavender envelopes to Marya. The single line was in French, a language spoken but not written by the semi-literate Betsy: 'I must leave St Petersburg but will return soon.' There was no signature.

Just as Marya feared for Stephan's safety, so he feared for hers.

Christmas trees spread their piny fragrance.

After the New Year, the Imperial Family travelled south to their new palace in the warm flower-scented cliffs overlooking the Black Sea. Because of the omnipresent fear of bombs and other terrorist assaults, there were two identical blue-and-gold Imperial trains: until the last minute nobody knew which would carry the tsar and tsarina. When their Majesties boarded the second train, the Countess Paskevich, as one of the retinue of ladies in-waiting, lumbered after them.

Paskevich moved into the flat on the Fourstatskaia. He commissioned the great Impressionist artist Serov to paint Marya's portrait, whiling away the tedium of her sittings with his sparkling acerbic conversation. He took her to the latest cabaret at the

Aquarium, went with her to the Maryinsky Theatre for the Imperial Ballet's performance of *Swan Lake* with Nijinsky. They heard Rimsky-Korsakov conduct his own *Golden Cockerel.* They heard Chaliapin's basso profundo reverberating to the cheapest balcony in *Boris Godunov* and a recital by the golden-haired child prodigy, Vladimir Horowitz, whose small feet barely reached the piano pedals.

During the long winter nights Paskevich made love with tireless skill. While her heart was dead she had often responded passionately to him; now she felt not even a hint of desire. Paskevich was her adversary in an undeclared never-mentioned battle whose prize was her heart, mind and body.

Betsy, feather-brained except when it came to the transactions between men and women, understood Marya's more frenetic shopping excursions, her impatience, her occasional outbursts of temper; yes, Betsy comprehended exactly what would happen when Iskra returned to St Petersburg.

She broached the subject when the curtain was about to rise on a matinée performance of this week's new French farce at the Michel Theatre. 'Darling Marya' — she reached for one of the cream chocolates on the velvet ledge of her box — 'you simply must take ballet lessons.'

They had been discussing a certain young

countess and her handsome escort. Marya had never quite accustomed herself to the way that Betsy flittered like a hummingbird between subjects. Lowering her opera glasses, she asked: 'Ballet lessons?'

'I never saw anyone in more need of a good ballet mistress.'

The orchestra blared the opening chord of 'God Save the Tsar', and as the two young women rose to their feet Betsy's perfumed blonde head touched Marya's.

'Darling Marya, Iskra's absolutely too divine. So romantically brooding. In my opinion the time is perfect for you to branch out. Discreetly, of course. I can't recommend Madame Chkiedze highly enough,' Betsy murmured. 'Eons ago she was a *première danseuse*. She's near the Rossi Street colonnade, not far from the Imperial Ballet School, but on a back street. Her studio's downstairs; it opens on to a garden with a gate to the alley. Nowhere could be more private. Madame's a tyrant about dance, but she's not a prude. There's the sweetest little boudoir right off the changing-room, and she's quite darling about letting certain of her students use it. Shall we drop by her studio after the performance?'

The same afternoon Marya arranged for thrice-weekly ballet lessons. Handing Madame Chkiedze the first month's fee, she felt a thrill go through her, as if Stephan had touched her hand.

The Lenten season halted all social activities, including the Friday Nights. Paskevich, however, received visitors, ruddy-faced men wearing fine wool shirts belted at the waist and loose trousers thrust into highly polished boots — the rustic Tolstoyan garb affected by the landed gentry. The meetings took place behind the closed drawing-room doors.

'What on earth do you discuss for hours with those hobby-horse farmers?' Marya asked irritably. Stephan's prolonged absence was wreaking severe damage on her nerves.

She sat at the vanity unit buffing her nails while Paskevich, who had just emerged from a long conference, lounged on the bed.

'Grain,' he said. 'We discuss grain.'

'Wheat? Rye? Barley?'

'Corn as well. I buy for his Majesty.'

'The tsar? A grain broker?'

'Scarcely a way I'd describe his transactions,' Paskevich said. 'Quite simply, our bond issues don't cover military outlays. If he levies more taxes, there'll be riots. So the crown buys grain to resell.'

'Profiteer?'

'If we don't handle the transactions, merchants will. What about your spring wardrobe? Have you told Bézard he's profiteering?'

'If I don't get new clothes, I won't starve. If

the price of bread goes up, the workers don't eat.'

'Do I hear echoes of your friend Iskra?'

Marya's hand trembled as she set down her gold-topped nail-buffer. 'Iskra? Oh, you mean the scribbler. Betsy's beau.'

'He's a Socialist, isn't he?'

'How should I know? Betsy and I never talk about politics. And how did you get into such a boring subject anyway? You know I loathe politics.'

A few days passed before Easter. Paskevich's crested railway carriage was hitched to the train that travelled south to the Crimea, where his sprawling villa stood amidst hundreds of acres of carefully tended vineyards. Protocol obliged him, as Minister of Finance, to celebrate Easter with the Imperial family — and his countess.

Marya and Boris were part of the vast joyous congregation attending the midnight service at St Isaac's, the cathedral whose immense cupola-topped gold dome and four smaller gold domes commanded St Petersburg's skyline. The interior, with its freshly cleaned icons and bas-reliefs, its walls and pillars of malachite, lapis lazuli, porphyry, could easily accommodate the fourteen thousand worshippers. Peasants in homespun caftans and bast boots, middle-class families with well-scrubbed children, befurred Society groupings — everyone in the gilded cathedral stood holding a burning candle as the mighty liturgical choruses swelled exultantly. Just before midnight, the metropolitan, his mitre blazing with jewels, led golden-robed bishops and bearded priests into the frosty spring night. The entire congregation followed bearing their candles. Like a glittering golden snake, the vast procession wound around the cathedral square. Returning, the metropolitan peered through the doors as if looking into the tomb of Jerusalem. The great cathedral was empty. Turning, flinging wide his arms, he proclaimed in a loud, exultant bass voice: *'Kristos Voskres!'* Christ is risen.

'Voistinu Voskrese!' roared back the congregation with such enthusiasm that candles flickered or went out. 'Indeed, He is risen.' People wept, laughed, embraced.

Miss Dunning, a Lutheran, having celebrated the holiday more staidly at the German Reformed Church on the Bolshoya Morskaya, was waiting in the festively decked apartment. The dining-table had been extended and was covered with savoury and sweet delicacies. The cook — she had replaced the alcoholic French chef — had been among the worshippers at St Isaac's: without pausing to take off her bright-green calico headscarf, she set to work slicing her renowned *kulik,* the enormous Easter loaves made with dozens of eggs and pounds of butter.

Traditionally at Easter everyone was

made welcome. Most households considered 'everyone' to include only family and friends. The Alexievs, however, were young and lighthearted and generous. All night long their door opened. The neighbourhood servants. Yuri, the taxi-driver came with his arthritic mother. The poor folk who lived in nearby attics and basements brought their children. Thin young clerks from the lowest ranks of the Finance Ministry gathered at the buffet. Bézard's designers and apprentices arrived in one perfumed, chattering group. The knife-sharpener, the herring woman, the shop assistants, messenger-boys, the cripples who begged at the corners of Fourstatskaia. The elegant Friday Night habitués. Whether clad in rags or in sables, the guests were embraced by Boris and Marya with the three ritual kisses: blessing, welcome and joy.

Betsy, her blonde hair rumpled from visiting so many homes and receiving so many kisses, said in Marya's ear: 'I heard from Iskra. He'll be in Petersburg next week.'

Behind a closed door a piano tinkled Chopin, accompanied by the little *thud, thud* of dancing feet. A row of pink-and-white tutus hung like crumpled carnations, shoeboxes were scattered everywhere, odours of sweat, rosin, powder and cologne permeated the changing-room.

'How did you come up with the idea?'

Stephan asked. He had just arrived. 'This as a meeting-place?'

'Betsy.'

'Good old Betsy. I should've guessed.'

'Madame's got her winter clothes in the boudoir, but as soon as she's finished packing away everything she's promised the room to us.'

'You're blushing.'

'When I put in my request I must've been lobster-red. Madame handed me the key and told me tartly that patience is much lacking in my character. Now tell me about you. Where've you been all this time?'

'A wild-eyed revolutionary like me answer that?'

Behind his bantering tone, Marya heard an unhappy wariness. 'You don't need to tell,' she said.

'In Moscow, organizing. At the first rally more than a hundred students joined the Democratic Reform Party.'

'Is that why you were exiled, that kind of recruiting?' Her voice was high and thin. 'Next time will it be a Siberian prison?'

'Marya, calm down.'

'They caught you twice before; they could easily catch you again. Stephan, you mustn't take any risks —'

'If somebody doesn't take a few chances,' he interrupted, 'the old injustices will last for ever. The pogroms. The poverty. The inequities of class. The police spying and brutality. Our entire empire prostrated before one man. This is the twentieth century, Marya, and you're an American. Surely you see that Russia needs hauling out of the Dark Ages.'

'You're a marvellous writer, Stephan —'

'And I can sway Russia with more soppy novels?' he asked. 'Marya, listen to me. I can't plonk myself down at a desk. My life has no meaning if I'm not working with the others towards clipping the claws of the fat archaic Romanov eagle.'

'You sound so angry. As if you've got a personal vendetta against the tsar.'

He gripped her shoulder. 'Nicholas isn't my enemy,' he said. 'The Autocracy is.'

'Stephan, I didn't mean to raise your hackles. It's only that I worry —'

She was interrupted by a scratching sound.

Madame Chkiedze's boudoir and dance studio ran along the rear basement three steps down from a high-walled little garden which was shaded by a huge horse chestnut. A fluffy red Pomeranian was clawing against the French window. Darting back up to the garden, the dog raised a leg to the trunk of the huge tree.

'That's to inform us we're trespassing on his property,' Stephan said.

Their shared laughter broke the tension.

'He's Petipa, after the choreographer,' Marya said. 'Watch out. This Petipa's a biter.'

Stephan drew her close against his side.

'I'm going to die if I don't kiss you soon.'

His breath against her ear penetrated her body, melting her bones. For several moments she closed her eyes, allowing sensation to carry her, then she turned to his kiss. As in any good fairy-tale, his kiss transformed her. Once again she was the American girl of the Verballen Imperial Waiting-room, tremulous, young, yearning, innocent.

The door to the studio was opening. They pulled apart quickly. Smoothing down her ballet dress, Marya introduced Stephan to Madame Chkiedze.

'Strakhov?' The tiny, erect old woman stared down her arched nose at him. 'Many years ago when I taught at the Imperial School, there was a student called Strakhov.'

'Irena. My sister.' Unaccountably, Stephan flushed. 'She died when I was a baby.'

'Yes, I remember. Her death was a great loss to the ballet.' The wrinkled face was inscrutable. 'Unusual-looking girl with great ambitions. Could dance forty fouettés.'

It was clear from Madame Chkiedze's tone that she had felt no warmth for Stephan's sister. Marya later decided that this ancient antagonism lay behind the ballet mistress's continued refusal to grant them the boudoir.

Marya and Stephan fell into a routine, arriving on Monday, Wednesday and Friday just after three, when Madame Chkiedze embarked on her afternoon lesson. This gave them almost an hour together on the weathered marble bench under the tree. They could be seen from the long window of the studio, which meant no kisses.

Some afternoons desire dizzied Marya, driving her mad with restless impatience. At other times, sitting in the rustling green shade with pink petals from the candle-shaped blooms falling about them at the smallest breeze, she believed herself in a miniature Garden of Eden.

She learned a great deal about Stephan. He never joked about his ideals. He had a romantic streak. He was haunted by ghosts that he refused to discuss. He was brave but not impulsively so. For the most part they talked about inconsequential things — a book he was reading, a Russian drama she'd seen at the Alexander Theatre, the visiting Royal British naval squadron which clogged the Neva. Tacitly they avoided Paskevich's name and seldom used the future tense. Stephan never mentioned his parents or his dead sister, the ballerina. He always wore the same shabby suit. Marya had assumed him poor until she heard through Betsy that he supported a large soup-kitchen in the Vyborg district.

'Did your parents leave you the money for it?' she asked.

'My father was a professor,' he responded tersely.

'Do you use your royalties from *Days of Freedom*, then? I'm prying, I know that; but, Stephan, it hurts to hear things about you third-hand.'

'The novel is illegally printed, so it hasn't earned me a kopek. Sometimes my other writing pays a little. That's what I live on.'

'Isn't sponsoring the soup-kitchen expensive?'

To avoid her grey questioning eyes, he bent to scratch Petipa's ruff. *I can't tell her,* he thought. But why not? *I'm ashamed.* It was that simple. He was ashamed of his father, ashamed of being a bastard. He feared being less in her eyes.

'What a Sphinx!' she cried. 'Why can't you trust me?'

'It's you who shouldn't trust me.'

'There! You're being cryptic again.'

'Hardly cryptic. I shouldn't be here, putting you at risk.'

'Are you being followed?' she asked in alarm.

'No, no, of course not.'

The studio door opened. 'Madame's ready for me,' Marya said, getting to her feet. They embraced awkwardly, aware of possible watchful eyes.

'I never loved anyone before,' he said in a low voice. 'Bear with me if I'm not good at it.'

'You're wonderful. It's me. I shouldn't keep pushing you. Friday?'

'Of course Friday.'

Watching her float down the three steps, diminutive and graceful in her calf-length cloud of tulle, he thought of the long years when he had dreamed of her by night, fictionalized her by day. Even his repugnance for Paskevich and her extravagant way of life couldn't diminish that love. He wanted her so much that he ached, yet in a cerebral way he was grateful that they lacked privacy. Making love would blind him yet more to his obligations.

If only I were free.

Stephan had been manacled by invisible chains since he had read the scrawled, misspelled letter that changed his identity. Those first months after he'd learned the truth he'd been a madman: he would, had it been possible, have torn himself in two to drain away his Romanov blood. Later, he supported any exile group that preached a non-violent overthrow of the Autocracy. He had made a promise to himself that he would have no personal life until the double-headed eagle was toppled from its lofty perch. Yet he bore no animosity to Nicholas II, his half-brother.

Stephan wasn't blind to the psychological overtones of his politics. He understood that he was engaged in a dubious battle with that long-dead narrow-minded giant, Alexander III, who had so carelessly sired bastards. Stephan's self-knowledge in no way lessened his obsession. He had chosen his *nom de plume,* Iskra, the spark, because until

Russia was no longer an Autocracy he would consume himself.

He felt guilty about stealing these hours with Marya.

The piano started, and Stephan glanced inside. She was stretching at the barre. He felt equally guilty about meeting her in this hole-and-corner way. Oh, how he longed to wrench her away from that ugly caustic Monarchist! Some day, some day . . .

With a sigh Stephan let himself out of the back gate and into the empty, rutted alley.

Chapter Twenty

The piano ceased in mid-bar.

'Pas de bourée!' Madame Chkiedze's tyrannical old voice cut through the closed door. 'No, no no! That right arm looks like a broken broomstick!'

It was Friday. Marya glanced at the round clock on the wall. In less than ten minutes her lesson would start. Where was Stephan? He had never been late; he'd promised to be here. *What if he doesn't show up? Today of all days.* Today there was no need to hurry back to the apartment. Raymond Poincaré, the president of France, here on an official visit, was being honoured with a reception at the Winter Palace, and Paskevich was attending it and the small private dinner-party later.

At a rattling bang on the garden door, she jumped.

Stephan stared at her through the glass. His jacket was unbuttoned, and his chest heaved. The flesh of his face seemed pared back.

She ran to the door, sliding the bolt.

'Got trapped in the alley,' he gasped. 'Okhrana. I'll go upstairs and out the front door.'

'They'll be on the street, too. Stay.'

'I can't put you at risk.'

'Don't be an idiot.' Marya was reaching for the small package wrapped in the previous day's *Birzhevye Vedomosti*, crumpling the newspaper into the waste-paper basket as she dropped the lamb chop near the excited Pomeranian. Fishing the hitherto unused key from her purse, she said: 'In here.'

The boudoir was a jackdaw's nest. Posters from Madame Chkiedze's illustrious prime overlapped on the walls, souvenirs imprinted with names of world capitals crowded together on the tables, open escritoire drawers spilled yellowed clippings. And everywhere lay coils of old-fashioned knitted undergarments. The odours of Madame's musky perfume and candied violets were overwhelmed by the sprinkled peppercorns that Russian women believed fended off moths.

A pair of coffin-sized, finger-smudged cardboard boxes stood side-by-side. One, topped with green stars, was closed. The other lay open.

'Get in.' Marya sneezed.

'I shouldn't.'

'There's no other hiding-place. Hurry!'

Stephan obeyed. Too tall to stretch out, he curled on his side. Marya hastily covered him with folded layers of antiquated underwear and put on the lid with the pink galaxy.

She relocked the door and was at the bench retying her slipper when a sweat-drenched figure emerged from the studio with a dancer's proud duck-footed grace. Marya hurried inside, curtsying.

Madame Chkiedze, a tiny, imperious man-

265

darin figure, inspected her with cold disdain. 'Mademoiselle Alexiev, are you mocking me? Please to curtsy again. Again. Again.'

The studio door was flung open.

Marya, facing away, bent deep in the curtain-call position, heard the raucous breathing. Raising her head surreptitiously, she glimpsed at the mirror behind the barre. At another time she would have been amused by the reflected pair. The one with the pointed beard was tall and skeletal with a balding pate; while the other, short and full-bellied with clean-shaven bulging cheeks, had a thick shrub of black hair that glinted with sweat.

The tall gaunt intruder snapped out the Okhrana's official title: 'Department of Political Police.'

Madame Chkiedze, spine and grey chignon in perfect alignment, responded: 'You are interrupting a lesson.'

'A terrorist was seen entering your back garden. He's not there now.'

'Then, he must have climbed over the wall,' the ballet mistress said.

'Impossible. Our men in the alley would have seen him.'

'He hasn't shown himself inside,' Madame Chkiedze said in her most acid voice. 'Ask Mademoiselle Alexiev. Ask my accompanist.' The piano-player slouched over the keyboard, a cigarette dangling from his mouth. 'Or check with Madame Pavlova —

she was my previous student.'

'Iskra, he calls himself. Tall, well set up, young. Black hair, a business suit.'

'I've told you already that I have not seen your terrorist. What about you, Miss Alexiev?'

Marya came out of her curtsy. 'If anyone had come in,' she said, 'Petipa would've let us know.' Petipa, yapping furiously, was darting around the mismatched Okhrana pair's legs. The shorter policeman aimed a stubby boot; the lap-dog retreated, whimpering. 'As you can tell, our little fellow's quite the guard dog.'

The skeletal Okhrana officer gave her a sour look, then turned to the ballet mistress. 'We'll need someone to show us the premises.'

Madame Chkiedze said in a tone of exasperation: 'Mademoiselle, if you would be so kind? Needless to say, I won't charge Count Paskevich for the lesson.' She turned to the plain-clothes men. 'My pupil's guardian is the Minister of Finance.'

At this the fat man clapped his handkerchief to his dripping forehead.

His tall companion showed no sign of intimidation. 'Let's get going, miss. Time is of the essence.'

Marya, cradling Petipa in her arms, swept by the police into the changing-room. 'Are you going to stick knives in these?' She waved at the tutus. Her insolence was disconnected from the banging and jolting of her heart.

'We're only doing our job,' the shorter policeman whined.

The tall companion was trying the locked door. 'Open this.'

'Madame's sanctum sanctorum? I've never been inside. How thrilling. Will you be safe if I set Petipa down?'

To use her own key would be incriminating: she took her time returning to the studio for Madame's key. As she opened the boudoir door, the shorter policeman pulled out a grubby handkerchief, sneezing. The taller man glanced at the clutter, pointing to the huge cardboard boxes.

'What're those?'

'At the risk of encroaching on your territory, I'd say from the evidence . . .' Her nose itched. Pulling her lacy scrap of handkerchief from her bodice, she gave an exaggerated sneeze. 'I'd say that Madame appears to be storing away her winter clothing.'

'A man could hide in one.'

'Your terrorist can close boxes from the inside and lock doors from the outside? Did he study with Houdini?'

A bony hand pointed to the green-adorned lid. 'This one first.'

As Marya took off the lid, black motes of pepper danced upwards. They all sneezed, including Petipa, who retreated to the studio. Marya removed the topmost dress, a grey-and-brown striped broadcloth. Shaking out the folds, she laid the garment on a chair. With the same elaborate concern she transferred a heavy wool skirt, a cape lined with astrakhan, a jacket. With each garment, more pepper filled the air. By the time the box was empty, the stout policeman was contorted into an asthmatic fit.

His tall companion, also sneezing, turned to the other box, where Stephan was hidden. 'Now this.'

Marya buried her face in her handkerchief to hide the terror before she edged off the lid. 'It appears to be Madame Chkiedze's lingerie,' she said. 'Shall we go through it, too?'

He pressed a bony hand on knitted undervests, sneezing. 'The old girl's right; he must've escaped next door — or upstairs.'

As the two men hurried up the staircase to Madame's ground-floor apartment, Marya's leg muscles went limp. Holding on to the wall, she tottered back to the studio.

'Madame, you were wonderful.'

'Those *muzhiks* wasted enough of our time. Miss Alexiev, we have work to do.' She raised her chin towards the accompanist, who lowered his hands in a thunderous chord.

Marya was the final student of the day. Counting slowly to twenty after Madame Chkiedze and the pianist had disappeared upstairs, she returned to the cluttered boudoir. Locking the door behind herself, she called softly: 'It's all right, it's safe.'

Stephan climbed out of the box, sneezing

269

violently again and again. Marya opened the window, and a cool breeze swept through the room. As she smoothed clothes back into the box, his sneezing abated.

'What nerves you've got.' He was brushing off his suit. 'You were superb.' He kissed her forehead and moved to the door.

'Where are you going?'

'Be serious. Haven't I pushed you and Madame Chkiedze close enough to the fire?'

'Leave now and we'll be in the flames. There are men stationed all around.'

'What if those two come back?'

'Wait until dark. Believe me, this is the last place they'd search. You should have heard them sneezing!'

'I did. With the greatest of envy. Me, all I could do was —'

He held his reddened nose.

'The boss looked like an experienced guillotine operator. I almost passed out when he felt the underwear . . .'

'You sounded so cocksure.' He put his arms around her. 'My brave darling, you're shaking.'

'I was positive he'd feel you in there.'

Kissing her hair, he said: 'It's over.'

'They're looking for you; you're never safe, never, never—'

He stopped her with a long kiss.

The kiss changed to explicit caresses. His hands engulfed her breasts, then slid down her side, pressing hard through the tutu against the curves of her hip bones. His touch was wholly different from Paskevich's, less skilled, urgent yet somehow mysterious, unfamiliar yet at the same time as intimate as her fantasies of him — his touch ignited her. Her mouth still wide open to his mouth, she took a backward step, toppling on to the chaise-longue, drawing him down with her. Only the distant aromas of musk and pepper, his odours and her own filled the universe — that and their gasping breath as they pressed against each other. He raised himself to open his trousers. She wriggled out of her ballet tights, yanking them off together with her lace-embroidered silk pants and letting them fall to the floor. Her eyes were squeezed shut. As she reached for him, her rage of desire was pierced by a momentary self-judgement: she was acting the corrupt Little Alexiev of gossip. Was that in his mind, too?

'Ah, but I adore you,' he whispered. 'Always . . . I'll love you for ever . . .'

The brief dread faded, and she rose up to greet him.

Since Verballen she had borne and lost a child, Paskevich had tutored her in carnal pleasures, so how was it that nothing had changed between her and Stephan? Her body, flushed and burning, moved as rapidly as his; and almost immediately that waiting stillness, the exquisite stillness that precedes orgasm, held her in thrall. She gave a gasp of surprise. The wildness of her pulsations obliterated everything, even the instrument of her joy: Stephan himself.

Her ears continued to tingle long after their breathing had quietened.

'I love you,' she murmured, her tongue tracing the faint scar on his cheek.

'If only I could wake up and see you every morning.'

'Stephan, come home with me. California's a beautiful place, golden and warm. Lots of writers live there. And can you really do anything here, Stephan? Be honest. Will Russia ever change?'

'It will. It must.' He put his finger on her mouth, caressing the soft upper lip. 'Darling, probably it's not fair to ask you this, but would you stay here with me? Be married here?'

'Yes.'

'There's every reason you should say no. You just saw what my life can be like —'

'Already trying to back out?'

He moved a bit apart from her, and said with low sincerity: 'Marya, before, when I said I'd love you for ever, I meant it.'

It was close in the fusty overcrowded boudoir, but Marya's skin rose in goose-pimples. She was remembering Paskevich's words: *I'm your husband, Marya. If you ever let any man but me near you, I'll make you long for death.* She thought briefly of his uncanny ability to read her mind; of his vindictiveness, which could be either polished or roughly brutal. Languid from love, with Stephan wrapped around her,

Paskevich seemed a secondary problem, an obstacle she could manage.

'Sweet,' Stephan said, kissing her.

This time they made love without haste, tenderly.

Afterwards she drowsed. Holding her, Stephan was struck by her trust in him, that she could sleep in his arms. That she had never questioned his past or his background.

I'll tell her about myself, he thought. Yet, as he tried to phrase the story of his birth, he knew he couldn't say the words aloud, even to her. It was as if he, from his marrow, were part of a shameful, treacherous lie. She shivered, and he drew up a heavy cloak. *I'll tell her after we're married.* His thoughts shifted to the unfairness of involving her in his fate, then to what he must do after he left this haven.

When Marya awoke, darkness had fallen and a grass-scented breeze drifted from the open window. Stephan had covered them with Madame Chkiedze's astrakhan-lined cape. The pepper itched in Marya's nostrils, and she knew that to smell the homely spice would always bring memories of love.

'What's the time?' she murmured.

He reached for his watch, angling the face towards himself. 'After nine. I had no idea it was this late.'

'Doesn't matter. I'm free tonight.'

'Marya, I've been thinking. St Petersburg's too dangerous for me.'

'You ought to lie low for a bit.'

'Not too long. Probably a few weeks. One thing's certain. We can't meet here any more. When it's safe, I'll send word through Betsy.'

After they were dressed, he took Marya's face between his hands and pressed soft lingering kisses on each of her eyelids. 'Promise me', he said, 'not to be reckless.'

'If you make the same promise.'

'I'm used to quicksand. But you aren't.' Stephan's voice went low with venom. '*He's* clever, Marya, and dangerous.'

At the French window, he kissed her quickly. The thick grass swallowed the sound of his footsteps. In the darkness, she wouldn't have known he was gone if it hadn't been for the subdued creak of the gate.

Feeling her way up the staircase to Madame Chkiedze's apartment, Marya let herself out of the front door. Under the corner street-lamp, a gypsy woman wailed a lovesong, continuing to sing as she scooped up a coin tossed from a window. An elderly couple walked slowly with short steps. A plump servant stood in a doorway. A peaceful street scene. Marya, who had been anticipating watchful-eyed police, gave a sigh of relief and started home.

Under the Rossi Arcade a trio of young dancers moved gracefully, pretending to ignore the ogling Guard officers. An audience laughed at the Petrushka puppet show. A group eating ice-cream from the nearby cart circled a dancing bear. Green, blue, yellow, white and red balloons floated above a vendor.

Marya hugged her light cape around her and drifted slowly in the direction of the Fourstatskaia flat.

Chapter Twenty-one

Since none of the tenants kept a motor car or a carriage, to see a horse-drawn cab waiting wasn't unusual. No lights showed in Boris's window, or in Miss Dunning's. Her brother was out, and Aunt Chatty was probably in bed.

Marya climbed the stairs and unlocked her front door, raising both arms and stretching like a languorous cat before starting down the unlit corridor towards the pale glint from her open bedroom. She paused at Miss Dunning's room, wondering if she ought to tap and invent an explanation for her tardiness.

'She's at the Rachmaninov recital with your brother,' Paskevich said.

Marya gave a little cry of surprise.

'My dear, pardon me. I didn't intend to startle you.' He stood at the far end of the corridor, a swaying shadow with the glint of glass in his hand.

Marya had often witnessed Paskevich consume heroic quantities of vodka, brandy and wine with no visible effect. How long had he been drinking? How drunk was he?

To disguise the apprehension rippling through her, she spoke more frostily than she intended. 'Why aren't you at the reception?'

'Now, there's a fucking fine tone to take

with the man who foots the bills.'

Angered, Paskevich adhered with mocking over-embellishment to the nobility's code of manners, the sole exception being that hideous night in the Crimson Palace. Determined not to show her fear, Marya held her head erect and went down the corridor. She could smell the reek of perspiration and liquor; she saw that his tail coat and brocade vest were unbuttoned, his dress collar and tie missing, the stiffly pleated shirt open to show his strong wrinkled throat and a delta of black hair. An eccentric pity clutched Marya. 'You haven't waited for me to have dinner, I hope.'

'Yes, I'm certain that is your most cherished hope.'

Marya went to her dressing-table. Perfume-bottles had been shoved aside and toppled to make room for a tantalus. The cut-crystal bottles labelled brandy and whisky were empty; and the vodka, which occupied the middle space, was missing. 'I'll tell the cook to fix a meal for you,' she said.

'I'm not hungry. What about you, my dear? Have you dined?'

'I . . . I had a late tea with Betsy.'

'An exceptionally late tea. It's after ten.'

'Such a lovely evening. I decided to walk home.' She glanced towards the cubicle where Klazkha slept. 'Where's Klazkha?'

'Such a lovely evening. I imagine the pockmarked prostitute followed your example and took a stroll.'

Marya realized then that the apartment was abnormally silent. 'Where are the other servants?'

'I gave them the evening off.'

Coming up behind her, he gripped her shoulder. She saw his reflections repeated to infinity by the triple mirror. The glitter in his small bloodshot eyes, the way his lips were drawn back over his teeth — his expression was the same as on the night he'd brutalized her. Then, she'd been too naïve and young to recognize a man tortured beyond endurance. Releasing her so abruptly that her teeth clicked together, he wove back to the bedside table for the vodka-decanter. Filling the glass, he said: 'What time did you take tea with our dear baroness — isn't that the title the blonde public cunt prefers?'

'After my lesson.' Marya's voice wavered.

'Those toe-dance lessons! So you went from your prized ballet tutorial to your cherished friend's house?'

In San Francisco, the boarding-house landlady had owned a tomcat and a parakeet. The tabby would sit absolutely motionless, golden eyes fixed on the brass cage where the bird fluttered. With equal force Marya had despised the poised all-powerful cat and the terrified bird.

She set down the comb. 'You know everything, don't you?'

'One thing I've never been, my dearly beloved, is stupid.'

'Have you had me watched?'

'I?' His broad nostrils flared, and hauteur crackled in his tone. 'I?'

'You've suspected all along, haven't you?'

'At the risk of sounding egotistical, sweetest one, I do understand women. And you, my pet, are not adept at infidelity. You've been either totally absent-minded or wildly chafing at the bit. I do confess to a problem understanding what you see in that insufferable boy. Handsome enough, true, but how can you bear all that fervent high-mindedness? No, don't try to argue. I've ploughed through that sickeningly naïve novel. Liberty triumphs. Justice rules. He cribs from Goethe, doesn't he? Well, what can one expect of these well-educated revolutionaries? Tell me, does your precious "Iskra" realize that he's acting as the instrument of his own destruction?'

'He wants reforms, that's all. He's a pacifist; he's not trying to destroy anyone.'

'Merely his own class. And the monarchy.'

'He wants Russians to have the same equality and freedom as we have in America. Universal suffrage.'

'Tell me, can he possibly believe that the unwashed masses, given half a chance, wouldn't indulge in cruelties and repressions that would put Attila the Hun to shame? Is that young man of yours so completely blind to human nature? Does he honestly believe that, if the monarchy fell,

Russians would turn into altruistic vision-
aries?'

'He lacks your cynicism.'

'Some might call it common sense. Ah well,
he's an even bigger fool than he appears if
he discussed politics with you in Madame
Chkiedze's garden.'

'How did you know that's where — ?' She
stopped, flushing. 'The police told you.'

'My charming Marya, the last thing I would
do is involve myself with the Okhrana. Vul-
gar scum, all of them. No, my information
came from the old servant-woman you persist in calling an aunt.'

'Aunt Chatty? She's not a servant. She's
Mother's second cousin.'

'That doesn't speak highly for your family
tree, does it? But there I go, forgetting that
your mother served train passengers.'

'Being a Harvey Girl was considered an
honour. And I don't believe Aunt Chatty
would tell *you* anything.'

'No? When you didn't come home after
your lesson today she fell into a panic. She
telephoned my offices and spilled her fears.
She believed you might have been arrested
because you'd unwittingly become involved
with radicals via our ardent novelist.'
Paskevich threw his head back, draining the
glass. 'By the by, Marya, you never mentioned that you'd met him before. And neither did your brother.'

'Boris has no part in any of this.'

'I never suspected it. He has the brains to

keep a soft berth when he finds one.'

'Boris isn't a sponger.'

'What description would you prefer? A weakling? A self-indulgent gambler? A hedonistic pimp who lives off his sister's earnings? A hypochondriac?' Paskevich held up a hand to halt her sisterly protests. 'Let's not digress. I haven't finished answering your question. After Miss Dunning had finished whimpering and panting in my ear, I put her mind at ease. All was well, I said, adding an explanation that you and I had . . . *private* plans for the evening. Since the old woman's remarkably prudish about your means of keeping cream cakes and champagne on the family table, I had no difficulty convincing her to take the box at the Maryinsky with Boris. Then I telephoned your dear friend, Betsy. She vowed she had no idea where you were, but I encouraged her to chatter on until she'd filled in the details of what I already knew about you and the great novelist.' Emptying the remaining vodka into his glass, Paskevich tossed the decanter on to the bed. Trickling dregs darkened the needlepoint cushions. 'I take it our highly esteemed author is the other candidate for fathering the dear departed little bastard?'

Lally . . . Marya closed her eyes. Tears squeezed behind the closed lids.

'So he is,' Paskevich said thickly, and drank. Dropping the empty glass on the bedspread, he lurched across the room. Standing behind the vanity stool, he elaborately flexed his fingers. Hands too large for a man his height. Virile black hairs tangled between the knuckles and at the strong wrists.

'Paskevich, you're very drunk.'

'Foolhardy of you to point it out. But, then, you've never lacked courage.' He flexed his hands again. 'Aren't you the least curious whether or not I'm about to inflict great torment on you?'

'I wish to God you would. Maybe enough pain would stop me from remembering Lally.'

'You are aware, aren't you, that, whatever I choose to do to you, as a minister to the tsar I'd be immune from investigation? Besides, as my mistress, you're ranked as a prostitute, and whores are murdered or maimed daily without the gendarmes wasting a minute's time on investigation. So, you see, it's within my power to despatch you in an interesting variety of ways.' He curved his tensed fingers around her throat. His ruby and diamond cuff-links gleamed in the mirror. 'But I swore never again to hurt you physically. Besides, there are more refined punishments.'

'You mean . . .' She faltered. 'Iskra?'

'According to Miss Dunning, his real name is Stephan Strakhov. Why should I dirty my hands on Mr Strakhov? Enough police are after him to do the job.' Paskevich leaned down, breathing the odour of stale liquor at her. 'The apartment will be closed.'

'Is that my punishment? But I've always wanted to leave here . . .' Her voice faded. The birds on the Chinese wallpaper seemed to be fluttering their wings in denial. That divan bed where Paskevich had roused her passion, that armchair where he'd sat to grip her hands and guide her through her worst labour pains, the window where he'd held her as they'd mourned Lally's death — how much of her life was invested in this room?

'You were saying?'

'Paskevich, I've cared for you,' she said in a quaking voice. 'I've cared deeply. When Lally was alive, I often wished there was a way to prove she was yours. I respect you. I admire your brilliant mind, your immense knowledge, your wit. I enjoy . . . going to bed with you. But the night Betsy brought Stephan here I knew nothing had changed between us. After that . . .' She got to her feet. 'It was dishonourable to stay with you.'

'Then, we're agreed.' He handed her the short capelet that she'd dropped on the chair. 'Come.'

'Now?'

'It's all arranged.'

She swallowed hard. Wherever he was taking her was bad, very bad. 'First I must find Klazkha, write a note to Auntie, and to Boris.'

'They're no longer my concern.'

It was then that her mind flooded with the ramifications of what was happening.

Paskevich would assuredly toss her brother out of the Ministry. Boris, with his weak chest! The apartment closed? How would Aunt Chatty live? Boris wouldn't be able to help her. And what about Klazkha? With her yellow card and without a reference — a reference that Paskevich wouldn't write — she would never find a job.

Pleading with him was unworthy and, anyway, useless. Marya fumbled in her purse for the money she had won on a horse. 'Paskevich, everything I own belongs to you. But I was lucky at the Hippodrome.' She extended the folded banknotes. 'This'll be enough for Boris to give Klazkha a few months' wages and pay Aunt Chatty's passage back to San Francisco.'

Paskevich hit her hand. As the slap rang out, banknotes scattered soundlessly across the silk-woven rug. His face twisted with such pain that she reached out to steady him.

He stepped back. 'I gave my word never to hit you again, but that was how I'd punish a child. You're such a thoughtless child, Marya. You give impetuously, like children do. You give to the old woman. You give to that brother of yours. You risk your life for servants and cripples. You bestow your body on that good-looking boy. Why? You have clothes, jewels, money, lessons, anything you wish.' He drew a hoarse breath. 'You even admit to caring a little for me. So why, for a few minutes' pleasure, did you toss it all away?'

'Love', she said, 'has no reason.'

He gave a strangled laugh. 'Again we're agreed. Now, come along.'

She glimpsed her reflection, lips white, the eyes wide with fear. Was she such a coward that she'd go meekly? *He's too drunk to chase me.*

Darting across the room she evaded his out-thrust arm. She lifted her skirt above her knees, racing down the corridor, pausing briefly to yank the front-door handle with both hands. Then she was taking the steps two at a time. Paskevich's patent-leather evening pumps thundered behind her. She was at the bottom step when the heel of her left shoe twisted. As she reached out for the marble balustrade, his hand encircled her wrist like an iron manacle and he pulled the arm behind her back. She bit her lip to keep from crying out.

Her capelet fell to the floor, and she could feel his breath hot against the back of her neck. He twisted her arm more cruelly. His lips pressed against her nape. 'Never again,' he whispered. 'Never to hold you again. Oh, my dearest love, can you imagine how much I hurt?'

Marya stopped fighting. He loosened his grip, bending to retrieve her wrap.

Paskevich travelled in vehicles gilded with the family crest — his railway carriage, his red-lacquered sleighs, limousines, carriages. He never used public conveyances. Yet as they emerged from the building the waiting cabbie jumped down, obsequiously doffing the tall cylindrical oilcloth cap with a copper buckle that all droshky-drivers wore. Paskevich ignored him, handing Marya into the shabby vehicle, taking the seat opposite her. He gave no directions — he must have already told the driver their destination. The blinds were drawn, so she had no idea where they were going. A little earlier the streets had been alive with voices, laughter, traffic, tram bells. Now the silence was so intense that the city might have fallen under the spell of an evil sorcerer. Though the air in the droshky was unpleasantly close, goose-pimples covered her body.

They swerved around a corner. She reached out for the strap, continuing to grip it. The dank tarry odours, the lapping of water, the creak of boats hitting softly against a dock told her they were travelling beside a canal or river, which meant nothing. St Petersburg straddled forty-two islands.

The hoofs took on a hollow note long enough for her to know that they were crossing the broad Neva. They clipped on a bit further. The cab eased to a halt.

'Let's see your pass,' a man's voice shouted.

The driver's voice called from above: 'It's Count Paskevich.'

'Yes, and I'm Tsar Nicholas.'

Paskevich snapped up the blind and thrust out a blue slip of paper. 'The superintendent is expecting me.'

Then Marya saw the shadowy grey-brown walls that thrust up thirty feet.

They were at the Peter and Paul Fortress. That first morning in the Crimson Palace, Paskevich had pointed across the Neva at the grim fortress, telling her its history. It had been a prison for centuries. In one of the cellars Peter had ordered the torture and death of his heir, of his own son, Tsarevich Alexis. Those suspected of opposing the Autocracy often didn't go before a judge but were held incommunicado in the bastions, sometimes for years, until a secret commission decided their fate: through the centuries these thick walls had soaked up the cries of the Romanovs' foes. The tradition continued.

By day traffic flowed through the fortress's tree-shaded courtyards and worshippers filled the cathedral. By night the gates were locked.

The sentry squinted at the pass, then saluted. 'My humblest apologies, your Excellency.'

The next time the droshky halted the driver dismounted, lowering the step with a loud clack. They were in front of a vine-covered stone house. Paskevich handed her down. Marya's bones seemed fused, and she swung her legs from the hips. They passed under a lamp-post. In the glare his set face was as white as polished marble.

They were admitted into a long hall by a slack-jawed young duty guard. His uncertain moustache appeared pencilled on, his grey uniform was pulled across his soft-looking paunch. Covertly he eyed Paskevich's rumpled dinner-clothes, Marya's pretty spring outfit, his glance lingering on her breasts and ankles.

'I am Count Paskevich.'

'Yes, your Excellency. The superintendent's waiting for you upstairs, first door to your right, Excellency.'

Paskevich's slow footsteps echoed up the staircase. A piano halted in mid-cadenza.

The jailer relaxed, grinning at her. 'Two years back,' he said, 'we got so many of you students the fortress was called "The University".'

'I'm not a student,' Marya said.

'A political, ain't you? The same thing.'

Paskevich was already coming back downstairs. He extended a tiny plain white cardboard box. 'This is yours. You have the superintendent's permission to keep it.'

He watched her drop the box in her purse before handing the guard a document bearing an official seal.

The guard's lips moved as he scanned the writing. He looked up. 'She's being sent *there?*'

'Can't you read?'

'Yes, Excellency.' The guard shouldered his rifle. 'This way, you.'

Marya, fearing for her ability to walk, conjured up a vision of the guard tossing her over a shoulder like a sack of potatoes. The image struck her with lunatic merriment. Her lips formed a smile. As they turned into a narrower corridor she looked back. Paskevich hadn't moved. His heavy shoulders quivering, he gazed back at her, then bent his head, covering his eyes with his hand.

She and the guard moved down the long, rough-plastered hallway, their footsteps echoing. Halting, he jangled the keys of a windowless cupboard-like room lined with open shelves. Garments made of coarse unbleached white fabric, calico stockings and kerchiefs were folded above clumsy boots.

The guard seated himself at the desk, leaning back importantly as he opened a huge ledger. Dipping a nib in ink, he held up the document Paskevich had given him. 'Marya Fedorovna Alexiev, right?'

She nodded. He referred to the document half a dozen times as he printed her name in the ledger.

'Date . . . May the seventeenth . . . 1914.' His cheeks wobbled with the effort as he wrote. 'Class?'

Startled, she echoed: 'Class?'

'Are you a peasant or what?'

'My father was a hereditary noble.'

'Good luck for you. Privileged classes get a bigger food-allotment. So you're Orthodox?'

This didn't seem the time to go into her

religious doubts: she nodded.

'Any possessions?'

'Just my clothes.'

'Empty your purse.'

She had forgotten about the tiny card-board box. As it spilled out, the lid fell off. She gave a little cry. Paskevich had returned Stephan's ring.

'Looks like glass,' the guard said. 'A lady like you ought to wear something fine and glittery.'

The ancient sanded diamond, as big as a robin's egg, made her feel as if Stephan were here, holding her. Was it only a few hours since their naked bodies had been entwined in a messy room that smelled of mothballs and pepper? She shrugged. 'A souvenir, that's all. The superintendent said I could keep it.'

'Down here *I* make the rules.' The guard blew out his cheeks several times, then nodded. 'Go ahead, it's yours.'

Not thanking him, she slid the ring on her thumb.

He was at the shelf. 'One skirt, one jacket,' he muttered, pulling down the items. 'One pair boots, one pair calico stockings, one calico kerchief.' He moved back to the table, dropping the armful. The boots clattered on to the floor. Printing the list in the ledger, he blotted the page, then looked up.

'What's keeping you?' he said.

'Change?' Her voice rose into a squeak. 'Here?'

'No, at the Winter Palace.'

'Then, would you please step outside?'

'Can't,' he said cheerfully. 'If you escape, it's my backside. We got a responsibility to watch prisoners.'

'Where's the wardress?'

He grinned. 'None on duty at night.' He had come around the table and was so close that his odour of onions and rancid sweat engulfed her. A large pimple blossomed under his scraggly moustache.

Reaching out, he touched her hair. 'Like a kopek fresh from the mint,' he said. 'Only some grand duke or nobility as rich as God could afford to toss away a pretty little piece like you.'

'He'd have you flogged if —'

'He ain't never going to hear another word about you. Not where you're headed.' There was a fleeting pity in the dulled eyes. 'The Trubetskoi Bastion.'

'Oh my God,' Marya whispered.

The fortress had six bastions.

Peter himself had supervised the construction of one, while the other five were overseen by his five closest friends and named after them. The bastion built by Prince Trubetskoi had become the most infamous prison in all Russia. In the Trubetskoi solitary confinement was enforced so rigorously that the unfortunates held there who didn't succeed in killing themselves generally went mad.

'It ain't my decision,' he muttered apologetically. 'Now, put on your uniform.'

About to be entombed alive, she asked herself what difference it made whether this lout saw her naked. Turning towards the shelves, with numb fingers she began undoing the pretty pearl buttons of her blouse. She heard the panting gasps behind her, and understood what was happening. Dizziness and humiliation oozing through her, she willed herself to continue to undress.

Rhythmic grunts were drowned by a carillon. The Peter and Paul Cathedral marked the hours of St Petersburg with three different tunes and a cannon-burst at noon. It must be midnight, for the discordant chimes were ringing out 'God Save the Tsar'. As Marya drew down her petticoat, she felt a spurt of warm sticky wetness against her buttocks. Her head seemed to be rising above her. She welcomed the engulfing darkness.

She came to on a thin pallet. She wore the prison uniform, jacket on backwards, skirt awry. The coarse stiffness of the fabric surrounding her limp flesh made her feel like some boneless mollusc encased by its shell. The boots with stockings thrust into them were beside the cot. She could feel something smooth against her cheek. Lifting herself up, she saw her own embroidered, filmy linen camisole. At this paradoxical generosity of the guard, she gave a long-drawn-out sigh.

The high-set barred window admitted scarcely enough dirty light for her to see the long, bleak cell. Heavy grey felt was glued to the floor, and the same thick fabric covered the wire mesh that screened the walls. She knew about the felt. The prison authorities used it for solitary confinement, so that prisoners were thwarted in their attempts to tap out messages to their fellow-prisoners.

She was buried alive.

Lying on the prison cot with tears oozing down her cheeks, Marya thought of Paskevich as she'd last seen him, one hand covering his face to hide his weeping.

1914

TSAR ORDERS MOBILIZATION ALONG AUSTRIAN BORDER

St Petersburg Gazette, 29 July 1914

GERMANY DECLARES WAR ON RUSSIA

St Petersburg Gazette, 1 Aug 1914

Chapter Twenty-two

Marya heard the faint jingle of the Judas-window being opened. There was nothing, not so much as a gleam at the spy-hole, yet she was on view like a zoo animal to the watching guard. Standing immobile, she waited until the metal had clinked down before making a fist to shatter the skin of ice on the chipped enamel bowl. Washing her underwear, she bit her lip at the pain radiating from her chilblains.

Stiff, swollen red finger-joints, though, weren't her true pain.

With nobody to speak to, nothing to occupy her, not a book, not a deck of cards, no way of marking a calendar of sorts, she was like an insect caught in amber, trapped for ever in unanswerable questions.

Had Paskevich consigned her to this living death for as long as she continued to breathe? Or would she be released tomorrow? What was going on in the world beyond these thick soundless walls?

How were they faring, her loved ones?

Badly, of course.

But how badly?

They're no longer my concern, Paskevich had said. She was certain that he'd cut Boris from his 'desk' at the Ministry. Her brother with his weak chest and frequent illnesses would have difficulty obtaining even a mediocre position. Marya doubted whether Paskevich had given Boris her winnings to buy Aunt Chatty's passage home. How was the elderly spinster, a Californian accustomed to mild winters, holding up in this cruel cold without the well-fed stoves of the Fourstatskaia apartment? And what of Klazkha? Had she been forced back on to the streets?

Marya groaned involuntarily as she wrung icy water from her petticoat. *Stephan*... Her cruellest fears were reserved for Stephan. Paskevich had said there were so many police on his trail that capture was a certainty. Had her beloved been transported to some brutal Siberian penal colony? Was he ill? Wounded? Was he still alive? He could, for all she knew, be going mad in the oubliette adjacent to hers. An irony that would surely appeal to Paskevich.

As she draped her wet underwear on the end of her cot, the blur of tears made the dangling pieces appear to be the pale limp ghosts of earlier prisoners. Turning away, she reached for the ring which dangled from her neck on a camisole ribbon. Rubbing her thumb over the smooth diamond as she would Aladdin's lamp, she said aloud: 'God, if You do exist, let Paskevich suffer in hell for all eternity.' As the words creaked out, she thought of an accurately thrown rock frightening away the crow on Lally's coffin, the magnificently bound books in Josip's banged-together shelves, the bald head bent as he'd wept in the warden's hallway. Paskevich had always been an enigma to her, and an enigma he remained. Even more bewildering were her responses to him. He had locked her in this tomb, yet she could no more hate him than hate her own arm, liver or heart.

Rage, though, came easily. Rage had sustained her through the blazing summer, the autumn when endless moisture dripped from the vaulted stone ceiling and seeped through malodorous felt. Rage sustained her in this endlessly dark winter.

A key turned. Hinges creaked. The heavy door opened.

It was the slack-jawed warder who had admitted her: a few weeks ago he had started showing up every third day to guard her during her routine fifteen-minute exercise period. He extended a grey prison cape.

'Thank you,' she said, taking the heavy dank wool. 'Tell me, is it very miserable out there?'

Though any recognition of the prisoners' humanity was forbidden, his insufficient moustache quivered in a hint of a smile. She beamed. Her resentment towards him had long ago vanished. What did a little masturbation really matter when this was her kindest, most generous friend. *Friend?* she thought as she pulled the hooded cape over her shoulders. *I really must be going mad.*

Normally two guards sat at the table in the vaulted corridor with the high windows; today there was only one. Outside she found another deviation. The bulky young corporal stationed in the sentry-box had been replaced by an aged policeman. With his oversized blue coat touching the ground, his cheeks hollowed, his mouth puckered from toothlessness, he appeared far too geriatric to be a gendarme.

The long courtyard, formed as it was from the high walls of the Trubetskoi Bastion and thirty-foot-high palisades, never saw sunlight. Plodding around the uneven cobbles, avoiding the ice puddles, she thrust her chilled gloveless hands into the cape pockets.

Her left fingers encountered something.

In the old impetuous days of freedom, Marya would have immediately pulled out the small object. Now she rubbed it surreptitiously. Paper? Yes. Folded paper. Walking faster, she pressed the wad into her palm. It seemed a century before the bells jangled out the quarter-hour and her friend returned her to the cell with the black-painted number 15. He took the cape from her.

The slop-bucket encased in wood to the left of the door had been emptied, fresh water was in the ewer, and a wedge of black bread had been tossed on the floor as if to a dog. Following her usual routine she first ate the sour heavy bread. Waiting a few minutes, facing away from the door as she always did to relieve herself, she cautiously took the wad of paper from her sleeve. Her chilblained fingers shook as she tore a corner from the thin cheap paper.

If you are Marya Fedorovna Alexiev, give the guard something to identify yourself. He is loyal to Klazkha's friends.

Marya leaned back against the mildewed felt. She sat like that with her arms crossed over her joyous, rapidly beating heart for several minutes. Then, using her teeth and aching fingers she ripped an inch square from her wet camisole. Klazkha would surely remember ironing the rosebuds no matter how faded and frayed the embroidery.

Three mornings later, the slack-jawed guard — friend of Klazkha's friends, her own dearest friend — returned with a cape. She shoved the scrap of cloth in the pocket.

The rest of the week gales swirled snow. She marched around her cell with her jaw clenched in frustration at not being taken outside. The storm ceased. She was keyed up with excitement as her door opened. At the sight of the short, bearded Latvian guard, she felt an agonizing shrivelling within her chest, as if hope were an organ being surgically removed.

Days passed with no sign of her friend the guard. Mists clouded the fortress, and during her exercise periods she could hear the creaking grumbles of ice cracking on the

Neva. One day her meal was a hunk of *calatchi,* the sweet white bread that compassionate merchants distribute to prisons on Easter Sunday. Marya recalled the Easter egg hunts in Golden Gate Park, and the lavish night feasts on the Fourstatskaia. Resurrection, she decided, was a fraud, and the note a cruel hoax.

One morning the slack-jawed guard stepped inside with a cape. Thighs watery, she pulled on the heavy garment. She could feel folded paper. As she circled the courtyard, the soft west wind ruffled her hair like a caressing lover. Back in her cell, she went to the corner with her slop-bucket. Hunched over, she read the pages in her lap.

(My name is Ovruch. As Klazkha Sobchak's friend, I am taking down her dictation, so think of this letter as coming directly from her lips to your ears.)

Dear Marya,
You can't know how good it makes me feel to know you are alive and breathing even if in that horrible place.

The very morning you disappeared, Count Paskevich's man hammered an eviction notice on the door. The other servants all got a month's salary and hand-wrote references, but they never stopped whining and squawking about being dismissed. It was all due to you, Cook said. She'd heard from some high-ups at the Crimson Palace that you'd run off with some South American. Me, Miss Dunning and Boris, we decided that you was with Iskra. He was gone, too. Nobody, not even the baroness, knew where he was, and so you being with him made sense. Anyway, I needed to find work, and Boris jumped in and right off got me a position as laundress with a lady friend of his. He rented a nice big room for poor Miss Dunning —

Poor Miss Dunning? The letter trembled in Marya's fingers.

— and he landed himself a job playing secretary to some rich big shot taking a trip to the United States. After a couple of months it seemed like fate, his leaving Russia before the war come.

(This is Ovruch speaking. Your brother is indeed lucky to have escaped the Capitalist Monarchist war. What a débâcle! Bloody Nicholas squanders lives without a care — our losses in Prussia alone ran to over three hundred thousand, and the casualties in this new Polish campaign are so immense that the numbers are censored. If anyone speaks out, he's packed off to jail for being defeatist. We Bolsheviks have distributed a pamphlet asking questions about the tsarist butchery. Your friend Iskra

wrote it. Incidentally, Klazkha reminds me to tell you he's safe, but nobody knows where.)

'Alive!' Marya whispered. 'He's alive!'

Then she reread Ovruch's interjection. A war? He had sketched the marginal details, seen from his own political stance. A war? Paskevich, while doing everything in his power to raise money for the Army, at the same time had been warning Nicholas that losing to Japan in 1905 had been highly detrimental to the throne and another war might be catastrophic. Who was involved besides Germany and Russia?

The questions seemed inconsequential compared to the pencilled personal news.

I put off the bad news as long as possible. What with no more money come from Boris, I found poor Miss Dunning a smaller place in Vyborg.

Marya shivered. Vyborg, that blighted industrial area, home of the St Petersburg Fever Hospital.

Her heart went worse. My boss, a good sort even if she does have a different man in her bed every night, let me do the laundry off the premises; she even got me some extra jobs. So I could work and sleep in the room with Miss Dunning. Ovruch and my new pals

*helped pay for the doctor and the medi-
cine, but nothing helped. Just before she
fell asleep that last time, something
strange happened. She opened her eyes
real wide and said: 'I see her, Klazkha.
I see my bright, pretty little bird trapped
in some awful stone cage.' And in the
morning she was gone. She passed in
her sleep, so she had no pain.*

*Remember this. I promise you won't
be there much longer. I'll move heaven
and earth to get you out. I owe you my
life and I pay my debts.*

    Klazkha Sobchak

Shoving the letter inside her jacket,
Marya fell on the cot. Her joy at the good
news had evaporated, and she was remembering the childhood comfort of Aunt
Chatty's soft vanilla-scented bosom, remembering the fluffy kindness and the
lack of judgemental morality about Lally's
birth, the lovingly smocked little dresses.
Well, now Lally had a warm lap to nestle
in.

Alone, with nobody to share her grief,
Marya couldn't control her great shuddering
sobs. The guard who flipped open the Judas-window on the hour paid no attention
to her prolonged tears. Hysterical sobbing
was routine among those confined in the
Trubetskoi Bastion.

Long ago, Paskevich had warned Marya
against straying: *I'll punish you until you'll*

305

wish you were dead. Understanding her completely, he had unerringly selected the cruellest punishment for her.

Exile from humanity.

Chapter Twenty-three

'What're her chances?'

'My girl, she's in the Trubetskoi Bastion.' Ovruch's voice resonated deep within his enormous chest. 'Nobody breaks out of the Trubetskoi.'

'You'll come up with something.'

'Pah!' Ovruch mimed spitting. 'Klazkha, our task is to deliver the proletariat from the oppressors, not to help the parasites.'

'Parasite? I told you how she took me in from the streets! How she done all she could for Josip! How she lost her little girl because *she saved my life!*'

At Klazkha's unprecedented vehemence, Ovruch focused his attention on her. Seemingly unaware of his scrutiny, she flicked her iron delicately across the pleats of a dress-shirt.

They were in her place in the Vyborg slums. The ten-by-twelve room had marginal light from the narrow window and was crowded by the ironing-table, a chair and a cot, and stacked wicker laundry-hampers, yet as far as Klazkha was concerned her home compared favourably with the Malachite Hall of the Winter Palace. For the first time in her life, she had a room of her own with a key to lock her door.

'We're comrades,' Ovruch said slowly. 'I respect your judgement. But that doesn't alter the fact that she's in the Trubetskoi. And I'm no magician.'

'You're tops at the secret stuff,' she retorted without a hint of flattery in her tone.

'Let me think.'

With his luxuriant brown beard resting on the embroidery of his immense peasant blouse Ovruch appeared as relaxed as a hibernating bear. It was this lack of tension that inspired confidence. Klazkha, distrustful of the entire male sex, had permitted him to enrol her in the outlawed Bolshevik Party. Within the highly splintered, discordant left, the Bolsheviks, numbering less than fifteen hundred members, were a minor if violent force, wreaking the most destruction and making the most noise, although the Mensheviks, Social Democrats, Kadets, the Democratic Reform Party, which Stephan had founded, were all far larger.

The size of his party was the only small thing about Ovruch. Six foot six, broadly built, as he lounged on the cot with his back against the wall and his bast boots thrust out, he dominated the room. At the age of twelve he'd been taller than most men, and when the police had beaten his father for no good reason he had assaulted the gendarmes, felling two. As punishment, the boy had been sentenced to eight years' hard labour. In Siberia he had spun into the orbit of an ugly, brusque, hereditary nobleman from Sembirsk: Vladimir Ilich Ulyanov. Like many revolutionaries, Ulyanov had taken a pseudonym: Lenin. Lenin's ideology vibrated a tuning-fork within the peasant youth. He, too, saw the evils inherent in class, religion and Imperialist nationalism; he, too, believed in the worldwide rule of the proletariat. Lenin drilled his young disciple in Marxist dialectic; and Lenin's schoolteacher wife, Krupskaia, taught the oversize peasant youth to read and write. Now that Lenin had once again been exiled, Ovruch was a spokesman for the Bolshevik Central Committee.

Klazkha was far from his most perfect recruit.

She refused to take part in the bank robberies that financed the party; she argued against bomb-throwing and balked at carrying a gun at demonstrations; she never mouthed Marxist dogma. Her sole political conviction, that women were equal to men, was the narrowest plank in the Bolshevik platform. These negatives, though, were far outweighed by two pluses. She was closemouthed. She was a laundress. Party members carried their bundles here, exchanging messages without arousing the suspicion of Okhrana spies.

Klazkha went to the samovar, pouring a glass of tea for Ovruch. For several minutes while he slurped the hot liquid through sugar cubes her iron sizzled on damp linen. Her uncommunicativeness met with the big man's approval.

'It'll take a lot of brainpower and hard work,' he said finally.

'Then, you will help her?'

The floorboards creaked as Ovruch rose. 'Don't get your hopes too high. All I promise is to try to come up with something that the party'll go along with.' Shrugging into a smelly sheepskin jacket, he let himself out.

Klazkha smoothed a wrinkled nightshirt on the padded table, her face relaxed. Had she been impractical enough to go in for taking her emotional temperature, she would have discovered a feverish elation. The party rank and file seldom disagreed with Ovruch's suggestions.

Two days later, Ovruch dropped a pair of sweat-odoured peasant blouses near the door. 'It seems', he said, 'that we're not the only ones looking for this Alexiev woman here in Petrograd.' At the outbreak of the war, in the first white heat of patriotic loathing against all things Germanic, St Petersburg had been renamed Petrograd. Most of the inhabitants continued to use the old name, or simply 'Peter'. 'Why would the American ambassador be interested in her?'

Klazkha's arm continued its rhythm, giving no clue to her astonishment. Could Boris have prompted concern at the embassy? Before leaving Russia he'd talked repeatedly of searching high and low for Marya — but, then, Boris was full of talk. 'Her and her brother was born there,' Klazkha said.

'And you never mentioned it?'

'Why should I? Right away when she was born her father put the name down with our people there. She's Russian.'

'I'm not sure that's the American law.' Ovruch tugged his beard thoughtfully. 'And her friend Strakhov is still keen for her. Paskevich's mistress and Strakhov . . . It's astounding.'

'They met on a boat, when she came over here.'

'It'd save time, my girl, if I didn't need to worm the facts out of you.'

'You Bolsheviks trust me because I keep my mouth shut,' Klazkha said. 'Iskra and the Americans — what're their chances of finding her?'

'In the ambassador's case, an embassy flunkey asked a few questions of some minor bureaucrat and came up with nothing. As for Strakhov, there's not much chance he'll discover any more.'

'How's that?'

'You know the Democratic Reform Party. What a bunch of white hands!' 'White hands' was the working-class denigration of those who'd never performed manual labour.

Klazkha's admirably red hand eased the point of the iron along a collar. 'Iskra's got a lot of brains. He'd be a big help.'

After a pause, Ovruch's massive head nodded. 'You're right. You and me, we haven't the time for the footwork. This war is the opportunity we've been waiting for. What better time to convince the proletariat to unite than when the oppressors are sending them to the slaughter? Let Strakhov run around organizing the Alexiev woman's rescue.'

Two months after this, the revolutionary cause was unwittingly boosted by the tsar. In August 1915, Nicholas reached two decisions that would reverberate across the Empire and down through history. First he closed the Duma. The Russian parliament was a sop to the people, without power; yet, even so, the existence of the feeble body was seen as a hopeful signpost by many of the educated. Disbanding it threw divergent groups — the liberals, the *intelligentsy*, the bourgeois merchants and the workers — into the same pot. Nicholas's second fateful choice was personally to head the armed forces. His mother, the Dowager Empress Marie, as well as his brothers, uncles, cousins, pleaded with him to change his mind. Eight cabinet ministers signed a protesting letter of resignation, and the former Minister of Finance, Count Paskevich, came out of seclusion to point out to the sovereign that His Imperial Majesty completely lacked strategic military experience, and furthermore with the regular army decimated by a series of disasters — including the loss of Russian Poland — the army he would lead was a shapeless wad of untrained, unarmed peasant conscripts. With the tsar as commander-in-chief, any and all of the inevitable future defeats would be laid at the palace door, thus placing the status of the Romanov dynasty in jeopardy.

In the face of such an outcry, the tsar wavered. He sought divine guidance. In the Peter and Paul Cathedral, a few hundred yards from where Marya lay tossing with fever in her cell, Nicholas and his empress knelt beside the plain marble tombs of his Romanov ancestors. It is possible that Jehovah advised His anointed one to stand firm, or equally possible that Alexandra murmured a reminder that to permit lesser beings to alter a monarch's decisions assuredly would lessen the Autocrat's power, which it was his sacred trust to hand down intact to their son. That same evening, wearing simple khaki blouse, blue trousers and polished boots, the tsar departed for Field Headquarters — Stavka in Russian.

He left a capital that simmered with misery.

Silent weeping crowds gathered daily along the Nevsky Prospekt, where closely printed casualty-lists were pasted on the shop windows. Medicines cost a hundred times what they had at the start of the war; rents were catastrophically high; and, since there weren't men to work the fields or enough railway wagons to transport civilian supplies, when women went out with their shopping-baskets they found hugely inflated, unaffordable prices and empty stalls.

A far greater Okhrana presence couldn't halt the acceleration of strikes and demonstrations.

In October, the far-left Bolsheviks joined with the moderate Democratic Reform Party in a protest march on the Peter and Paul Fortress.

The sound of the door opening awoke Marya. A tin bowl sloshed as it was thrust inside, a wedge of black bread thumped. The door clanged shut.

In the earlier days of Marya's imprisonment hunger had ruled her. Now she was apathetic about food. Rolling over sluggishly, she closed her eyes again. *No wonder I'm sleepy; they're putting some kind of poison gas in my cell.* As she thought this, the idea took root in her mind as fact. *They've been gassing me ever since I heard from Klazkha.*

Months earlier, Marya had destroyed the letter in the only way available to her, by chewing and eating the pages. In those early days she had existed on a cloud of adrenalin. As spring had eased into summer without any further sign from the outside world, though, the vitality of hope oozed from her and she fell prey to physical ailments. In August, when the tsar had departed for Headquarters, when her cell had turned into a Turkish bath, heat rashes had erupted across her torso. The untreated dermatitis resulted in a fever. On her recovery, she had decided that the letter had been a figment of her fevered dreams.

A key was scraping in the lock. She pushed herself up on her elbows. The brownish water masquerading as soup was gone, as was the hunk of bread. Frowning, she tried to recall when she had eaten. The sound of rain had stopped, too. When?

And what was that faraway rumbling? Thunder?

The door creaked ponderously. The slack-jawed guard stood on the threshold extending the wool cape.

'I can't go today,' she said. The prison inactivity, once tortuous, now was as sweet as a lover's embrace. 'I'm not up to it.'

He narrowed his eyes urgently.

'It's miserable out,' she croaked. 'I'm ill again.'

He shook the cape. *What a silly matador*, she thought, closing her eyes. Then she heard male voices. The guards never talked when her cell door was open. *They've relaxed the rules, and that means there's a letter.*

Again the preposterously far-fetched idea became fact. Standing so rapidly that she dizzied herself, she thrust her bare feet in the boots and tied the calico scarf over her tangle of hair. Grabbing the cape, she flung it around her shoulders.

The two guards looked up from their greasy cards, calling out: 'Keep inside, Yuri.'

'*Da*, it sounds like trouble out there.'

'What *are* you, a pair of girls?' jeered her guard.

As Marya emerged into the chill grey courtyard, she thrust both hands in the pockets, anticipating the feel of paper.

Nothing . . .

She let out a groaning sigh. Head bent, shoulders slumped, she trudged through the puddles that formed where the cobbles had sunk. The thick grumbling sounds intensified, drowning out the rattle of traffic.

Slowly it came to her that the approaching rumbles weren't thunder but the roar of a marching crowd.

Soldiers?

Yes, soldiers.

The German armies are invading St Petersburg, she decided. Why else would the toothless old gendarme huddle deeper inside the sentry-box? The unaccustomed racket assaulted her ears. To muffle the blast, she held both hands against her scarf.

Nothing could shut out the howls and disorganized chanting. The bellowing shouts were Russian.

'Freedom for the politicals!'

'Freedom for the prisoners!'

'Freedom for the victims of capitalism!'

The ancient guard slunk backwards into the Trubetskoi Bastion. Marya was trotting now, an excited hamster in its cage. The hopes that had fired her months earlier were blazing again.

Fists pounded against the iron-barred gate; then a heavy weight reverberated, as if a battering ram had been used, or maybe a man had flung himself against the barrier. The rain was needling harder.

'Open the prisons! Open the prisons!'

The command reverberated inside her skull.

Without a glance at her guard, she flew towards the gate. She didn't feel the rusty iron as she pulled the bolt. The gate burst inwards with such force that a nail spun from a hinge. She was thrown back on to her hands and knees. Surrounded by an explosive stream of boots, she crawled against the wooden palisade.

'Marya!'

A tall man shoved and elbowed his way through the jam of packed bodies.

Unquestioningly she accepted that Stephan had come to save her.

Chapter Twenty-four

Five minutes after the gate was opened a squad of mounted police galloped into the courtyard. Under the rearing hoofs and slashing whips the demonstrators panicked, shoving, hitting, trampling one another in an effort to retreat through the narrow gate.

By then the prisoner was gone.

Klazkha emptied another steaming kettle into the round wooden bath. Her sleeves were rolled up, and a blue-and-white-checked oilcloth apron protected her clothes. 'Too hot?' she asked.

'Sheer heaven . . .' Marya slipped deeper into the steaming water, relaxing a few moments before she gripped the edge of the bath and sat upright. 'You're positive Stephan'll be back?'

'Wild horses couldn't keep him away. In my life I never saw nobody more concerned.' Klazkha kneeled on the gritty floor, ladling water over the curls that snaked down Marya's back. 'Let's hope a good vinegar rinse will untangle this mess.'

'Are the Okhrana after him?'

'He's fine. Absolutely fine. Now, sit back down and hold this cloth over your eyes.' The sharpness of vinegar filled the warm air.

'Why did he run off then?'

'He explained.'

'Everything happened so quickly that some of the things he said didn't stick in my memory.'

'How much do you remember of it all?'

'I was in the courtyard, a huge crowd burst in, and Stephan was there. We got into a taxi and he pulled me on to the floor. We stopped somewhere — I think it was on the Kamenoi Ostrovski — and he whisked me into a closed droshky and then we were here. Klazkha, where is this?'

'The Vyborg Inn. It's right across the street from my place, so I'll be popping in to visit.' Klazkha couldn't prevent the reedy quaver in her voice. That first glimpse of Marya had shaken her to the core. Marya, bone-thin under filthy, drenched prison rags, red-gold hair a dripping rat's-nest, mud splattering the lovely face. Klazkha had muttered to Stephan that he should come back later, she'd take over. Half-carrying Marya to this bathroom, a recent tin-roofed addition off the inn's back porch, Klazkha had counted five more kopeks into the dimwitted bath-boy's palm to pay for extra hot water.

'Will you just look at them crinkled fingers. You been in there long enough. Come on, ups-a-daisy.'

With a supporting arm, she hauled Marya, rosy from the hot water, out of the deep bath, enveloping her in a frayed towel warm from the stove. A long strip of mirror was propped against one wall. Marya peered at her steam-clouded reflection and saw a skull face, sunken eyes, bone arms and legs protruding from the cylinder of towelling. A stick figure drawn by a child. 'Oh my God! No wonder he ran off.'

'You been locked up for over a year. Nobody else would look half so gorgeous.'

'Gorgeous! A mummified skeleton.'

'Marya, a lot of things is changed, but one thing you can rely on. I ain't one for flattery.' Klazkha had brought along her own nightgown, coarse muslin and far too long for the petite Marya. Tying a pink ribbon around the improbably narrow waist and blousing out the top, she draped a shawl borrowed from the landlord's daughter over the thin shoulders, then gently combed out the wet curls, snipping off the worst knots. While her hair was being tended to, Marya sat by the stove listening to rain on the tin roof, a gently soporific drumming.

'Better get you to bed,' Klazkha said. 'You're nodding off.'

'I was thinking about the guard.'

'Yuri's his name.'

'He delivered your letter, did you know that?'

'I gave it to him with my own hands. He belongs to Ovruch and my party. The Bolsheviks.'

A prison guard, a laundress and a *muzhik?* How strange. The left-wingers as a general rule were like Stephan, university-educated. Many were well-to-do, and quite a few belonged to the aristocracy. Marya, isolated for so long that she no longer differentiated between interior and exterior dialogue, was ruminating aloud.

'Maybe that's true for them others,' Klazkha said. 'But mainly us Bolsheviks is workers.'

'Oh.' Marya turned her head to look at Klazkha. 'Have you heard from Boris?'

Klazkha, who had already reiterated her limited information, patiently went through it again, finishing up: 'Mr Alexiev, he always lands on his feet. No need to fret about him; he's safe and sound in America.'

'His chest always gives him trouble in the winter!' Marya's voice dropped to an urgent whisper. 'And, besides, if he were well, he'd have written to Auntie.'

'He did, you can be sure of it. But, with the war and all, the post's something terrible. Besides, who's to say what poor Miss Dunning's old landlady done with her letters?' Klazkha was adjusting the shawl over damp red hair. 'Come on, let's go upstairs.'

The third-floor bedroom was warmed by a tall, antiquated corner stove. From the ceiling dangled a single flickering bulb. The oak cross angled above the bed was dusty, and the draught from the opening door stirred dust-mice across the linoleum.

Klazkha's nose twitched. 'Needs a good pail and scrubbing-brush in here,' she said.

'Ah, Klazkha, just smell that food . . .'

The small table was crowded with a meal extravagant for poverty-stricken Vyborg at any time and mythical here since the war's escalating inflation. Marya, resting on the bed, nibbled a slice of dark bread spread thinly with brined sheep cheese — all that her stomach would tolerate. Klazkha sat at the table and helped herself to sausages, pickled onions and a slice of rich cheese pie, cutting everything on her plate neatly and methodically before taking her first bite. She had just finished mopping up her plate with bread when a loud knock rattled the door. She answered, drawing back the bolt. Ovruch's bulk filled the doorway: he remained immobile, gaping at Marya.

Klazkha gave that old face-splitting grin. 'Did I exaggerate?'

Marya's hand was engulfed by Ovruch's huge one. 'Before, you were a drowned little sparrow. But, Marya Fedorovna Alexiev, you're a beauty.'

Where had this giant peasant seen her? Marya smiled uncertainly before she recalled. 'You were there at the Trubetskoi,' she said. 'How can I ever thank you enough?'

'No need for gratitude,' he retorted. 'I've been a guest of the tsar's myself.'

'Where's Stephan?'

'He'll be here soon.' Ovruch helped himself to the bulk of the sausages and cheese pie. 'Now, don't try to talk. What you need is rest.'

Obediently Marya lay back and closed her eyes.

'What did you do with her uniform?' Ovruch asked with a full mouth.

'It's them rags in the corner.'

'Good. I'll drop the whole bundle in the Neva . . .'

The voices and rain lulled Marya. It seemed impossible that she could sleep before Stephan showed up; yet, exhausted from the turmoil and relaxed by the hot bath, she kept drifting off.

'Look at her,' she heard Klazkha say. 'Dead to the world.'

'Do you know what that little one did? She unlocked the gate for us. And then, when the crowd started to go for Yuri because of his uniform, she jumped in front of him, throwing out her arms to protect him.'

Marya had no recollection whatsoever of aiding her friend.

'That's her all over, thinking with her heart.' Klazkha sighed. 'If only she'd use her head.'

'I'll never forget the sight, her facing down a mob.'

'And her just skin and bones.'

'She'll fatten up. It's not her body that concerns me. It's her mind. How was she with you?'

'She rambled a little but she's nothing bad.'

'My girl, nobody who's been inside the

Imperialist's solitary confinement comes out the same . . .'

Marya was asleep.

Crouching on the scarred wood floor, she shrank from the workmen's boots that whirled and kicked out in a batteringly loud Cossack dance. The dancers meant her no harm, somehow she knew that, yet she couldn't quell her dread. She quivered to escape; yet, no matter how fiercely she willed herself to get up and move, her muscles remained leadenly locked. Abruptly the cavorting leaps ended, the dancers separated. She could see a window and a muddy yard beyond.

Stephan, blindfolded, wearing a dingy uniform, stood against a stained, pitted wall. At a shouted command, a line of ragged soldiers lifted their rifles. Took aim. Shots rang out. As the cracks reverberated within her skull, Stephan's body jerked and sagged, painting fresh crimson on the wall behind him.

Opening her mouth in a scream, Marya awoke. Her bones ached, and the pain cut above her eyebrows like a too-tight leather thong.

Stephan rose from the pine table to sit on the bed. 'Sleeping Beauty wakes,' he said tenderly. 'When I got back yesterday you were already out of it.'

His smile was warm, his grip firm, his weight sagged the mattress, yet the nightmare still held her captive.

'They shot you,' she whispered.

'Nobody's shooting at you, darling. There's no need to be afraid; you're safe now.'

'It's *you* who's in danger. The firing squad shot you.'

'A bad dream.'

'There was blood, I tell you. Blood everywhere.'

'Hush, it's all right. I'm here with you. See?' He put both arms around her.

She closed her eyes for a few moments, letting the reality of his solid body seep through her. Maybe the execution had been an ugly dream. 'Were you writing before?'

'Yes, a leaflet for the Democratic Reform —'

'Pamphlets are dangerous.'

'Marya, listen to me. There is no firing squad. And I've done this kind of work since the Revolution of 1905, and I was only fifteen then. I'm still in one piece.'

'That other time, you barely got away . . .' At the memory of him sneezing under Madame Chkiedze's peppered wool bloomers, she chuckled.

'There, that's more like my Marya.' He spoke with the faintest hint of gruffness, as if warding off tears. 'Right now it's time for your lunch — or, rather, breakfast.'

'I'm not hungry.'

'Your stomach's shrunk. You need to eat small amounts every couple of hours. I'll run down to the kitchen.'

As he left, a large marmalade-coloured

tomcat squeezed past him, jumping on Marya's bed. The cat's shoulder had been torn, his ear was ripped, and above one eye was a gash that resembled an oddly misplaced mouth. Marya tenderly stroked the battered animal.

'When I was little they called me Gingergirl. And you've the same colour hair, sort of, so you're Gingerboy,' she murmured in English. 'You've been in a major battle. They tell me I'm not right in the head. We're made for each other, Gingerboy.'

By the time Stephan returned with the tray, the cat had retreated under the bed. Marya lay with the covers thrown off, thrashing as she slept. When Stephan touched her cheek he could feel the heat pouring from her skin.

Dreams of death swept over Marya like ocean waves, one nightmare after another. Awaking drenched in sweat, she would feel as if her head were a pain-buffeted kite somewhere high above the bed. Time no longer moved sequentially. Sometimes Klazkha would be sponging her down with cool water. Then Stephan would be holding a spoon of bitter-tasting medicine to her mouth. A heavy-jowled doctor sombrely shook his thermometer. In her worst delirium, she cried out for Paskevich. It was Paskevich — father, lover, husband, avenger — who had locked her into this eternal punishment, therefore only Paskevich could release her.

One minute a sheen of sweat would cover Marya's woefully thin body, and Klazkha or Stephan would frantically sponge her down; then she would be racked with shivers, and they would pop heated towel-wrapped bricks around her and pile on blankets. She whimpered and groaned, she muttered phrases, she cried out for people — Stephan, Boris, her parents, Miss Dunning, Klazkha. She wanted Paskevich most frequently. Yet even as she urgently called the hated name Stephan could not find it in his heart to be jealous. His Marya barely made a bulge in the covers, her face looked two-dimensional, flattened by illness, and much of the time her glittering fevered eyes looked right through him. She was so frail, so near to death, how could he be jealous?

Then the fever broke, subsiding rapidly. On the fifth morning after her escape she awoke with clear eyes and sweet breath. Gingerboy jumped back on to the bed.

By afternoon she felt well enough to ask Stephan to puff the pillows and help her to sit up. Her face was yet thinner, but her temperature was normal and she was coherent. Scratching the cat's orange ruff, she asked: 'Is the inn safe?'

'Absolutely safe,' he said. 'The police aren't looking for you. Or for me.'

She turned her head on the pillow. 'How do you know?'

'A *chinovnik* high in the Department of

the Interior — he has a desk that oversees the police department — joined the Democratic Reform Party a couple of months ago. Which should give you a clue how bureaucrats feel about the Government since the war started. Anyway, he passes on useful information to us. There have been no memos about searching for me, and nothing whatsoever about an escape from the Trubetskoi Bastion. In fact, there's been no mention within the department of any disturbance at all.'

'That makes no sense.'

'There's been a decision to sweep anti-tsarist activities and morale-lowering matters under the carpet. And your escape from Russia's most closely guarded prison might be construed as both. Who knows? And the censors have been alerted, too. The papers haven't printed a word about the protest march on the Fortress — not a word. Anyway, you're in no danger.' He took her near-translucent hand, kissing it. 'God, Marya, if you just knew how frantic I've been. All that matters is that you get well quickly.'

'I promise,' she said, snuggling back into the pillows.

By the following morning she was able to pay attention for a longer span, and talking no longer hurt her vocal cords.

'What happened after you left Madame Chkiedze's?' she asked.

'Police were waiting in the alley, but I gave them the slip,' he said. 'The owner of a barge let me hide in the hold, and I got clear of Petersburg.'

A ferociously bowdlerized version of his escape from the city. It was true enough that he had slipped through the cordon in the alley; however, the police had caught up with him near Teatralsnaya Square. Slamming him with their truncheons until he fell to the pavement, they crammed him in with other prisoners *en route* to the dreaded police headquarters on Gorokhayava Street. By the greatest good fortune, a fire halted the Black Maria. The flames spooked the horses, and as they bolted Stephan managed to open the rear door of the lurching wagon and jump out. He barely noticed twisting his ankle as he fell, but he was hobbling by the time he reached the Fontanka Embankment. The master of a coal-barge, horrified by bruises inflicted by the police, hid him. The barge was heading west towards the Russian Duchy of Finland. Stephan wanted to go east. When they were well away from the city, he bandaged his ankle so that it would support him and set off for Omsk where he had friends. Station masters, as he knew only too well, generally acted as Okhrana spies, so he limped along the hot dusty farmland for days until he considered that he was remote enough from St Petersburg authorities to risk boarding the train.

'I got to Omsk the same week that Nicholas declared war. Marya, I tried to contact you

— oh God, I tried. I sent telegrams and letter after letter — care of Betsy, care of Madame Chkiedze. There was never a single response. The silence had me terrified. So I came back here.'

'Here? The Okhrana were after you.'

'I was beyond caring. First I went to Betsy's apartment. There were open trunks everywhere. She'd just arrived home from the Crimea with her grand duke and a handsome new chauffeur. A jolly *ménage à trois.* She told me that at first she was positive that you and I had run away together. But then she began hearing from everybody that you were in South America. Your brother and Miss Dunning were gone, too. I decided that Betsy, being Betsy, had mixed up her continents and that the three of you had packed up and gone home to California. It fitted in with what I knew about Paskevich.' Stephan's intonation was frigid. '*He'd* resigned from the Ministry and left the city.'

Marya lay back in the pillows trying not to think of Paskevich the last time she'd seen him, that twisted expression of misery.

'Then I went to see Madame Chkiedze,' Stephan was saying. 'She told me she'd never received my letters.'

'Did the Okhrana intercept them?'

'Who knows? The postal system in the provinces has always been a disaster. And with the war it's a hundred times worse. Madame Chkiedze said — I can still hear her scornful tone — "The Little Alexiev no longer lives in our war-torn land. She is enjoying life on the Pampas with her new *cher ami.*" '

Marya sat forward in the bed. 'And you believed that?'

'By then I'd heard it all over Petrograd.' He was at the window, and his sigh clouded the pane. He rubbed with his palm to see out. Sleet obscured Klazkha's building across the way. 'The story was universal. You'd taken up with an immensely rich South American. There were even the minor discrepancies that make gossip seem true.'

'Oh, Stephan.'

'I cried a lot. Bitter tears, I'm ashamed to say. Then returned to Omsk and started a newspaper.'

'Illegally, of course. Why must you always put yourself in harm's way?'

'Somebody had to tell the country that our troops were sent into battle untrained and unarmed. Marya, in a little over a year of war the Germans have slaughtered more than two million of our soldiers. Anyway, I tried to bury myself in putting out the paper. But in spite of what I'd heard about you — and believed on a rational level — my heart refused to be convinced. So I came back to Petrograd again. On the journey here we kept being shunted over to let troop-trains pass. It's not only the peasants who are cannon fodder. The High Command arms junior officers with bayonets. Bayonets! To lead their men against German heavy artil-

331

lery! So many of my friends and colleagues at university are dead.'

Marya's immediate thought was one of selfish gratitude that he was safe. Then she sighed, recalling the gorgeously uniformed young guests with whom she had flirted at her Friday Nights. *How many of them are alive?*

By October the rivers and canals that laced St Petersburg were darkly turgid, a prelude to freezing, and Marya had recuperated enough to feel like a prisoner in the small bedroom. But her only clothes were the two long-sleeved muslin nightgowns that Klazkha had supplied and the fringed shawl borrowed from the landlord's daughter. Each time she tried to broach the subject with Stephan, she found herself tongue-tied. Wouldn't such an appeal for clothes revitalize his memories of her as the Little Alexiev, kept woman?

Klazkha noted the problem, typically keeping her own counsel until she had a solution. One icy morning when Stephan had gone off to a planning session with Democratic Reform leaders at the university, she dropped by the Vyborg Inn.

'Yesterday I was delivering some shirts over near the Nevsky Prospekt,' she said. 'And who should I bump into but that handsome Mishenka.'

'Mishenka! Is he still with Monsieur Bézard?'

'That goes without saying. An old married pair, them two. Seeing him set me thinking . . . The way spoiled rich women change their minds, there might be a thing or two left over at that fancy dressmaking shop of theirs. Size don't matter. Nobody's thinner than you, and we can always take in seams.'

Marya, picturing Stephan seeing her in some elegant creation, gave her old musical laugh. Then her shoulders slumped. 'I don't have a rouble to my name,' she sighed.

'I got a bit set aside.'

'Klazkha, that's dear and generous, but I can't take your savings.'

'If you want, we'll make it a loan.'

Marya stroked Gingerboy's tattered ear, reddening with embarrassment as she said: 'Monsieur Bézard's always been tremendously expensive. And Lord knows what his prices are now. You've told me how even the prices at the flea markets on the Voznesensky Prospekt have soared out of sight.'

'No sense wasting our time talking about money until I find out what's what at the Frenchie's.'

Listening to Klazkha's tale, Bézard alternated between horror that Marya had been in the dreaded Fortress and contrition that he had believed the relentless tattle about 'the Little Alexiev and her millionaire gaucho'.

Tugging his waxed moustache, he said:

'But of course. Sometimes a husband gets tight with the purse-strings, or a lover de-camps after the fittings and garments are left.'

'I won't be able to come up with near what they're worth.'

'My good woman, you're talking as if Marya were a mere customer.' He spoke in ag-grieved tones, then raised his palms expres-sively. 'She's my friend.'

That same evening he packed a carpet bag and hailed a droshky. As the horse clipped by the Vyborg's derelict blocks of flats, splashing and bouncing over open sewers, passing through clouds of sulphuric smoke from the belching factory chimneys, Bézard took out his cologne-scented handkerchief and held it delicately to his nostrils. Frown-ing into the darkness, he pondered why that bright, lovely free spirit had been locked up in a political prison. And why, liberated, had she flown to this slum?

At the Vyborg Inn a receptionist thrust a candlestick at him, muttering: 'Electricity's been cut off again. She's room thirty-five.'

The door was opened by a tall man. The flaring candle revealed a face that Bézard considered typical of Russian aristocracy: high cheekbones, deep-set eyes and a nar-row arched nose. As the younger man apolo-gized in educated tones for his abrupt departure all mysteries unravelled for Bézard. Hadn't he himself warned the charming young American years ago that in

334

view of Paskevich's implacable nature she must abandon every thought of her first lover, the young radical? Well, so much for good advice.

Marya was thin, so thin.

The fawn twill suit, rejected by the piano-legged heiress to a munitions fortune, needed taking in by half. Mouth full of pins, Bézard fitted the jacket and skirt, raising the narrow fox-trimmed hem to show Marya's slender ankles in the latest style from Paris. Though intensely curious about the details of her imprisonment and release, he asked no questions. She volunteered no answers — indeed, she said little. She'd been such a lively thing, and this poignant new quiet caught in his throat.

At ten-thirty, when the electricity flickered back on, Klazkha, who had brought her iron, was pressing the extra blouse and Marya was smoothing the freshly fitted skirt over her hips. After the hideously coarse uniform, the cheap muslin nightgowns, this fine English twill felt softer than angora wool. 'Soon I'm going to find some kind of work,' she said to Bézard. 'It'll take a while, but I'll pay —'

'Pay? These clothes are a dead loss! And, now I see how slim and chic you are, there's a brown coat that's also been left on my hands.' The coat, part of a Montenegrin princess's trousseau, could be copied by his workshop in a day.

Klazkha had lugged up the bathroom mirror. Marya, eyes sparkling, twisted this way and that to inspect herself from all angles. With an enchanting glance out of her past, she smiled at the couturier. 'What a Merlin you are! You've transformed me from a waif to a grand duchess!'

Chapter Twenty-five

The following morning Marya dressed in her new finery and laced her second-hand boots, which fitted remarkably well considering that Klazkha had bought them from a barrow, and was fussing with her hair when Stephan tapped on her door. His bedazzled eyes told her as eloquently as his words how she looked. He took her arm, squeezing it against his side, and as they descended the staircase side-by-side they were sharing the same thought: they hadn't yet made love.

It was late for breakfast, a few minutes to ten, and they had the dining-room to themselves, so they picked a table in the window-bay where sunlight dappled the vase of dusty wax roses.

A tall woman in a grey nurse's cap had paused in the hall. Peering at Stephan's back, she stepped inside. Her bulbous nose and a brownish birthmark on her receding chin were redeemed by her warm smile.

Stephan introduced her as Madame Valentina Taurit. 'We bumped into each other in the hall yesterday,' he explained to Marya, adding: 'We were at university together.'

'I was one of the bluestockings at the Bestuzhev Higher Courses for Women,' Valentina Taurit said with rueful humour. 'That was before I fell in love with a medical student and married him. So much for my education.'

'But, Sister Taurit, you had already studied a great deal,' Marya said admiringly. 'To be a nurse.'

'Don't let the uniform take you in. I'm a mere Volunteer War Nurse. The training takes all of six weeks. But I do have a lot of duties, so after my husband went into the Army I closed up the flat and moved in here.'

Marya said impulsively: 'What you're doing is marvellous!'

'Me? Ah, Miss Alexiev, it's our Russian soldiers who're marvels. They never complain. It breaks my heart, listening to them pretend that the most horrible wounds are nothing.'

'This damn war!' Stephan said. 'What's wrong with the human race? Why can't we learn that violence is never the answer?'

'I couldn't agree more. Yet — and God forgive me — this is the first time in my life I've felt truly useful. Ah, how good it is to be needed.' The flat-faced maid was limping over with a battered serving-tureen. 'But here's your breakfast, and I mustn't be late for my shift.'

As the tall ample figure in the grey uniform moved around the tables and disappeared into the hall, Marya's gaze followed.

'There's a pensive expression.' Stephan ladled the inevitable buckwheat gruel into their bowls.

'I was remembering . . . Stephan, when I was eleven my idols were Florence Nightingale and Clara Barton. I began informing one and all that when I grew up I was going to be a nurse. One day Father sat me down for a talk. Poor Father, he never put on airs, he was gentle and polite to everyone. So it came as a shock when he told me in a serious tone that nurses belonged to the working class and surely I was old enough to realize that becoming a glorified hospital servant-girl brought shame on him. The deepest kind of shame. Oh, how wretched he made me feel! So naturally I got fresh. I pointed out that I was an American, and *we* didn't have silly regulations about class — why, Mother had been a Harvey Girl. And the way things were, with money so tight at our house, I'd need a job, too. Father was the mildest person imaginable, yet suddenly there he was snorting fire. I was his daughter, he barked, an Alexiev, a hereditary noblewoman! And not another word, not one more word of this disgraceful nonsense about scrubbing bedpans!'

'If this confession is leading up to an announcement that you're volunteering, Marya, remember this. You still need quite a good deal of nursing yourself.'

'You've healed me completely,' she said, smiling.

'That's good news.' Glancing around the dining-room to make sure they were alone, he bent across the dusty wax roses to touch his lips to hers. 'Tonight?' he murmured.

'Tonight . . .'

Gingerboy curled around their legs with a purr, then departed, the wintry sunlight wavered on their loosely connected fingertips. *Tonight . . .*

'You're so beautiful,' he said. They were on her narrow bed, his arm under her neck.

Her earlobes and fingertips were still glowing. 'You don't know how terrified I've been.'

'But why?'

'I'm so scrawny, skin and bones. And you seemed so . . . well, *uninterested.*'

'You're exquisite. And I didn't want to push you until you were completely well. But don't think it's been easy.'

She kissed his hand, smelling the odours of their love; he pretended to bite her shoulder, and their laughter sounded softly in the darkness.

'Do you', Stephan asked, 'believe in fate?'

'A poet's question! Yes, I suppose I do believe in destiny — at least, my Russian side does.'

'Then, listen with that ear.' He kissed the lobe, and whispered: 'Somewhere in the universe there exists a great misty book which tells the past, present and future. In it our names are inscribed together.'

'Is this another proposal?'

After the briefest hesitation during which he thought of her feverish muttering for

Paskevich, he asked, 'Is there any reason you won't marry me?'

'None.' Running her fingertips down his naked thigh, she gave a throaty laugh. 'Under the circumstances, what else can I say but yes?' She expected a chuckle.

Instead he said in a low voice: 'I should be ashamed. You'd be sharing your life with a landmine.'

'I'm on the Okhrana's list myself.'

'You're not,' Stephan said. Then he wondered if she had forgotten what his contact in the Department of the Interior had told him: the name Marya Fedorovna Alexiev was nowhere to be found in the police files. 'But as my wife you'll be on it.'

'Then, mark it in your misty book that we're officially engaged.'

'My work — I won't be able to make much of a living.'

She thought of his mysterious legacy that supported a soup-kitchen, hesitating briefly before she said: 'One of the reasons I love you is your idealism.'

'A quality that's debatable.' Though he spoke lightly, he spoke from the heart. Before he'd read Irena's letter, his ardour to reform Russia had indeed been quixotic. Since that night in the Moscow apartment, though, every cell in his body had become a battlefield. The genes of his liberal, artistic maternal forebears were locked in mortal combat with those of his cruel, all-powerful paternal lineage. He no longer viewed himself as a crusader for social reform, but as a son out to topple his father's omnipotence.

Holding Marya tighter, he started to explain all this. But the longer a humiliation has fermented in the dark, the more potent it becomes. Added to that, Stephan was a solitary and, except in his writing, he had immense difficulty lowering the drawbridge to his interior world. His mouth went dry, his tongue swelled. He couldn't form a confession. Instead he tugged at a strand of her hair, saying: 'Shall we set a date?'

'Stephan, maybe it's not such a good idea for *you*.'

'What do you mean? I adore you.'

'A couple of weeks ago Klazkha brought over a pile of those rubbishy gossip-sheets, old ones. There was an article about' — her voice went down — 'Paskevich. It not too subtly brought up his great affection for his American ward. We both know how it would affect the Democratic Reform Party if the members heard that your wife had been Paskevich's mistress. That kind of gossip is death in politics — and the party means everything to you.' She pressed closer to him.

Even as he began tracing the delicate knobs of her spine, he couldn't prevent the thought: *She's postponing our marriage because she's still entangled with Paskevich.*

'What was that last one?' Klazkha was asking.

342

Marya blinked in puzzlement at the unbound papers in her hand. How could she be in Klazkha's room with its smells of hot damp linen and charcoal when a moment earlier she'd been across the street in the Vyborg Inn finishing a request to enrol in the Volunteer War Nurse training programme? Hadn't she just signed 'Marya Fedorovna Nizhni'? (Though she wasn't wanted by the police, she and Stephan had concluded it would be tempting fate to take the tram to the City Hall on Nevsky Prospekt to replace her documents under her real name, so he had obtained top-notch forgeries.)

Klazkha's room, never bright, was sunk in gloom. Outside, large feathery flakes were falling. It hadn't been snowing before.

'Ain't it something, the way Stephan strings together words?' Klazkha continued the intricate dance of her iron on one of Bézard's ruffle-necked nightshirts. 'Go back over that last bit, will you?'

'Klazkha, how long have I been here?'

In reply, Klazkha set her iron on its side and came to touch a roughened palm to Marya's forehead. 'Cool as a cucumber,' she pronounced. 'When you was ill and thrashing around in the bed, I never knew where your mind was. Since then, a few times you stopped talking for a while, then started up on a whole new tack.'

'You're saying I've been having blank spells?'

'Seems like it.'

'How long? How often?'

'It's only a few minutes. Four times. Maybe five.'

Marya had considered the dropped stitches during her illness as part of her high fever. To hear that she'd been having lapses since her recovery was bad news, very bad news indeed. 'Don't tell anyone.'

'Then, you'll explain how things are to Stephan?'

'I just can't bear for him to see any more of my faults,' Marya burst out.

'He worships the ground you walk on,' Klazkha said. 'It just ain't right, not telling him.'

'Promise not to say anything?'

After a long pause, Klazkha nodded reluctantly and returned to her ironing.

Neither of them spoke until Ovruch stamped in. Snow floured his bushy moustache and beard, falling in white clumps as he shed his immense sheepskin coat. Klazkha mopped the linoleum while he towelled his beard, then returned to folding sheets into a wicker basket. 'Ovruch,' she asked, 'the prisoners released out of solitary, you said they wasn't right.' At Marya's furious glance, Klazkha studiously inspected a pillowcase for creases. 'What was wrong?'

'Different problems. Some doubted themselves. Some fretted about every little thing. Some shrank into themselves. Or were terrified to leave their home. And of course all were run down and caught every stray germ that came along, like Marya did.'

'What about memory?'

'One woman didn't recognize her own children. A man had forgotten his alphabet. Why? Are you worried about Marya?'

'She's not,' Marya snapped.

Just then a loud banging rattled the door. It was the half-witted boy who delivered the heavier laundry-baskets. As Klazkha slowly gave the instructions, Ovruch continued to gaze thoughtfully at Marya.

Three days later it was Klazkha's birthday.

Marya planned a surprise party with the same gusto she had put into arranging her elegant Friday Nights. She cut strips of newspaper, gluing them into chains to drape around the walls, she arranged the table with plates, tea-glasses and a small, exorbitantly dear *kulik* that she had gone all the way to the Nevsky Prospekt to buy — her first tram ride since her release. She rearranged everything when Ovruch brought his contributions: a block of farmer's cheese, white bread and a big jug of wine.

The guest of honour tapped.

'Happy birthday!' sang the trio. 'Happy birthday!'

Klazkha took in the decorations, the food, the wine, the package on Marya's bed. 'A party,' she said gruffly. 'I ain't never had a birthday party before.'

'How old are you?' asked Ovruch.

'Nineteen,' Klazkha said.

'Impossible,' Stephan said. 'You're far too mature and sagacious.'

'Writer's words,' Klazkha muttered, but she was smiling.

While they dug into the food, a bitter wind came up, rattling the closed shutters and sending draughts through the double-glazed windows.

"What a winter this'll be.' Ovruch pared off more cheese. 'Crops'll fail everywhere.'

'Why sound so jolly about it?' Wine had brought a flush to Klazkha's cheeks.

'What could be better as far as we're concerned? When enlisted men go hungry at the front, we radicals can point out that the rich are dining on caviare and pheasant breast. We'll describe palace menus to war widows making their children's soup with grass and earth.'

'There's a man for you!' Klazkha snapped. 'What woman would sound so cheery about starving little ones?'

'The tsarina's a woman,' Ovruch said. 'I haven't heard that she weeps for our Russian children.'

'Of course she does. Ain't her own boy sickly?'

'Pah! That German woman's rotten through and through. She tells Kaiser Willie our troop movements, then laughs at our losses. She sleeps on silk sheets with Rasputin, then opens the grand duchesses' bedroom doors and watches him debauch her own daughters.' These defamations, voiced in every level of Petrograd society, were delivered good-naturedly.

Stephan put down his glass. 'The tsarina's a complete prude, Ovruch, and you know it.'

'All right, she wears a tight corset, but we won't spread the word. Comrades, I tell you again that we couldn't wish for a better situation. The tsar trots off to play soldier at Headquarters, so we can blame him for the millions of casualties. He leaves behind his German wife to rule the country, and she's mesmerized by Rasputin and does exactly what he tells her, replacing decent capable men in government with his corrupt creatures. What better allies do we need?'

'The Democratic Reform Party refuses to cash in on the Army's defeats or to broadcast lies about the empress.'

Ovruch turned to Marya. 'You were in the Trubetskoi. Tell us. Did they show such gentlemanly scruples there?'

Recalling her chilblains, her fevered illness, her wild loneliness, she said softly: 'Ovruch is right, Stephan. You can't tie your hands. You have to fight with all you've got.'

Ovruch nodded and rested his bearded chin in his hand, watching her for another few moments. Then, as if he had filed away necessary information, he said to Stephan, 'Marya understands. Whatever weapons there are, we use them.'

'Even if you contribute to the German

victory and leave Russia in ruins?' Stephan asked.

'Pah, Strakhov. What sort of talk is that? Or d'you have a quarrel with the German workers?'

'No, of course not.'

'Then, you see my point, don't you? This war isn't our battle.' Ovruch paused. 'Our battle is to get rid of the bloodsuckers, the whole miserable bunch of them, with any means given us. That way there'll be no tsars or kaisers or kings to slaughter us in another of their Imperialist wars.'

'We in the Democratic Reform believe the tsar's necessary. With so many different peoples, we need a figurehead to hold us together.'

'Forget all that prettified manure about a constitutional monarchy, Strakhov. It's impossible. If you want a free proletarian government, you can't keep a Romanov as your Little Father.'

Stephan's response to this political argument was out of character and proportion — or so it seemed to Marya. Fists clenched, he jumped to his feet. The abrupt motion jarred the table. His glass fell. Ovruch rose, too. Stephan was a tall man. The bearded giant towered over him. The two men breathed heavily, glaring at each other across a growing stain of crimson wine.

For long seconds there was only the muted roar of the fire within the stove. Marya, too, was caught up in the emotional melodrama.

Clasping her upper arms, she thought of that summer night when Paskevich had been empowered by his birth to escort her into the living death of the Trubetskoi Bastion. 'Stephan,' she said slowly, 'you've always said your deepest conviction is that everyone is born equal. How does that square with an aristocracy and an autocrat?'

Ovruch gave her a beam of approval. 'Exactly.'

To avoid appearing to side with him, she added: 'Of course, that question, for what it's worth, is coming from an American.'

Stephan blinked as if coming awake, and began to scrub the spilled wine with his handkerchief. 'Sorry, Klazkha,' he muttered, 'I'm letting politics ruin your party.'

'Don't worry about it. And the wine'll come out with salt and cold water.'

To smooth over the awkwardness, Marya presented the birthday gift, a heavy, nearly new maroon shawl.

Klazkha's eyes were wet as she draped it around her shoulders. 'You shouldn't have.'

Ovruch refilled their glasses for another birthday toast, then started to sing 'Volga, Volga'. As the other three chimed in, he draped his thick arm over Stephan's shoulders and smiled at the two women. The acrimony had vanished. The foursome sang folk-songs until the occupant of the next room banged on the wall.

The next morning a letter arrived from the Pokrowski Hospital accepting Marya Nizhni in the Volunteer War Nurse training programme.

Chapter Twenty-six

As Marya hurried down the hospital steps she leaned to her left to compensate for the weight of a bucket whose sloshing liquid gave off acrid fumes of carbolic acid. In her free hand she carried lethally long scissors and a jar of petroleum jelly. Hair covered by a white scarf that tied at the nape of her neck, her grey-striped uniform concealed by a long white surgical gown, she might have been mistaken for an operating-room sister if it weren't for the small enamel pin with the emblem of the Russian Volunteer War Nurse. She had received her diploma three days earlier. Her nursing career, though, had begun the hour she entered the Pokrowski Hospital, when she had been assigned to washing feet and clipping toenails for the walking wounded.

Reaching the ground floor, she pushed open a swinging door black-painted: 'AMBULANCE WARD. STAFF ONLY'.

In peacetime, visitors had entered the Pokrowski Hospital through this gallery with its grandiose arched ceiling and large, evenly spaced windows. At the far end an immense gilded Romanov eagle hovered above the pair of outsize doors which both stood open. Beyond, in the courtyard, stood horse-drawn ambulances from which an ant-like stream of stretcher-bearers were unloading casualties: already rows of wounded lay on the stone floor. Half a dozen nurses were at work cleaning wounds. *Sanitars* were already carrying the prepared men upstairs, where they would be examined by the surgical unit.

Marya breathed shallowly while she acclimatized herself to a stench whose foulness rivalled the fever hospital during the cholera outbreak. The odours of long-unwashed bodies, dysentery, urine, blood, vomit and death were underscored by the vile sweetness of rotting gangrenous flesh. Groans, coughs, retching and muttered curses rose to the arches; a drummer-boy roughly jolted from his stretcher gave a high prolonged shriek of agony.

The sister in charge, a dourly efficient Estonian, gave Marya a glance, jerking her thumb towards a mud-caked bundle. The conscript couldn't have been more than seventeen. Orange lice paraded on his incipient beard and across the filthy blood-soaked rags wadded over the left side of his face. His right eye gazed trustingly up at her. As always when the wounded looked at her with this faith, she bit back saying that her uniform was a fraud and she was an ignoramus with six short weeks of training.

Instead she gave the boy one of the reassuring smiles that seemed to ease pain. 'I'm getting you ready so the doctors can look at you,' she said. 'Let's take the bandage off your face, all right?'

He gave a nod.

Marya picked up the scissors, swishing the blades through carbolic acid before she began to cut. The stiff cloth seemed to have become part of his flesh.

He groaned.

'Sorry,' she said.

'Nitchevo, Sistriza,' he said in a weak hoarse voice. It's nothing, Sister.

With a reassuring pat on the shoulder, Marya left him to get warm soapy water to loosen his improvised dressing. The slash from his eye to his jaw didn't appear infected. She was about to leave when he pointed to his feet. He hadn't been issued leather footgear, and as she sawed at the peasant bark boots the odour of rotting flesh grew unbearable. Her throat filled with bile; she stared at his black frostbitten toes. Dark lines already traced his feet and ankles. Gangrene. Upstairs some harried doctor would immediately despatch the boy to the operating-arena, where both feet would be amputated.

As *sanitars* carried him off, a Cossack was jolted down beside her. Horseflies hovered on the blood-soaked cloth wrapped around the stump of what had been his right arm. While Marya washed his maggot-ridden flesh he kept calling for his mother. After that the Estonian sister summoned her to help with a conscript who held his exposed guts. Marya then clamped ether to the nose

353

of a red-bearded peasant who'd been castrated by a landmine.

When finally the last of the convoy was borne upstairs, crones wearing the shapeless smocks of ward maids shuffled in with buckets of disinfectant to scrub the length of stone floor and the three Volunteers were free to leave. It was more than two hours after the end of their shift.

Marya lingered outside the staff door with her grey uniform cape pulled close around her. Limp with exhaustion, throat aching from holding back her nausea, she drew painful yet refreshing breaths of icy air. She was in no rush to get home to the Vyborg Inn. Tonight Stephan was at the Obukhov Weapons Factory discussing the Democratic Reform Party with any worker who cared to listen. So she would stay alone in their room studying a textbook on abdominal wounds. Inevitably her mind would tangle with fears that the police were raiding Stephan's impromptu recruiting session. If she dozed off, she would dream of the Trubetskoi Bastion.

A gust of wind tugged her long veil across her face. She was pushing aside the length of white flannel when she saw a frail hunchback lifting the hem of his worn astrakhan coat as he minced towards her. There was something familiar about the curve of spine and small, neatly pointed grey beard.

'Mademoiselle Alexiev,' he said.

At this use of her real name, she glanced quickly around. There was nobody nearby. 'Yes?'

'I have the honour to deliver this.' He extended an unaddressed envelope.

When she didn't reach for it he turned his head. The tortoise-like motion jolted her memory. He was one of the numerous elderly hangers-on who roosted along the endless corridors at the rear of the Crimson Palace. Freezing air reached into the pit of her stomach. What an idiot she was! Amid the swarming transients in the slummy anonymous Vyborg district, and at this huge impersonal hospital nursing under her alias, with no mention of her in the police files, she had lulled herself into believing that she was safely hidden from Paskevich.

'The message is important.' The hunchback's eyes were moist and pleading.

Taking the blank envelope with the embossed crest, she tucked it in her cape. 'Thank you.'

'It is, I believe, of immediate concern to you.'

She ripped open the envelope, taking out the single sheet: 'I must speak to you on a matter regarding your brother.'

The powerful commanding strokes of unsigned handwriting dizzied her. It took several heartbeats before she thought: *Boris. Oh, my God. Paskevich knows something about Boris.*

She had no idea whether or not her brother

had remained in the United States, but it seemed likely. Fretful about his health and general well-being, she had dithered over attempting to find him through the American embassy, finally abandoning the idea. What if some over-zealous State Department employee turned over Marya Nizhni's request to the Okhrana? She had also considered enlisting the aid of a New York reporter Stephan knew, but the American was too jovial, a loose-tongued boozer.

'His Excellency', said the old man, 'has left his equipage at your disposal.'

Marya hurried towards the Rolls-Royce. As the car merged with the jam of vehicles on the Troitsky Bridge, twilight made the Crimson Palace appear to be floating in a blood-red haze, and she realized that she hadn't paused to consider that the note might be enticing her into a trap. Yet obviously Paskevich knew where she was; so, if he'd wanted her back in the Trubetskoi Bastion, wouldn't he simply have tipped off the police? Furthermore, he was above lying. What did it matter, anyway? She was incapable of ignoring a message, no matter how vague, about her brother.

In the courtyard a moon-faced butler greeted her. 'Miss Alexiev? Count Paskevich is occupied. He begs your indulgence until he's free.'

'How long will that be?'

'A courier has just arrived from His Imperial Majesty.' The servant was taking her cape. 'His Excellency requests you make yourself comfortable. If you'll follow me?'

Marya wanted to shout angry refusals into the round pink face. But how could she yell when the butler was so patently obeying orders? She followed the plump liveried back up the branched staircase — how bitterly the serene burnished opulence contrasted with the ambulance ward — to the rooms she'd used during her first weeks in St Petersburg. The panelling had been covered in white silk; the warmth of apple-wood logs crackled in the fireplace, drawing artless perfume from the massed white hothouse roses.

The bathroom door was open, and the water running. A short woman bent so far over the Delft bath that her smartly tied apron bow appeared a butterfly perched atop the black bell of her skirt. She turned off the taps and set down the bath oil before she bobbed a curtsy.

'Good afternoon, Mademoiselle Alexiev,' she said in French. 'I am Marie Antoinette, like the queen, but everybody calls me Toinette. Ah, your uniform — some poor soul has left his blood on you. But do not worry. While you bathe I will get out the stains.'

Scarcely hearing the rapid French chatter, Marya stared at the collection of crystal perfume-bottles. They had been her pride in that other life in the Fourstatskaia apartment. *Why did Paskevich save them?*

357

Why these re-furbished rooms? Is this his form of a Barmecide's Feast before I'm whisked back to that solitary hell? Her every instinct was to flee. But how could she leave the Crimson Palace before hearing about Boris?

Toinette helped her undress and climb into the scented water. Marya's skeleton was less prominent, but she still considered herself a rail. Toinette, though, praised the slenderness, the whiteness of her skin, keeping up the flow of compliments while she held out the hot bathtowel and then fastened new silk lingerie that fitted to perfection. How had Paskevich known her smaller size?

Toinette was highly skilled.

'Do you work for the countess?' Marya asked.

'I was engaged only last week, so I never had the privilege of meeting the poor lady.'

'Poor lady?'

'But surely you know? Countess Paskevich was taken from us more than six months ago. Both empresses paid last respects.' Toinette rattled on, listing grand dukes and grand duchesses and other dignitaries who had attended the funeral. 'Ah, what tragedy — the count left without even a child to comfort him in his hour of grief. But at least he's blessed with friends like you, mademoiselle.'

'I've been out of touch.'

'But of course. In your own country. I hear

how you came back through Finland to aid our war effort. Such bravery! Such patriotism!' Curling-tongs and compliments were applied to Marya's hair.

So Paskevich's wife was dead. And these rooms prepared. Clothing ordered in the correct size. Questions filled Marya's head, but the plausible answers skimmed like dragonflies, refusing to alight.

'Will you wear this?' Toinette held up a pale-green silk dinner-dress trimmed with deep-emerald bugle beads. 'Or this.' Rose satin with a small train.

'I prefer my uniform.'

'It will take me some time to iron that dry. But there are other gowns . . .' Toinette's skirt seemed attached to wheels as she glided through the windowless dressing-room flinging open armoires. Marya's hands, roughened from disinfectants and harsh hospital soap, caught on the delicate fabrics as she moved aside the dresses. Momentarily she felt betrayed by Bézard, then she saw the thick satin labels of Madame Brissac, the supreme arbiter of Russian fashion. Marya drew out the plainest gown, navy with white collar and cuffs. Toinette buttoned and adjusted, producing a triple-strand pearl dog-collar. Marya's slenderness, the rosy pearls and simple dark dress produced exactly the opposite effect from that she had intended.

Toinette clasped her hands, breathing: "Très élégante!'

At a tap, the maid glided to the door, returning to say: 'Mademoiselle Alexiev, his Excellency is free now and requests the pleasure of your company.'

All at once Marya's mouth was dry, her heartbeat erratic. She wore Stephan's ring with adhesive tape wound around the band to keep it on her middle finger. Rubbing the smooth diamond as if it were a good-luck charm, she squared her shoulders.

Chapter Twenty-seven

Paskevich sat at his desk. Slowly he set down the bound report with TOP SECRET red-stamped diagonally across the cover. His clever, monkey's face grew pale and drab: at the hospital Marya had seen this same sallowness in patients suffering an internal haemorrhage. Nervous tremors were slithering down her own back. Too much had passed between them for her to remain dispassionate. Not only the long, silent entombment in the Trubetskoi Bastion but also the times she'd been infected by his passion and thrashed naked in his arms, their shared laughter, Lally's birth and death, his obsessive love. Edging warily over the threshold, she gave a little jerk as the door closed softly behind her.

'Good evening, Marya,' Paskevich said. 'Won't you sit down?'

'I'm not staying.'

His pale lips quirked into a reproduction of a smile. 'Then, let me say quickly how lovely you look. That dress is exquisite on you, et cetera, et cetera. Why the frown? You no longer enjoy compliments on your appearance? Then, let me praise you for renouncing worldly comfort in the Vyborg and playing ministering angel at —'

'All right, all right. You know everything

I've been doing. Now, what's this about Boris?'

'But how can we let almost two years pass without comment?' There was a shade too much facetiousness in his voice. 'Aren't I meant to apologize for your restful holiday in the Trubetskoi?'

Recalling her felt-lined sepulchre, Marya closed her eyes. 'It was as you hoped, Paskevich. I longed for death.'

'If it's any consolation,' he replied in a low tone naked of sarcasm, 'so did I.'

Why can't I hate him? 'I don't pretend to understand the game you're playing — the rooms, my bottles, the wardrobe — and I don't want to understand. I'm here for one reason. To hear about Boris.'

He reached into the pocket of his dinner-jacket for a battered-looking envelope taped across the top. 'Opened by our censor, not me,' he said.

Circumspect as if she were taking meat from between a lion's paws, Marya went slowly to the desk, grabbing the crumpled letter, retreating immediately. Though she had vowed to herself to leave the Crimson Palace the instant she discovered Paskevich's news of her brother, seeing Boris's familiar scrawl destroyed her intentions. Moving towards the cabinet filled with jade miniatures, she tore away the tape.

The letter, three pages of sporadically mis-spelled English on Waldorf Hotel stationery, was heavily censored. *'My dearest Marya, I trust this will get through . . .'* She sped by a blacked-out phrase. Boris wrote that, knowing she had left St Petersburg with another man, he disliked using the Crimson Palace as a mail drop, but he had exhausted every other hope of communication. He had already told her about himself many times, but since he had never received a reply he would start all over again.

After weeks of unsuccessfully scouring the city in attempts to learn her whereabouts, he had been offered a job by a friend.

I act as a secretary/guide to America. (Incidentally the cost of living in New York is way higher than in St Petersburg, and my salary doesn't go far.) My friend believes —

Censor's ink blackened the next two lines.

Anyway, I've joined the Knickerbocker Club and met some decent fellows, so life isn't fatally dull. How is Aunt Chatty? I never heard a peep from her, so obviously she's never gotten my letters, either. Marya, from following the war news about the —

Another long censor's slash.

Anyway, she must be worrying herself into a swoon every hour. What I'm say-

ing is the two of you must immediately come home to the good old USA. Not just for your own protection but because I miss you both terribly.

Marya wiped her knuckles across her eyes.

'Bad news?' Paskevich asked quietly.

'He doesn't even know Aunt Chatty's dead. He's lonely. Things aren't going well.'

'Is he still with Madame Orlovna?'

'Who?'

'He sailed to America with her a month or so before the war. She's the heiress of a Moscow cloth manufacturer. Divorced. Dabbles in painting, mysticism and men.'

Marya, who had been picturing Boris as a slave-drudge to a spoiled princeling, changed scenarios to Boris jumping through hoops for some rich, raddled old nymphomaniac.

She had forgotten how Paskevich could follow her thoughts. 'Actually, Madame Orlovna's decent-looking if a bit full-blown, or so I hear,' he said. 'Before they left for New York they had been lovers for a long time. He stayed with her whenever he visited Moscow. She entertained a great deal, there and at her country place. Imagined herself a *salonière* — a lot of high-minded talk, but also a lot of sexual frolics. Incidentally, I've transferred funds so Boris'll receive a monthly stipend.'

'Why?'

'Why not?' Paskevich went to the decanter, pouring her a glass of wine. 'Marya, I'm deeply sorry about Miss Dunning's death.'

Close to tears again, Marya sipped the sherry.

There was a tap on the door.

'Dinner,' Paskevich said.

'Thank you for the letter.' Putting down her glass, Marya stood.

'I took it for granted you'd dine with me.'

Marya couldn't ignore Paskevich's generosity to Boris, yet on the other hand there were the Trubetskoi Bastion, and the question why he'd redone her rooms, hired Toinette and ordered all those clothes. Honesty followed by a dignified exit seemed appropriate. 'Stephan and I live together — but you know that?'

The small dark eyes glinted. 'Another reason I insist you dine here. You must enlighten me about Mr — Does he prefer Iskra or Strakhov? What, precisely, does your idealist hope to accomplish?'

'If you ever went near the Vyborg district, you wouldn't need to ask.'

'The poor are always with us,' Paskevich said, rising to face her.

'Since when do you quote the Bible?'

'In this case it's apt. Tell me, has your ardent revolutionary ever considered the nature of Russian peasants? They've always sought out strength. They obey strength. They are awed by strength. They grovel before strength. For them, there are no good or bad tsars, only weak or strong. The last thing they want is the burden of freedom. Our peasants demand *vlast.*' Authority. 'Believe me, Russia and Nicholas would be far, far better off today if he came near to resembling the vicious bloodthirsty tyrant that the radicals have labelled him.'

'It's the system that's wrong.'

'System?' Paskevich tapped a cigarette on his Fabergé case. 'In America they invented a system. Here in Russia, our government is the tsar, and the tsar is our government. A supreme autocrat, that's our system. Nicholas might not be clever, but he's amiable and he means well. The war's already caused enough unrest. He needs whatever support we educated classes can give him.'

'All this is fascinating, but it's late,' she said.

'Russia is perched on top of a keg of dynamite.' Paskevich formed an acid smile. 'Doesn't it seem to you that Strakhov should protect the powder rather than ignite it?'

'After the explosion we'll have a freely elected Duma.'

'A democrary? Here in Russia?' Paskevich chuckled. 'Marya, take it from a man who's served in our government for a great many years, a revolution would bounce Russia into the hands of the leader of whichever party is the most brutal and repressive.'

'No,' she denied, thinking of Stephan. 'They're good decent people.'

'I agree. There are idealistic radicals. But

they won't be the men who take over. Consider our history. Bloodshed, starvation and the knout. If the Autocracy's overturned, there'll be a new ruler —'

'An elected official.'

He shrugged. 'If the concept of an election pleases you, then by all means let any new leader be elected. What's important is that he'll immediately set out to crush the opposition parties —'

'You would say that!'

'Marya, Marya, his secret police will make the Okhrana seem like benevolent nursemaids. He'll not only annihilate his fellow revolutionaries in other parties and probably in his own, but he'll also blot out anyone who might be a future threat to his power. And, of course, the nobility, the bourgeoisie, the intelligentsia, even the well-to-do peasantry will be crushed like hazelnuts.'

Her head tilted. Faintly from across the Neva came the chimes of the carillon of Peter and Paul Cathedral tolling 'Praise the Lord in Zion', the hymn that had marked the hours of her imprisonment. Paskevich's voice faded, Boris's letter dropped from her fingers, fluttering to the magnificent Bukhara rug. She blinked. The bells had ceased.

'What is it, Marya?' Paskevich was saying. Lines of concern creased his forehead. 'What's wrong?'

'Nothing.'

'You said something about the bells, but your eyes were blank.'

She noticed Boris's letter at her feet. Bending to retrieve the pages, she sank into the nearest chair. Carefully refolding the crumpled stationery, she asked: 'How long was I like that?'

'Maybe five minutes.'

She exhaled with relief. 'Right after I escaped from the Trubetskoi there were long stretches — hours — that I couldn't remember. I still have episodes, but they're far shorter.' How was she blurting out to Paskevich what she'd kept from Stephan? 'I suppose I behave fairly normally. People don't notice anything's wrong.'

'The change was obvious to me,' he said quietly.

'It's terrifying.'

He inserted a fresh cigarette into the amber holder. 'Have you heard of Sigmund Freud — the alienist?'

She shook her head.

'He's in the enemy camp. A Viennese. Freud believes that certain memories are too agonizing to bear, so to survive we bury them. But they don't go away. Instead, they manifest themselves physically. According to our good doctor, bringing the pathological out into the open is curative.' Paskevich tapped away cigarette ash. 'I'm not saying I subscribe to Freud's theory. Still, why not give it a try? After all, you're with the man who brought about your suffering.'

She looked at him, expecting that irritating half-smile. Instead he looked repentant and sincere.

'Tell me about the Trubetskoi,' he encouraged.

She sank back in the leather chair, and after a minute found herself spilling out details of the mind-destroying inactivity, the chilblains that thickened her knuckles in winter, the heat rashes of the summer, the sour mildewed bread, the faint clang as the metal disc dropped down on the Judas-window, the insane fears and hopes. Surrounded by a collection of priceless miniatures, she talked of silence so deep that it pressed against the eardrums like water, the loneliness that transformed her slow-witted jailer into her closest friend. She told of the smuggled letters that erected soaring castles of hope, structures that crumbled under the agonizing weight of months without word. From time to time she would stop to weep into Paskevich's handkerchief. The richly scented smoke of his cigarettes curled upwards. He never interrupted, never prodded, never questioned. When she groped for a word, he found it for her. She had no idea how long the old horrors spewed from her. Finally her voice rasped as if fingers were pressing on her windpipe. 'I spent the day with wounded coming directly from the front,' she said hoarsely. 'To them the Trubetskoi would be a rest cure.'

'One should never compare torments,' he said. Stubbing out his cigarette, he went to the door. Servants who had been waiting for well over an hour bore in the *zakhouski*. White-gloved hands rolled Sevruga caviare in thin blinis, her favourite. She played with one. When Paskevich led her to the table, she didn't protest. They were served wild mushroom soup, asparagus and melted butter, lobster in a white wine sauce, venison.

Both of them toyed with the sumptuous meal. Neither spoke. Paskevich's character always had eluded Marya: his moods, though, had become familiar. She had never seen him like this. As sluggishly miserable as she. He caught her watching him. Rather than lifting a quizzical brow, he snapped his fingers. The footmen departed.

He set down his vermeil knife and fork. 'Are you aware, Marya,' he asked, 'that you're the only person to hear my innermost soul?'

'When was that?'

'That first morning after we were together, I explained myself thoroughly, or so I believed at the time. Now it seems, however, that I've never fully understood my own persona. Before this evening my privilege was a God-given one. As the sun rises in the east and sets in the west, so it was an unalterable fact that the rest of mankind existed to serve us. They worked our fields, tended our homes, fought our wars, relieved our lusts. I never questioned it. Why would I? My rank was a genetic part of me, like my large hands and my baldness, my intellect, and I've never questioned possessing those. You, as one of the minor gentry, a woman, were a lesser being. There for my taking.'

'Were you so lofty?'

'Lofty?' He frowned. 'You aren't following me. Think of the toy poodle I gave you, the little dog who was crushed under a cart.'

Fifi, a white fluffball, had been presented to her in a beribboned basket shortly after Lally's death. Marya had trained Fifi to sit up and beg for titbits, she had walked the pretty little dog in the Admiralty Gardens, scolded her when she chewed slippers and messed on the rugs. And, of course, never once questioned Fifi's right to rule her own exercise, bowels, urinary tract and diet. How amazed she would have been had Fifi one morning stood up on her fluffy little hind legs announcing that they were equals and demanding control over her own destiny. Marya's eyes widened in comprehension.

Paskevich nodded. 'Yes, that's how I felt about you. You were mine to rule. Of course, this didn't prevent me from adoring you and your courage, your beauty, your wit, your pride, your spirit. How it infuriated me that I couldn't go to the land of the dead and bring back the child for you. Your infidelity drove me beyond madness. Yet never once did I question my absolute supremacy over you.'

'Now, though?'

'While you were talking, I loathed myself profoundly. For the first time I recognized what I'd done to you as a fellow human, not as my disobedient possession.'

The gleam of sweat on his pate, the sagging flesh of his throat and his halting tone affected her more than she cared to admit. 'When we have free elections,' she said, stabbing the flakes of the tiny puff pastry crescent, 'then one group of people will no longer be able to believe themselves the masters.'

'Marya, hasn't a word of what I've tried to tell you sunk in? Every species of animal has a pecking order. There will always be those who rule; always the strong will dominate the weak.'

'Exactly what will change under a fair government.'

'Never in this world. Dominance is nature's most basic law. Political concepts, speeches and slogans are so much whipped cream.'

'It's late. I'm too tired to argue.'

'What I'm saying is that I repent, sincerely repent, acting my own part in the vast injustice of creation.' Paskevich refilled the two green hock-glasses. 'The apology is personal, of course.'

The ormolu clock ticked away a minute. She nodded slowly.

'I'm absolved, then?'

'Yes,' she murmured.

'Unlike me, you don't weigh yourself down with grudges,' he said, and raised his glass to her. 'The Countess Paskevich is no longer with us.'

At this abrupt change in conversation, Marya gave a little jerk. 'Toinette told me. I'm sorry.'

'No need for pity. My late wife died in ecstasy. She was devouring a *croque-en-bouche.*'

Marya recalled the candlelit Khazan Cathedral, the stout bride freeing her veil from her diamond *chiffre* as the tsar led her to the altar. 'Must you make fun of everything?'

'Should I weep crocodile tears over a glutton? The doctors had warned her often enough.'

'She was your wife.'

'Never. I told you that the night of my wedding. *You're* my wife. It's time we legitimized the situation.'

Leaping up, she jarred the table. Crystal rang and china clattered as she cried: 'Are you out of your mind?'

'Merely rectifying a mistake.'

'You threw me into hell,' she said hotly. 'Stephan and I love each other.'

'Then, why haven't you gone through the formalities before a priest?'

'That's my decision.'

'Oh?'

'It's not as if I was secluded in a convent school before, is it? Anybody who has read the gossip-sheets knows I was your mistress. If Stephan married me, he'd destroy his credibility — his followers would see it as embracing the corruption and unfairness he's spent his life trying to change.'

'He's explained about himself to you, then?' Paskevich's smile was unpleasant.

Her questions about Stephan buzzed like a disturbed hive of bees. 'Of course he has!' She could hear the bells across the Neva chime out 'God Bless the Tsar'. The anthem meant it was midnight. Midnight? Stephan might already have returned to their room. 'And I'm going home to him this minute!'

'No.' Paskevich had come around the table to stand a foot from her. The diamond studs in his starched shirt glittered and so did his eyes.

'I love him,' she said, enumerating the reasons for her love as if she were holding up a shield. 'He's decent, scrupulously just, he gives everything away, he's honourable, uncomplicated and —'

'And you don't understand him at all,' Paskevich interrupted hoarsely.

His arms encircled her waist and shoulders. She flailed. Paskevich clamped her wrists, holding them behind her back. As he pressed her body against his she felt the buttons of his dinner-jacket, his diamond studs, his erection. 'You're part of me,' he muttered. His breath smelled of wine from the Caucasus, his tongue was forcing itself into her mouth. Remotely, as if from the highest balcony tier at the Maryinsky, she was aware that the scene they were playing illustrated the law of nature she'd so recently denied. A few are born to dominate. Even without his rank, Paskevich would have risen to the top because of his drive and energy, his intelligence and shrewdness, the force of his will. She had never hated him more. Trembling, angry, frightened, dizzy, she wrenched her hands free, pushing at his chest.

'Let me go.'

'Never,' he muttered. 'Never again in this life.'

'I hate you!'

He ignored her words, he ignored her weakly pummelling fists. His embrace tightened. He whispered obscene endearments, his hands cupped her buttocks and he pressed her backwards, his lips moving down the pearl dog-collar to the flesh below.

Chapter Twenty-eight

As Paskevich released her, she staggered back a step, holding on to a chair. The door had swung open, and Stephan stood there gripping the handle.

His shoes were muddy. Snow rested on his hair and the shoulders of his overcoat. As he looked from her to Paskevich, his mouth quivered, then the lines of his jaw hardened. Had he ever looked at her like this, his eyes as impersonal as flat blue pebbles?

The footman puffed into view. 'Excellency, this man rushed past the *dvornik*. Shall I call the guards?'

'Shut the damn door!' Paskevich barked.

The door closed with a thump.

'Why aren't you at the Obukhov works?' Marya blurted, realizing as she spoke that the question implied she had intended to use his absence for this visit. 'Stephan, I meant . . . What about the meeting . . . ?'

He said nothing.

'A letter came from Boris, and Paskevich sent word to the hospital. You know how desperate I've been.'

'Mr Strakhov. Welcome to my home.' Paskevich's politely formal greeting managed to convey amused indulgence. 'Boris *did* address Marya's letter here. I'm related to them, as you know.'

'Here, look.' Marya fumbled with the clasp

of her evening bag, holding out the pages. 'He's in New York.'

Paskevich tapped away an ash. 'I assure you that Marya's telling the truth.'

Stephan appeared to be examining the tiny Egyptian tomb figures. In truth, he was as oblivious to the millennia-old objects as to the melting snow that trickled down his forehead and cheeks. When he was ten, a supposed friend at the Moscow gymnasium had come out of the shadows to punch him hard in the stomach, and that's how he felt now — shocked, baffled, the breath knocked out of him. *So this is why she put off marriage. Paskevich. Yes, of course. Paskevich.*

'I should've sent a message to the inn,' Marya said. Her eyes were luminous with tears. 'Stephan, please, please speak to me.'

His gaze travelled from her coiffed hair to the pearls, the exquisitely fitted gown, the dainty silk shoes. The clothing made her yet more unapproachable: she was set apart by beauty, that most enigmatic gift. He made a gesture with his hands, spreading the palms. 'I don't know what to say without sounding like a jealous idiot.'

'I freely confess to having manoeuvered Marya here,' Paskevich said. 'When Boris's letter arrived a few days ago, I ordered clothes. This afternoon I had a note delivered to the Pokrowski Hospital. I refused to see Marya until she had changed. I insisted she dine with me.'

'But you didn't use force or chains, did you?' Stephan's face was expressionless.

'Stop talking about me as if I weren't in the room,' Marya cried.

Stephan turned his cold blue gaze on her. 'I can understand the attraction of the Crimson Palace,' he said. 'It's a million miles from the war.'

'You'll find me quite knowledgeable on that subject,' Paskevich said. 'I know exactly how asinine our military leadership has been. I'm aware that we've permitted our allies to use Russia as a decoy whenever they need to divert the Germans from their Western Front. I know precisely how short we are of trained officers, artillery, shells, rifles and bullets — I've proposed that the armaments factories be nationalized. I know that to transport supplies and men we need three point seven times as much rolling stock as we have.' Paskevich's recitation hovered between malice and amusement. 'And, as to the front, in my salad days I was awarded the Saint George Cross and the Saint George Sword. From your writing, though, it's clear that you're a pacifist, so military medals will scarcely impress you.'

'The poor are starving.'

'Ah, so this is a discussion of what you of the Left call the "class war",' Paskevich said. 'Well, not being of a suicidal nature, I refused to be the instrument of my own destruction. I'll not willingly turn over my

378

country to illiterate peasants. You see, I lack your generosity of spirit, my dear Stephan . . . Leonidovich, is it?'

At the questioned patronymic, Stephan blinked, startled, then coloured and said: 'I've interrupted your evening long enough.'

'One minute.' Marya held up a finger. 'Let me run upstairs for my uniform.'

'Marya, it doesn't take a genius to see that this is where you belong.'

'I belong with you!'

Stephan gave her a cold look. As he whirled around, his unbuttoned overcoat flared out. He didn't notice that he had toppled a Ming bowl. Priceless chinoiserie thumped on the carpet at the same moment as he slammed the door.

Marya started after him. Paskevich caught her arm.

'Let me loose,' she cried.

'He won't believe a word you say.'

Marya jerked free. She darted from the study. Both sides of the double staircase were empty, as was the hall below her. As she gripped the banister, the carved shell pattern digging into her palms, the heavy vestibule door slammed shut.

Paskevich, following her, ignored the silk-stockinged footman stationed outside the study. 'A sensitive young man,' he said.

'Why couldn't he have a little bit of faith in me?'

'My dear, he's so upright that for him everyday machinations don't exist . . .' His voice seemed muffled by distance. 'He's right: you belong here. Rest in your rooms.'

Stephan halted in the middle of the Troitsky Bridge. The sparse snow drifted through the circles of light cast by the lamp-post as he rested his gloved hands on the wrought-iron rail to stare down. With its thin white coat of snow, the icebound Neva appeared solid enough; but the tram tracks that crossed the river in winter had not yet been laid, and no sledges had ventured out.

How much force would be needed to break through the ice to semi-frozen water? Would a body hurtling downwards do it? He commanded himself to stop being maudlin. Yet he felt as lost and betrayed as on that night in Moscow when he'd read Irena's letter.

I always knew he would take her back, Stephan thought. *Take her? That's not fair, is it? She admitted she went willingly to the Crimson Palace. Because of Boris, she said. True? A lie? How many nights while I've been shouting myself hoarse at meetings has she been there? How often has she worn those clothes, then taken them off for him? How often have they made love?*

Oh, God, God, why didn't I play the caveman, ruin her coiffure and drag her out of that perfumed overheated study by the hair? She said she wanted to come with me. What did it matter if it were true, or how long she'd be with me? I'd have had her. All along, I knew she'd let herself be bought by the richest, most cynical type of reactionary, so why do I keep expecting her actions and motives to be so damn pure and high-minded?

Why is the world so ugly? Why is life so cold? Has my heart always been a crippled animal thrust out of the herd? Is that why I'm always alone? Or is being solitary an inherited curse?

Without any plan in mind, he reached an arm around the ornate lamp-post, climbing on to the base. He poised there, the iron chill penetrating his sleeve as he gazed through the darkness at the bed of soft bluish snow.

'Zdrastvuj!' Hello.

At the sound of a man's voice Stephan jerked out of his dismal reverie.

A gendarme in a long blue coat was peering up at him. 'Not thinking of something rash, are we?'

'Wanted better view of the Neva, thas all.' Stephan slurred his words.

'A bit too much celebrating, eh? That bootleg stuff'll fell an ox.' At the onset of the war, in the hope of increasing productivity, the Government had ceased distilling vodka — a state monopoly — but no amount of police surveillance could control the illegal stills. 'Come on down here, and we'll walk on over to the tram-stop'

Stephan permitted himself be led across the bridge towards the silhouetted cathedral, whose spire rose like an unsheathed sword above the fist of the Fortress where

Marya had languished. Whichever direction he went in Petrograd, he would be reminded of her.

Klazkha awoke to the jarring clatter of her cheap alarm-clock. A quarter to five. Not indulging in another minute of rest, she wrapped herself in the birthday-present shawl and grabbed her water-pitcher. Outside her door she stumbled over a large box. Josip, poor dead Josip, had taught her to recognize her name. Holding her candle lower, she saw KLAZKHA SOBCHAK printed across the cardboard. No client, Bolshevik or regular, would have left the box here where it could be snatched by thieves. What was inside? Klazkha viewed curiosity as a weakness, so she kicked the box into the room and hurried to the ice-covered water-butt. Returning, she washed and pinned her plait into an uncompromising bun. Only then did she open the carton.

A heady odour of eau de Cologne filled the room. Marya's fur-trimmed suit, two blouses and the heavy coat had been squashed inside amidst a tangle of stockings and underwear, with the leaking scent-bottle on top. Klazkha's forehead creased in a perplexed frown. Marya would never ruin her clothes like this. *It must have been Stephan.* But why? What had got into him to do such a thing? At this hour nobody was about at the Vyborg Inn, so she couldn't go across the street and find out what was what. She smoothed the clothes and scrubbed the scent stains as best she could before starting her own work. She was ironing a sheet when the door shuddered under frantic banging.

'It's me!' Marya cried. As Klazkha unslid the bolt, she rushed in, her face as grey as her nurse's cape. 'Have you seen Stephan?' she asked in a high voice.

'No, but when the alarm rang, them things' — Klazkha indicated the clothes hanging on the door-hook, the lingerie now neatly folded into the carton — 'was already outside the door.'

'Oh, my God . . .'

'What's this all about?'

Marya blurted out a disjointed tale that included a letter from Boris at the Crimson Palace, fancy clothes, a French personal maid and being tricked into accepting Paskevich's invitation to dinner. 'When Stephan showed up I told him about the letter, and so did Paskevich,' she finished with a sigh. 'But who can blame him for having his doubts? It does sound concocted.'

'I believe you,' Klazkha said. 'But he's a man, and men always think the worst of women.'

'You would say that!' Marya sank on to the free space on the cot. 'Oh, Klazkha, I'll never see him again.'

'He'll get over it.'

'He's always despised me for living with Paskevich . . .'

'Then, he hid it really well. You should've seen him working to get you out of prison, and fretting like a lunatic when you had the fever.'

'He's paid up on the room.'

'Then, you'll stay here until you get your bearings.'

'I'll bet he left a note and the landlord just forgot to give it to me.' Marya rushed out.

Klazkha reached for her shawl, hurrying through the dawn to catch up.

The landlord lounged against the desk. 'Strakhov rang at an ungodly hour. Couldn't wait until morning for me to tot up the bill. And now he's gone, and so's the cat.'

'Gingerboy?' Marya said dully.

'Not hide nor whisker of either of 'em.'

'What about a forwarding address?' Marya asked.

'Didn't ask. Never do. The less I know, the less I can tell the Okhrana. Come to think of it, they must've been after him. He looked fair beaten.' The landlord picked his teeth, displacing a stringy substance from between his molars. 'If the cat comes back, want me to fetch it across the street?'

Marya wore that dazed expression.

Klazkha replied for her: 'We'd be grateful. Let's get on back to my place, Marya.'

As they emerged on to the slushy pavement, a tall, crested motor car oozed around the corner. The chauffeur honked

the horn continuously, and workers rushing to the factories made a path, stopping
to gape. The magnificent vehicle came to
a halt.

Paskevich emerged. 'Come, my dear,' he
said to Marya.

'Remember what he done, putting you in
prison,' Klazkha whispered.

'Get into the car.'

'Don't get mixed up with him again,'
Klazkha muttered.

But Marya was already moving towards
Paskevich. As slowly as if she were under-
water, she let him hand her into the velvet-
lined car.

Klazkha knew when she was beaten —
and, besides, the count intimidated her.
Shivering, pulling her shawl tighter over
her bosom, she watched the gleaming phe-
nomenon toot its way through the crowd.

Chapter Twenty-nine

The Tsar's Village — Tsarskoe Selo in English — had begun with a single unpretentious stone house, the retreat designed by Peter the Great's wife for her hard-driving illustrious husband, growing into an aristocratic metropolis of thirty thousand inhabitants. The town was serviced by two pairs of railway tracks from Petrograd, which lay fifteen miles to the north. The public line continued on into southern Russia. The private line veered off, disappearing behind the endless iron-work stockade that enclosed three palaces, stands of evergreen forest, artificial lakes and hills, orchards heavy with fruit, roads meandering across velvet lawns between follies that included an authentic crimson pagoda. Battalions of servants tended this hermetically sealed Wonderland, home to Nicholas, Alexandra and their five children. Since the war they had been protected by ever-increasing numbers of gold-helmeted Imperial Guards and a swelling garrison of Cossack horsemen.

Beyond the main entrance to this stronghold ran a broad avenue lined with homes of the Imperial courtiers, estates that since the onset of the war were also more and more heavily fortified. A squad of sturdy gatekeepers with Browning pistols tucked into their bright blue sashes guarded the Paskevich grounds.

The dacha, originally built by Catherine the Great for her oversexed young Paskevich bantam rooster, had been enlarged innumerable times until the original 'cottage' was the smallest wing, a delightful maze of rooms furnished with the hotchpotch acquisitions of well-travelled generations.

Marya's favourite spot was the east-facing morning room: the deep-set windows were glazed with old, unevenly blown glass whose lavender tint softened the harsh summer light. On this particular afternoon in June she perched on the window-seat holding a book.

Paskevich had been summoned to the palace — the first time that she'd been left to her own devices since she had become his countess.

They had been married that same day he'd come for her outside the Vyborg Inn.

Twisting the unadorned platinum band, she attempted to recapture the memory of Paskevich sliding it on her finger. Try as she might, she could not conjure up any memory of the ceremony: either she'd been having a blank spell or — more likely — she was engulfed in the ice age that followed Stephan's departure. All she knew of her own wedding was hearsay evidence. Toinette chattered often about the chic elegance of having an evening ceremony in one's own private chapel while the staff of the Crimson Palace murmured in reverent awe of witnessing the patriarch himself conduct the sacrament.

Marriage . . .

Paskevich's uxorious attentiveness made her wonder if he were willing her to forget Stephan — an impossibility — or cramming experiences beyond imagining into a brief space of time. Each night before he led her into the frescoed dining-room he would present her with jewellery: some nights before they came downstairs he would fasten an heirloom around her throat or wrist or on her earlobes, great barbaric pieces with the chill of an ancient world; at other times as they ate their *zakhouski* he would casually hand her a case that held a contemporary masterpiece by Fabergé or Sazanov.

Paskevich kept his modern art at the cottage, and he would lead her through halls and rooms, pausing at naïvely brilliant or gauzy paintings to show her the difference between various French Impressionists or to explain the foibles of German Secessionists, Russian Moderns until the artists as well as their works sprang to life. The full-length portrait that Serov had painted of her several years earlier glowed against the mahogany panels of the drawing-room. It amused Paskevich to have easels set up in various parts of the grounds. She daubed like any amateur. His confident, apparently unplanned brushstrokes slashed across the canvas, imbuing landscapes with the same vivid shimmering light as the best of his collection. He danced masterfully. On warm evenings the gramophone would be cranked on the terrace and they would tango, he twisting her, turning her, bending her backwards almost to the crazy paving; at other times the elderly string trio would play waltzes as he whirled her across the marble squares of the ballroom. Later, the curtains undrawn and the gleam of a summer night silvering their naked bodies, he would make love to her. He was as insatiably erect as a Priapus. She responded unwillingly to his inventive skill and electric ardour, later wondering how she could be in love with one man yet gasp like a frenzied houri with another.

At the rumbling of wheels on gravel, she turned. Four matched black horses sped by pulling an open carriage with a pair of bewigged footmen hanging on behind. The slight distortion of antique glass added to the sense that she was looking into an earlier age. The scarlet equipage belonged to the Imperial household and the Palace livery was unchanged since the reign of Catherine the Great, whose now-fossilized protocol the Court still adhered to rigorously. For Paskevich to be driven to and from the Alexander Palace in a Court carriage was a singular honour noted — and envied — by every aristocrat currently in residence at Tsarskoe Selo.

The morning-room door opened, and

Paskevich came in, the bejewelled order of St Vladimir ablaze on his formal frock-coat. With an over-elaborate bow, he said: 'The empress sends her regards.'

'What did she want?' Marya asked.

'My pet, you can't still be fretting that she'll swoop down on you for moral turpitude?'

'You yourself told me what a prude she is.'

'The guilty flee where no man — or woman — pursueth. Her Imperial Majesty has no idea of your unsavoury past.' He took Marya's hand. 'I give you my solemn promise that she won't shove you back into the Trubetskoi.' He could drop her imprisonment easily into conversation while she was assiduous in avoiding the subject. 'My summons had nothing to do with you.'

'Then, what?'

' "A matter of grave national concern." ' Paskevich used a prim falsetto. 'First she lectured me on what every illiterate in the empire knows. We can't transport our troops, grain rots in the fields, our factories can't get raw materials — but why should you be bored, too? Finally she came to the crux. "Russia is being strangled by our inefficient railways, don't you agree?" "Nothing could be more true, your Imperial Majesty," I replied. She was transparently waiting for me to elaborate. So I pointed out that we wouldn't be in this pickle if she hadn't pushed for the appointment of our current Minister of Transport. What a dunderhead! Anti-Semitic to the point of lunacy. Imagine, he turned down an excellent plan to finance thousands of miles of track simply because a Jew suggested it!'

'You didn't say that to her!'

'But I did. In a delicate way, of course. She retorted that Rasputin, her spiritual adviser, had praised the minister as a devout and faithful soul, loyal to the monarch.'

'Where was it all leading?'

'The minister, alas, is in failing health and has handed in his resignation. I've been sounded out as his replacement.'

It took Marya several moments to digest this. 'Did Rasputin suggest you?'

He laughed. 'Hardly likely. All I can tell you with certainty is that I'm expected to perform miracles.'

'You *are* clever.'

'My dear! That sounds suspiciously like a compliment.'

'Will you do it?'

Her hand was still in his, and he raised it, kissing her wrist. 'I explained to her that I'm on my honeymoon.'

'I've never been able to avoid a fight, even an already forfeited one,' he remarked that evening as they strolled in the side-garden. 'Aren't the lilacs incredible this year? Such perfume.'

'Is that a *non sequitur* or are you being cryptic?'

'Not at all. I'd much rather stay here with you and smell the flowers.' His clever-ugly face twisted in a self-mocking smile. 'But, alas for me, I am what I am.'

'Didn't you tell me once that serving in Nicholas's Cabinet was as meaningful as reciting the alphabet backwards?'

'Probably. It sounds like me.' Putting his arm around her waist, he said ruefully: 'But, in war as in love, lost causes are my speciality.'

Three days later Paskevich left for Stavka, the tsar's military headquarters.

Marya stood on the platform of Tsarskoe Selo station gazing expressionlessly after his train until the trail of black smoke had been absorbed by the cloudless blue sky. With the final fading of smoke she felt a sharp snap at the base of her skull, as if certain vital nerves leading to and from her brain had been severed.

Paskevich had orchestrated every aspect of their marriage. The next few days she wandered through the half-hundred rooms, staring with equal blankness at paintings and bizarre antiquities plundered from exotic locales. She found herself locking and unlocking the little red leather jewel-box that held Stephan's ring. She left in Toinette's plump capable hands the clothes and jewels to lay out for the ridiculous daily sequence of changes, five in all, and let the chef write out the menus. She picked at the elaborate meals placed before her.

Mornings she spent in the study, where the robust aroma of Paskevich's tobacco lingered. She sat at his desk, unable to force herself to write even a few lines in response to his daily letters from Stavka. She did write to Boris, who, rotten correspondent that he was, had sent her a single belated congratulatory note on her marriage. Clock hands circled with tedious languor.

It must have been a week after her husband's departure when she heard two housemaids chattering in the hall. Holding her pen, she eavesdropped with a total lack of curiosity until she realized they were discussing her.

'Poor little thing,' one was saying. 'With the Master gone she's a lost soul.'

'In a trance,' the other agreed.

'Ah, how she adores him! And he her.'

'Why not, after that last dragon? Are all Americans as beautiful as an icon? Imagine what floggings we'll get if she goes into a decline.'

'Don't even think it! Quick, say a prayer to the Holy Virgin to avert evil.'

Why am I mooning about? Marya wondered; then she thought: *I'm a Volunteer War Nurse. There are military hospitals in Tsarskoe Selo.*

St Vladimir Hospital, as the discreet

393

bronze plaque stated 'Under the Patronage of Her Imperial Majesty', was a health spa compared to Pokrowski. Rather than travelling from the front packed into cattle-trucks, the wounded were transported on fully equipped sanitary trains, also endowed by the empress, arriving shaven, clean, lice-free, with freshly dressed wounds. Many were officers, and of these quite a number were tended by their own batmen or valets. When General Brusilov's Galician offensive was launched in June, however, conditions at St Vladimir's darkened dramatically. The wounded flowed in until there was no space between cots, and pallets were jammed in every passage and hallway. The staff were brutally over-burdened.

The ladies of Tsarskoe Selo discharged their patriotic obligations by organizing charitable bridge luncheons rather than enrolling as Volunteer War Nurses. Countess Paskevich, therefore, was welcomed with surprise and warmth.

Aware that her husband, like her father, would see an uncrossable abyss between the nobility and the nursing profession, Marya avoided mention of hospital duties in her infrequent letters to Stavka.

She was spooning cabbage soup into the young lieutenant whose entire face, including his eyes, was heavily bandaged when a red-headed messenger-boy barged into the ward to give her a folded note:

Have you a few minutes for an old friend? I am in the garden.

Ovruch

The porch and grass were crowded with pale convalescents shuffling about in khaki slippers and bathrobes. Ovruch, wearing a voluminous white linen blouse collared and belted with brilliant peasant embroidery, towered over the wounded like a huge, obscenely healthy, upright bear. She had not heard from him, or from Klazkha via his pen, since her marriage. They were her link to Stephan.

'Ovruch, oh, Ovruch, how good to see you.' She stood on tiptoe to press her cheek against his beard.

'You look beautiful,' he said, adding in his usual mild tone: 'But this place stinks of the Capitalist war.'

'I can't be gone long — a sister's covering for me — but why don't we take a walk?'

They ambled in companionable silence along the broad avenue that led towards the Imperial gates. Lumpy clouds sagging across the sky produced an oppressively humid heat; but Marya, cooped up for hours in the fetid wards, felt refreshed by the scent of roses and watered shrubs that drifted over walls of the estates.

'How's Klazkha?' she asked.

'Starting a committee of women comrades.'

'Good for her.' Marya gazed up at a leafy

lime branch where a bird trilled. In a murmur she asked: 'And Stephan?'

'Who knows? He's in Galicia.'

'Galicia?' She halted. They were directly in front of a tall gate carved with Muscovite designs. 'You mean with Brusilov's army?'

'The idiot went to the recruiting office in Vyborg Square and enlisted.'

'Because of me?'

'He never said. But he was a pacifist before you ran back to the Crimson Palace, Marya! To marry one of Bloody Nicholas's top henchmen!'

Marya was silent, waiting until they had passed the stone gatehouse where four burly men had been eyeing them.

'Ovruch,' she said, 'remember when Klazkha asked whether prisoners in solitary confinement had difficulties afterwards? You warned her to expect all kinds of cracked behaviour from me, including memory lapses?'

'Are you trying to tell me you had a mental blackout and woke up married?'

'I'm not positive,' Marya said honestly. Swallowing, she launched into an explanation of why she had gone to the Crimson Palace and how Stephan had found her there. 'He stormed out — not that I blame him. But for a long time I was in a complete muddle.'

'Poor little one,' Ovruch said.

The calm empathy brought tears to Marya's eyes. 'It was impossible anyway.

Stephan and I are nothing alike. He's given his life to a great cause, he's completely incorruptible. And you know me, a frivolous grasshopper.'

'Why put yourself down? You're far more one of the people than he is. Who's his family anyway? He never talks about them. What are they? Some great land-owners?'

'Oh, come on.'

'Why not? He talks and acts like the high and mighty.'

'He lives on what his writing brings. And his father was a Moscow art professor who just got by.' *So where does it come from, the wherewithal to keep the soup-kitchen going?* Branches rustled overhead. She raised her nurse's veil, letting the slight breeze cool her neck. Despite her sense of disloyalty to both her ex-lover and her husband, oh, how good it was to talk about Stephan. 'Is he an officer?'

'He didn't go that far wrong.'

They halted to watch an ambulance. Muf-fled groans came from within as the horses trotted over a rut. Was Stephan being jounced to a field-hospital where conditions were foul beyond comprehension? Was he alive?

Ovruch was watching her. He took her arm, guiding her across the street to a high pink stucco wall that ran uninterrupted by gates for nearly a quarter of a mile. 'Marya, I want you to consider this carefully before you answer. Where do your loyalties lie?'

'Politically, you mean?'

'What else?'

'There's no need to think, then. I'm the least political creature in the world.'

'You aren't enjoying this Imperialist blood-letting, are you?'

'What a question!'

'You hate tyranny, don't you? And believe every man and woman should have an equal chance?'

'Of course, but —'

'Then, now is the time to bring your beliefs to reality.'

'Are you trying to enrol me in the Bolsheviks?'

'Only if you're committed to the international class struggle,' Ovruch retorted. 'But all the groups representing the proletariat could use information from somebody close to Bloody Nicholas.'

'You mean . . . spy? Ovruch, you can't be asking me to be a detective with Paskevich?'

'Why sound so horrified?'

'He's my husband.'

'Just because some lazy useless priest' — he spat noisily — 'waved a little incense and said a few words when you weren't in your right mind doesn't mean you are yoked to him.'

I'm his wife. We share a past both good and evil. We're of the same blood. Our lives are inextricable, tangled in so many ways that I cannot fathom. 'Ovruch, I can't spy on him.'

'Why not? He shoved you into that hell on earth easily enough.' Ovruch paused, and when he spoke his voice rumbled from his massive chest. 'Listen to me, little one. The day of reckoning for this rotted empire is coming. The Romanovs and their toadies have watered the earth with our blood and fertilized their wars with our bones. But this time they've slaughtered too many millions even for our long-suffering Russian workers and peasants. I tell you, Marya, Bloody Nicholas's cronies and all the others feeding at the same trough will learn a bitter lesson when the proletariat rule.'

'The worst thing about you Bolsheviks is your slogans,' she said with a smile.

'I didn't come to Tsarskoe Selo to joke.' A motorized truck emblazoned with red crosses was coming towards them. Gripping her arm below the elbow, his huge spatulate fingers digging into her grey-striped uniform, Ovruch nodded towards the approaching ambulance. 'Marya Fedorovna, there are the results of this Capitalist-Imperialist war. Does your husband give a damn about the massacred millions? Do any of the other pampered drones? I tell you it's time to choose which side you're on.' He released her.

She rubbed the bruised flesh through her sleeve. 'I can't ever see people the way you do. I'm not saying I'm right or excusing myself but I simply can't love or hate according to politics or patriotism. To me each person is an individual case.' As she spoke, she accepted that her emotions would be far more disciplined were she able to follow a doctrine that applied rigid classifications. A good radical, a vicious Monarchist, a wishy-washy liberal. Or, like Klazkha, to lump all men as the enemy. Picking a leaf and tearing it along the veins, she said: 'It wouldn't do any good for me to try to get information from Paskevich. He can see right through me and he'd know exactly what I was about.'

They turned back to St Vladimir's. As they neared the hospital's grey wood sprawl, Ovruch said: 'Marya, you're my friend, and I say this in friendship. Go back to your own country. In America, for the time being any-way, you'll have the luxury of standing apart from the world struggle.'

By the end of the afternoon, when Marya reached the Paskevich 'cottage', the clouds were a blackish purple. She was being for-mally served her solitary dessert when the first lightning flared, and during the ensuing peals of thunder rain began pounding on the roof of the broad veranda.

As she climbed the stairs to her rooms, a great bolt of lightning split the universe and the electricity went off. At this moment of blackness, she heard the front door burst open. The rain-scented darkness rushed around her, and she was chilled with an atavistic fear of invisible beings that dwell in the night. Her heart dragged in time with the long, slow-fading growls of thunder. A wild blue flash zigzagged, silhouetting the short heavy-shouldered figure.

'Paskevich?'

In response he stamped up the stairs, pulling her against his rain-drenched suit in a crushing embrace.

The night's pleasures had drowned out the storm and made them both languorous, so they breakfasted in bed. The earlier downpour, rather than cooling the air, had intensified the humidity, and the bedroom remained oppressive even after Paskevich had ordered the butler to open the windows. Nibbling on a fresh roll spread with butter churned this morning, Marya rested back in the pillows while Paskevich told her he had returned home with the emperor, who was sympathetic to newlywed ardour.

'You're unusually quiet,' Paskevich said.

'I was thinking . . .'

'About what?' His quick dark eyes were fixed on her.

She shifted on the rumpled sheet so that their legs were no longer touching. The tray wobbled, and she reached out to prevent the bud vase from falling. 'The war,' she said. 'At Stavka do they care that there are so many casualties?'

'Quite a number of whom you've seen at St Vladimir's?'

'You know I'm working there?'

'Oh, I've known from your first day, but have been waiting patiently to be informed.' He spoke with sardonic detachment as if he were floating above the besotted spouse and the young wife who kept secrets from him.

'I should have mentioned it.' Marya ruefully touched his stubbled jaw. 'Tell me about Stavka.' A question that came out easily enough but she knew would have made her face burn had she gone along with Ovruch's request. 'Is the railroad knot being untangled?'

'Why, splendidly. I make my suggestions, and His Imperial Majesty listens. He peers carefully at my maps which show pins where rolling stock is needed and where track must be repaired in order to ship Brusilov the supplies he desperately needs, and to transport raw materials to the factories, to bring food to the cities. I write down names of *chinovniks* who could expedite matters. He gravely takes my lists. And — Marya, you won't believe this miracle — he actually promoted one of my recommendations. That's an excellent percentage, isn't it? One out of five hundred?'

'Who does he appoint, then?'

'He relies on the pouch.'

'What do you mean?'

'The pouch, the leather pouch that sometimes brings your letters, and always the tsarina's.'

Now Marya did flush. 'I just don't have much to write about.'

'*She* always does. She writes to her Nicky two or three times a day.'

'Maybe her advice is good.'

'And maybe bears can fly. She repeats what Rasputin tells her. She's convinced her holy man can look through flesh and bone to spot a "good soul", which in both their eyes means a fanatical Monarchist with an inclination to kiss Rasputin's smelly feet. Mundane details like senility, dishonesty and inept stupidity don't enter into their calculations.'

'She went to the trouble of appointing you.'

'*Touché* — but, my dear, remember I'm from a long line of consummate courtiers. It's in the blood, knowing how to deal with hysterical, meddlesome royal bitches.'

'Aren't you being hard on her?'

Paskevich had been heaping strawberry jam on a bite of *buloshki,* and now he popped the morsel in Marya's mouth.

'Do you know the real reason Nicholas dissolved the Duma?' he asked. 'They were debating the Rasputin problem. The Romanovs all keep warning Nicholas to rid himself and the empress of their greasy "spiritual counsellor", so now he avoids his brothers and seldom visits his mother. Can you believe it? The Imperial Family and the Empire torn apart by one filthy, lecherous Siberian peasant?'

'Is it that bad?'

'Worse.' Paskevich shrugged his thick shoulders. 'My pet, the only words of wisdom my father passed on to me were "Never discuss politics in bed with a pretty woman".' Dishes rattled as he lowered the breakfast-tray on to the white linen towel beside the bed. Putting his arms around her, he said: 'Welcome me home like you did last night, my dearest.'

Later in the day, after receiving a telephone call from the matron, Marya stormed into her husband's study. The secretaries scuttled out.

'You sent in my resignation!'

Paskevich wore his most irritating smile of amusement. 'Do sit down, my dear. The afternoon's too hot to bolt about.'

'How dare you! St Vladimir's needs me.'

'Oh, we've done our bit. I've endowed thirty-seven hospitals for the military.'

Briefly taken aback by this hitherto unmentioned largess, she rallied: 'There are not enough nurses by a long shot.'

'Then, why not send your maid to do good works one or two mornings a week?'

'She has no training.'

'While you — stop me if I'm wrong — have an all-encompassing medical education of six weeks of lectures.' He leaned back in his chair. 'Marya, you're my countess, not a ministering angel.'

'I knew you'd be just like my father.'

'For once Alexiev was right,' Paskevich

said. 'So let's get this straight. You will not change soiled linen for peasants or empty their bedpans or —'

She never heard what else he forbade. She had slammed the study door behind her.

Paskevich had been home four days, and they were in the summerhouse sipping lemonade, when a stout Imperial equerry puffed along the path, his bulbous perspiring face the same crimson as his cape. Doffing his feathered, tri-cornered hat with a deep bow, he handed Paskevich an envelope crested with the Imperial eagle.

Our train will return to Headquarters at four this afternoon.

Nicholas

'So soon?' she said.

'Does that mean you'll miss me?'

She would, but recalling his high-handed foreclosure of her nursing career, she said: 'I'll be bored, that's all.'

He laughed, his eyes glinting maliciously. 'Good. You can amuse yourself by writing long letters to your adored husband.'

Chapter Thirty

Without nursing or Paskevich to fill her days, Marya was battered by fears for Stephan: she worried about his safety just as she had when she was buried in the Trubetskoi. Then, though, ignorance had fuelled her fears, and now she knew too much.

Stephan was with Brusilov's army.

Earlier this year, the French and British, planning for the Somme offensive, had set about coercing their Russian ally into taking the burden off the Western Front by launching a simultaneous attack on the Austro-Hungarian armies in Galicia. The tsar, as commander-in-chief, had fallen in with the strategy, giving command of the Galician campaign to General Brusilov. A superb tactician and meticulous planner, yet also a dashing warrior, Brusilov had routed the enemy in every battle. These victories, however, came at a high cost. The death toll was appalling, severely wounded jammed every hospital. Marya had nursed Brusilov's men, the blind, the crippled, the catatonic, the gas victims coughing out what remained of their shredded lungs, the limbless.

If Stephan were a casualty, as a resident of Petrograd he would be listed there. Every afternoon that hot and disastrously triumphant August, Marya was on the Nevsky

Prospekt scanning the long, hastily printed lists.

Jotting a note to her husband, she mentioned casually that she was on the train going into town for a bit of shopping.

Paskevich fired back: 'Buy whatever you want. Buy more than you want. But have the merchants come to you in Tsarskoe Selo. Reports of unrest have been pouring in from Petrograd. If you feel absolutely compelled to shop there, take the car and keep Ilich with you at all times.'

Ilich, the under-chauffeur, one of the brawny young men from Paskevich's estates who served as guards, was romancing the buxom parlourmaid, the household gossip. The last thing Marya needed was to have her preoccupation with casualties broadcast among the staff.

She shredded the letter into a waste-paper basket.

Paskevich's next letter started: 'Marya, you tore up my last letter, didn't you? Remember this, then. You are my wife, and as such have a legal obligation to obey me. I do not permit you to endanger yourself. You may not go to Petrograd. This is an order. Stay away from Petrograd.'

Male heads turned after Marya. The floating white linen of her summer dress gave an illusion of coolness as she moved across the station square. Heat rose from the cobbles through the thin soles of her shoes as she made a wide circle around the equestrian statue of Alexander where knots of disgruntled men lounged. With little in the way of raw materials reaching armaments factories, more and more workers were being laid off.

Reaching the Nevsky, Marya took the shady side, folding her parasol to avoid jabbing anyone in the mass of unemployed loiterers, frazzled women lugging string shopping-bags, water-sellers, vendors with trays of useless gewgaws. A ragged urchin tugged at Marya's skirt. The instant she dropped a coin into his grimy paw, jostling waifs surrounded her. She gave until she had no more change. Moving on, she paused to stuff a five-rouble note in a blind veteran's cap, she overpaid for one of the fanned-out cigarettes in front of a legless sailor, she selected a pencil from the tray of a one-armed Cossack. Her mind was all smoke and flame and regret as she conjured up the long, narrow room at the Vyborg Inn and Stephan with tears on his cheeks as he sat at the table drafting a leaflet that urged the tsar's government to follow the example of all other civilized nations and grant pensions to wounded veterans, war widows, war orphans.

As she neared Doblin's Butter Shop she became part of the waiting crowd. Jumping on tiptoe, she glimpsed a bow-legged corporal pasting up long, tightly printed sheets that covered the entire window and part of a wall. A Georgian crossed himself. 'May God have mercy! Today's list is a mile long.' A modestly dressed older woman collapsed in tears, and a young boy whose jaw trembled drew her from the crush.

Marya nudged her way forward, glimpsing her haunted reflection in the window glass.

There were no Strakhovs.

Relief blurred her vision as she passed the Europa Hotel on her way to the upper-storey tea-salon where she and Miss Dunning had often taken Lally. In a poignant reverie, she dawdled over an exorbitantly priced éclair and a pot of coffee. Her table overlooked the Nevsky. The boulevard below was a river of caps and kerchiefs, hardly a hat to be seen: even in wartime the upper classes fled during the summer, leaving the city to the poor. Trams disgorged shabby families, servant girls strolled arm-in-arm with sweethearts on leave, a one-armed veteran kneeled on the pavement to chalk gawdy likenesses of the emperor and empress. A hurdy-gurdy appeared, burbling while the dressed-up little monkey held out a cap to the circle of spectators: despite the crowd's obvious poverty, kopeks flipped into the miniature fez.

Iron shutters began clattering over shop windows. With a start Marya realized that the wall clock showed five past seven. The train to Tsarskoe Selo left in less than thirty minutes.

On the Nevsky, traffic had come to a halt. Children were being hoisted on to shoulders, and heads turned expectantly towards a rhythmic tootling and drumming.

The band swung smartly by, followed by mounted Gardes whose immaculate white uniforms and glossily curried, high-stepping horses couldn't have contrasted more sharply with the group of Russian conscripts in leg irons. Unshaven, unkempt, wearing ragged filthy uniforms, the captives staggered and lunged to keep up the rapid pace — a difficult task hampered as they were by their shackles and the long, heavy chain that linked them together at the right wrist.

'Papa, why're they all trussed together like that?' piped a child.

'Deserters,' the father explained. 'They're being paraded, then they go before a court martial.'

'If you ask me,' shrilled a woman's voice, 'it's the wrong way round. The ones who ought to get their necks stretched are the rich smug cowards on their fine horses.'

'The Gardes're here to defend us.'

'Defend us, hah!' a factory worker bellowed. 'They're garrisoned in Petrograd for one reason: to protect that German bitch and her greasy lover. Them poor souls in chains, they shed blood for us.'

'And what's their reward? Hanging.'

The good nature of the crowd had curdled into anger on behalf of the deserters. The briskly played march couldn't drown out insults shouted at the Gardes, who stared fixedly above their horses' ears. A drunk lifted his porter's smock, cackling as he urinated in a steady stream across the chalked Imperial portraits. A narrow-shouldered eel of a grocery clerk slammed a long, hooked pole against the flag blazoned with a Romanov eagle, and as the fringed cloth rustled downwards more than a few cheered.

A tiny, shawled crone crossed herself. 'It's God's will that the poor suffer.'

'Nothing to do with God, old woman,' snapped the thin grocery clerk. 'It's the rich. They bleed us dry, the rich.' He glared at Marya.

Suddenly aware that her pretty summer dress and gauze-swathed white Leghorn hat made her as conspicuous as a beacon, she edged her way towards a side-street. A blow caught her in the small of the back. She stumbled into the gutter. Her hat flew off. Fingers shaking, she bent to retrieve it. A motherly-looking peasant woman aimed a foot at her buttocks.

Laughter bubbling around her, Marya crumpled.

Her jaw hit the stone kerb. Dazed, surrounded by milling bast boots and crude iron-toed shoes, she felt herself sliding backwards into the Trubetskoi courtyard. There, surrounded by demonstrators' feet, she had looked up to see Stephan. A second kick, this one involuntary, sideswiped her ribcage. *Get up,* she commanded herself

411

woozily. *Get up! Stephan's with Brusilov's army and there's not a chance he'll appear like a vision in shining armour. If you stay down here, you'll be trampled to death.* She managed to push herself up on to her knees, then callused hands were drawing her to her feet.

'Thank you. I'm ever so grateful —'

'No time for yammering,' muttered the short bulgy-eyed man who had helped her. 'Get away from here. Go!' He jabbed her between the shoulder-blades.

His shove and her own fear propelling her, she pushed her way back to the alley, which was not crowded. She began to trot, edging around a barrow that reeked of stale fish: the fishmonger and his three customers swivelled to watch her. Not realizing that it was the blood flowing down her forehead and jaw that attracted their interest, she fled mindlessly until her lungs were ready to burst. Reaching a barrel that held cholera-safe, boiled water, she slumped forward from the waist like a sprinter who has passed the finishing tape. With each shuddering gasp a dagger of pain cut into her lungs. Her brain synchronized with her exhalations, spurting out thoughts that were peculiarly rational. *The kick must've cracked a rib. There's blood on my dress. Yes, my forehead and chin were cut when I fell. I've lost my purse. I have no money, no return ticket. Anyway, with those angry workers it's a mistake to go within a mile of the station.*

Where, then? How far's the Crimson Palace? A pair of white-capped, white-collared sailors, ordinary seamen, were heading towards her. She jogged in the opposite direction, zigzagging towards the Crimson Palace.

Her feet burned with every step. Each breath tormented her.

She was in a well-maintained neighbourhood. Few lights showed at the windows — the inhabitants must be in their country places. The droshky clattering towards her seemed a mirage until the horse defecated — the pungent, hay-like aroma of reality. The driver reined at her signalling hand.

'The Crimson Palace,' she said.

Lifting his tall buckled cap, the driver squinted down. 'Rushed out after a fight with your man, did you, eh? Well, my damaged pretty, first show me the colour of your money, then I'll take you to the Crimson Palace.'

About to respond that she was the Countess Paskevich, she recalled the ugly crowd. 'There was a disturbance on the Nevsky, I got hurt and lost my purse. But don't worry, you'll be paid when we get there.'

'Paid when I get there.' Falsetto-voiced, he mimicked her. 'That old chestnut? Not bloody likely.' He flicked the reins, and the mare jumped forward.

Marya's chest felt as if it was encased in an iron maiden, her heels were blistered and her thighs wobbled like rubber as she

413

limped up the side-steps of the Crimson Palace. She banged the immense brass dolphin. The door stayed shut.

Summoning her last reserve of strength, she tottered the quarter-mile to the courtyard entry. This time a *dvornik* edged open the door. Peering through the crack into the White Night, he raised a bottle. His arm dropped before the vodka reached his mouth. 'Countess,' he muttered. 'We weren't ess-pecting you . . .' Opening the door wide, he slumped drunkenly on to his stool.

She kicked off her tattered shoes, leaving them adrift on the dimly gleaming ocean of parquetry.

No lights came on in her rooms. A servant must have pilfered the electric bulbs. Dust-sheeted furniture lurked like hump-backed predators. There was no response to the service bell. With a whimpering grunt, she shoved down the folded mattress and collapsed on the bare ticking.

'I'm sorry, Paskevich,' she said in a flat drugged tone. Her broken rib was taped, the cut on her jaw sutured, the graze on her forehead covered with a plaster.

Paskevich, telegraphed by the frightened housekeeper, had just arrived from Stavka.

'No more so than I,' he retorted.

'Sorry . . . you had to come so far . . .'

His eyes glittering, he watched her sink back into her laudanum-induced slumber

414

before he stalked from the room.

He administered a beating to the grizzled footman who had deserted his post in the hall. The buck-toothed girl hired to tend the bellboard prostrated herself, attempting to kiss his well-polished shoe, but he dismissed her without references. The *dvorniks* he beat with his trained fists before despatching them as well as the housekeeper, who had enjoyed a snug berth at the Crimson Palace for over twenty years, to the rotting, never-used palace that crouched in the gloomy depths of the Paskevich forests on the upper Volga.

When he returned to Marya's room, her mind was still imprisoned by the opiate but she was sitting propped with cushions while Toinette, summoned from Tsarskoe Selo, chattered as she arranged flowers on the vanity unit. As Paskevich came in, the maid discreetly glided to the dressing-room.

He gripped the footboard. 'Why were you here in Petrograd?'

Emanations of her husband's unsated rage reached through Marya's drugged lethargy. 'There was a disturbance on the Nevsky.'

'I ordered you to stay away,' he said. 'Now, answer my question.'

She bit back the response, *I came here to find out whether Strakhov — Stephan — was on the casualty-lists.* 'What's so wrong with doing some shopping?'

'Merchants must have more forbearance nowadays. So much shopping, and thus far I've received no bills.'

'Don't take that tone with me. I'm not a servant.'

'A shame, that.' Paskevich continued to scrutinize her. 'I have a meeting with Sir George Buchanan. When I return you'll tell me exactly what brought you here.'

After he had left the room for his discussions with the British ambassador, she lay staring out of the window. Flocks of sparrows wheeled across the hard blue sky.

I'm going closer to Brusilov's army, she thought hazily. The decision made no sense: she'd have no information about Stephan there, while here there were the casualty-lists with their grim news — or absence of news.

When she awoke the next morning, the decision, whether or not it was logical, remained firm.

Paskevich came by after she had nibbled on her breakfast, by now his anger no longer spraying in all directions. He placed a flat leather jewel-case from Sazanov's on the bedside table.

She didn't open it. 'It was a mistake to come up to town. But, without you around and without nursing, I was going crazy.' She drew a breath. 'When I'm well I'll apply to Princess Hélène's field-hospital.'

He gave her another of those long, unreadable glances. 'In Galicia, isn't it?'

'Yes,' she said, and flushed.

The following day Paskevich received a telegram that Tsar Nicholas had summoned his ministers to an urgent cabinet meeting at Stavka. In farewell he took Marya in his arms, holding her a little apart so as not to crush her taped ribcage. 'I hate to leave like this.'

'Since the emperor can't rule without you, I'll have to make do.'

'Marya, as soon as you're well, go back to Tsarskoe Selo.'

Caught up by the tenderness of his grasp and the naked concern in his eyes, she didn't argue with the way he was side-stepping her resolve to nurse at the front. 'You're my lord and master,' she said.

Cocking an eyebrow, he laughed.

By the end of the week the bruises on her face had dwindled and it no longer hurt to breathe. Monday morning, she awoke with a sense of purpose. It was not yet seven, and Toinette wouldn't bring her breakfast for two hours. With her taped chest it was difficult to raise her arms to dress. She buttoned a loose sailor-blouse over her camisole and squashed on a tam.

She took a motorized taxi to the vast flat where Princess Hélène lived and administered her hospital. Despite the early hour, secretaries bustled and typewriters clattered.

The princess's grey hair was drawn back into an uncompromising bun, the stern expression of her brown eyes was magnified by gold-rimmed spectacles. Because of the early hour, she offered rolls and coffee. 'It's a pleasure to meet you, Countess Paskevich. So kind of you to call. Especially in view of your accident.'

'I'm completely recovered,' Marya interjected.

'What good news.'

'I'm here to offer my services.'

The princess took a sip and set down her cup. 'We have many kinds of fund-raising activities.'

'I want to nurse.' Marya slid her Volunteer War Nurse diploma in and out of her bag, not giving the princess time to see her alias.

'I'm afraid we can't use you in the hospital.'

'It's true that Volunteers aren't fully trained, but I've had nursing experience — quite a lot of it.'

'Your qualifications aren't the problem.' The princess removed her spectacles, appearing less authoritarian. 'My child, you're American, and possibly you don't know our laws. Here every wife is legally her husband's ward. A few days ago Count Paskevich did me the honour of a visit. Need I say more? I must bow to his objections.'

Anger pounded at Marya's temples. Paskevich had done more than side-step her decision, he'd tried to bury it. Well, she had an answer for that! Thanking Princess

418

Hélène, she took a droshky to Znaminiskii Square where the Bureau for Military Hospitals was located. She gave a harried clerk the diploma and matching false identification documents that Stephan had procured.

At six-thirty that same evening Marya Nizhni was boarding the train to Pskov.

Chapter Thirty-one

Pskov, some hundred miles south-west of Petrograd, was well behind the lines. However, the War Department had designated it 'Nursing Headquarters for the Front', requisitioning all public buildings to serve the wounded. Marya, assigned to Military Hospital No. 5, formerly the Girls' Ecclesiastical School, knew within her first hour that the two other hospitals where she had nursed were earthly paradises compared to this. The over-crowding, the abominable food, the lack of sanitation and the indolent corruption sickened her, but it was the cheeky disregard for life that drew her rage. Those in charge exuded the belief that wounded officers were sent there as an annoyance to the staff, while enlisted men were expected to do their duty and die.

In her first letter to Paskevich, Marya apologized for her moonlight flit, requesting that he address any letter he might send to Sister Nizhni.

Within two days his answer was in her hands.

My dearest,
There is no need to beg my pardon. We will discuss how to better the conditions at Hospital No. 5 upon your return

to Tsarskoe Selo. I long to hold you.

Dearest Paskevich,
It's impossible for me to leave. The need for nurses is worse by far than imagined . . .

In every war the conditions are worse than anyone can imagine . . .

I have been promoted. And to go from Volunteer to Head Operating Theatre Nurse is a real coup.

It is a useless gesture to play ministering angel, Marya. You are to return home. I order you to return to Tsarskoe Selo.

You of all people know how immense the casualties are. The need for nurses is desperate. There are never enough surgical supplies. Please sell my pearls and other jewels and forward the proceeds.

I, as your husband, control all property within the marriage. The pearls, therefore, are not yours to sell.

I am ashamed to have made any request on behalf of those who give their bodies and lives to protect elderly, privileged men behind the lines.

She received no answer.

421

My dearest Paskevich,
When I wrote that letter I was seeing red. Those were ugly things to write. But supplies and nurses are so desperately needed here.

To Countess Paskevich,
This is to inform you that a million roubles have been placed at the military's disposal for use in hospitals in the Petrograd area. His Excellency has requested that I remind you that even though you have elected not to remain under his roof you are still his wife and he expects you to conduct yourself as befits your station.
I am respectfully yours,
T KISHINSKY
Secretary to
Count Ivan Arkadievich Paskevich

Marya was reading this icily dictated letter in the quarters she shared with two other Volunteers. Though much envied by the regular nursing staff, who were billeted in town more than a mile's walk away, the stone-floored basement cloakroom was far from heaven. The dankness and odour of earth pervaded everything, coat-pegs were the only place to store clothes, the straw pallets attracted insects.

Marya reached for the coal-oil lamp. It was ten o'clock in the evening. Time to relieve the ward sister. Spying was the favoured sport in Military Hospital No. 5, so she thrust the letter in the blazing furnace, which she passed on her way upstairs. Pinned to the main hall's bulletin-board was the front page of the *Pskov Evening Gazette:* 'BRUSILOV'S VICTORIOUS ARMIES SETTLE IN FOR WINTER.'

The columns below were heavily censored, but everyone in Pskov knew that the blanked-out passages were criticism of the tsar. For the first time Nicholas was being publicly lambasted. On 27 September, after Russian casualties in Galicia had topped a million and a quarter, the empress had nagged her husband into silencing the victorious bugles. Brusilov, cognizant of who had halted his advance, openly expressed his angered frustration. His troops, rather than being grateful that their slaughter had ended, chorused their general's complaints. In Pskov, as elsewhere, the hitherto revered Nicholas was derided as a hen-pecked cuckold, and boorish jokes about him swarmed thicker than the flies.

Marya had reached the buff-painted door to the former gymnasium, now the ward for officers below the rank of major. Most of the old aristocratic officer corps fertilized the war's earlier battlegrounds, and the great percentage of the wounded in this large gym were sons of the petty bourgeoisie or peasants commissioned in the field.

The bulldog-faced ward sister marked her place in her yellow-covered novel and rushed out rather than conferring with her replacement, as was the regulation. Marya, wiped off the stained trolley, loading it with the medications and equipment she would need on her round. Setting her lamp on the upper shelf, she wheeled between closely ranked cots that receded into the shadows as she passed. The murmurous sounds of restless tossing, snores and creaking cots were punctuated by sobs and groans from the gas cases. Chlorine gas suffocated its victims. Mustard gas destroyed both inside and outside, the entire skin surface oozed, the lungs wept away their mucous membranes, the destruction of the stomach lining brought on continuous vomiting. The wounded bore their agonies with incredible stoicism. Come nightfall, though, suffering assumed physical dimensions, turning into a shaggy beast ready to pounce on the vulnerable with excruciatingly sharp teeth. Most deaths occurred on this shift. Marya never could reconcile herself to death. She took each death, no matter how welcome or inevitable, as a refutation of her nursing ability.

One of the more remote cots was surrounded by a canvas screen. A screen could mean either that the patient was recovering from surgery or that he was dying. Last night a diminutive Muslim had lain there comatose. Taking her lamp around the screen, she saw that the Muslim had returned to Allah's bosom.

The new case, a tall man, appeared to be sleeping, but you could never tell. As she bent over him shadows veered wildly and her lamp nearly fell.

He opened glazed and luminous blue eyes. 'Marya,' he said without surprise.

Carefully setting the lamp on the metal commode, she kneeled. Face rigid, lips quivering, she murmured: 'Stephan.'

'Been expecting you,' he said.

'Who told you I was nursing here?'

He shook his head. Despite the heavy dark stubble, he had the look of a weary bewildered child. 'Just expected you.'

She touched his forehead, feeling the heat. But the remark didn't necessarily mean he was delirious. Wasn't that why she was here? To look for him among the wounded?

'The light . . .' he whispered.

'Does it bother you, darling?'

'Glows . . . makes a halo round your face . . .' His breath came more rapidly as if he were struggling to draw air into his lungs.

She reached for his wrist. Under her fingertips the pulse raced, rapid and weak. She shook the thermometer, carefully edging it under his arm. A hundred and three point seven! She took the chart clipped to the foot of his cot, scanning it.

'Strakhov, Stephan Leonodovich, Capt. Infantry. Field commission. B. 18 April 1889. Unmarried. Parents dec. No next of kin. Bayonet wound traversing chest. Left lung

pierced. Prognosis, guarded. Surgery performed by Dr Golder.'

Golder. Thank God, Golder.

Golder was the only trustworthy surgeon
in the unit. The chief often operated in a
drunken stupor, three of the staff were well-
meaning incompetents, another had a case
of nerves so bad that his scalpel shook. And
then there was Golder. A touchy Jew from
Minsk with a broad, clean-shaven Slavic
face, Golder insisted that his instruments
and draping-cloths be sterile. The other doctors called him 'Our Fuss-budget Israelite'
to his face.

For a brief moment she thought of Golder,
and what she knew about the obstacles he
faced. Russia had always been legally as
well as socially anti-Semitic. Legislation restricted the Empire's millions of Jews to the
Pale of Settlement, a strip of land that ran
from the Baltic Sea to the Black Sea: to
travel or live elsewhere in the Empire they
must request a pass. Only a handful of their
children were admitted to Russian schools,
and the Russian language was not permitted to be taught in their own primary
schools, which effectively barred them from
a higher education. Dr Golder had attended
a Russian primary school as part of the
minuscule quota.

'Marya?' Stephan whispered. 'Come here.'

Replacing the charts she returned to kneel
at the head of the cot. As they gazed at each
other, the reflection of the shaded oil-lamp

glowed in both pairs of eyes. All that was extraneous had been swept away. The bitter scene at the Crimson Palace, her marriage, the mask of secrecy he wore. Pride, hurt, jealousy, the war, politics, all went by the board. The smells and sounds of desperately ill men in the overcrowded ward vanished. All that existed was the joy of seeing each other. *How simple things are,* thought Marya.

'I love you,' he murmured.

'And *I* love *you.*'

'Marya . . .' His voice was so faint that she had to bend to hear him. 'Why the screen?'

'Because you were operated on today.'

'Am I . . . going west?'

'No! You aren't!' she whispered fiercely. 'I won't let you die!'

'The Germans! Look out for the Germans!' shrilled a terrified voice.

'Have to finish my rounds. Be back as soon as I can.' She clasped his hand. He attempted to return the pressure, but his hand fell back. Close to tears at his weakness, she murmured: 'Rest. Don't try to stay awake till I get back.'

'Screen . . .'

She folded it for the night orderly to move.

Later, she tiptoed across the hall to the dispensary, glancing around before she slid the key from her pocket. Nurses were not meant to have keys. The unit's chief, the drunk, exchanged surgical supplies for imported whisky, the matron bedecked herself

427

with jewellery bought with laudanum, so Marya had no compunction when she pilfered medication for the wounded in her care. Pocketing a phial of aspirin, she returned to the ward. 'These'll bring down your fever.' She lifted Stephan's head so that he could swallow.

At six the generators throbbed and the overhead lights blazed. It was time for the shift-change, but nurses and orderlies straggled in over the course of the hour. Normally when they were all on duty, Marya would totter down the stone stairs to her makeshift bed. Today, she ran to Stephan's bedside.

His temperature had dropped to a hundred. In her delight, she clasped the thermometer overhead, her swollen feet moving in a little jig.

Patients and nurses turned to gape.

Halting her exhibition, she said: 'Captain Strakhov's an old friend . . . of my brother.'

She dragged a chair over to his bed. Later, she repeated the same explanation when she questioned Dr Golder.

'Your brother's friend is a lucky man, Sister,' the doctor said in his precise Russian. 'An inch higher and the bayonet would have severed the main artery. Now we must be on guard for infection.'

Marya drew a shuddery breath. The death toll from infection at Military Hospital No. 5 was notorious.

Chapter Thirty-two

The matron, a stickler when it came to nurses' decorum, was not in the least fussy when it came to sterile procedures. Marya tended Stephan herself: she changed his dressings, flinching as she syringed out the gory wound with peroxide filched from the dispensary; she boiled his pus-filled drainage tube; she scrounged new lint dressings.

Four days after their surgery, the men were carried upstairs to the erstwhile headmistress's office: here, to the tune of screamed curses, orderlies ripped off bandages so that the surgical team could examine their handiwork. Marya went upstairs with Stephan, easing off his dressing with a lotion that gave off a heavy aroma of chlorine. Dr Golder bent over his neat tiny stitches, then nodded to the orderlies, who grappled the half-naked Stephan from the table. Stephan couldn't repress his drawn-out groan.

The brevity rather than the roughness of the examination disturbed Marya. Once Stephan was safely back in his bed, she returned upstairs. Golder, the only doctor on the team without an office, sat on a bench in the corridor as he made out his reports. 'You told me yourself that Captain Strakhov's wound could easily become infected,' she said in a low angry tone. 'That puffiness looked suspicious to me. What about septi-caemia?'

'Possibly you would be reassured', Dr Golder said, clipping his words, 'if one of the other surgeons took over.'

How could she have forgotten his touchi-ness? 'I didn't mean that as criticism. Why, Dr Golder, you're the best there is here. By miles.'

'Sister,' the matron said, and sombrely drew her upper lip over her long, yellowish teeth. 'It has come to my attention that you are spending a great deal of time in the Junior Officer Ward. By now you are well aware of the regulations against familiarity with the patients.'

'If you mean Captain Strakhov, he's an old friend of my brother's.'

'In my hospital we obey the rules. Nurses neither form sentimental attachments nor renew friendships. Each patient is treated the same.' The matron fingered a pearl ear-ring recently exchanged for the week's sup-ply of opium pills. 'And, Sister, as you also know, regulations state clearly that nurses' skirts must touch the floor. Please let down your hems immediately.'

As Marya closed the green baize door, her eyes filled with angry tears. That this larce-nous martinet had power over her, over Stephan — over all the helpless wounded unlucky enough to be sent to Hospital No. 5! Knuckling away her tears, Marya stuck out her tongue at the door.

After the midday meal — watery bortsch, salt fish and black bread followed by stewed prunes — she returned to the former gymnasium.

A gloomy afternoon with rain pecking at the windows, the ward was filled with shadows. Stephan was shaved and sitting up. Wearing a wide-collared hospital gown, he might have been posing for a romantic chiaroscuro painting of a poet — say, Eugene Onegin.

'Surprised?' he asked. He was pale — so pale that the little scar — her scar — stood out like a pink thread.

Swallowing, she said: 'It's much too early for you to be sitting up.'

'I'm better,' he said. 'Much.'

He reached for her hand. His grip was stronger, and she felt a shock of warmth go through her body. Her breath caught. They gazed at each other for a long minute. Then the door opened and orderlies wheeled in carts with the chamber-pots. Marya, without a farewell, went to help them.

Stephan watched her recede. He still saw her eyes — *twin silvery moons,* he thought. How could he feel this clean steely passion? Had useless emotions like jealousy and bitterness been cauterized by the battlegrounds? This thought led him, unwillingly, back to visual images: bodies in the contortions of the damned; limbs sticking up from the mud; men who dwelled in sodden trenches until the mire, their uniforms and flesh became a single brown element; weaponless men ordered to capture Big Berthas; men evaporating into a red haze. At times he'd been convinced that he should befriend the hordes of fat grey rats: they were all that flourished at the front.

He had found himself incapable of blaming the enemy, or his superior officers — even the inept and arrogant. Russia was ruled by a Supreme Autocrat, and therefore it followed that responsibility could fall on one pair of shoulders alone. He glanced at the tsar's photograph, which hung tilted downwards between windows, a position in which the protective glass refracted light and the bearded benign features were difficult to make out. *My half-brother . . . No man should ever wield so much power over other human beings.*

He meant no evil to Nicholas, yet since reading Irena's scrawled letter it had become an obligation of his blood to remove all Russian rulers from omnipotence. Stephan's right hand clenched involuntarily, as if he were taking an oath.

That night, after Marya had finished her rounds, Stephan asked: 'What's happening at the front?'

An often-repeated query in the wards. Although Marya would have imagined that the patients would have lost interest in the cataclysm that had maimed them, taken their limbs, sight, lungs, sex organs, they followed the war with wholehearted avidity.

'I haven't been paying much attention,' she said.

'Did you ever?' Though his retort wasn't particularly humorous, it was a reminder of their shared past, and they both smiled.

'I'll bring you a newspaper.'

There was only one liberal paper available locally, the *Pskov Evening Gazette*, so she slogged into town under bleak low-hanging clouds to buy it. Stephan scanned the four smeared sheets, rereading an article on the second page which revealed as false slander the rumours that Rasputin, 'spiritual adviser to the empress', had met with the empress's brother, Prince Ernst of Hesse, to discuss a separate peace between Germany and Russia.

'Spreading a rumour by denying it is an old trick,' he told Marya. 'If this story got in, the censors are losing control.'

'I've noticed that the talk's openly anti-tsar now.'

For a moment his eyes were veiled and dark shadows cut into his face. Then he let the newspaper rustle to the worn floorboards. 'Marya, you must've realized why I enlisted.'

'Of course I do,' she said with a sigh. 'It still cuts me to ribbons.'

'Don't feel that way. I haven't regretted my decision. Not that I've changed my mind

about pacifism. What could be more sense-
less than this wholesale misery and death?
But the Army's given me an opportunity to
live with working-class Russians and peasants.'

'And how many opportunities to get killed?'
He shrugged. 'I should've trusted you.'

'Who can blame you? If only I hadn't let
him . . .' Her voice trailed away. In the two
weeks that Stephan had been in the ward
neither of them had mentioned Paskevich,
yet he was always beside the cot, a shapeless, formless yet dominating presence.

After a few moments he said: 'I sometimes
wonder what happened to Gingerboy.'

'He's on the next of his nine lives, enjoying
the attention of a pretty Manx.'

Despite their chuckles, Paskevich's aura
remained.

At the end of the week there was a hail-
storm, but foul weather couldn't stop
crowds from lining the streets to welcome
Brusilov. At Military Hospital No. 5 the
general was greeted with applause and
cheers. Tightly corseted, grey moustaches
fiercely waxed, he marched ahead of his
aides into the Junior Officers' Ward. With
a borrowed safety-pin, he fastened a newly
minted Cross of St George to Stephan's
dressing-gown before reading in a loud pa-
rade-ground voice how the decoration had
been earned: Marya learned that Stephan
had received his near-fatal wound rescu-

ing a wounded private from no man's land.

During the warm months Pskov, with its new extensions bulging like warts from the *de facto* hospitals and rows of ugly military shacks, with the normal twenty thousand population swollen by a hundred thousand wounded and thousands of hospital personnel, resembled a vast grimy prison-camp. The first snows restored Pskov to its early splendour as a trading crossroad. Snow hid the new tin roofs and blanketed the makeshift additions, snow settled on the fortress ruins and tumble-down medieval city walls until they appeared whole again, snow covered the ancient squat churches with uneven walls melted into the ground. At Military Hospital No. 5, snow hid the gravel of the erstwhile playground, snow disguised the hastily thrown up kitchen unit and glistened on the bare branches of the cherry orchard that sloped towards the river.

On a sunny morning Stephan ventured outside with Marya. Slowing her pace to his, Marya guided him along the cleared path to the promontory. Below them the gelid Velikaya river wrestled with the narrower, livelier band of the Pskov river — a battle that showed in thin white streaks of surf above the swirling grey and near-black waters. Lifting a hand to shelter his eyes against the dazzle, Stephan gazed first at the town, where feathers of white smoke rose from white buildings, then at the illimitable distances of tree-etched whiteness.

'Laugh, if you want, at my chauvinism; then ask what happened to the pacifist,' he said. 'But as far as I'm concerned a country like this is worth fighting for, dying for.'

'Stephan, you aren't returning to the front?' She tightened her grip on his arm. 'You can't. You're not strong enough.'

'Stop worrying. Next week I'm being mustered out.'

'Oh, thank God.'

He turned to look at her. 'Marya, I never would have made it without you.'

'Tit for tat. You nursed me after you rescued me from the Fortress.'

'Ovruch co-ordinated the rescue, and Klazkha did most of the nursing,' he said, pausing. 'There's another difference, love. Now you're married.'

'Separated.'

'Do you see him giving you a divorce?'

'He will. He must!'

'Marya, he's already shown his colours. He'd rather throw you back in the Trubetskoi than let us be together.'

Centuries ago, a monastery had been built on the small island formed where the rivers met. A monk shuffled from the derelict cloister, leaving a trail in the fresh-fallen snow. Marya watched the slow progress of the brown-robed ancient. Years ago, Paskevich had told her that she was his unto death.

Stephan was watching her face. 'So we

agree,' he said, 'this has been an interlude?'

'There must be a way —'

'Marya, stop deluding yourself. He's not going to let you go.' Tears intensified the blue of Stephan's eyes. 'You aren't missing much. I'm what you Americans call a lone wolf. And I'm fairly single-minded; that means I'll never rest until Russia's changed.'

'Whoever replaces Nicholas will be worse.'

'That's Paskevich talking.'

If her cheeks had not already been crimson from the cold air, she would have flushed. 'Must you bring him into everything?'

'He's part of you; the two of you are tangled together like those rivers,' Stephan said, gazing at the mingling waters below them. 'We've had this time together, and I'm grateful. These few weeks have been a miracle.'

With the last two sentences his voice had altered, and the low huskiness acted on her as always. Yet — and maybe it was the cold air penetrating her cape and clothes — she experienced not only desire but an actual physical sense of loss.

He looked into her face and put his arms around her. They clung together like lovers, like mourners at a funeral, not caring that the ancient monk was witness to their embrace.

Chapter Thirty-three

Dear Marya,

When Stephan told me you was a full-time nurse in Pskov, I almost fell down. I had no idea you wasn't still dallying at it in Tsarskoe Selo. Stephan says you're a regular angel of mercy and the wounded recover because your smiles is the best medicine there is. But, then, he always did have a way with words. He didn't mention Count Paskevich, and I didn't ask no questions, but I guessed that you must've escaped the bald buzzard! Good for you!

Can you believe it? Me, Klazkha Sobchak, sending you a letter? Not that I do my letters anywhere near as fine as poor dear Josip, but I can write, and read books, too. It's come about like this. I'm part of the Bolshevik Women's Internationale. One of us is a schoolteacher, and she gives classes. That's how it is with us. We share whatever we got. Which ain't much.

Have you heard about the dreadful shortages here? The baker at the corner says when he gets flour there ain't no wood to heat his ovens, or when he's got the wood there ain't no flour. You can imagine the queues for bread. Yesterday I waited all night in a blizzard for a quarter-loaf and was lucky to get that. Some waited nearly as long and went home with nothing. Life is awful for women with families to feed.

It's not easy getting out laundry when you have to spend hours scrounging for fuel to boil the linen and heat the irons. Luckily one of the Women's Internationale is married to a wood dealer and sometimes he helps me out.

We women're part of the Bolsheviks, but already we got 107 members on our own. Our aim is to get women a fair deal. Our motto's 'Equal Pay for an Equal Day'. Like it?

Write soon and tell me your news — printing is easiest for me to read. And remember, whenever you are in Petrograd, you have a place to stay.

Regards from
Klazkha Sobchak

Marya ran her forefinger along the uneven scrawl as if touching the pencil marks brought her in physical proximity with her friend. Refolding the thin, lined paper, she tucked it in her pocket. It was time for her shift.

Dr Golder bent over one of the stained porcelain sinks outside the school lavatories. The knitted surgical cap pulled over his wavy beige hair, the mask pulled down around his throat, and the long surgical coat were thin and frayed from frequent boiling.

She took the sink next to his. The smell of carbolic soap was strong as they scrubbed their fingernails.

Displaying uneven teeth, he gave her one of his rare, surprisingly warm smiles. 'You'll find seven post-operative patients in your ward tonight, Sister.'

She was his only friend in the hospital, and he kept this friendship on a strictly professional level. She had gleaned, though, that he was thirty, unmarried, an agnostic, a Socialist. He appeared impervious to the staff's taunts and slights, but she had noted a studied expressionlessness on his broad features as anti-Semitic jokes were passed around or religious slurs entered into the conversation.

As he reached for his towel, his forehead wrinkled into a frown. Then he nodded, as if he had reached a decision.

'I probably should not tell you this, Sister,' he said. 'I belong to the Jewish Socialist Bund. It's outlawed.'

'Now should I warn you that I'm an Okhrana agent?'

He didn't smile. 'There are half a dozen in the hospital.' Lowering his voice, he muttered: 'Rasputin is dead.'

She dropped the soap. 'Rasputin dead?'

'I received a coded telegram from Petrograd.'

'But the lines are down.'

'They were repaired yesterday,' he said.

'I didn't doubt you,' she said hastily.

As they went up the basement stairs, he

whispered: 'The body was found in a canal.'

'Was it an accident? Or murder?'

'I have told you all I know.'

They had reached the vestibule. An orderly lounged smoking a cigarette, butts scattered on the floor around him. Dr Golder stared at the mess, small muscles moving in his nose. As they climbed the empty upper staircase, he said: 'A hospital should never be slovenly.' He glanced around to make sure they were alone before adding in a low voice: 'Forgive me if I am wrong, but I believe you share Captain Strakhov's conviction that Russia must change?'

She nodded, her smile lifting her soft upper lip.

'It is wrong to celebrate death, but this murder is excellent for us.'

'Not so fast,' she said. 'You want Socialism. And, being an American, I hope Russia'll become a democracy.'

'But you, the captain and I all want an end to the tsarist oppression and injustices. Rasputin guided the Romanovs. Mark my words, Sister, his death will leave them at loose ends.'

The press was forbidden to print the news. The censor's power, though, had lessened to a point unthinkable a few months earlier. The front page of the *Pskov Evening Gazette* was filled with columns about the immense crowd that gathered at the ice-covered Moika Canal in Petrograd to watch as the

441

police dredged up the bullet-ridden, bludgeoned corpse of a Siberian peasant. And what other Siberian peasant's death would have occasioned such interest?

The story, read aloud in the Junior Officers' Ward, was drowned out several times by cheers. In the enlisted men's ward, Rasputin detractors expressed boisterous satisfaction while his partisans defended the slain 'monk' with equal vigour. 'That's what happens to any of us who raise our heads,' wheezed a badly gassed corporal. 'The higher-ups chop it off.'

Among both enlisted men and officers there were expressions of dismay that 'the German woman' hadn't been slain with her 'lover'. And, despite threats of punishment, only a few voices joined in the post-supper 'God Bless the Tsar.'

The winter of 1917 was the coldest ever recorded in Pskov.

That December the hospital furnace and stoves blazed continuously, overheating the wards until window-frames cracked and draughts whistled everywhere. A snowfall blocked all roads. Isolation shattered all remnants of discipline. Matron was openly flouted. Nurses hitched their faded uniform skirts well above their ankles, fluffed their curls to show outside their white kerchiefs and coyly undid the top two buttons of their bodices. At night, rustles and gasps came from ward cots while the bewhiskered cleaning woman, reputed to be a sorceress, did a brisk business in love potions and herbs that induced spontaneous abortion. Orderlies peddled rubbing alcohol tinged with cherry extract to the patients. Scuffles broke out between Monarchists and Revolutionaries. And the photographs of the tsar presiding over each ward were covered with spittle.

When the snow stopped, Marya and her fellow-Volunteers floundered through the deep snow into town. They found a similar breakdown of order. Gendarmes were striking because their wages wouldn't buy food. Editors of all three newspapers refused to submit their copy to the censors, and the Rasputin story was being openly reported. The murder had been committed by Felix Yusopov, a handsome, immensely rich, effeminate young prince married to the tsar's niece, and his accomplice was Grand Duke Dimitri, the tsar's blood nephew. A blurred photograph on the front pages showed the tsarina prostrate on Rasputin's grave in Tsarskoe Selo.

When the snow was finally cleared from the tracks, the surgical chief was suffering fits of delirium tremens and one of the five other surgeons was ill. The remaining doctors couldn't keep up with wounded flooding into the hospital. Golder taught Marya to perform minor operations, his steady hands demonstrating on a corpse. Marya swayed dizzily the first time she amputated a gangrenous frostbitten toe, but soon — or so she wrote to Klazkha — she went about the job as calmly as a cook carving a roast. The nursing staff had always been short-handed, so she continued her ward duty. She always felt tired.

On the first Thursday night in February, she returned to her ward desk, reaching out a hand to push back her chair.

A sudden pain burst under her left shoulder-blade. The torment was so unexpected and so intense that she didn't dare move. Standing with her arm extended, scarcely breathing, she resembled a statue.

'What is it, Sister?' called the insomniac cadet.

Marya couldn't respond.

He shuffled into the hall, bawling: 'Help! Help!'

Two minutes later Dr Golder was running in, pyjamas flapping under his uniform-coat. By now Marya's agony had relaxed a little and she was slumped into the chair. Adjusting a screen around them, Golder popped a thermometer into her mouth. His broad face intent, he moved his stethoscope over her chest and back.

'Dry pleurisy,' he diagnosed.

'A good night's sleep'll fix me up. I'll be fine.'

'Sister, I am the doctor. Country air is what you need. Do you have relatives to care for you?'

She thought briefly of Paskevich. 'My brother's back in America. He's my only family.'

'Pardon this intrusion,' Golder said. 'However, you have mentioned that your father was a Russian, and it is obvious to me that you come from a high level of society. Surely you know somebody with a country home?'

There was such compassionate kindness in his voice that Marya felt tears welling in her eyes. 'My dearest friend lives in Petrograd.'

Golder assumed the friend to be wealthy. 'Well, if you promise to rest in bed,' he said in his precise way, 'Petrograd will be adequate.'

Chapter Thirty-four

Three days later Marya was getting off the tram in Vyborg Square. A sudden blast of chill north wind caught her by surprise. Skidding in the icy slush, she fell. When she started to walk again, she picked her way carefully, holding her small valise with one hand, using the other to hold her flannel headgear protectively over her nose and mouth. She moved beside a snaking line which ended at Vyborg Square Bakery. The sign, a plump round loaf with a curl of steam, mocked the women stamping their feet and clasping their arms in an effort to keep warm. At every corner a sign was posted: 'IT IS FORBIDDEN FOR CROWDS TO GATHER.'

Reaching the Vyborg Inn, Marya wearily recalled her happiness there. She staggered up Klazkha's rickety steps, pounding on the door.

'Hold on!' Klazkha called over the rattling of the bolt. Her smile shone. 'Ain't this just like you — seven hours late and as impatient as ever.'

'The train was delayed . . .' Marya closed her eyes.

'You're shivering enough to shake down the house,' Klazkha said gruffly. 'Come on inside before you freeze.'

Klazkha's laundry was heaped neatly in a

corner. Two long, broad strips of red canvas covered the floor. Across one Klazkha had painted in black: 'IF A WOMAN IS A SLAVE THERE WILL BE NO FREEDOM.' She hadn't finished the second. 'LONG LIVE EQUAL RIGHTS' shone wetly, while the rest of the sentence, FOR WOMEN!, was feebly outlined in pencil.

Marya's flannel veil had frozen to a starchy stiffness. Unpinning it, she let her heavy cape drop. An immediately offered glass of hot tea eased the pain in her lungs.

'You look awful,' Klazkha said.

'After a night on the train, do you expect me to be turned out like a grand duchess?'

'No need to get on your high horse. I'm telling the truth.'

Marya changed the subject. 'What're the signs for?'

Klazkha was refilling Marya's glass at the hissing dented samovar. 'Next week my bunch, the Women's Internationale, is having a protest. Hundreds of other women've promised to march alongside us.'

'In this cold?'

'Marya, you're stuck there in the Pskov hospital; you don't see real life —'

'Death is what I see.'

'Stop being so touchy. I know how hard you nurses work,' Klazkha said. 'But you have no idea just how bad things is here. No food. People starving and freezing to death. Women are sick to death of not having a say. Some of us're painting signs

447

that say "Bread for our children".'

'At the bakery on the square . . . longest line . . .' A coughing attack interrupted Marya.

'Drink your tea,' Klazkha said with a worried frown.

Sipping, Marya kicked off her shoes and lifted her icy damp feet towards the stove. 'Klazkha,' she asked quietly, 'do you know where Stephan is?'

Klazkha hit her head. 'Stupid me. I meant to tell you first off. Three days ago — you won't believe this — when the Duma opened who should be a deputy —'

'Stephan? But how?'

'All I know is him and Ovruch both won a seat.'

'Ovruch, too? But aren't opposition parties outlawed?'

'They couldn't stop 'em from getting in. The people is that angry. The only trouble is that the tsar has still got the power to dump the Duma whenever he wants. Men, they're like little boys playing games! Why? Are you going to look Stephan up?'

'No. It's over.' Marya gave a long sigh.

Klazkha glanced at Marya, but if she had any comment she let it pass. 'If that ain't the strangest thing, him showing up in your ward,' she said. 'He credits you with saving his life.'

'I can't tell you how sweet and nice it was. We never talked about the bad things; we scarcely mentioned the war and politics. I never gave a thought to the future.'

'When did you ever?' Klazkha shoved a gnarled twig in the stove. 'There goes the last of the wood. Wrap the quilt around yourself while I finish my signs.'

The room was dark by the time the paint dried. Klazkha folded the canvases. She had been talking about her foray into politics, trying to make her voice colourless, but it was obvious that Klazkha Sobchak, child labourer, child prostitute, laundress, personal maid, took immense pride in being at the helm of the hundred or more members of the Women's Internationale.

Klazkha, on her side, was noting Marya.

In the days when Marya was Miss Alexiev, she was kind and generous — hadn't she risked everything to give her, Klazkha, the lady's-maid job? — yet at the same time a gorgeous, preening tropical bird with her expensive clothes and furs, her jewellery, her parties. Klazkha, while pretending to frown at flirtatious vanity, had taken immense pride in her employer's looks and conquests. After the months in solitary confinement, though, Marya's altruism had crowded out her frivolity. *She's a tiny little thing, and she's just not sensible, the way she's taken on the troubles of the world,* was the way sensible Klazkha's thoughts ran. *No wonder she's exhausted.*

A kick shivered the door. 'Open up,' Ovruch boomed.

Switching on the light, Klazkha unbolted the door.

Ovruch no longer wore *muzhik's* clothes. He looked a prosperous bourgeois in his karakul hat, karakul-collared topcoat and outsize, handsomely cobbled boots. The most startling transformation, though, was his bushy beard: it had been barber-trimmed below his reddened cheeks and cut into a pointed goatee like the one sported by his idol, Lenin. Balancing birch logs on his shoulder with one hand, he held a covered plate that smelled meltingly of cheese and yeast.

'A *khachapuri* to celebrate the first night of your holiday,' he said.

'Food, fuel — the privileges you deputies get,' Klazkha said tartly. 'Well, go ahead. Shove one of them logs in the stove so we can be nice and snug while we eat.'

Despite Klazkha's analysis, Marya had a great deal of hedonism left in her, and she savoured the cheese pie, her pleasure un-dimmed by the memory of a cheese pie eaten across the street on the night of her rescue from the Fortress.

'Marya,' Ovruch asked. 'Do the wounded know there've been lavish dinners and balls in Petrograd?'

'It was in the papers that the British Military Mission is here to discuss war strategy.'

'Discussions, pah! There are lines of cars and court carriages outside the theatres and palaces, women in furs and diamond tiaras, dinner-parties at the Hotel Europa, champagne at the fanciest nightclubs — does that sound like military talks? You'd never guess this was a city where people starved and froze. You can be sure none of them gives a thought to how many die on Brusilov's battlefields.' The cadenced voice rumbled with undertones, as if the speech were being delivered in some large draughty auditorium. 'The people are angry.'

'The truth is,' Marya said, 'the wounded are still up in arms that Brusilov was ordered to stop his advance.'

'Not all of them,' Ovruch said.

'Marya, you're all done in.' Klazkha spoke in the same concerned, bullying tone she'd used as a lady's maid. 'Ovruch, I got to put you out the door; there's still these things to finish for the march.'

Klazkha had not prayed since Josip had died. She had not entered a church since Lally's funeral. On a most basic level she agreed with the Bolshevik pronouncement that religion was the opiate of the people. Yet the day before the march she gripped coins and went inside the Church of the Holy Trinity: as poverty-stricken as the rest of the Vyborg district, the church was freezing cold, with icons so begrimed by candle-smoke that it was impossible to tell more than the outlines of the holy faces. Klazkha lit a candle, prostrating herself on the stone floor in front of the cross.

She prayed for good weather. She prayed that the women workers from the textile plants and the rubber plant and the women yellow from slaving in the shell factories would join the march. She prayed that nobody would be hurt. At this point a memory swam into her mind. During her time on the streets one of the clients had demanded that she strip and lie on the floor begging for kopeks while he kicked blue bruises across her thin unformed body. She stirred on the icy stones, and a not entirely original thought occurred to her: *What's praying but a fancy form of begging?*

Getting to her feet and brushing off her coat, she left the church. Frowning as she walked home, she went over every detail of the protest march and decided to call a last-minute meeting of the other organizers. 'I'm leaving nothing to luck,' she told Marya.

But luck was with her. The cold spell broke on 23 February, the day of the demonstration.

The wind came from the south, a light warm breeze that raised the temperature. The morning was as sharp and clear as the first bite of a tart apple. The sky was cloudless. The sun shone in benediction on gilded domes and frost-encrusted rooftops. The Women's Internationale marchers were joined by grandmothers cooped up too long by the freezing temperatures. Housewives ground down with trying to put food on the table for their family anticipated a bit of sociability. Schoolgirls played truant. The fuel shortage closed the Putilov factory: female workers, angered by the loss of wages, learned about the demonstration from *Rabonitsa* and joined the chattering flocks who gathered throughout the city.

Vyborg Square was packed. Above the sea of scarved heads was a spume of crimson flags and banners. Soprano voices sang 'God Bless the Tsar'; the national anthem was drowned out by louder singing of the revolutionary 'Marseillaise'. Klazkha's group squeezed through the crowd, distributing red armbands.

Marya, a red badge pinned to her nurse's cape, was crushed against the Tsar Alexander equestrian statue in the centre of the square.

'Hold this, will you?' Klazkha shouted, handing Marya her banner. She scrambled on to the pedestal, gripping a leg of the bronze horse before she retrieved the pole. She waved the red canvas energetically above her head.

The crowd quietened.

'Women! Comrades!' Klazkha shouted. 'Today we're united. Today we let the Municipal Council, the Duma and Tsar Nicholas himself know we're not going to be slaves any more!' With an effort, she raised the heavy banner above her head, and the soft wind fluttered the canvas to display the slogan: 'IF A WOMAN IS A SLAVE THERE

WILL BE NO FREEDOM.'

After a long, deafening roar of approval, Klazkha lowered the flag. 'What are we going to say?' she shouted.

The Women's Internationale screamed back: 'That we're not slaves!'

'And who is it we're telling?' Klazkha bawled.

'The City Council, the Duma, the Little Father!'

'And what else will we tell 'em?' Klazkha yelled.

The Women's Internationale flapped banners with slogans, and there was a deafening cacophony of voices, the most repeated words being 'Give our children bread! Give our children bread! Give our children bread!'

When the screaming quietened, Klazkha cried: 'Let's get a move on. March in ranks. Don't let anything scare you. And, if we run into Cossacks or police, remember: women stand together, firm and proud.'

Marya, in the front ranks beside Klazkha, was borne along by the crowd. As they approached the Bolshoi Sampsonievsky Prospekt, they saw the dozen or so Don Cossacks waiting. The mounted men spread out across the broad avenue and began slowly riding towards the marchers. At a shouted order, lethal whips were unhooked from saddles.

'Shame!' Marya shrieked.

Others joined in. 'Shame . . . Shame . . . Shame!'

At another signal, the riders stopped, and the sergeant trotted alone towards the crowd. He was very young and wore his hat tilted jauntily over his right eyebrow. Teeth gleaming in a smirk, he reined his horse until it reared above the front row of marchers. Marya linked arms with Klazkha and a big seamstress, using all her strength to prevent the crowd from thrusting her forward.

'Nikolai!' shrilled a voice from behind. 'Nikushka, it's me, your mother. None of this nonsense, *boychik*. Let us move on!'

The Cossack turned as crimson as the piping on his uniform and lowered his whip.

Laughter rang out as the identity of the Cossack was repeated. The red-faced young sergeant turned his horse and trotted back to the squad.

The police had granted the women permission to march on the Town Hall, the belief being that at most there would be a hundred women. It had never occurred to anyone — not the officer who had granted the permission, not the councillors who had agreed to listen, certainly not the sensible Klazkha — that there would be a mob this vast.

Streams of women in the narrower streets joined the river of female humanity flowing down the broad avenue. More banners waved; there were louder shouts for bread, for votes for women, for an end to the war. Hastily despatched mounted police were breaking up even the smallest knot of onlookers. The police, however, were powerless to stop the women. They crossed the Neva and paraded down the Nevsky Prospekt. The crowd grew yet larger. At the red-brick clock-tower of Town Hall, Klazkha stopped. Women crowded around the Russian-Byzantine Chapel of the Vernicle, women climbed on to the steps of the six-columned Grecian portico of the Feather Stalls. Many of the merchants in the long, colonnaded feather-market were women: they closed up to join the demonstration. Marchers pushed forward, jamming Mihaelevsky Street, climbing on the portico of the Roman Catholic Church, shoving against the Europa Hotel. Klazkha stood atop the Council building steps. Waving her arms like an orchestra conductor, she synchronized the shouting.

'Come out, Councillors! Come out! You promised to hear us! Come out and listen!' Sun melted icicles on the eaves that jutted from the clock-tower, and the dripping water darkened her red headscarf. 'Listen to what we have to say.'

They had chanted almost an hour before two of the paired second-storey windows opened, and a quartet of Council members in heavy overcoats showed themselves. The immense crowd grew silent.

Klazkha and other chosen leaders took turns slowly calling out their requests.

'We need bread for our families.'

'We need fuel.'

'We need a living wage.'

The dumpling-shaped member of the Council had continued smoking during the recitation. Now he took the cigar from his mouth. 'Good ladies,' he boomed in a politician's rounded tones, 'as men, it delights us to hear from the fair sex. It was good of you to take the time from your busy lives to brighten further this fine afternoon.'

'We don't want sweet talk, we want bread.'

'Good ladies, there is a war on —'

'Bread, give our children bread.'

'Equal pay!' shouted munition workers, yellow as canaries from tetrachloride. 'Equal pay for equal work!'

The dumpling-shaped politician, who knew a way out when it came his way, gripped the balustrade with leather-gloved hands. 'Salaries are determined by your employers,' he boomed. 'Now, if you'll excuse us, dear ladies, we must return to our appointed duties of running this great city.'

He and his fellows returned inside; the windows closed.

'Bastard!'

'Condescending arsehole!'

Cries spumed up from the angered women. Flags and banners waved. The police gingerly tried to edge the crowd back down the Nevsky. The women refused to budge. They stood for another hour, swaying as they sang hymns. By now the setting sun cast redness across the statues of saints that topped the Catholic church.

457

'It's too cold for you to be out with that pleurisy of yours,' Klazkha fretted. 'You go on home.'

'Leave?' Marya pulled the cloak tighter around herself. 'Now? Are you crazy?'

A French window opened again. This time an Orthodox priest appeared. The lights behind him outlined his mitre, darkening his bearded face to a shadowy blur. The shouts diminished; many women crossed themselves.

'My daughters.' His basso profundo tones carried like an opera singer's to the far reaches of the crowd. 'Have you forgotten your Christian duties as our Lord's weaker vessels? Are you not ashamed to be loitering here when it is time to make dinner for your babes and the husbands you vowed to serve and obey?'

'Make dinner with what?' somebody shouted.

But the cries were dispirited, for the air was now so cold it froze in the lungs and, indeed, there were husbands and families waiting.

A Chevalier Garde major appeared beside the priest. 'Good women, either you go home willingly or we'll be forced to make you disperse.' He raised his rifle, aiming at the evening star.

At the sharp retort, the crowd splintered into a hundred thousand fragments, scattering down the side-streets or into the Feather Stalls. Klazkha and Marya were caught in the stream hurrying along the Nevsky Prospekt.

'We didn't need to do what the priest told us,' Marya said.

'Marya, it wasn't him; it's the women. I don't want none of them hurt.'

Marya walked silently past the barred and dark English Tea Room, scene of leisurely teas with the 'baroness'. Where was the stupid charming Betsy now? Marya pulled her uniform cloak tighter around herself.

Slipped under Klazkha's door, there was a telegraph from Matron: 'URGENT YOU RETURN TO HOSPITAL.'

Klazkha insisted on accompanying Marya to the station. They set out before five. Though it wouldn't be light for hours, groups of striking workers were already milling around. Women stood under the lamp-posts of Vyborg Square handing out red cockades and armbands. There were no police about. The cobbler's door had been broken down, and men and women were rushing out with armloads of boots and shoes. In Vyborg Square a bespectacled student clung to the equestrian statue haranguing bundled-up men to march for 'Peace, land, bread'.

'That's Ovruch and the Bolsheviks' slogan,' Klazkha said.

The women's march the previous day had set off their husbands and sons. In the crowded tram the conductor, a burly Estonian, planted a wet kiss on Marya and Klazkha's lips, refusing their kopeks. 'Today all women ride for a kiss, and all strikers ride for a handshake!'

The tram jarred to a stop at the Liteinyi Bridge. It was barricaded and guarded by soldiers in badly fitting khaki uniforms. 'None of the bridges is open today,' the lieutenant called. 'Orders of the military commander.'

'Fuck the military commander!' shouted the thick-set Estonian conductor.

The lieutenant lifted his sword overhead. At this signal, his men kneeled, aiming their rifles.

Some passengers dropped to the floor in sobs. An old laundress shrieked in terror.

'Fuck the Army.' The conductor jumped from the tram step. 'This way, comrades!' He slithered down the embankment, followed by a good half of the passengers, including Marya and Klazkha. Men and women alike heaved their shoulders against the embankment fence. Planks toppled. Marya, buoyed by a defiant schoolgirl excitement, skidded hand-in-hand with Klazkha across the broad frozen Neva.

The Estonian conductor commandeered another tram, and all passengers joined in singing 'Comrades, Boldly in Step' as they clanged through the predawn darkness.

The station square was filled.

'Down with the war!'

'Down with Bloody Nicholas!'

'Down with the German woman!'

The cold morning air was clouded with breath and unfocused violence. Shoving their way through the crush, Klazkha and Marya pushed into the relative calm of the station.

At the Pskov platform Klazkha said: 'Sorry it wasn't more of a rest cure.'

'I'm better, aren't I?' Marya responded. 'Klazkha, thank you for everything.'

Klazkha slowed and gripped Marya's arm. 'Thank me? Ain't a day passes that I don't think of all what you did for Josip, and how dear it cost you.'

At this reminder of her charming, wilful little daughter, Marya winced. 'You've repaid me a thousand times over.'

When she reappeared at the window for a final wave, the train was starting. Klazkha ran alongside. 'If you ever need anything, come to me,' she shouted. 'I owe you my life.'

Chapter Thirty-five

'I sent no telegram,' the matron said, waggling a disciplinary forefinger with each word.

'It was signed with your name, Matron.'

'Lies and more lies!' The matron's face was flushed and swollen with hostility. Her perfume reeked as cloyingly as ever, but she had left off her jewellery. 'In the last few days everybody has been inventing lies about me. As if I've ever done anything but work hard! I've run a respectable hospital!' A drop of spittle landed on the desk. 'Sister, your veil is crooked!'

Marya wearily adjusted her head-dress. The journey, instead of taking twelve hours, had taken three days, and she hadn't yet fully recuperated from her pleurisy. She was too exhausted to wonder who had sent the message, or why the halls were filled with ambulatory cases hobbling about in bathrobes and the orderlies were gathered with their heads together. Excited chatter crackled beyond the open doors to the wards.

Upstairs in the bandaging-room, Golder welcomed her with a brief harassed nod, and finished dressing a shoulder wound. After the patient had left, he explained that he was handling the caseload on his own. 'The chief has passed out in his office; the others are in Pskov to see the Imperial train.'

'The tsar's here? But why?'

'He is no longer in charge.'

'I can't believe it! He's finally given up being commander-in-chief?'

'Far, far more than that.' Golder's broad Slavic face was suffused with exaltation. 'The hour has finally struck,' he said sombrely. 'He has just abdicated.

In much the same way that the French Revolution had begun with the women's march on Versailles, so the overthrow of the Romanov dynasty was sparked by the women's march on Petrograd Town Hall. The following morning's random lawlessness, which Marya had witnessed before she left the capital, marked the onset of a hunger riot. Mobs had swirled down the Morskaia and along the Nevsky Prospekt, converging at the huge opulent Gostinyi Dvor where they had looted and vandalized, beating any shopkeeper who attempted to protect his merchandise.

The Volynskii Guard Regiment was called out. Forty rioters were killed, hundreds more wounded. By nightfall the city had returned to normality. Guests thronged to Princess Radziwill's brilliantly lit palace on Fontanka, the Maryinsky filled with ticket-holders for the Efrem Zimbalist recital, Café Cubat served seven-course dinners to smartly tailored profiteers.

The situation was well in hand, or so the Petrograd military commander telegraphed

Nicholas, isolated five hundred miles away in his Field Headquarters. Alexandra, immured in Tsarskoe Selo, jotted another of her innumerable letters to her husband: between descriptions of their children's measles she mentioned the riots. 'Another example of young people out for excitement,' she wrote. 'As soon as firm measures were applied, typically, the hooliganism ended.'

Paskevich, in the capital for conferences with the French and British ambassadors, however, viewed the disturbances with a far keener eye. At midday he despatched a telegraph to the tsar:

PETROGRAD GARRISON OF 160,000 MADE UP OF RECENT CONSCRIPTS STOP UNTRAINED, UNDISCIPLINED PEASANTS STOP WILL MUTINY BEFORE THEY FIRE ON THEIR FELLOWS STOP IF POLITICIZED, RIOTS MIGHT BECOME A REVOLUTION STOP YOUR IMPERIAL MAJESTY MUST DESPATCH LOYAL TROOPS FROM FRONT TO MAINTAIN ORDER STOP DO NOT DELAY STOP

TOMORROW MIGHT BE TOO LATE

Paskevich's message — completely at odds with the other soothing communications — violated both court etiquette and government protocol by giving a direct command to the Autocrat. Nicholas tore up the cable.

By the next dawn crowds had already flooded out. Now, though, radical organizers peppered the main thoroughfares. Red armbands were distributed, red flags spumed, red banners with revolutionary slogans were held high, anti-war placards waved. Breath rose in synchronized clouds as the multitude bawled revolutionary ditties.

This time several regiments were called out.

At the order to fire on the crowd, a recruit wavered, then turned his rifle on his lieutenant. As the young officer toppled slowly from his horse, the long grey regimental line remained kneeling with their rifles fixed. There was a preternatural stillness in the air, like the stillness in that long moment before a cracked dam finally gives way. Then, unprompted, the newly recruited soldiers were on their feet, running to mingle with the people. The mutiny spread instantly. The garrison became part of the mob, throwing open armouries, lynching officers. A huge, unhemmed red flag was hoisted above the Winter Palace, official residence of the tsars. The unchecked swollen mob split like a vast amoeba, swelling and dividing again. Beneath the canopy of black smoke could be heard the nervous rattle of machine-guns.

By now Nicholas had received further telegrams pleading for swift deployment of loyal regiments. He brooded indecisively about attacking his own subjects until well after midnight before issuing the command to deploy troops from the front to Petrograd. Then he set off for the capital himself. Normally an honour guard stood at attention on every station platform along his route. On this journey, he went unsaluted.

When the gold-trimmed blue Imperial train chugged into Pskov, the platform was empty except for the provincial governor and a bearded general wearing galoshes. The two men assailed Nicholas with tales of defections to the revolutionary cause, stories of betrayals from every class, rumours about the vile behaviour of the mobs. Any politically astute monarch would have realized that the turbulence was still localized and could be squashed by further infusions of battle-seasoned regiments. It is known that Nicholas, a family man, was consumed by anxieties about his children's measles and fretful about his family's safety. He was also a deeply religious fatalist, and it is possible that this uprising seemed to him the will of God. He composed a letter of abdication.

Without a tsar, the vast bureaucracy died quickly. Within weeks, the Empire was like a cut earthworm, a hundred thousand *soviets* — or committees — each wiggling separately.

Everywhere people were setting up committees to govern themselves. Military Hospital No. 5, now autonomous, was administered by an executive committee formed by delegates of various internal committees. Ostensibly the doctors' committee wielded the same power on the executive board as any other committee — nurses, cleaning staff, orderlies, kitchen staff — yet, as under the old regime, the surgical unit was the top of the pyramid. And why not? The doctors were educated, city folk, political sophisticates. Besides, they operated the outpatient clinic which treated the local peasants: the fees were paid in the food and fuel that enabled the hospital to survive.

Golder and a rotation of the three Volunteers were assigned to run the clinic.

As usual, Marya arrived for her duty a full hour before the clinic door opened. The cook, as diligent as he was ill-natured, already sat scowling behind the long table where he collected fees — several heaps of muddy potatoes, a cackling white rooster with its feet tied together, huge heads of wilted cabbage, bundled faggots, pathetic little bouquets of onions and garlic.

Golder was sweeping the clinic floor — once again the maids' committee had voted to strike.

'Here.' Marya reached for the twig broom. 'Let me.'

He relinquished the handle with a brusque nod that told her he was in one of his touchy moods. He remained curt while tending the sick and injured. When the door was finally locked again, Marya scrubbed the examining-table.

'Sister Alexiev?' Golder was tending the

spirit-lamp under the sterilizer.

Marya's brush ceased to move as she turned questioningly. Though long ago she had confided her real name to Golder, even in private he rarely used it.

With small jerky movements he adjusted the flame. 'I have mentioned you to a trusted comrade rising high in the Provisional Government. Deputy Ovruch.'

'You're Ovruch's friend? But you're a Socialist, not a Bolshevik.'

'We are all comrades in the fight against oppression.' Golder took off his spectacles. 'I had no idea you were married.'

Flushing, she said: 'I'm not. I mean . . . that is, I'm separated from my husband.'

'Count Paskevich?'

'Yes.'

'Your private life is not my concern.' Holding the glasses to the steam, Golder polished the lenses with rapid precision. 'However, a reactionary Monarchist does seem a surprising choice for you.'

The old inexplicable loyalties pulled at Marya. 'He's not a reactionary,' she snapped.

'A former cabinet minister?'

'He's a brilliant man. He knew that if the Autocracy fell we'd end up in this snake-pit.'

'The road to an equal society is not smoothly paved.'

'Did Ovruch tell you anything else about me?'

468

'Nothing. He did say that his invitation to you to become a party member still holds.' Golder jammed on his glasses. 'Taking into account your marriage, my own advice is to return to America.'

'The hospital's under-staffed. I'm needed.'

'That,' Golder said, 'is up to the executive committee.'

'So you'll tell them,' Marya said bitterly.

'They have every right to know.'

Marya stalked out of the dispensary. As she slammed the door, her legs went weak and she sank on to the three-legged stool that had been used by the testy cook.

Golder emerged. He stood on the far side of the table, hands dangling at his side, his fingers fluttering up and down his blood-spattered surgical coat in a little tattoo of awkward misery. 'I would never, never disclose your personal relationships,' he said. 'But surely you understand, Marya, that I had believed you gave me your full trust. And hearing of your secrecy — learning the identity of your husband — has been a shock.' Maroon splotches showed on his wide cheeks. This was far and away the most personal speech he had ever made to her — and the only time he had used her given name. 'A considerable shock.'

He cares for me. No. He's crazy about me. Marya looked down at the floor: the strew of sunflower-seed husks resembled lice. Until now it had been easier to suppress the knowledge of Golder's feelings, but the signs had all been there. Hadn't he nursed her diligently, sat up with her during the worst of her fevers? Hadn't he 'liberated' opiates and chicken legs for her? As a Jew, he was unpopular enough to have been shot for the thefts. 'I should've confided in you,' she murmured.

'After Strakhov arrived, it seemed obvious that he was the one you cared for. Handsome, well bred, cultured, tall, a poet — a famous novelist. What chance did I have?' Shrugging, Golder pulled over a chair and sat across the table from her. 'Now I feel doubly foolish, learning that you are married and devoted to your husband.'

After a long pause, Marya murmured: 'Paskevich is a distant relative. In San Francisco we were poor, my brother and I. Broke, as a matter of fact. Dead broke when he brought us over here.'

'Then, circumstances forced you into marriage?' Golder asked gently.

To cauterize his apathy, she said: 'If you want the truth, I became his mistress. I was quite notorious. He gave me everything my frivolous heart desired — jewels, furs, servants — that's why I was his mistress.' Abruptly she stopped, shaking her head. 'I'm not being honest again. It's true that Paskevich appealed to my pleasure-loving side, and he *did* coerce me into the relationship — and into the marriage, too. Yet also there's something . . . well, something overwhelming and magnetic about him. It's not

470

just his intellectual brilliance. Everybody who ever met him respects him, but he doesn't give a damn whether they do or not. He's like a diamond, impervious, with the inborn strength to do exactly as he pleases. He has his own code. He deals with people ruthlessly. Oh, I'm making a hash of this. He's unique. If you want the entire truth, I've never exactly understood my own feelings for him.'

'Sometimes emotions are inexplicable,' Golder said stiffly.

'Well, now you can tell the executive committee the whole story.'

'I was piqued before. Hurt. As I said a few minutes ago, this is between us and the four walls.'

'Then, we can keep on the way we were? As friends?'

'It would be dishonest to say you could ever be simply that to me.' He gave a sad rueful smile. 'But, yes, I will remain your friend always.'

The nurses billeted in Pskov had always envied the former cloakroom, so it was no surprise when the committee of nurses voted that the three Volunteers had been cosseted long enough and others were now entitled to the dank basement cloakroom. The Volunteers would live in town.

Golder, who had also been exiled to Pskov, often joined Marya as she trudged through the cold spring rains or the frigid

471

mists that hovered across desolate un-ploughed fields. He had always been cir-cumspect, but since his declaration he was even more so: he limited the talk to their caseloads.

One evening, as they slogged back to town along the muddy unpaved road, he said nothing whatsoever. A black crow cawed overhead. There was the grumbling of ice caught in the swollen spring torrents of the unseen Pskov river. Their boots squished in the ruts.

'Is anything wrong?' she asked finally.

'I have been wondering if I ought to tell you this.' He stared towards a distant tumble-down wall. 'Count Paskevich has left the country.'

Her boot slipped in a puddle. 'Paskevich?' She regained her footing. 'How on earth do these rumours get started? Paskevich would never leave Russia while we're still at war. Never.'

'This is no rumour. He went last Friday in a sealed train through enemy territory. He is in Switzerland.'

Paskevich had often said that the Swiss were the most boring people on earth. But . . . hadn't he gone to Zurich before sailing for England? Unconsciously Marya gnawed her soft upper lip as she entered the ice age of Lally's cholera and death. Yes, there had been something about opening a secret ac-count that only he and members of the tsar's immediate family would have access to. Or did she have the facts mixed up with another of his numerous transactions as Finance Minister?

Golder was watching her. 'Doubtless he has secret funds there.'

That baffling admiration for her estranged husband prodded her. 'He hardly needs to be secretive,' she said coldly. 'He has interests in lots of places.'

A cart was coming towards them, big wheels spraying up mud. They moved from the path to the tall wet weeds. 'I didn't mean to snap at you,' she said. 'It's just too astonishing to believe, that's all.'

'Some further news of interest to you.' He fumbled with gloved hands inside his army topcoat, bringing out a tattered copy of *Socialism Today*. He handed it to her.

They had reached the tumbledown wall. Leaning against the worn stones, she flipped open the paper, glancing at the headline: 'President Kerensky Exhorts Front Line Troops to a Continuation of Conflict. Minority Bolshevik Party Takes to the Streets in Anti-war Disturbances.'

'More riots?' she asked. 'It's only been two months since the tsar was deposed.'

'The Provisional Government is shaky, and the war is as unpopular as ever. The story's on the next page.' He took the paper, reading: ' "The Democratic Reform Party's leader, Deputy S.L. Strakhov, calls for a coalition to end the war honourably." ' He gave her the page. 'Strakhov's always attempting to convince the Duma to stop bickering and act for the general good, not for their party goals. Some members call him the conscience of the Provisional Government.'

She smiled with pride. 'That sounds exactly like him.'

'Being a conscience,' Golder said gravely, 'means that he is willing to go against the general opinion for what he considers right. He speaks out publicly against those in high places whom he believes in the wrong.'

The paper trembled in her hand. 'The way you're talking . . . is he in danger?'

'I can put it this way. If he were still on the battlefield, he would be earning more medals.'

That year spring came late, and was so brief that winter seemed followed immediately by summer. In July the Bolsheviks staged a coup. Kerensky, president of the Provisional Government, using loyal troops, quashed the *putsch* without difficulty. Lenin fled to escape arrest, but Ovruch and Trotsky hid in Petrograd where they encouraged the party faithful.

A cold September fog enveloped Petrograd, but inside the Putilov works a darker haze came from the dust thrown off by soft cheap coal.

In the vast hall, the lines of pulleys and wheels were still. Workers leaned against their benches, gazing up to where Stephan

474

straddled a metal girder. He was delivering an election speech.

'. . . first item on the Democratic Reform platform is to seek an honourable peace with Germany,' he was saying. 'Then we'll be able to use our full resources to bring food to the cities and —'

'This manna from heaven, how do we pay for it?' interrupted a heavy-bellied machinist. 'With that money the Provisional Government sends out still joined?' Inflation had increased at such a hectic pace that banknotes were distributed in sheets that people cut for themselves.

'All wages are good for nowadays is wiping your arse,' shouted the machinist's benchmate.

At the echoed roars of laughter, the chairman of the *Fabsavkomy* climbed on the cart used to transport metal, kicking his boot rapidly, speeding along the track to the hecklers. 'Quieten down, you Bolshie hyenas,' he roared in a tone worthy of Chaliapin. 'Our speaker's here to tell us why we should elect his candidate. Give him a chance.'

In response, the pair banged their screwdrivers against the metal bench, a clatter that made it impossible to hear. Half a dozen Democratic Reform members stamped over to the disruptive duo, quickmarching them to the factory door. The pair gave a final shout of the Bolshevik slogan, 'Bread! Peace! Land!' before they were ejected into the fog.

In the quiet, the foreman called up to Stephan: 'We've heard a lot of hot air about the election. But nothing about how it'll work.'

'Yes, what's it we're meant to do?'

'You know that the voting's scheduled in Petrograd for November the twelfth?' Stephan asked. In other parts of the Empire, the polls would open on later dates. Capped heads were bobbing below him. 'Well, between now and then you have to educate yourself about the candidates. All you men over twenty will cast your ballots — you'll be told where the voting takes place — and your women will go with you.' At the irate murmurings, Stephan said: 'Friends, it's only fair to let the women vote. That's what this revolution is about. Having a government chosen by one and all. I'm here to ask you to mark your ballots for the Democratic Reform Party. I honestly believe we'll do the best job of bringing an honourable just peace with the Germans. We pledge that everyone will have adequate food and fuel. We will see that your children are educated, and that each of you is given the identical opportunity as the highest person in the land. The same justice. The Democratic Reform Party has a goal of fairness and equality for everyone, and that is why you should vote for us.'

Stephan spoke firmly even though he knew that his party was too weak to capture more than a dozen seats. He was confident, however, that the majority of votes would be cast for moderate parties who would form a coalition.

The height dizzied him, yet looking down at the pale oval faces lifted towards him he spoke in a strong assured tone that penetrated every corner of the immense munitions works, reaching into the soot-blackened corridors where green-capped office clerks had gathered to listen.

His throat ached by the time he left the Putilov works. While he waited for his bus he bought a glass of hot grassy tea from a vendor. The fog smelled, faintly, of sea-salt, reminding him of the Channel steamer.

Marya . . .

Talk was rife that Paskevich, like many another tsarist official, had bribed his way out of Russia. Stephan knew the talk to be true. Yet he hadn't attempted to contact Military Hospital No. 5. Why hadn't he admitted Marya back into his life? Or at least written to her? Why?

Because this is the most crucial hour of our history, he told himself. *Now is the time for action.* A less pompous inner voice added: *And, besides, who knows where my Okhrana files are?* He wasn't positive that the Okhrana knew the true identity of his father; but tsarist secret agents, carried away by their own omnipotence, had infiltrated even the most august bedrooms. Stephan's file had been among the many that vanished the previous March, when the squat yellow

Okhrana headquarters had been stormed by angry mobs. *If it fell into the wrong hands, I'm a walking bomb.*

The horse-drawn bus emerged from the mist.

Stephan jumped off at the Tauride Palace, where the Duma met, turning in to nearby Tverskaya Street, where he lived. At the fishmonger's he was forced off the pavement by a mass of noisy ragged children, waifs who earned a few kopeks by holding a place in the food queues. These had begun forming earlier and earlier. In Stephan's opinion, the increasing ineffectiveness of the Provisional Government could be measured by the growing length and duration of food lines.

His building was five storeys tall, with a handsome mansard roof and intricate stonework balustrades that pigeon droppings transformed into marble.

'Welcome home, Excellency,' said the creaky sour-breathed *dvornik*. 'Your visitor, he come by a while ago, and I let him into your rooms like you said. Nervous one, he is, twitching like a rabbit all the way upstairs.' He peered up at Stephan, curiosity in his rheumy eyes. 'Lots of odd folks dropping by to see you.'

'He sits on the same committees. You know how many committees there are these days.' Escaping the inquisitive old man, Stephan hurried through the vestibule. In the unswept and unheated hall, a little poodle yelped on a lead tied to a doorknob. The old aromas — beeswax polish, rich cooking, French perfume — were supplanted by Revolutionary cabbage, rancid oil and burning peat. The sourness of wet rot grew heavier as Stephan climbed upstairs.

The sharply pitched walls of his garret were lined with water-stained copies of the same poster, an idealized woman in Russian costume raising a banner scrolled, 'JUSTICE FOR ALL WITH THE DEMOCRATIC REFORM PARTY!' A narrow alcove held the ironwork bed; in front of the low-set oriel window stood a table desk. The visitor bent over writing.

His name was Pyotr LeFort. In the early days, LeFort had been the most radical member of the Democratic Reform Party; but as years had passed he'd inched to the right, and since the Revolution he'd been haunted by generations of LeForts who had loyally served their tsar. To elude his feelings of guilt, he had just visited Tobolsk, where the deposed emperor and empress with their five children were kept under house arrest. Earlier, they had been detained in Tsarskoe Selo; but, after the thwarted Bolshevik coup in July, Kerensky had decided that this was too close to Petrograd — not only were the Romanov family in proximity to mobs roused to blood violence by the extreme left factions, but they were also far too available as a rallying-point for Monarchists. Tobolsk in western Siberia was a provincial capital mouldering far from the railway line.

As Stephan closed the door there was scampering in the walls.

'You have rats,' LeFort said breathily. 'They terrify me, rats.'

'They're not my favourites, either. Well? Did they get the money?' Before LeFort's departure for Tobolsk, Stephan, enslaved by substantial ghosts of his own, had handed over a purse filled with gold coins for the ex-tsar.

LeFort glanced nervously around the attic as if the flourishing tribe of rodents might hear and report the conversation. 'It's not so easy, Strakhov. They're prisoners in the governor's mansion; they're never allowed out; they can't have visitors; their mail is opened. I had no way to contact them. Then Soloviev showed up.'

'Soloviev? You mean Rasputin's son-in-law? He's there?'

'Yes. And he has ways of contacting their Majesties. Others get messages through sometimes, but Soloviev claims that his are the only ones their Majesties trust.'

'Because of the Rasputin connection,' Stephan said with considerable bitterness.

'There's no other explanation. Believe me, this Soloviev's a shifty-eyed pig. Anyway, a few days later he slipped into my hotel room. Their Majesties, he told me, had graciously accepted our contributions for the "snow troop" operation.'

'The what?'

'You have to understand that fortunes are gathered to help the Imperial Family escape. As as I can tell, Soloviev's concocted this scheme to get his hands on every kopek.' LeFort's plump shaking fingers twiddled the pencil. 'His story is that the entire family are to be spirited off in a troika by Whites.'

'The plot's a good idea.'

'Strakhov, what a poet you are, building castles in the air.'

'Why do you say that?'

'Soloviev is a scoundrel and he is in charge. The simple truth is that I'm a coward. I shivered the entire time I was in Tobolsk — ragged soldiers at every corner, peasants who spat at anyone in respectable clothes. I couldn't leave fast enough. So I let myself be gulled by the shifty swine. He's got our money, and not a damn thing's going to change for the Imperial Family.'

'Maybe it's better this way. What if they *had* attempted to escape and been caught? Then they would be in the soup.'

'In the soup? Oh, what a dreamer! They're already in hell. Bad enough mosquitoes the size of buzzards in the summer, winter gales that literally freeze the blood, but that's not the half of it. The walls and fence of the governor's mansion are covered with the vilest cartoons about the Imperial Family. The empress and grand duchesses see this filth every time they go near a window. His

Majesty saws his own firewood while the crudest sort of peasant guards make jokes and spit. They're helpless.'

'Kerensky will protect them.'

'Oh, Kerensky's a decent sort. But he'll be kicked out in the election.'

'Why so negative?'

'Why? Strakhov, we've unleashed the Antichrist. Anything that's not vile is doomed, doomed.'

After LeFort had left, Stephan sat at the desk. LeFort had left behind a note: 'Tobolsk. Conditions of Imperials, Soloviev. My culpability.' A stutterer, LeFort overcame his handicap by outlining any important conversation in advance. Stephan struck a match. As he dropped the flaming scrap in the cold stove, he thought: *The Revolution's succeeded. We've done away with the Okhrana. Yet here I am, still burning papers.* He returned to the desk, slumping with his face buried in his icy palms. Darkness fell, and the nocturnal rats scurried forth from their hole, pattering around the attic. Stephan didn't move.

Though far more hopeful about the future than LeFort, continuing to believe that soon Russia would have a just and equitable government, he wasn't thinking about politics. His convictions were like the lights across the street, glimmering through the fog, mocking him like insubstantial ghostly creatures. The Willys.

The truth stood out real and stark; he

could actually see in block letters the words: YOUR BROTHER.

Nicholas was his half-brother.

Stephan's wound ached, and he pressed his hand to his abdomen. He had taken part in banishing his brother as well as his innocent nieces and nephew to a living hell.

Church bells chimed eight, the hour when a three-course dinner was served in the Tauride dining-hall. Like most delegates, Stephan usually downed the meal hungrily. Tonight, though, he stayed at his desk brooding about Tobolsk.

Chapter Thirty-six

Although many Russian soldiers refused to fight or deserted, the war tottered on. Wounded continued to flow into Military Hospital No. 5. The doctors, though, itched to return to their homes. On a rainy night in mid-September, at the end of a marathon vodka-drenched session of the executive committee, the surgical unit pushed through a decree: the hospital was closed.

Twenty-five of the severely wounded, with Marya and Golder in attendance, were jostled to Petrograd, where a yawning Provisional Government functionary deployed the ambulances to a general hospital not far from the Petrograd Stock Exchange on Vasilevsky Island. At the overcrowded hospital, Marya and Golder cajoled various committees, finally procuring beds for their charges on condition that she join the staff as a nurse rather than as a Volunteer, and he become part of the hospital's depleted surgical unit.

Nursing sisters had less time off duty than Volunteers. It was two weeks before Marya's first free day. She went with Klazkha to 'get a look at the Duma in session'.

'You ain't pulling any wool over my eyes. What you want to look at is Stephan,' Klazkha said as they made their way through the Tauride Palace.

Neither the Catherine Hall's soaring dimensions nor the proximity to the seats of power intimidated the spectators' gallery. Mothers nursed their infants, children played noisy games of tag up and down the stepped aisles, families gnawed black bread and onions, card-players hunched over their greasy deck. In these bleak autumnal days, tickets were obtained for warmth and shelter rather than to observe the democratic process.

Below, officials were ambling on to the dais, taking their places. Where the tsar's portrait had once presided now hung an immense, theatrically posed full-length photograph of President Kerensky: the glass covering it was streaked with spittle.

'Down there. See?' Klazkha pointed to a pair of empty places in the first row of the balcony. 'Them two must be ours.'

'You really *do* have pull. These seats are marvellous.' Slipping off her uniform cape, Marya leaned over the rail. 'Do you see him?'

'No; and I don't see Ovruch, neither,' responded Klazkha. 'The thing I don't understand is why you don't drop by Stephan's place. I showed you his address, printed right on top of the Democratic Reform newspaper, plain for everybody to see.' Klazkha's throaty inflections bespoke pride in her newfound literacy.

'In Pskov we agreed, he and I, that it was impossible between us. Remember, I told you.'

'Oh, so you did.' Klazkha was unbuttoning her ancient black overcoat with the frayed neck and cuffs.

Marya had hoped for a chance to say Stephan's name. With a sense of loss, she accepted that Klazkha — sound, practical Klazkha — wasn't about to pursue any feminine discussion about the pros and cons of visiting Stephan.

From here it was too far from the podium to see faces clearly, but the first speaker, short and beefy, wore a uniform with puttees wrapped around his thick legs. In a booming monotone he vilified President Kerensky. The hubbub in the gallery increased deafeningly, and the deputies moved around talking in one another's ears. After an interminable harangue, the speaker backed away from the lectern.

The chairman banged his gavel. 'I call on S.L. Strakhov.'

Stephan's desk lay beneath the gallery. At the exact moment he strode into view, the sun emerged from the clouds, burning through the grimy windows with rays of legendary brilliance: it was impossible to see with any degree of clarity. Marya leaned towards the lectern as if the rising and falling timbre of Stephan's voice controlled the tidal rhythm of her breath. She had no idea what he was saying.

Then thick grey clouds obscured the sun. Despite the distance, she saw Stephan with vivid clarity.

He was looking directly at her. Warmth surged through her body, and this warmth was the only sensation she felt. *I'll go to his place,* she thought. *Of course I'll go there.* Later she was uncertain whether it was impulse or predestination that had made the decision.

The clouds ushered in a storm that broke in late afternoon.

Stephan, who had just returned home from pleading with the Duma to let the Romanovs emigrate, listened to the hailstones drum against the round window. Still wearing his overcoat and knitted mittens, he sat at his desk peering down at paper which was a dim rectangle in the gathering dusk. He was meant to be totalling the cost of a final election broadside, but inside his head words kept clamouring. He took a fresh sheet:

When Autumn sheds her saffron clothes,
We will find a shelter in the woods . . .

Absorbed and intent as if he were listening to faraway dictation, he slashed lines across the page. A gust of wind drove the hail more fiercely, drowning out the tentative tap at his door. At the second tap, he looked up and sighed. The poem, such as it was, would die in embryo, unable to survive the harsh air of the outside world.

He opened the door, and in that first moment he felt only a prickling confusion. Had his poem, which naturally was about Marya, summoned her into being? Then happiness blossomed until there was no room for anything but pure elemental joy.

'Marya . . . up in the gallery . . . there was a nurse in the gallery . . .'

'I knew you saw me,' she whispered.

They gazed at each other, then he shook his head as if casting off the spell. 'You're drenched. Come in.'

Leaning against the door to unlace her soaked boots, she blurted: 'Paskevich is in Switzerland.'

How typical of Marya to dive into the most difficult part of the conversation! Smiling, he said: 'Yes, I know. What about you? Aren't you meant to be in Pskov?'

'The hospital voted to close. Dr Golder and I came here with some of the worst cases. What a journey!' Easing off a wet boot, she glanced around the garret. 'Are you . . . uh, do you live here alone?'

'Have I found somebody else? What do you think?' Rewarded by her incandescent smile, Stephan could feel his pulses race. They gazed at each other until footsteps on the narrow stairwell impinged on his zany rapture. 'Marya, put your boots and cape back on,' he said. 'You shouldn't be here. It's not safe.'

'But Paskevich's in Switzerland. I don't understand why — running's not like him. But he can't get at us.'

'It's me I'm talking about. I'm dangerous for you.'

'You? Everybody in the Catherine Hall was spellbound when you talked; people say you're the most respected member of the Duma. And Klazkha, she never exaggerates, she says you're as good as elected to the Constituent Assembly. Who could be safer than you?'

His chest tightened. *Tell her, tell her. It's not fair, it's completely unjust to keep her in the dark.* Yet there he was equivocating. 'What about you? The wife of a tsarist minister? You ought to be home in America with Boris.'

'I'm Sister Nizhni to everybody but Ovruch, Klazkha, and you. Oh, and Dr Golder knows, too.'

'Petrograd's full of people who might recognize you.'

'Bah. Nurses are anonymous.' She drew a breath. 'Now, explain. Why are you a threat?'

Pressing his hands on the veneered desk, he looked down at his whitening nails.

'Stephan, don't you understand? I'd walk through fire for you. Why are you playing these games with me?'

There was such hurt, tenderness and genuine perplexity in the soft voice that he wanted to weep. What was the matter with him anyway? He loved her, he trusted her with his life, so why couldn't he explain himself to her? The question answered itself. *I've hugged my wound so tight for so many years that it's turned gangrenous and stinking. God, how ashamed I am of being his bastard — of being his son.* 'David Francis, the latest American ambassador, is a gentleman of the old school. One look at you will convince him that he's back in the age of chivalry. He'll get you back to America no matter what it takes.'

'I'm not leaving Petrograd.' The silvery eyes glittered with tears. 'Stephan, you don't have to tell me anything at all. I want us to be together again. There. No pride. I've said it.'

'Oh, Marya, Marya.' He repeated the name in a ragged despairing voice.

A rat scurried in the sloping wall, then there was only the rattling hail. Marya's heavy stockings were a darker grey at the feet, and she left wet prints on the floor as she crossed the attic to him. She halted before they were touching but she was close enough for him to feel emanations of heat from her slight, tenderly curved body. With a groan he reached for her, holding her close, kissing her eyelids, her forehead, her lips. The room was icy, the hail noisier, but the real world was here in her body and his own. Lifting her slight weight, he carried her to the alcove and fell with her on the bed.

October the 24th passed like any other day in the hospital. The admitting nurse reported at the lunch-table that twelve assault victims, most of them elderly, had been brought to the emergency bandaging-room. When Marya glanced out of the ward window she saw children on their way to school, and the customary line of bundled women inching with excruciating slowness towards the bakery.

During the night, though, she was awakened by reverberations that rattled every window in the nurses' dormitory. With each jolt, brightness streaked from the Neva towards the Winter Palace, now President Kerensky's home and the seat of his interim Provisional Government.

'May God have mercy on us, it's artillery,' cried the operating-room sister who had served at a field-hospital. The nurses yanked their capes over their nightgowns and raced across the courtyard to the hospital proper, where the night staff were in the hallways exchanging wild rumours: German troops had captured the city, Monarchists had taken over, the Anarchists were blowing up everything, Nicholas was back in power and destroying the city that had destroyed him. No further salvoes were fired. Everybody straggled uneasily back to their duties or to bed.

In the morning a teenage cadet with a bullet wound in his thigh was carried into

Marya's ward. Between bitten-back whimpers, the boy told her that he had been guarding the Winter Palace when the barrage came. 'It was the Red sailors on the *Aurora*. They fired at the palace,' he muttered. 'They only fired blanks, but after that a big mob rushed inside. The heads of the Provisional Government told us cadets to surrender, they didn't want bloodshed. I held up my hands like you're meant to, but some stinking peasant shot me anyway. The Bolsheviks arrested everybody in the Government.'

'What?'

'Sister, you're all white.' The boy began to sob. 'I'm going to die, aren't I?'

'Of course you're not. But if you don't stay calm you'll disturb your stitches. Later, we'll drain the wound.' Frantic about Stephan, she didn't know what she said, but the boy relaxed.

Just after the lunch-carts were wheeled in, Klazkha came into the ward. As she hurried between the high-legged tight-packed cots quite a few men looked up from their watery gruel — her body, as always, attracted male attention. Ignoring the appreciative remarks, she handed Marya a single sheet of blurred newsprint. It was printed only on one side:

TO THE CITIZENS OF RUSSIA
The Provisional Government has been deposed. Government authority has

passed to the Petrograd Soviet of Workers and the Military-Revolutionary Committee . . .

The task for which the people have been struggling — the immediate offer of a democratic peace, the abolition of landlord property in land, worker control over production, the creation of a Soviet Government — this task is assured.

Long Live the Revolution of Workers, Soldiers and Peasants!

'Them Bolsheviks, they took over Petrograd real easy,' Klazkha was saying. 'They just told the guards everywhere to go home, then posted pickets. Can you believe it? Practically no shooting, and now they got all the government buildings, the railway stations, the post offices, the telephone places, the banks and bridges, everything.' Klazkha might be a Bolshevik, but red was not her colour. Her toneless voice held not a hint of triumph at the party's bloodless successful takeover.

'The cadet, the boy in the first cot, was at the Winter Palace. He said that the entire Provisional Government was arrested. Is that true?'

'The Cabinet, they was carted off. They was almost lynched on the way to jail, but President Kerensky escaped.'

'What about the Duma?'

'Ovruch says Lenin wants them to stay. If

you ask me, I think them Bolshevik bigwigs want somebody to blame if things go sour. That way they can run things in secret, with nobody to account to. That's men for you.' She glared around at the enfeebled prostrate veterans. 'Power and no responsibility — ain't that exactly what all of 'em wants?'

'Stephan —'

'Don't take it personal, Marya; he's not as bad as most.'

'Have you heard anything about him?'

'I come the minute this paper was out.' Klazkha touched Marya's arm and said a bit too heartily: 'Don't you worry. That Stephan, he can take care of himself.'

Marya went crazy for the next two days, then she was off duty.

The area around Tverskaya Street was crowded with haranguing speakers and placard-carriers: the entire civil service had gone on strike against the new Bolshevik regime.

'Delegate Strakhov's not back yet, and he didn't tell me where he went,' Stephan's *dvornik* said, adding in a wheedling quaver: 'But I'll bet he tell you more'n me what he's up to, eh, Comrade Sister?'

The next weeks there was no word from Stephan — and no news of him, either; the only newspapers now distributed were the Bolshevik *Pravda* and *Izvestia*, and they printed stories of Bolshevik candidates exclusively. Whenever Marya was free to leave the hospital, she jumped aboard an over-burdened tram or bus. The *dvornik* reported there was no word, no word, each time questioning her slyly about Stephan's past.

Once Golder accompanied her. As they left the building, he said quietly: 'The old man is a spy. In the past, half the doormen were Okhrana spies, and now they are being recruited by the Reds. Best not to go there again.'

Advice that Marya was incapable of heeding. Climbing to Stephan's attic, she would deride herself as a pathetic little dog sniffing her absent master's clothes, but she couldn't stay away.

At the end of November, blizzards swept down from the North Pole, the worst storms ever recorded in the city, one blinding snowfall succeeding another, and many who ventured outside froze to death. For safety's sake, the hospital committee voted that the staff could not leave the buildings.

On Christmas Eve, while the wind howled and shrieked, she found an unsigned note under her pillow. 'Dearest, I am safe and will contact you as soon as I return to Petrograd.' She held the mysteriously delivered scrap of paper to her cheek; it was the most precious Christmas gift she had ever received!

The nurses' and doctors' committees voted to strike if they were cooped up another day. The storms continued; however, the executive committee had no choice but to rescind its order.

Chapter Thirty-seven

Tverskaya Street hadn't been cleared. Drifts buried the ground-floor windows. The stalled white-blanketed motor-bus resembled a sleeping polar bear. A narrow foot-path was carved in the shoulder-high snow. Marya picked her way along the path, her nose and mouth covered with a thick muffler, her cold-anaesthetized feet encased within three pairs of knitted socks and outsize felt snow-boots.

She was trudging behind an equally muffled man who carried a bundle over his shoulder. Concentrating on avoiding the icy patches, she took a while to recognize him.

'Stephan!' she shouted. 'Stephan!'

He turned. Stared. Then they were floundering towards each other. Clumsy in the layers of clothing, they embraced, pulling back to gaze in wonderment at each other. The frost whitening his hair and eyebrows increased Marya's sense that it had been decades since she'd last held him.

'It's you, it's really you.' Her whisper seemed too low to form the great clouds coming from her mouth. 'I've been frantic.'

'But didn't you get my message?'

'At Christmas. Where've you been?'

'Moscow. They fought the Bolsheviks in Moscow. At least, the military academy cadets and students did. I ran in circles like a rabid dog trying to pull the Liberal parties together. Hopeless. Absolutely hopeless. Talk about fiddling while Rome burns — they keep on with their old arguments while Lenin steamrollers ahead. His goal is total undivided control, and he won't lose a moment's sleep if in the process he destroys Russia —' Stephan broke off. A trio of unkempt Red Guards had turned the corner and were slogging through the pristine whiteness. Their boots, which made shrill angry sounds in the snow, were invisible, so that the bouncing rifles slung over their shoulders seemed to be propelling them.

Stephan retrieved his bundle. 'Come on, let's get inside.'

Marya didn't budge. 'Stephan, every time I've been to your place the *dvornik*'s acted cagier and cagier.'

'Old Dmitry? You're imagining it. He and I are friends.'

'Dr Golder says he's a spy.'

'He did?' Stephan said. 'What a hopeless case I am, thinking friendship matters any more. Come on, then, we'll sneak in the back door.'

The garret, marginally warmer than the street, was sunk in gloom, the sole light coming from a rubicund glow that penetrated the rimed oriel window. They sat on the edge of the bed with the heavy dusty quilt around their shoulders.

'Klazkha doesn't think they'll stay in power, the Bolsheviks,' Marya said. 'Golder agrees with her; he says they'll be gone before Easter. But I'm not so hopeful. I hear the wounded keep repeating, "Peace! Land! Bread!"' *Why am I prattling this way when all I want is to kiss him?* 'A fine slogan, even if they don't mean a word.'

'And to think that I've spent my life unleashing these cynical liars!'

'They aren't all like that. I see Ovruch at Klazkha's and he's the same as ever. Even in these storms he's been seeing that food gets through to the hospital.' As Marya spoke she remembered Paskevich's acid amusement as he'd warned her that the idealistic revolutionaries never were the ones who grasped power. *Paskevich is brilliant — Paskevich has left Russia.* 'Stephan, the Revolution's gone sour. Now's the time to leave the country.'

'Exactly what I told you before.'

'Can you get us forgeries?'

'It's impossible for me to leave now.'

'Why? You said yourself that you couldn't do any good here.'

'There are people in Tobolsk I must help.'

'People? Who?'

'My . . . family.'

Her body went stiff, inflexible. 'You told me you had no family. Tobolsk? That's where the Romanovs are.' She turned to peer at him.

Stephan couldn't look away.

There was something terrible about the still white face so near his own. Reared by an artist, Stephan had always considered beauty a pleasing attribute. The ancient Greeks, though, had understood that certain aspects of beauty are too excessive for the mortal eye to look upon. Gazing at her, he was unable to breathe. It was as if a boa constrictor had wound around him.

I'll surely die, suffocate to death if I don't tell her now.

His hands clenched the quilt so tightly that a feather escaped, drifting upwards. 'Years ago I found out . . .' His throat tightened.

'Yes?'

'I didn't know until after we'd met . . .'

'Stephan!'

'I swear I didn't know then.' Lips scarcely moving, he mumbled out Madame Strakhov's dying request, his discovery of the hidden letter. 'I'd sworn to destroy the papers unread. But this envelope was addressed to me. My name. So it wasn't wrong for me to open it . . .' Looking into that terrible beauty, his throat again tightened.

She touched his sleeve.

'My sister had written to me,' he muttered. 'My dead sister. At least, I'd always been told that she was my sister.'

As he spoke, Marya sat more and more rigidly until their bodies no longer touched. Her neck prickled, her insides went numb, yet perversely she was unsurprised. Hadn't his revelations been foreshadowed often enough? The jeweller, Sazanov, remarking that the sand-rubbed diamond had been owned by an ancient and powerful family, Paskevich's mocking deference that night Stephan had followed her to the Crimson Palace, the barricade of secrecy he had erected.

'So the tsar's your half-brother.' She reached to her throat for the braided thread, drawing out the ring. 'And this belonged to the Romanovs.'

'I had no idea when I gave it to you. *He* sent it when I was born. And the money came from him, too.'

'You're the son of Alexander the Third,' she said.

'A silly schoolgirl was seduced by a creaky lecher.'

'Who cares how old they were?' Anger, irrational and overpowering, swept over Marya: without realizing it, she had switched to English. 'The point is you're one of the Imperial Family.'

'I never saw him. He never contacted me —'

'How could you have kept something so major — so vital — from me?'

'If you only knew how many times I tried to get the words out.'

'Oh, what an idiot I am!' she cried. 'Am I such a flibbertigibbet that you couldn't trust me? Or don't I mean enough to you?'

'Stop it!' He jumped up so swiftly that the bed swayed. Going to the desk, he gripped the rail of his chair to control himself. 'Marya, stop blaming yourself. It's me. Even about silly minor things I've never been able to be open about myself. I don't know how I got this way. Maybe it was having "parents" ' — he set the word apart — 'who were so much older; maybe it's inherited from *him*; or, more likely, it's an individual shortcoming. But for as long as I can remember I've had this sense of otherness, of being alone on an island. Any personal question seemed groundwork for an invasion. Forced to talk about myself, I felt as if I had to hurl each word across the mined water. Later, after the letter told me who I was, it seemed fair and just that I was set apart. Wasn't I the son of a despot? I deserved to be cut off.'

'We lived together in Vyborg,' she pointed out.

'Yes, and not telling you then was worse than any lie.'

'You're not a liar.'

'Try to understand how I felt. All my life I'd idolized my father — or, rather, my grandfather — and adored my mother — my grandmother. To me they represented the highest principles. Justice. Sincerity. Integrity. Then I discovered they'd lied to me every day, every hour, each minute of my life. My real mother was a feather-brained dancer. My real father was the man I most despised in the world: a narrow-minded cruel despot. I ached for revenge, but all four of them were dead. I was a wolf without vocal cords caught in a trap of rage and anguish, silently howling to the uncaring moon. I hate myself, Marya, and it was unbearable to have you hate me, too.'

Across the dim garret she could see the gleam of tears on his cheeks.

'Hush, darling, hush,' she murmured, and went to draw him back to the bed. Pulling him down on to the unsheeted mattress, she had a swift unwelcome memory: 'Leda and the Swan', a painting of a rosy mortal woman embracing a deity in the guise of a swan. Then he was kissing her throat, and pleasure took over. It had been a long time.

She was off duty until midnight, so they decided to have supper at Constant's. The waiter, resplendently uniformed in gold-braided green, retreated to the warmth of the kitchen, and only a few distant tables were occupied, yet they found themselves whispering in lower and lower voices.

'Tobolsk is a crazy idea.' Marya was using her fingers to detach the particle of fish on the spine of the *vobla;* these tiny, skeletal salt fish along with heavy bran-laden bread were now the staples of Petrograd diet. A scrap of bone cut into her gum and she took a sip of water. 'What could you do there?'

'Call it salving my conscience.'

'Why on earth should you feel guilty?'

'Nicholas isn't a monster like . . . like his father. I never intended to destroy him or his children . . .' His undertone faded.

The waiter was returning with two silver-nested glasses of tea on a massive silver tray. They didn't speak until the steaming beige water was set before them and their bone-strewn plates were carried away.

'How soon,' she asked, 'are we leaving?'

'We? What are you talking about?'

'Siberia. We'll need travel documents.'

He leaned across the table. 'You're not coming with me.'

She ignored him. 'Golder has a friend on the new transportation committee.'

On 5 January, Stephan marched along the snowy crowded Shlapernaia in a solemn procession of the First Constituent Assembly. The Tauride Square was crowded with armed Red Guard, artillery, machine-gunners. The only entrance to the palace grounds was through a narrow wicker gate, where the delegates were scrutinized and patted down — procedures repeated by Latvian Red Guards before they entered the palace. They gathered uneasily in the Assembly Hall. Through the windows came the chatter of gunfire. The Red Guard were firing on the triumphant crowd. Stephan bit back his cry of betrayal. At the same time relief flooded through him. Marya wasn't out there. She was on duty at the hospital.

Non-Bolshevik delegates were drowned by hisses and boos from the packed gallery. After several hours a Bolshevik delegate jumped to his feet shouting: 'I refuse to take part in this charade. The Constituent Assembly is made up of capitalist tools, hire-lings of bankers, hyenas who feed on the workers and counter-revolutionaries.' This was a signal for all the Bolshevik delegates to march out. After their departure, the hall quietened, and delegates read interminable maiden speeches.

At four in the morning, shots rang in the gallery.

'I have been instructed to inform you that all those present should leave the Assembly Hall because the Tauride Guards are tired,' a round-faced Bolshevik sailor shouted. After an exchange with the chairman, the sailor raised his pistol, firing into the air. 'I request that the Assembly Hall be immediately vacated.'

'We'll reconvene in an hour,' the chairman roared.

Stephan waited with several hundred other delegates at the immense buffet which was filled with empty vodka-bottles. Heavily armed men, mostly sailors and Latvians, clanked about. Within the hour, a young man came to stand at the doorway. Cupping his hands, he trumpeted that he was Comrade Sverdlov. 'The Central Executive Committee has ratified a resolution,' he bellowed. 'The Constituent Assembly is dissolved. Now, go on home.'

Pulling on his overcoat, Stephan felt hollow, as if he were sliding from a rope bridge that had just given way under his feet. *So it ends,* he thought. *The only freely elected parliament in our history is dissolved after one night.*

'Sister Alexiev tells me you wish to travel.' Golder's articulation was more careful than usual. 'In which direction?'

The doctor, Stephan and Marya all wore shawls over their hats and coats as they crouched on foundation blocks. Floorboards had been chopped away, and the partially destroyed roof showed patches of lead-coloured sky. This was one of the wooden houses that the Bolsheviks had commandeered to be torn down as fuel.

'I'm going east,' Stephan said. There was a desperate ring to his words.

Golder assessed him. As a patient in Military Hospital No. 5, Strakhov had been pale and weak, yet imbued with purpose. Golder had, of course, been jealous on Marya's account, yet at the same time he had been filled with admiration for the wounded captain, the epitome of a gallant poetic revolutionary. That idealistic optimism had vanished. The eyes looking warily from shadowed sockets were a startlingly intense blue, the high-planed face was more angular, and despite the ridiculous shawl this new, darkly restless despair was maybe more attractive, certainly more in keeping with the times.

'How far east?' Golder asked.

'Siberia.'

'That creates a problem. Nobody quite

505

knows what is happening in Siberia. A great deal of fighting — the Czechs, Whites, Greens, Anarchists. Official policy is to issue no travel passes to Siberia.'

'It's my home.' Stephan was fumbling in his pocket with a gloved hand. 'Here's my passport.'

Siberian landowners invariably lived in the western cities; they left the boggy vastness to peasants — and Strakhov did not come from peasant stock, Golder would stake his life on that. Raising the passport to the light, he examined the indented seals. 'Forgery?' he enquired.

Strakhov shrugged assent.

'Excellent work. Where in Siberia do you wish to go?'

'Tyumen.'

Tyumen, a small town on the Siberian railway line, was a jumping-off point: most people travelled there after the ice broke up, when steamers could ply the Tura river. 'Is Tyumen your final destination?'

'Tobolsk.'

At this Golder adjusted his steel spectacles. 'Even more of a problem. The Romanovs are there.'

'So I believe,' Stephan retorted stiffly.

'And Sister Alexiev is to travel with you?'

'It's far too risky,' Stephan said.

'Name one thing that isn't risky now?' Marya cried.

Golder knew better than to argue with his wilful American love. Shrugging his shoulders, he raised his gloved palms, an immemorial gesture of helplessness, one of the rare times he displayed any overt sign of his Jewish heritage. 'Two sets of passes,' he said. 'Let me see what can be arranged.'

The Bolshevik clerks who bumbled around in the magnificent suites of the tsarist bureaucracy had little schooling; quite a number of them were illiterate. Obviously they avoided paperwork. Golder's contact, however, was a high-ranking administrator from the Central Committee.

Two weeks later, at the fuel-ration house, which was now cannibalized to the rafters and beams, Golder handed over the sheaf of profusely stamped documents, then produced two long slips of paper. 'These are tickets on a secret train.' He spoke with justifiable pride. Tickets on scheduled trains meant one fought to climb on to the roof or cling to the couplings. 'You'd better hurry over to the Nicholas yard to keep your place.'

'Now?' Marya cried.

'There will already be a crowd. The departure time is early tomorrow morning.'

'But what about my promise to stay on at the hospital?'

'I will explain to Matron later.'

'And there's Klazkha and Ovruch — I must say goodbye —'

'It is unwise to advertise comings and goings,' Golder interrupted forcefully. 'Collect your clothes as if you are spending time with a friend. No farewells. Just walk away from the hospital.'

Marya jammed her few possessions into her valise. Golder was waiting for her outside the staff door. Glancing around to make sure they were alone, he said: 'Some things for your journey.' He opened his medical bag and took out a bottle of kerosene. 'This will keep away the lice. Never forget that a single bite from one infected louse could mean typhus.' He also produced a small phial of aspirin and a loaf of white bread — gifts so rare that they must have cost him many months' salary.

'You're our guardian angel,' Marya said shakily. 'Take care of yourself, Pavel.'

His ears reddened at her use of his first name. With sincerity unbecoming in an avowed atheist, he said: 'May God watch over you in Tobolsk.'

1918

Our task is to overthrow the world.

LENIN

For us, all is a question of expediency.

OVRUCH

There has never been a civil war without executions.

LENIN

Chapter Thirty-eight

The train travelled with agonizing slowness, draughts blew between the crudely planked boards of the goods-wagon, the toilet was a chamberpot in a blanketed corner, but the rail part of the journey was luxurious in comparison to the time they spent on the seatless woven Siberian sledge — the *koshevy*. On the afternoon of the fourth bone-jolting day, as Tobolsk came into view, the passengers burst into cheers.

Tobolsk reminded Marya of Pskov. Here, too, the ruins of ancient fortifications rose at a meeting of two rivers, and the thick-walled onion-domed churches were equally antiquated. Tobolsk, however, had a primitive nature unique to Siberia. The shops and public buildings were decrepit and un-painted, the tumbledown log huts were caulked with mosses so that they appeared as one with the surrounding forests. Scrawny feral pigs rooted in yards protected by woven willow fences. Peasants and be-grimed priests reeled drunkenly on the main streets.

At the Tobolsk Grand Hotel, a frame building adorned with the splintered remnants of window-boxes, Marya shed her wraps and leaned her aching bones against the desk while Stephan handed over their documents: a new law compelled Tobolsk innkeepers to submit the documents of prospective lodgers to the authorities before renting a room. While a russet-cheeked porter ran the papers over to the town hall, Marya and Stephan sipped tea under the covert gaze of hotel guests clustered near the stove. With their stubbled cheeks, brightly coloured shirts and loose trousers tucked into bast boots, they might have belonged in the Siberian landscape — that is, if their clothing weren't so new. The group watched quite openly as the landlord haggled over the embroidered ribbons that Stephan had packed for barter: on the journey nobody had accepted paper money, everything was either gold or exchange.

The porter led them to a room with a stove that rose to the ceiling and a high-legged bed. Nothing else, not even a washstand. Dizzy from the vodka-laced tea, groggy from the heat, too weary to recognize hunger, Marya kicked off her worn felt snow-boots and collapsed into the deep soft mattress. Within seconds she was asleep.

She woke to a low insistent tapping.

Drowsily she pressed Stephan's shoulder. 'Wake up.'

'I'm awake,' he said in a low voice.

'Somebody's out there.'

'One of those clowns by the stove.'

'Find out what he wants, then.'

'My darling, lovely, impetuous Marya.' He reached an arm around her. 'Tobolsk is crawling with Monarchists who see the Romanovs as holy icons to be rescued and restored to the throne, as well as Anarchists who wish them dead. There are spies and counter-spies. Whoever our visitor is, he'll be wanting me to commit myself.'

'Maybe it's a messenger from your . . .' Although they were whispering, she left the word 'brother' unspoken.

'More likely one of Soloviev's people.' Stephan, embarrassed, had never explained about the gold that had been pocketed by Soloviev. 'That thieving cheat's got the empress's total trust, poor deluded woman.'

'If he's the only way to contact the Romanovs,' she mumbled, yawning, 'then we'll have to deal through him.'

The stealthy taps ceased, and the floor creaked softly.

'He's gone,' Stephan said. But Marya had already fallen back to sleep.

During the night, she stirred from her dreamless slumber. Stephan was not there. Conjecturing that he was using the indoor lavatory, the landlord's greatest pride, she snuggled back into the feather-bed. When she awoke in the morning Stephan was breathing slowly and evenly at her side.

The *koshevy* had taken its toll. As she got out of bed, every muscle in her body protested, and her thighs were so tight that it was torture to descend the rickety staircase. The landlord's stout young wife cut them great slabs from a loaf of moistly rich, sweet-sour brown bread redolent of the earth and set out bowls of pickled river fish and thick, golden soured cream.

'Sheer heaven.' Marya sat back with a sigh. 'Absolute bliss.'

'I was famished, too,' Stephan said. 'Now for a bit of exercise.' He kept his tone purposefully casual.

'Walk?' Marya groaned. 'I can barely totter.' She blew him a kiss. 'See you later.'

The hotel perched beside the frozen Tobol river on the north side of the market-square, a sloping field large enough to accommodate numerous farm-carts and peddlars' wagons. Although this was Tuesday, market day, and the sun was a brazen disc in the hard blue sky, there were less than a dozen vendors in the square. Women as squat as dumplings in layers of winter clothing shoved to make their purchases. Mangy dogs and scrawny pigs snarled and squealed as they fought for offal. On the river, a trapper bent double to haul a sleigh piled with blood-rusty pelts. Peasants in matted furs slipped into the shop on the corner, emerging furtively with earthenware jugs of *samogen,* the potent Siberian illicit vodka.

The previous night when Stephan had sneaked out of the room — thank God, without waking Marya — the square had been deserted. He had been on his way to the apothecary's shop. Treb answered, his black-haired legs like spindly sticks below his nightshirt. An early recruit to the Democratic Reform Party, Treb was astonished when his old mentor told him what brought him to Tobolsk. 'You're here to help Nicholas? You, Iskra, who dedicated your life to ending the Autocracy? You're not in your right senses, and I draw the line at playing messenger to lunatics.' Stephan had talked in low passionate tones about the increased jeopardy of the Romanovs under the Bolshevik regime. Eventually Treb had scratched his bony ankle, promising to send word to the governor's mansion. The pharmacist's conduit was a client, Dr Eugene Botkin, the Imperial physician who had accompanied his deposed patients into exile. 'Don't expect anything,' Treb had warned. 'The Romanovs are as wary as ferrets; and, frankly, there's no reason why they should trust you, an exiled radical, a member of the Provisional Government's Duma.'

Back in the room, beside the soft-breathing Marya, Stephan had decided that his odds might be increased if he displayed himself outside the governor's mansion where the Romanovs were imprisoned. But he had worried that Marya would insist on going into danger with him.

Well, that problem solved itself, he thought as he crossed the square to a wide snow-covered street whose freshly painted sign was unique in dilapidated Tobolsk: FREEDOM HOUSE AVENUE. Freedom House was the post-Revolutionary, never-used name for the governor's mansion.

Though grander than anything else in town, the governor's mansion was unpretentious. Built in a vaguely classical style, with regularly spaced window-embrasures set into the limestone, the second storey was adorned with a porch too narrow for use. Guards clustered on the steps, and more guards strolled back and forth by the carriage-gate, which was open, giving a view of a side-yard where firewood was stacked taller than a man — LeFort had said the tsar sawed the household's firewood. The newly built fence was covered with obscene graffiti.

Stephan couldn't help making involuntary comparisons with the Winter Palace and the other Imperial palaces that he had seen photographed — the villas, the hunting lodges, the enchanted self-contained world of Tsarskoe Selo. But why should he feel guilty? A little over a year ago, all Russia had belonged to Nicholas Romanov, which was certainly a greater evil.

The smaller peak-roofed building opposite, which Treb had told him housed Botkin and others in the dwindled entourage, was guarded by a handful of peasants wearing red armbands on their matted furs. At the moment they were boisterously offering advice to a wizened little fellow-sentry as he chalked the finishing touches to an oversize cartoon of a woman in a royal tiara being mounted by a bearded monk with an enormous penis.

The guards on the steps of the governor's

mansion were watching Stephan. He strolled deliberately, yet more grateful that Marya was not here. If she were, he would have been incapable of walking in these calmly measured steps.

He went uphill a few hundred yards past the mansion, halting to look down at the frozen river junction before he turned back.

'You!'

One of the guards at the governor's mansion was waving in his direction with a 7.62 millimetre Nagant revolver. As Captain Strakhov, Stephan had carried the identical gun: the weapons issued under Nicholas were now being used to imprison him.

'Yes, you!' bawled the guard. 'No dawdling around here!'

Stephan continued at the same deliberate pace. The guard's arm straightened. Snow exploded near Stephan's boots. As the echoes of the shot faded, a curtain stirred in a second-storey window.

Stephan had no idea who was looking out, but from the stealth of the motion it seemed likely that the observer was a member of the Imperial Family — his Romanov kin.

The next morning Marya was able to walk in a stiff-legged gait. She circled the market-place, exclaiming over the small straw-nestled eggs, the limp frozen carrots and gnarled potatoes, the muscular red hams with hairy hocks, the squawking chickens dangling by their legs, the furry rabbits.

Throwing out her arms, she cried: 'What handsome lucky people the Siberians are! Did you ever see anything so prosperous? All these wonderful things just waiting to be bought!'

And, in her company Stephan did find the colours and shapes of the foods extraordinarily vivid, the odours enticing, the Siberian voices mellifluous, the chill air exhilarating. Marya's silvery eyes sparkled. 'Do we have enough ribbons to barter for one of these hams? I'd love to take one back for Klazkha. She's so practical she'd make it last until summer. But I think a cheese would be better for Dr Golder. Oh, do let's go back and look at the cheese-stand.'

Her cheeks were pink, the lovely face glowed in the cold air. She bubbled with enthusiasm, warmth, life! How could he ever have been glad of her absence?

'Your prescription will be ready at four this afternoon.'

The note was delivered by a scampering girl as Marya and Stephan warmed themselves at the hall stove. Stephan stared at the paper until the small precise writing blurred. This was the code he and Treb had decided on if a reply were sent from the governor's mansion. Stephan had counted on waiting a minimum of a week. To have the message delivered and answered in less than two days? Too good to be true. A trap? Would he find Red

Guards waiting to arrest him at the apothecary's shop? He had known Treb for years, and trusted him, but Russia had been smashed and old friendships lay in shards amid the other debris.

'How does anyone know you're here?' Marya asked in a low anxious voice.

'It's from Leo Treb, an old friend. I spotted the name on the pharmacy sign on my walk, and dropped in to see if it was him. And it was.' Hating himself for the glib reply, a mingling of truth and prevarication, he got to his feet. 'He was busy then, but now he has time for a drink.'

'I'll pop along with you.'

'What, and interrupt reminiscences of the good old days?'

Just then one of the putative spies shoved through the double doors. In the sudden draught, Stephan picked up his coat. He wanted to tell her that if he wasn't back by dinner time she must return immediately to Petrograd, yet he knew that such a warning would only convince Marya that she must accompany him — an argument that might be overheard.

'I'll try to keep it short,' he said.

A clock was chiming four as he arrived at the apothecary's shop. Treb, in his white coat, was talking to a woman with a bandage around her jaw. Interrupting his own rapid flow of advice, he said: 'Ah, Comrade. You're a bit early. The prescription's still in my laboratory.' He nodded meaningfully at the beaded curtain. 'If you don't mind getting it yourself?'

Stephan glanced around at the shop with its white glass jars marked in Latin and its dispensary cabinet with labelled drawers. Everything seemed normal. Excitement showed on Treb's squarish red face, but there was no sweat on the narrow forehead. The woman held her hand to the bandage, covering what appeared to be a genuine toothache.

Nothing appeared amiss. But all at once he was recalling that one hot morning during the Brusilov offensive he had stepped into a seemingly normal, shady birch grove only to have German bullets hail around him.

Then, he'd been under orders to advance, and now his mission was the same. He had to contact Nicholas. Drawing a shallow breath, he moved behind the counter. The beads jangled, swaying behind him as he climbed six steps and stepped into the darkness. The smell of drugs and medicinal herbs, intense below, was overpowering.

'I thank you for your promptness, Monsieur Strakhov,' a man whispered in French, the language of the Court. 'And I apologize for the lack of lights, but this is safer for us both.'

Stephan's pupils expanded. He saw that he was in a corridor less than two feet across and eight feet long. To his left, a waist-high ledge held open jars and marble mortars and pestles. At the far end of the narrow pharmacy was the shadowy outline of the speaker. A short plump-bellied man in a dresscoat.

Nicholas didn't send a note, he sent an envoy, Stephan thought. *The very first recognition of my existence from my father's line.*

Closing the door, he continued to hold the porcelain knob. He needed it to maintain his balance.

'Dr Eugene Botkin at your service,' the other man said. 'Time is short, and we have much to discuss.'

Chapter Thirty-nine

'Since Monsieur Treb passed on your most kind offer, his Majesty has been so kind as to discuss the matter with me at great length.' There was a pedantically earnest note in the cultivated voice.

'I never expected a reply this soon.'

'The Heir needed a few pills for his cold.' In fact — or so Treb had informed Stephan — the boy was suffering from painful internal bleeding; however, even in the dark night of exile, the former tsar and his wife clutched at the secret of haemophilia. 'I came by yesterday with the prescription. We in the entourage are permitted a certain amount of freedom; but, alas, the Imperial Family are not. These Revolutionary swine!'

'Before we go any further, Dr Botkin, you had better know that I was one of those swine. I was exiled for my sins, and later served in the Provisional Government.'

'Yes, his Majesty told me. He also said you were never a Terrorist.'

Nicholas knew about him . . . 'I had no idea he was aware of me.'

'For many years.'

Struck dumb, Stephan sank on to a chair. Dr Botkin followed suit. Facing each other this way, their knees almost touched.

'His Majesty went over my instructions several times,' Botkin said. 'The first matter of which I was to inform you concerned his father. When the late tsar lay dying, he entrusted certain . . . well, *delicate* aspects of his private life to his oldest son.'

Delicate aspects of his private life. What an old-maidish euphemism for the huge lusty tyrant's by-blows.

'His Majesty asked me to explain that in your case he fulfilled these . . . *filial obligations* to his late father by arranging that you were not excessively punished for your youthful escapades.'

Stephan clenched his hands to hide the tremor. 'And I thought I was brilliant or lucky when the Okhrana didn't torture me or pack me off to a Siberian labour-camp,' he said bitterly.

'There is no need for self-reproach, Monsieur Strakhov.'

'But there is, Doctor, there is. Short of restoring him to the throne, I'll do whatever he asks.'

'Might I ask why you've made this turn-about?'

'Believe me when I say that what I intended was to make Russian society more just, not to force him and his loved ones into captivity.'

'You uncorked an evil genie, and you wish to make amends — that's it, then?'

'Exactly.' Stephan paused. 'It's more than that. He watched over me, and anything I do for him can be considered repayment.'

'Good. And you will obey his wishes?'

'You have my word on it,' Stephan said. 'Anything that's within my power, I'll do.'

'There are certain preliminaries that must be covered before the Imperial Family can . . . emigrate.'

'Tell me what he wishes me to do.'

'And you will obey?'

'I give my promise. I'll do whatever he asks of me.'

The bell jangled below as the door slammed shut. There was a window behind Botkin. The faintest twilight came through the closed shutters, throwing wan stripes across the plump face and tightly pursed lips. When no further sounds came from the shop, Botkin flipped a handkerchief open, mopping at his forehead. 'Tobolsk can give one a terrible case of nerves. Pardon me for being abrupt and not conversing more, but the sooner we can get to his Majesty's request, the sooner we can leave, don't you agree?'

'Absolutely. What does Nicholas ask of me?'

'A certain gentleman is being detained in St Petersburg. In the Kresty Prison. The sovereign wishes him freed.'

'A rescue?'

'Is that the only way you can get him released?'

'I'm *persona non grata* with the Bolshevik regime myself; I have no power, none at all. But I'll do my best.' Stephan frowned. 'A prisoner? It's hard to fathom how a prisoner could help the Imperial Family.'

'His Majesty didn't confide that.' Briefly the apothecary smell of the small room was replaced by the odour of soap and peppermint as he leaned forward to whisper: 'But he stressed that getting this personage to Zurich was vital.'

Stephan frowned, baffled. He could only assume that the prisoner was an incarcerated grand duke, one of the Imperial Family. But why Zurich? 'It won't be easy. As I said, I'm powerless and so are my fellow-liberals.'

'Are you backing down?' Botkin asked curtly.

'No, of course not. I gave my solemn word. I'll do my utmost.'

At a soft creak on the staircase, Stephan and Botkin were both on their feet.

There was a tap, and Treb's voice. 'Dr Botkin, you've been here almost half an hour.'

'I'm putting on my things,' Botkin responded, and reached for a fur-lined coat neatly hung on a wall hook. 'The prisoner will be heavily guarded. It's Count Paskevich.'

'*Paskevich?*' Stephan gripped the ledge.

'He was close to his Majesty. A minister in his cabinet.'

'Hasn't anyone here heard? He's already in Switzerland; he left Russia in the summer.'

'He came back in December. He's been in the Kresty since he set foot on Russian soil.'

'Surely there would have been rumours — something?'

'He's being held incommunicado so Trotsky can pick the time to use him for a show trial.'

A low urgent voice came from outside. 'Dr Botkin!'

'His Majesty can count on you, then?'

'I gave my solemn word.'

'Forgive me for repeating myself, but I must make the importance of your task clear. Before I came here, both their Imperial Majesties whispered several times how imperative it is to the entire family that Count Paskevich reach Zurich.' Botkin's palm was wet as he gripped Stephan's hand in a fervent farewell.

Stephan waited in the medicinal-odoured darkness: doubtless Botkin was being watched, and following him out would incriminate not only both of them but the Romanovs, Treb and Marya, too. 'Paskevich, Paskevich, Paskevich,' he whispered the name until the syllables made no more sense than Nicholas's urgency to rescue the man — if he needed rescuing.

Marya paced the hall with increasing impatience as she awaited Stephan's return. Finally she got her outdoor things and asked the landlord for directions to Comrade Treb's pharmacy. The door was locked, but a gas-lamp inside showed Stephan and his friend leaning on the counter, a vodka-bottle between them.

As they returned to the hotel, Stephan explained about his interview with Botkin. Ashamed of shutting her out until now, he used a crisp tone to tell her about Nicholas's unceasing protection, and his impulsive vow to perform whatever task the former tsar set for him. 'Of course, when I promised, I had not a clue what he wanted. I'm to get Paskevich out of the Kresty.'

'Paskevich is in prison?'

'Or so Botkin says.'

Marya pulled the uniform cape tighter about her. 'I told you he'd never run away.'

'Everyone except you,' Stephan said, 'and of course the sad little Court tucked away here, believes that the heroic count is already safe in Switzerland.'

'Oh, that dumb stupid jealousy of yours!' Marya stamped her boots on the hard-packed snow. After a few steps, she asked: 'Why is he so important to them?'

'Botkin didn't have time to explain. I assumed you would know.'

They crossed the dark empty market-place in silence. At the hotel the long trestle table had been pulled out and the plump landlady was ladling soup. Marya and Stephan hurried to their places. During the meal, the landlord, winking, made remarks about honeymoon tiffs. Marya's face was white, her expression abstracted. Though she'd often pondered about Paskevich's whereabouts, she made an effort to keep her ques-

527

tions bottled up: just hearing her say her estranged husband's name raised a knot in Stephan's jaw and brought an impersonal chill into his voice.

Paskevich is in prison, she thought. *And it's my luck that of all the men in Russia it has to be Stephan who's promised to get him out.* But why was Paskevich's rescue urgent to the Romanovs? Trapped in this Siberian backwater, surely they knew their hardship could only grow worse under the Bolsheviks. Why not enlist Stephan to help in their own rescue?

She was toying with her *pirozhki* when her memory spoke to her.

As they left the table, she put her hand on Stephan's arm. 'The moon's almost full. Such a lovely clear night. Let's walk before we turn in, shall we?'

Twin lines formed between his eyes. She stared meaningfully at him. He nodded. They negotiated the hard-packed snow of the deserted embankment for several minutes before either of them spoke.

'This is the coldest night I can remember.' Stephan's carefully noncommittal tone told her it was a question.

'There's a tiny hole in the wall over the bed that I'm positive wasn't there before. We can't talk in the room.' She moved more slowly as they entered the darkness cast by a long row of peak-roofed boathouses where barges and steamers waited for the spring thaw. She slipped.

Stephan gripped her arm.

'I know why the tsar needs Paskevich,' she murmured, and felt his grip loosen, but she went on: 'Years ago, just before my Lally died, he sent Paskevich to London and Paris — he was Minister of Finance then — to float government bonds. He also sent him to Switzerland.'

'Why?'

'Nothing that happened in those weeks is very clear, but I remember thinking it was a totally bizarre reason: he was to open one of those secret accounts for Nicholas. As I recall, only Nicholas, the tsarina and their children had access.'

'What about Paskevich?'

'Oh yes, him, too. It might have been some bank rule or other that whoever sets up the account can get at it.'

Emerging from the black shadows she could see his expressionless profile silhouetted against the cold blue light of the Siberian moon.

'It all fits together,' he said. 'Nicholas is convinced that this "snow troop operation" of Soloviev's will work. He'd hand over his own money to the swine.'

'Why are you so convinced Soloviev won't help them?'

'Anything's possible,' Stephan said. 'And I admit that all they need to do is get out of Tobolsk. After that the Monarchists would be there. They'd use him — or the boy or any of the grand duchesses — to get back into power. I don't pretend to know what's in Nicholas's mind, but let's hope that's not what he wants. Because, if it's to sit on his throne again, he'll surely die, and so will his wife and children.'

'It's all so sad. Will you help them?'

'Stop pushing me,' he said with sudden anger. 'I already gave Nicholas my promise. But, believe me, Kresty Prison isn't where we'll find your husband. He's living somewhere like Monte Carlo, enjoying the sunshine, winning at the tables and so forth. Wine, women, song, courtesy of the Romanov secret bank account.'

'Can't you see how irrational you're being? Stephan, it's you I love, I always have, I always will.'

'Marya, you were the man's mistress for years,' he said in a low pent voice. 'You married him. You're still married to him. I fail to see why my jealousy is irrational.'

Chapter Forty

'Paskevich?' Klazkha exclaimed. 'In the Kresty Prison?'

'I'm not positive. Somebody said . . .' Marya's voice faded. 'If you'd find out whether he's there, it'd be a tremendous favour.'

'Why should you care? Personally, it's the best news I've heard in months.'

'I . . . I'd like to help him get out.'

'Are you crazy! He threw you in the Fortress and now he's stuck in the Kresty. Tit for tat.'

'Nobody should be locked up.'

'That's you all over, never holding a grudge. But as far as I'm concerned this whole thing's like turning one of them hourglass clocks. Before, he snapped his fingers and got whatever his heart desired — palaces, his own private train, motor cars, fine wines, fancy foods, them little dust-gatherers he collected. He strutted around like a dressed-up monkey, giving orders in that smirky voice of his. He *owned* people just like there was still serfs. He owned *you*, Marya, and don't deny it. Well, now the sand's turned over and he's at the bottom. Good, I say. Good! I ain't stirring a finger for him.'

'You know all the top Bolsheviks, so it's no big effort to ask around!' Marya snapped, bursting into tears. She was too tired for self-control or reason.

Slow as the journey to Tobolsk had been, the return trip had taken twice as long. In Tobolsk they had waited for well over a week before the wall-eyed Tobolsk travel commissar agreed to sign the documents that Golder had procured earlier. The *koshevy* ride had been even more bruising. The rail journey was so monotonous that the slow-moving days blurred together. Only one incident stood out in Marya's mind. As the train was climbing the gradient of the Ural Mountains, talk in the crammed compartment turned to the peace treaty just signed in Brest-Litovsk. A waxen-faced scrawny boy in a student's uniform had worked it out that the Bolsheviks had ceded the faltering Germans sixty million souls and the Empire's richest farmland as well as three-quarters of the coal and iron deposits. At the next halt, the thick-set man in the Persian-lamb coat had beckoned over two of the Red Guard escorting the train. They had marched the student from the carriage. With passengers watching, the man in the fur coat had fired his pistol three times in rapid succession. The frail body had crumpled, blood oozing into the snow with a few frozen droplets scattered like raspberries in the whiteness.

Klazkha was peering at Marya's midriff. 'Marya, you ain't . . . you can't be . . . '

'Pregnant?' Marya's tears ceased as quickly as they had begun. 'I forgot.' Throwing back her cape, she fumbled under her apron to unwind a long rope and release the large ham. Ceremoniously she handed it to Klazkha. 'A gift from Tobolsk. I guessed that everybody would think the same as you did — and it worked. Not one thief tried to snatch my tummy.'

'This whole ham ain't for me?'

'Well, it'd be nice if you gave Pavel Golder a slice. On the journey we finished off most of his cheese.'

Klazkha prudently yanked down the blind before she hid her gift in a hole behind the unlit stove. Marya looked. The room seemed large and barren without rolls of wet linen, stacked wicker hampers, irons upended on the stove. Klazkha's former clientele, reduced to menial jobs, couldn't afford the luxury of clean clothes, so she plied her craft in the laundry behind the basement dining-room of the Smolnyi Institute; nowadays the sedate academy for aristocratic girls roared and seethed in its new role as Bolshevik headquarters.

Klazkha replaced a floorboard. 'It's never made no sense to me why you keep going back to Paskevich. Him! The rottenest of the whole rotten bunch. If I didn't know better than to put any stock in magic or suchlike nonsense, I'd say he'd put a spell on you.'

'Is it at all possible that he's in the Kresty?'

Klazkha said grudgingly: 'Lots of nobles and old-time bigwigs is locked up there.'

'God, now Stephan'll be poking round and asking questions.'

'Stephan? I'd've imagined him the last person to be looking for Paskevich. Them two's always been a pair of roosters fighting over you.' Klazkha's pale blue eyes inspected Marya. 'But you're dead on your feet. I got an errand or so to do. Lie down and get some sleep. We'll talk when I get back.'

It was dark when Klazkha returned. Pushing a wad of rags against the door to block the draught, she gave that old face-splitting smile.

'Well, you could knock me down with a feather,' she said. 'He is in the Kresty. Now, take some good advice. Leave him to rot.'

'Is he in solitary confine—'

'He's there; that's all I know.'

On their return to Petrograd, Stephan had gone immediately to Vasilevsky Island, where he had roomed as a student. The boarding-house had been collectivized, but the landlord and his wife remained as managers. Because Stephan was an 'old and cherished friend', they let him and Marya have the last available space, the sewing-room. As they sat at the kitchen table filling in the necessary papers, the wife leaned forward, whispering that if, in addition to the wad of Kerensky rouble notes that were the official rent, their old friend Strakhov threw in 'something private' she and her husband would forget to mention his comings and goings to the authorities. Stephan unwrapped the last wedge of the Siberian cheese.

The sewing-room — actually an alcove off the second-floor landing — overlooked the pillared rear of the Academy of Sciences, a fine view that was its sole amenity. The window-ledge served as night table, the narrow daybed was far too short for Stephan, the faded maroon curtain that hid them from the stairs did nothing to drown out voices and footsteps, nevertheless they slept heavily.

After a breakfast of barley gruel, they returned to the alcove. Leaving the curtain open to foil any lurking eavesdroppers, Stephan whispered: 'Today I'll go round to my old haunts. See if I can find out what's happening in the Kresty Prison.'

Would he learn that Paskevich had been beaten? Tortured? Starved? Mutilated? Lenin's new secret police, the Cheka, outdid their tsarist predecessors in brutality. Suddenly fear stabbed her. 'Stephan, that's dangerous!'

'I'll only talk to my old colleagues.'

'If they were in the Provisional Government and kept their jobs, it means they're probably turncoats —'

'Believe me,' he interrupted, 'the last thing I plan to do is get myself locked up trying to help Count Ivan Paskevich. You'll wait here for me?'

'I thought I'd pop by to see Pavel Golder.'

'The hospital? Now it's my turn to say take care.'

He kissed her goodbye and Marya paid for a bath. Only cold water trickled into the yellowed coffin-sized tub, but after all those days on the train she was desperate. Shivering and all goose-pimples, she wielded the loofah energetically and scrubbed the sliver of soap into her hair.

The icy bath followed by a vigorous towelling banished her anxieties. She left the boarding-house buoyant with anticipation about seeing her friends at the hospital, especially Golder. Yet when she reached the Spit, where people waited at the paired maroon Rostral Columns and below the granite steps of the Stock Exchange for trams, she felt a prickling between her shoulders as though fate were tapping her. The starting-bell was being rung on the Finland Station tram. The Finland Station was a short walk from the Kresty Prison. Running, she jumped aboard.

She had no plan whatsoever.

The Kresty Prison, blood-coloured brick capped with crenellated domes, squatted on the Arsenalnaya Embankment as malignly as ever; but there were gouges in the limestone of the entry arch where the Romanov double eagle had been prised loose, and the sentry-boxes were covered with posters of Lenin. The young sentries responded to

Marya's confident manner — and her smile. They waved her inside, where she joined the inevitable queue.

The official picked at his stumpy yellow teeth with a sliver of wood as he studied her documents. Examining her through the grille, he said: 'So you're an American, eh?'

'Also Russian.'

'That's the important side.' He shuffled through the papers. 'Where's your pass? I don't see it here.'

'Pass? Isn't this where I get one?'

'Of course not. You have to go to Cheka headquarters for that. Where've you been, Sister? Tchicago?' He grinned at his own witticism.

'Pskov.' She fluttered her lashes with the coquettishness she had used on high-born admirers at her Friday Nights. 'Are you saying I made this whole hideous journey for nothing?'

'Which prisoner you got in mind to visit?'

'Ivan Paskevich.'

'Him? You came all the way to Petrograd to see him? That filthy tsarist rat? That land-owning turd?' A grudging respect for Paskevich managed to seep through the insults. 'Why would a pretty little thing like you want to get in the same cell with a bloodsucker like him?'

'He had me locked up. See?' Pointing to a line on her identity card, she read: ' "Former Political Prisoner." He buried me alive in the Fortress, in the Trubetskoi. There wasn't a

537

single hour in solitary that I didn't long to see the tables turned.' Her voice shook with sincerity. 'How I dreamed of seeing him in the same agony!'

The warder showed his little corn-kernel teeth in a broader grin. 'I got a bit of pull around here,' he said, beckoning across the hall to a short dishevelled guard.

Marya followed the little man across a courtyard patrolled by several pairs of Red Guard. Looking up, she saw machine-guns. They halted, and two soldiers held their rifles on Marya as a grey-haired female guard, a classic *babushka* with huge grandmotherly breasts, felt her for weapons.

Finally they were admitted to the cell block.

Marya began to shudder uncontrollably. An animal thing, this panic. She was thrust back into the Trubetskoi Bastion. Not only could she smell the dank odour of human degradation, but she could also taste it, feel it on her skin, experience it deep within her.

The rumpled guard jingled an old-fashioned ring of iron keys to unlock a heavy door. 'Fifteen minutes,' he said. 'Shouldn't be any problem; but, in case there is, give a yell. I'll be right out here.'

As the door opened Marya had a confused impression of yet stronger odours, a space not much larger than a tomb, marrow-chilling cold, narrow bunks with cards laid out on the lower.

The two players had risen.

Paskevich badly needed a shave, his business-suit was grimy and rumpled, his linen filthy, yet he stood as erect as ever, and the clever monkey's face shone with lively vigour. This must have been his bearing as a hard-fighting young officer. 'No retreat' Paskevich, wasn't that his nickname?

The door clanged shut behind her.

'Am I dreaming?' he said, gripping her hands. 'It can't be you, Marya.'

'Comrade Sister, please.'

He laughed, then dropped her hands, saying in French: 'My dear, allow me to present my cellmate, formerly Baron Manhukin of the Department of the Interior. Baron, my wife.'

The baron's baggy morning-suit showed that he had once been extremely corpulent. 'Countess.' Bowing politely, he said: 'I apologize, but it's not possible to give you and your husband privacy, so ignore my presence.' Heaving himself into the upper bunk, he picked up a book.

'This cell is the last place you should be,' Paskevich said with mock severity. 'Didn't you get my letter?'

'Which one?'

'I sent it to your Pskov hospital before the Bolshevik takeover. I mentioned that Lenin's the latter-day Torquemada, pure of heart and dedicated to equalizing mankind even if he has to slaughter every last human being to achieve his goal, starting with those of us who clean our fingernails. I told you to join Boris in New York.'

'The hospital voted to close down, so I never got the letter.' She shrugged. 'But what's the difference? When did I ever listen to warnings?'

'Touché.'

'Paskevich, how are we going to get you out?'

'You're asking my advice? You, the expert on prison escapes?' His small eyes glinted with malicious humour. 'If only they'd put me in the Fortress, consider the elegance of your revenge. Well, one can expect symmetry in art but not in life. I'll be out soon enough.'

'You will?'

'What a depraved man's dream you are, Comrade Nurse. That body, those eyes, those lips, the tantalizing wisps of red curls peeping out from the stern veil.'

'How will you escape?'

'The usual way. Feet first.'

'Then . . .' She took a breath. 'You've been tried?'

'The Bolsheviks are far too dedicated to freeing the proletariat from their chains to waste time on frivolities like the judiciary and courts of law.'

She lowered her voice to a whisper. 'It's imperative that we plan a way to get you out.'

'Who are *we?*'

She flushed deeply. 'Me. You. And Stephan Strakhov.'

'Ah, the Great Idealist.' Despite Paskevich's amused smile, twin pinpoints of misery showed in his dark little eyes. 'I must say his interest in my welfare comes as a surprise; but, then, I should have anticipated that his nobility extended even unto keeping an extraneous husband alive.'

'We don't have much time —'

'Marya, I forbid you to enlist your poet — or that pockmarked maid of yours — in hatching any form of plot.' He spoke with aristocratic coldness. 'I do not take aid from any jumped-up washerwomen or disillusioned radical scribblers. Is that clear?'

Marya saw red. Paskevich was of the bluest Russian blood, he'd been born with riches beyond calculation, even his jailers admired his courage, his intelligence was a many-faceted diamond, but how could he, locked up in this tomb, persist in considering himself a superior being?

Mouth quirking nastily as if he had read her mind, he said: 'No schemes. And stop frowning — you'll get wrinkles.'

Swallowing her anger, she murmured in an even lower voice: 'We were in Tobolsk.'

He peered at her with such intensity that she flushed again. 'Then, our noble poet's told you who he is?'

'So you *did* know?'

'Of course I knew, my dear,' he reproached. 'It concerned *you*. Do we *have* to waste time discussing him?'

'This isn't about Stephan.' She glanced at Baron Manhukin's back.

'Safe as the grave.' Paskevich spoke in a clearly audible tone. 'And just as unimaginative.'

'An . . . envoy . . . told Stephan that it's imperative to get you out of the Kresty. That's the first I knew you were here. Everybody swore you'd left the country.'

'Did you believe that?'

'No. I knew you.'

'Thank you again, my dear, for your confidence. It so happens, though, that you were wrong and the others had me dead to rights.'

'There's no time for games,' she snapped.

'But it's true. Kerensky arranged for a sealed train through Germany. Don't ask how, but he did. I went to Paris and London, suggesting to our gallant allies that it was in their best interests to send effective aid to Kerensky.'

'*You* backed the Provisional Government?'

'This was after the July Coup, and I'd accepted that the Bolsheviks were by far the greater evil. Well, you know how far I got with those efforts. I wrote to you just before Lenin took over.'

'Whatever possessed you to come back?'

'An old family tradition,' he chuckled. 'We Paskeviches are all buried in Russian soil.'

She had never understood her husband, and she still didn't, yet she accepted that he continued to find humour in everything, including his patriotism and his obsession for her: he was made of some adamantine element that remained unchanged even in this dank antechamber to death.

She whispered: 'Do you remember that bank account in Switzerland?'

'Ah, that's what's behind the rescue scheme. And I thought it was my own charming self.'

'Will you stop joking?' she hissed. 'They're desperate for the money, so —'

'Marya,' he interrupted. 'Did I ever mention that you're never more ravishable than when your temper's up?' He rubbed her lip. 'Yes?'

Yes.

He pulled her into an embrace, his fingers moving under her cape seeking the roots of her breasts, his erection pressing against her. He licked the inside of her ear breathing: 'Ever since you walked in I've been aching.'

Disregarding the dank prison cell and the page-rustling in the bunk, Marya arched her body against his. Her thighs parted, her bones melted, her lips opened for his kiss. A fraction of her brain seemed to be floating above them, a disconnected wraith unable to believe in her abandonment. How could she respond like this to the husband who had repudiated her? Shouldn't her traitor body, which belonged with her heart to Stephan, cringe with shame?

With an effort she wrenched away. Aware

of her own rapid breathing she mouthed: 'You disgust me.'

'Oh, absolutely. I can tell that by your pulse rate.'

Taking a step back towards the door, she said: 'It's your duty to get out of here.'

'Why?' He chuckled. 'Because your visionary lover tilted at the wrong windmills and ground his kin into flour.'

'Why keep bringing Stephan into this? When you took on that errand in Switzerland you obligated yourself.'

He stared at her for a long moment. 'I never thought to be reminded of my honour by a waitress's daughter.'

'Thank you.'

'It wasn't meant as an insult. Well, my dear, as they say, politics makes strange bedfellows. None stranger than this —'

The key was grating in the lock. He stepped back, giving the dishevelled little guard the same unseeing nod he'd bestowed on his servants.

'A thousand apologies, Excellency, but the visitor's time is up.'

Paskevich bowed to Marya. 'I can't tell you', he said, 'how I look forward to further such pleasurable breaks in my routine, Comrade.'

To her astonishment the unshaven face was alive with eagerness.

Chapter Forty-one

As Marya emerged from the ugly brick prison she was smiling. The first hurdle was cleared. She had convinced Paskevich. With a glance at the dense khaki-coloured clouds, she hurried towards the Finland Station. Taking her place in the line for Vasilevsky Island, she heard soft-voiced complaints that the tram was half an hour late. A few splattering drops rapidly multiplied into a downpour. Within a few minutes her cape was drenched and her optimism crushed. The Kresty had teemed with armed sentries, there were machine-guns on the roofs, and getting a prisoner out was hopeless.

The tram arrived. It was so crammed that the conductor didn't let anyone board. By now Marya's teeth were chattering, and she decided that Shank's pony was her only choice. The three or so miles to Vasilevsky Island wouldn't have been onerous, if it weren't for her boots. She had traded in the Tobolsk market-place, exchanging three lengths of embroidered silk ribbons for them and this was the first time she'd worn them. The supposedly weatherproofed felt shrank so rapidly that after the first mile Marya roundly sympathized with the millions of Chinese girls who'd had their feet bound.

The sudden downpour had slowed to a

drizzle by the time she hobbled by the small palace that had once belonged to Kschesin-skaya, *prima ballerina assoluta* — and mistress to Nicholas II before his marriage. After the February Revolution, the dancer had fled and her exquisite art nouveau building had served as Bolshevik headquarters until the July Coup, when the party had been ousted. Once again a hammer-and-sickle banner was hoisted. The dripping red flag reminded Marya of Ovruch.

A Rolls-Royce sped by, spewing filthy water and crushed ice across her cape. She vented her pain in loathing of the passenger, who could only be a high-ranking Bolshevik. The elegant vehicle jerked to a halt, then backed up. The rear window cranked down.

'Marya?' roared a familiar voice. 'Little one, is it really you?'

'Ovruch !' Marya plunged through slush to the car. 'Out of everyone in Petrograd, it had to be you! Coincidence of coincidences! I was just thinking about you, and hey presto! here you are. Am I a genie or a clairvoyant or what? But why am I being so sweet to you? Look at what your car's done to my poor uniform!'

Smiling at her happy effusions, Ovruch said: 'The least I can do is take you home.' He leaned forward to tap on the glass. The driver leaped out, flinging open the door.

Ovruch had entered yet another incarnation: high-ranking dignitary. The lustrously thick pelts of his sable hat and coat increased his considerable bulk. His beard was now shaven, revealing round cheeks and a large cleftless chin over which his moustaches swooped.

Asking where she lived, he boomed instructions to the driver. As the car eased forward, Ovruch unfolded a bearskin rug, wrapping it around her lap. 'A while ago I telephoned you at the hospital. The matron said you had a leave of absence for health reasons. I asked Klazkha about it. She said you'd been sick; that was all I could get from her. By then I was worried, so I telephoned your friend the Jewish Bund doctor for a full report. He told me you'd had another bout of pleurisy and were recuperating in the country, but he didn't know where.'

Until now, Marya had been easing off her boots under the rug while basking in renewed friendship. It had crossed her mind several times that Ovruch could magically solve her problem. Klazkha's wariness with a fellow party member, however, as well as Pavel Golder's evasions, tripped a warning signal. Mentioning Tobolsk would be a blunder, and asking for help with Paskevich would be disastrous.

'Yes, the pleurisy. It comes and goes. I got it the first time at the military hospital in Pskov, remember?'

'The effects of the rotten imperialist war stay with us,' he said. 'Little one, you must take better care of yourself. Why are you out in this nasty weather?'

'Don't scold me,' she said with a little laugh. 'The rain didn't start until after I left the house.'

'Are you still with Strakhov?'

'What a question! Of course I am.'

'Where is he?'

Giving a wave and a laugh, she again circled his question. 'Who knows? Writers! They're forever going off to peer at things.'

'Have you heard about Paskevich?'

His tone was noncommittal, but more warning signals flashed. 'We separated ages ago,' she said. 'What a hero he turned out to be, skipping out of the country.'

'He sneaked back to rob more from the people. We were waiting for him, though. He's in the Kresty Prison.'

'No! There's a turnabout — I'm walking around free and he's locked up. Let's hope he's there a good long time!'

'Now the proletariat rules, you don't need to worry; he'll pay for his crimes.'

'When will he be sentenced?'

'That's up to Comrade Trotsky. He'll prosecute at the trial.'

Trotsky, Lenin's second-in-command, was a flamboyant lawyer who could take Russian minds off the hunger and the cold when he performed that ever-satisfying courtroom drama of bringing down the high and mighty.

'Trotsky himself!' Marya said with a stiff-lipped smile.

'If you'd taken my advice and joined the

party, you'd have a front-row seat.' Ovruch was joking. Yet — and this might be her imagination — she saw watchful soberness in the round eyes.

'There's my turning,' Marya said, pointing. 'It's that sepia house with the bay window.'

Tolstoy Square had been paved in the antiquated way, with wood. The blocks were tremendously heavy and too damp to burn properly, yet fuel was so scarce that every morning a few more blocks were missing.

With a glance at the coffee-coloured muck, Ovruch said: 'I'll carry you. No, don't argue.'

Lifting her from the running-board, he held her a little too close against the solid heat of his huge body, and she was glad to be set on her feet on the front steps.

'You're a feather,' he said with an avuncular pat on the shoulder. 'This coming week we'll get together properly. You, me, Strakhov and of course Klazkha, just like the old days at the Vyborg Inn.'

She shed her infamous boots, pulling on dry stockings, then sat on the bed waiting for Stephan. It was dark and raining hard when he returned. His shoulders were slumped as he closed the curtain and draped his sodden coat on the finial.

'You're in the dumps,' she murmured.

'Remember how Circe could transform people into animals? Well, the Bolshevik Party knows the same spell. I went to the Tauride to see old friends — honest men who'd risked their lives for the Revolution.

549

Most of them have turned into rabbits and run. The rest have become swine. None of them would see me. Not one.'

'Oh, Stephan,' she sighed, 'I saw him. Paskevich.'

Stephan paled. 'You went to the Kresty?'

Stung by his icy tone, she snapped: 'Stupid me, I expected a pat on the back.'

'You couldn't have got a pass so quickly. Did you weep and plead with the guard to see your husband?'

'So that's it. Darling, you know it's you I love. Why be jealous of him?' In low rapid sentences, she explained how she had gained entrance to the cell and what had happened there — in her version she and Paskevich had chatted decorously as dowagers under the chaperoning eye of Baron Manhukin.

As the landlord's heavy boots rang on the stairs, she stopped, drew a breath. Pitching her voice stagily, she asked: 'Did you ever see such a cloudburst? But I was rescued. You'll never guess by whom. Ovruch.' At this name of new-minted importance, the landlord's tread slowed. 'He chanced to pass by in his car and insisted on bringing me home. Ovruch hasn't changed one iota. No side to him at all.'

Stephan also spoke his lines for the audience. 'Since the day he rescued you from the Trubetskoi Bastion he's been your devoted slave.'

'Oh, you,' she giggled.

The landlord's steps hurried around the landing, and his door closed. Marya counted silently to ten before she continued in a murmur: 'Ovruch says that Trotsky plans a big trial. This time he's got a perfect defendant: Paskevich will stand firm, the unrepentant aristocrat.'

Stephan bent to put newspaper under his overcoat. Not that he cared if it dripped on the rug, but he didn't want Marya to see his expression. She was right. He was jealous. No, he was eaten alive by the self-begotten monster. Left to his own devices, the last man on earth he would set free was her husband.

'How much would it take to bribe a guard?' Stephan asked.

'Which one?' Klazkha said. 'There's a whole prisonful of 'em.'

'When you rescued me only Yuri was involved,' Marya said.

'Yuri thought the world of Ovruch. They was like *that*.' Klazkha held up her hand, pressing together the second and third fingers of her grey gloves. The palm was darned and redarned. 'And times was different then.'

'Then, you agree with me,' Golder said. 'To get anyone out of the Kresty is impossible.'

'Neither of us is half-wits.' As emphasis, Klazkha rolled her eyes up to the dim heights of the Sennaya Market.

Once all St Petersburg had come here to

the Sennaya for feed, but now those who still owned a horse were forced to scrounge in the countryside. A century of animal odours still clung to the wooden walls. Far away a little group of merchants had set out antiquated corsets, ballgowns, ostrich fans and bureaucratic evening attire; understandably there were no customers. With its shadowy corners, the Sennaya was a perfect meeting-place, which was why Klazkha had suggested it.

Marya sighed deeply. 'So it's hopeless.'

'We-e-ll, I been doing some thinking about it.'

'So you do have a plan,' Stephan said.

'A bit of one. It ain't properly thought through.' Klazkha was being modest: she never put forward an idea until she'd considered it from all angles. 'The thing to remember is that with so much unemployment the streets is always filled with people looking for a bit of excitement. When a big shot like Count Paskevich comes up for trial, there's bound to be a big crowd. And that's what set me to thinking about something what happened a few months back. It was right after the October Revolution. Rations was getting smaller and smaller. It's got so I'm shamed by eating a decent meal at the Smolnyi, so I bring home my bowl to share around; I ain't saying it does good, but I feel better. Anyway, in those days we organized a big demonstration to the Smolnyi. To show solidarity, all us women went, even some that was awful sick.'

'I never heard about that,' Golder inter-jected.

'Them big shots covered it up; you'll see why in a moment. We shouted that we needed more'n one slice of splintery bread to give our families for supper. We shouted that we needed wood for our stoves. We shouted ourselves hoarse. And who should come out on the steps to talk to us but Ovruch. He stood there without no hat, talking about how things would be getting better now the people was in power. He blamed our being starving and cold on the exploiters and oppressors, the class ene-mies — you know how he loves to spout them Bolshevik slogans. Now, me, I knew for certain it ain't got nothing to do with the rich. The farmers, they won't sell for paper money. Even if they would, there just ain't enough railways to bring grain here to Pet-rograd. But you know Ovruch. Big, solid, steady. He convinced a whole bunch of the women. A few of us went on home, but the rest stayed in the freezing cold, getting more and more worked up against them upper-class folks. And when a Black Maria drove into the Smolnyi Square they swarmed all over it. They pulled out the prisoners. A family what owned a big apartment-house over on the Morskaia, the old parents, two grown sons and one of them's wife. They kicked and beat them poor souls to death.'

Marya shuddered.

'Didn't anyone try to stop it?' Stephan asked.

'Nobody could've. Them women was that savage. It's the hunger and worry.' Klazkha paused. 'Stephan, Dr Golder, if I got a bunch of us to act all wild and crazy about getting at Count Paskevich, what's your opinion? Would the Red Guards jump in to rescue him?'

The doctor rubbed his jaw thoughtfully. The thick stubble rasped: rather than using soap for shaving, he saved his minuscule ration to scrub for surgery. 'Shoot women, you mean? I should not imagine so.'

'I figure the same.' Klazkha nodded. 'Them big trials is all at the Tauride Palace, so they'll take him from the Kresty Prison across the Liteiny Bridge. On the far side of the Neva there's a burned-down palace. You know the one I mean, right on the embankment. It belonged to Grand Duke Serge. On the way to the Smolnyi sometimes I cut through there. From the front you'd swear that the whole place was destroyed, but at the back there's a private theatre left. One wall's tumbling down enough so you could move a wagon through and hide it.'

'A wagon?' Marya asked. 'Why a wagon?'

'One of us would throw a big shawl over Paskevich's head and a bunch would crowd around him, so it'd seem he was a woman like us. Our bunch would scuttle back into the rubble, like we knew we'd gone too far and was scared. We'd cover him with straw

554

and get the wagon back across the bridge. After that he could disguise himself, maybe put on a wig and skirts, wrap his shawl around his face and get out of Petrograd. Lenin done just that — pretended he was a woman after his July Coup went sour. Or we could dream up some other rig for him.'

'Klazkha, you're a genius,' Marya cried.

The two men responded more slowly.

'There are too many unknowns,' Dr Golder said. 'For example, Trotsky might decide to hold the trial in Moscow. Or, if it is at the Tauride, they might not take Paskevich by the most direct route.'

'Besides, it's hideously dangerous,' Stephan said. 'If the Red Guard do open fire, Klazkha, a lot of you could be killed. And they'll close the bridges immediately, so he couldn't escape anyway.'

Klazkha pulled her coat tighter around her. 'If one of you two men's got a better idea, let's hear it.'

Neither of them did.

Stephan glanced at his watch. A colleague had actually agreed to meet him this afternoon. 'A lawyer. Maybe he'll know if a show trial with Trotsky is on the docket.'

Klazkha had to return to work in the Smolnyi basement.

Golder, on his way to Vasilevsky Island, said he would see Marya home. Neither spoke of anything consequential until they reached Tolstoy Square.

As they picked their way across wooden

blocks, Marya asked: 'What do you honestly think of Klazkha's idea?'

'It *could* succeed.'

'You don't sound very certain.'

'I explained at the Sennaya. There are too many unpredictable elements.'

She sighed.

'Whatever needs to be done, you can count on me.'

'Thank you, Pavel.'

His hand tightened momentarily on her elbow.

Marya, perched on the window-ledge of the alcove, breathed on the pane and doodled numbers: 1,2,3,4.

1. Paskevich. A true aristocrat, he would never succumb to such an undignified escape-plan. Dressing as a peasant woman!

2. Stephan. True, out of guilty obligation he had given his promise to his Imperial half-brother, but could he wholeheartedly work to rescue a man who roused his loathing jealousy?

3. Golder. A dyed-in-the-wool Socialist, he despised the nobility — and he, too, had eyes for her.

4. Klazkha. She hated all men, Paskevich most of all for his long-ago efforts to push her back on to the streets.

Marya rubbed, and drops wept down the pane.

How could a plot with such reluctant conspirators succeed?

Chapter Forty-two

Since the Bolshevik takeover, Petrograd had walked on figurative tiptoe, talking more and more softly until it was pretty much accepted that anyone shouting or making loud noises was connected to the Government. Thus, on the following Monday, when the doorknocker sounded loudly and repetitively, a frisson travelled down Marya's spine. Reminding herself there were thirty or so other lodgers, she glanced at Stephan to see his reaction. Oblivious to the noise below, he continued to peer at the lines he'd been jotting in his notebook.

The banging ceased. After a minute there were footsteps. With a light tap on the adjacent wall, the landlady parted the curtains to show her thin taut face: as the former owner, she was both suspicious and under suspicion.

'A comrade brought this for you, Sister.' She extended an envelope: a red hammer and sickle glued over the embossed Imperial eagle did not completely hide the outspread wings. 'He's downstairs waiting for your answer.' She watched as Marya fumbled to open the heavy envelope.

To Marya Fedorovna Alexiev
I must leave for Moscow on Monday afternoon, but this morning I have some

free time. My driver will bring you to the Smolnyi Institute.

Ovruch

No mention of the promised reunion, not a word about Stephan, just a flat-out summons. Marya forgot her anxiety and the landlady's lashless inquisitive eyes. She thrust the note at Stephan. 'The nerve! As if I'd go without you!'

'Commissar Ovruch is being thoughtful; he knows how wrapped up I am with my writing.' As Stephan spoke he was rapidly slashing in his notebook: 'IT'S DANGEROUS TO REFUSE. HE'S TOO HIGH UP.'

'For once you could take time off,' she said petulantly. 'After all, he's more your friend than mine.'

'Yes, but you're the one he rescued from the Trubetskoi.' 'THE SMOLNYI'S THE ONE PLACE YOU MIGHT HEAR SOMETHING ABOUT THE TRIAL.'

Marya nodded. 'Yes, yes. Of course you're right.'

At the Smolnyi's pillared entry, Marya was greeted by Ovruch's chief assistant, a short, bespectacled young man whose educated accents contrasted with his worker's cap and rough corduroy jacket. He led her through the corridors lined with neatly clad, anxious-faced petitioners and parading Latvian guards. As they neared the folding doors of the chandeliered ballroom where a scant two years earlier girls of bluest blood had practised their waltzes and mazurkas, two shots rang out in rapid succession. Marya's guide held up a hand, halting her. The casual voices and typewriting machines fell silent. The Latvians stared around menacingly. The supplicants shrank against the walls. No further sounds came from the ballroom. After a few seconds the clatter resumed, and the Latvians began their pacing again. The petitioners, though, stayed huddled close to the walls.

Ovruch's anteroom was packed. The assistant elbowed a path through the crowd, ushering her into the inner office.

The desk where Ovruch sat signing papers was inlaid with ivory, ebony, gilt and semi-precious stones — a piece so magnificent that it must have been removed from the Winter Palace. Screwing on the top of his fountain pen, he crossed the large jewel-toned Kazakhstan rug to engulf her hands in his ham-like grasp. 'So. Here we are together again, just as I promised.'

His hands were warm, his smile welcoming, yet those two shots continued to resound in her head.

She thanked him for the car in a subdued tone, then looked around the sumptuous office. 'Very swank.'

'As we were saying the other day, the people now rule.' Indicating a gilded chair for her to take, he returned to the throne-like seat that matched the desk. 'Little one, we have a lot to discuss and there's not much time — I have a great heap of work to get through before Monday.'

'Yes, the note said that you were on your way to Moscow.'

'To arrange for offices,' he said. 'The news hasn't been released yet, but Moscow will be our capital.'

'You're pulling my leg!' she squeaked. 'The entire government can't just pack up and leave.'

'Pah, it not only can, it must. Petrograd's no Russian city, it's Tsar Peter's graveyard for Russian workers.' His voice deepened. 'The true heart of this country is the Kremlin. The party belongs there, little one, and so do you.'

Her jaw dropped, and her handbag slipped in her lap. So this was why he'd brought her to the Smolnyi without Stephan. 'I'd never live in Moscow!' she burst out.

'Why not?'

She had recovered. 'It's so dreary,' she said with a flutter of her eyelashes.

'With the Supreme Soviet there, Moscow will be the centre of all Russian life.'

'You'll rule from Moscow?'

'We'll follow the will of the people from there,' he corrected. 'The people demand change. Now that the exploiters are streaming over the Finnish borders, we will nationalize all wealth. We will nationalize industry, too. Think of it. Hundreds of millions of people guided by one central economic mechanism — the Supreme Economic Council — in Moscow.'

'It sounds thrilling,' she said, tilting her head with an expression of bright interest.

'Russia will have a different society from any the world has ever seen,' he said earnestly. 'Moscow will be the hub of that. And Moscow will be the centre of the international struggle.'

'Fight? Ovruch, I've seen enough to know we're bled dry. There's no way we can fight another war, much less a war with the entire world.'

'I'm not talking about artillery and bloodshed,' he said calmly. 'Russia will never take part in another Imperialist war. Our task is to spread the word to the proletariat that the future belongs to them. No matter where they live, they must follow our example. We will teach them how to overthrow their exploiters.'

'In some countries the workers are content.'

'Pah! How can the enchained be content? They need the party's guidance, that's all.'

That a small group who had seized illegal and tenuous power only a few months earlier should be planning world revolution was so ludicrous that Marya wanted to laugh. But Ovruch was watching her intently, and there was nothing in the least laughable about this gigantic peasant commissar. She glanced at the windows. Voices were rising from the courtyard. A crowd was gathering.

'Moscow will educate the proletariat around the globe about Communism. Has Klazkha mentioned that we've changed the name of the party? We're Communists now.' Ovruch leaned earnestly towards her. His coarse brown hair refused to lie slick although he'd glossed it with more oil than Boris had used in his dapperest days as a *chinovnik*. 'Comrade Lenin believes the world revolution will be waged within each individual country by the dedicated men and women who live there.'

And she had thought he wanted her body!

Maybe he did: his lips were parted and sweat glossed his forehead. But her body was only a tiny bit of what he wanted from her. He wanted her heart and soul, both of which — despite her father's fervid early tutelage combined with nearly a decade of living in Russia — remained stamped with star-spangled banners.

'You haven't convinced me that workers everywhere are set on overthrowing their governments; but, then, you're talking to an American capitalist.'

'Don't pretend you're the useless butterfly. Klazkha's told me you nursed her and her brother so Paskevich wouldn't send them to a filthy hospital. And you left his palace to tend the peasants maimed by Bloody Nicholas. You've proved over and over that you don't prosper with the rich or let the poor suffer.'

The voices below were now thundering

rhythmically, but she couldn't make out what was being shouted until Ovruch stamped across the carpet to fling open a window. A chill draught swept inside, filling the office with the chanted syllable, 'Bread, bread, bread'.

Ovruch leaned out. 'Ho!' he roared. 'You Latvians down there, are you asleep? Get rid of these counter-revolutionaries!' He remained there, watching for a minute or so, then slammed the window shut. Double-glazing muffled the shouts, the confused cries, the shrieks.

'These dissidents,' he said with honest sadness. 'Always they're trying to subvert the masses.'

Sun slanted across the desk. As Ovruch returned to his chair, the rays lit one side of his face. By contrast, the shadowed half appeared a dark metallic mask. Staring at him, Marya was hit by a thought. Until now, she was realizing, she had perceived only the brightly lit, benevolent side, the huge peasant who had helped rescue her from the Trubetskoi Bastion; and if Ovruch had delighted in the trappings of his ever-increasing power . . . well, she remained hedonist enough to understand his pleasure in such vanities.

How was it she had never noticed the zealot darkness?

'Don't look so bewildered, little one,' he said. ' "A revolution's like an omelette", as Comrade Lenin puts it. "To make one you must break some eggs." ' Taking her little sigh as an agreement with Lenin's recipe, he went on. 'Think of the excitement in Moscow! We'll be freeing the masses everywhere.'

'We?'

'You're the woman for me, little one. I've known it since the moment I saw you so brave and tattered in the Trubetskoi. And you'll remain part of me even while you're carrying the torch to America.'

'But . . .'

'You're thinking of Strakhov? Of course Strakhov. But, little one, the day of his softness is past. Democratic Reform, pah! His type of Revolutionary is heading for the Finnish border on the heels of the exploiters.' He paused. 'With me in Moscow, you'll be in the vanguard of the new world.'

'This comes as a surprise . . .' Where did that bit of triteness come from? Had she heard it in a theatre?

'I understand. A commitment to Communism is a serious matter. But I'm sure you'll come to Moscow. Telephone the Smolnyi when you're ready. My chief assistant will arrange the necessary travel papers. Oh, and remember, little one. He knows you as Sister Alexiev, not Countess Paskevich.'

She left the office walking stiffly, as if her body were sore and battered. That final mention of her real name, was it blackmail? He had spoken in his normal calm tone, yet what other reason did he have to say Countess Paskevich?

A door opened, and two officials emerged. Both were short and bald. The stouter was talking in the self-important tones of an underling with advance knowledge of big events. As he said the name reverberating within Marya's head, she moved more rapidly, keeping close behind them to eavesdrop.

'Paskevich . . . Yes, certainly public. Very public. Starts Thursday at the Tauride. You know Trotsky. As chief prosecutor, he'll open the whole bag of tricks. Any minute now you'll hear from people wheedling you for tickets. Yes, yes, I absolutely agree that *Pravda* and *Izvestia* ought to build up a trial of this importance. But perhaps your desk hasn't heard yet: this week we're forced to cut the fish ration.'

'Again?'

'Again. That's why time's of the essence. We must play the magicians. Divert them from what's going on. And it's brilliant actually. Can you think of any defendant who could divert their attention better than Paskevich?'

Chapter Forty-three

Friday, according to Russian superstition, is a melancholy day, and the Friday of the Paskevich trial appropriately dawned with a cold fog. By noon, however, a salt-odoured breeze had coaxed out the sun and was cavorting with the crimson hammer-and-sickle flags draped from random windows between the Kresty Prison and the Tauride Palace. The city, denied its customary joyous Easter by Bolshevik disapproval of all religion, was in the mood to come out full-force for an event of any kind. Along the crowded route, men hoisted small children on to their shoulders, pinch-faced ragamuffins squirmed through the crush for a better view, and factory girls flirted with the police, wheedling to be admitted beyond their cordon. Everyone wanted to get near enough to touch the cavalcade.

First came a truckload of Red Guards, then the three judges each riding in his own limousine with armed men on the running-boards and machine-guns poking out of the broken rear windows. Another truckload of soldiers. A dozen prison guards, three of them women, shouldered rifles as they marched ahead of the pair of sway-backed skeletal mules. More guards lurched on the splintery dray, one of the long vehicles without a rear rail used in autumns past to haul the great islands of floating logs from the canals to the bustling lumber markets.

The massive security, while not necessary, underlined the importance of the prisoner. But, even without it and the three days of relentless press build-up, the trial of a multimillionaire landowner from an ancient family, a man who had been an intimate adviser of Nicholas Romanov, would have been a major attraction. And, should the public need yet further proof that Commissar Trotsky had produced a defendant extraordinaire, there was always Paskevich himself.

Hands tied behind his back, he stood firm as the cart jolted over potholes, every now and then giving a sardonic nod. A Roman emperor in his triumphal chariot acknowledging the adulation of the plebs. His arrogance, rather than offending the crowd, won it. Onlookers waved small Bolshevik flags as he passed; children jumped up and down applauding. A few tentative cheers rose from veterans who had served under him.

'Good old "No Retreat" Paskevich!'

'Go for them civilian lawyer bastards, General!'

The exceptions to this collective good nature were the fair-sized group, a majority of them women, who pranced alongside the wagons. They shook their fists, bawling obscenities and threatening the prisoner with bodily harm, including castration. The tormentors for the most part were shabby if not downright ragged working-class folk. Only two wore unpatched clothes: the tall man in the neat business-suit and the pretty little nurse. Just before the parade reached the Liteinyi Bridge, Marya had led Stephan into the vociferous gang.

Her goal was to alert Paskevich that he might be rescued.

Marya herself wasn't positive there would be such an attempt. She hadn't visited Klazkha or Golder, and neither of them had contacted her. 'I've been involved in this kind of thing for years and, believe me, it's the safest way,' Stephan had said. 'We'll just have to take it on faith that Klazkha's managed to work out her plan.' At Marya's tentatively voiced idea of bribing a guard to warn Paskevich, Stephan had pressed a silencing hand over her mouth. 'Don't even whisper something like that.' With the greatest reluctance he had followed Marya when she'd jumped in with these jeering ill-wishers. As the hag in the buttonless army top-coat shoved ahead of them, he draped a protective arm over Marya's shoulder.

Darting a grateful smile up at him, she was struck anew by what his sworn guarantee to get Paskevich to Switzerland was costing him. Not the physical danger — though, of course, there was plenty of that — but the price of conquering his aversion and jealousy. The sunlight clearly showed his inner struggle. Those two narrow lines carved between his eyebrows were new, the high planes of his cheeks appeared carved in stone, his full well-delineated lips were compressed.

Marya turned to the wagon. 'Rotten, filthy bloodsucker! You and your lands and palaces! The day of reckoning's finally arrived!'

Paskevich paid her no more attention than he gave his other deriders. Marya clamped both hands on to the rough pine planks that slanted down at the rear of the cart. 'Tsarist! Monarchist!' The intensity of her scream abraded her throat but didn't attract his eye.

As the procession streamed off the bridge, she shoved ahead of the cart, scrambling on a carriage block to yell at the top of her lungs: 'Now you'll pay for throwing me in the Fortress!'

Paskevich was inclining his head in the opposite direction.

The embankment was packed. No good-natured merriment here. The predominantly female crowd was grim-faced, angry. As the cart went by, crude invectives swelled, growing higher and shriller until the cries were so inhuman that they might be passing through a great flock of disturbed crows.

Ahead of them, the crush of onlookers had pressed the police cordon inward. A bottle-neck. The guards marching in the front swung their rifle-butts to clear a path for the wagon. The wheels ground more slowly.

Marya grabbed Stephan's arm. 'Look!' she cried exultantly.

Ahead of them, on a great rubble-heap that had been the classical façade of the palace portico, was Klazkha.

Standing motionless amid the turmoil, straight and tall, she might have been a priestess of those fisher-folk who had once plied frail barks across this swampy network of rivers.

'Why do we need to wait for them lawyers and judges?' a woman was screeching.

'I say piss on these jumped-up tribunals!'

A factory worker reeking of garlic yelled: 'Street trial! Street trial! Street trial!'

Others took up the cry. 'Street trial! Street trial!'

'Street tri-i-al . . . !'

The police had linked arms against the surge, but the women broke through. By sheer force of numbers they separated the lumber-cart from the truckloads of soldiers. The jailers stopped trying to get the cart through, instead surrounding it and struggling to keep the vitriolic mass of humanity at bay.

'What's wrong with them fucking soldiers? Can't they tell what's happening?' shouted a jailer, his chubby face distorted by panic.

'How can they? These wolf bitches've cut us off.'

'We can't fight them all!'

'So let 'em eat his heart!'

Cannibalism might well be the goal of these maenads. Their faces were bloated and distorted, cartoon-like with blood-hatred.

570

Marya tottered, clinging to Stephan's waist. What if she were wrong about this being a rescue?

A guard flung down his rifle as he blubbered: 'Comrade ladies, don't harm me!'

Marya glanced at Paskevich. Nostrils flared as if his jailers' cowardice reflected badly on him, he stood erect. How could he not show the least trace of fear? The ululations were terrifying enough without the turmoil, the thick odours of sweat and violence, the mob which appeared on the verge of inflicting an unspeakable death not only on him, but also on anyone who tried to halt it. Marya gulped in air. To calm herself, she looked at Klazkha. Klazkha, her friend and protective priestess, standing there watchful.

The carter was slashing his whip at the thin stubborn mules, forcing them into the wall of women. The cart inched forward.

Klazkha thrust up both arms. It was this sudden and unexpected movement that caused Marya to look up from the riot.

In the building to the right of the burned palace, camouflaged by shadows of the window-embrasures, several figures were positioned. One was taller and broader than the others, a man as massive as Ovruch. But how could it be Ovruch? Ovruch was in Moscow, not in Petrograd. Marya's eyes narrowed, and the bulk swam into focus. Yes, Ovruch. But how had he known to be here? Had one of Klazkha's women been an informer?

In the shadowy light he poised there as immobile and watchful as a bear over a trout stream. Then, slowly hunching down, he rested a large service pistol against the window-ledge. Marya's gaze followed the direction of the barrel.

It was aimed at Klazkha.

'Klazkha!' Marya shouted. *'Move!'*

Her cry was swallowed by the screeched demands for a street trial.

'Klazkha, move!' Marya screamed again.

Abruptly Klazkha swung down her arms. In this same moment she ripped off her ruby scarf. Her long, straight brown hair, usually secured by a thick neat coil, tumbled down her back.

A signal.

Women grabbed the mules, women struggled with the guards, who one after another melted into the crowd on the Neva side of the embankment.

Marya was torn from Stephan's grasp. She screamed his name as she was whirled into the mêlée, and her protesting screams became part of the high-pitched babel. Panicky, she pressed herself against an axle. Around her were the boots and shawls and yanked-up skirts of women as they climbed the splintery spokes.

She looked up at Ovruch.

He was still aiming at Klazkha. But why Klazkha? Marya wondered in the split second. Why harm a worker, a party member?

A brief dazzling burst.

'Hurry, get the three of 'em,' Klazkha's voice was calling.

'Oh, thank God.' Marya was unaware that she spoke aloud. 'She's alive. She's safe.'

A gypsy-dark woman thrust a shawl over the white nurse's veil. Marya struggled to find Stephan. But a mass of womanhood was dragging her up the heap of charred wood, bricks and marble. The vulpine howls deafened her.

She never heard the second shot.

Chapter Forty-four

Klazkha didn't hear either of the shots.

The voices around her were too loud, and, besides, she was totally engrossed in the women clustered around Paskevich, Stephan and Marya. Why were they moving so slow? They knew there were only these few confused moments to spirit them to the fancy little private theatre where the hay-wain was. The Jewish doctor had showed up with it before light, wearing old clothes and leading the horse. Klazkha, who'd been there all night fretting herself sick with how to get away on foot, had felt like hugging him. Truth to tell, though, she hadn't been altogether surprised to see him. Although getting together had been risky, and they hadn't mulled over the details in the Sennaya Market, any man as besotted with Marya as he was must have worked out in his head what might be needed.

She didn't feel the bullet hit her.

There was no pain, no loss of consciousness. Yet all at once the energy was gone from her like spilled laundry water, and she felt herself slipping.

'Need to rest . . . '

Her mumbling went unheard. As she slid downwards, the women around, believing she had tripped, grabbed her arms, carrying her like ants with a tilted blade of grass.

What had happened to her? She tried to move her legs, but nothing happened. She thought of Josip, his poor feet trailing after him like rags.

Then all at once she was lying on something soft. A man's spectacles gleamed above her eyes. Marya's Jewish doctor? She felt his hands on her breasts. *Undoing my buttons. And in front of all my people. Men! That's how they are. Like animals. No, no, that's not it at all. Something stabbed me in the heart. A knife? No. None of the women would hurt me. It must have been something else. Anyway, I'm hurt. And he's tending me. But I already stressed he's got to rush them away. The Red Guard'll smell something fishy any minute.* She moved her lips, telling him to hide Marya and the other two under the straw, quick, and then move the wagon out. Instead of doing what she told him, he began to press down on her chest again and again, keeping time with that funny drumming against her ears.

Then Marya was behind him. Strands of that springy bronze hair were blowing from the shawl. Klazkha tried to reach up and push the curls out of sight. Her middle fingers twitched, but her hand refused to lift. She wanted to explain to Marya about how important it was to jump on the haywain. But what was wrong with them women? Every last one of them knew the rescue would fall apart like a dustball if they wasted a moment.

'Get in . . . cart . . . ' Klazkha shouted.

'What is it?' Marya bent lower. 'I can't hear you.'

'Go . . .' Klazkha dredged up a worry. On the Embankment, the women were already scattering. What would happen to all of them if this inner bunch was caught and the Cheka tortured them into confession? The Women's Internationale would be done for. 'Hurry . . .'

Marya didn't move. 'Klazkha . . . Hang on. Please hang on.'

Why couldn't Marya show enough common sense to get away? But when had Marya ever been practical? Years ago, would she have argued with Paskevich about employing a twelve-year-old with a yellow card as a lady's maid if she'd had common sense? Or would she have set foot in that room thick with the cholera? Marya had always been heart, a lot of heart, and not a single grain of common sense.

Why was somebody piling rocks on her chest?

Is this dying? Am I dying? Well, if I am, that's good and fair. I pay my debts, always. And I owe Marya my life.

'Klazkha, you're my best friend, the only true friend I ever had. I need you. Please fight. I need you. Everybody needs you.'

'Owe . . . you . . . my life . . .' Klazkha whispered. 'Always . . .'

What was the debt? The way her mind was all hazy she couldn't remember. All she knew was that she was overdue in paying something important. How freezing it was. Funny how cold this afternoon was, colder than it'd ever been in the heart of the blizzards.

And the light was all funny. Shrinking inwards until she saw only a gap of blazing whiteness. Then, at the end of that radiance, far, far away, Josip appeared on the crutches that Boris and Marya had bought him. 'My brother . . . ' Klazkha murmured to Marya.

Josip lifted his hand and waved. His wide happy smile welcoming her. Klazkha ran lightly towards him.

Pavel Golder sat back, his hands dripping with Klazkha's lifeblood. 'She's gone,' he sighed.

'You're giving up too soon!' Marya snapped.

'There is no time to waste,' Golder said. 'You must get into the wagon. *Now.*'

Marya ignored his urgency, pressing both hands on the lax scarred cheeks, blowing air into the mouth, tasting the salt of the blood that seeped out of the corners of Klazkha's mouth.

Most of the women, having played their parts, whispered a hasty farewell to their fallen leader or made the sign of the cross, then trotted around the tumbled wall and disappeared along the alley.

'Marya, there's nothing you can do.'

Stephan's voice. Mouth glued to Klazkha's, she shrugged his hands from her shoulders.

'The wench is dead.' Paskevich.

'We must leave.' Golder.

'Marya,' Stephan said. 'The Red Guard'll be here — they knew the plan.'

Marya's efforts at resuscitation ended with a gasp.

Paskevich had swung her up. The gaminess of his sweat surrounding her, she kicked and flailed. Ignoring her struggles, he climbed with her on to the cart, pushing her on to the floorboards. Stephan jumped on after them.

Marya sat up. 'I've seen men respond after —'

Paskevich gripped her shoulder as he said rapidly: 'The poor loyal devil will have tossed away her life for nothing *if you don't keep down!*' He yanked her next to him so roughly that she heard the back of her head slam on the wood. Stephan, on her other side, touched her reassuringly. Klazkha's lieutenants covered them. As armloads of hay fell on the cloth, Marya's body went rigid and pains darted from her chest down her left arm. *I'm not going to suffocate. Klazkha planned this carefully . . . I am not . . .*

Overhead, Pavel Golder's precise intonations: 'You cannot cough, or sneeze. And please keep still. Should anyone notice the hay move we are done for. We have a long distance to go, so relaxation is essential.'

The floorboards rose unevenly, hitting

578

against Marya's shoulders and spine as the cart lurched over the rubble. Thick straw-dust clogged in her lungs. She could hear shouts, and the pop of rifles. The noises faded. A straw poked against her forehead, tormenting her. Yet neither physical discomfort nor her panic symptoms alleviated the force of her grief. What were those last mumbled whispers? I owe you my life. She'd said that before, years ago in a putrid-smelling attic behind the Fourstatskaia Street apartment. *Klazkha, oh, Klazkha, look at where your punctilious book-keeping has got you . . .*

The rickety cart's unoiled axles groaned, the wooden wheels grated on cobblestone. Each time they turned a corner, Marya, who was sandwiched between the men, felt either her husband or her lover pressing closer to her side while she fell against the other. The cart careened and turned, gliding over stone and wood paving, bobbing along rutted alleyways, echoing across bridges until it seemed to Marya that she had wept for Klazkha beneath the thickly sweet hay for longer than her imprisonment in the Trubetskoi Bastion.

Finally they slowed and then stopped.

'Wait,' Golder whispered. The cart swayed as Golder climbed down. They eased forward slowly, halting again. Doors thumped shut. The hay was shifted, the cloth pulled away. Marya gulped in lungfuls of air.

Golder's lantern showed they were in a

cavernous stable. 'It is safe here,' he said. 'But I have promised to stay as briefly as possible.' Shadows were swaying as he moved to a corner. Setting down the lantern, he shovelled aside feed to reveal a laundry hamper with uneven black-painted lettering: 'Property of Klazkha Sobchak'. He took out a thick pile of folded woman's clothing and set it on the floor, then unpacked a blue university uniform and a sailor's short-jacket. Last of all, dun-brown porter's garments. 'These are for you, Count,' he said. 'I will return in no more than ten minutes.'

He led the horse out.

As the cart passed over the threshold, Stephan shut the doors and took the student's uniform up the loft ladder.

Paskevich had shaken out the ragged garments assigned him. With a shrug and a chuckle, he said: 'I'm reduced to the peasantry by your maid.'

At this mention of Klazkha, Marya stifled a keening sob. Grabbing the heavy heap of woman's clothes, she moved to the loft ladder. Stephan had ascended so lithely that she hadn't realized how far apart the rungs were. Her bulky armload made climbing impossible. Would Stephan consider her changing down here a defection? Ridiculous as embarrassment seemed in the midst of her grief and the precariousness of their situation, she could feel her face grow hot.

Paskevich was watching her. The lantern

cast a devilish yellow glint on his eyes before he elaborately turned his back to her.

She retreated to a corner.

Later she would question what had prompted her to keep on the nurse's uniform. Was it modesty in the presence of her estranged husband, or a hitherto unexplored area of practicality? She pulled the flannel petticoats, the voluminous skirt, the blouse over her other clothing. When she put on the filthy quilted jacket, she felt as bulky and round as any of the peasant women with whom she'd bargained on the Tobolsk journey.

The big door nudged open again. Golder coughed.

She emerged from her corner folding the grey cape into a bundle.

Golder was already spreading out the documents for Paskevich. 'Passports. Without photographs these were the best I could manage. Travel passes. These are quite genuine. Given any kind of luck, they should take you to the Finnish border.' He paused. 'Are you aware, Count Paskevich, of the Finnish situation?' At a negative response, Golder rapidly outlined that the Finns, having broken free of Russian rule, were now battling to expel Russian troops — a clash for independence that was hampered by the Finnish Bolsheviks. 'The Red Finns are strongest in the south,' Golder said. 'So the further north you cross the border, the better your chances of finding friends.'

The ladder creaked, and Stephan jumped down the last four feet. Wearing student's clothes, in the shadowy ochre cast by the lantern, to Marya he looked no older than he'd been on the Channel steamer.

'I almost forgot.' Golder pulled a crumpled kerchief from his pocket and handed it to Paskevich. 'Klazkha suggested winding this around your face as if you were suffering from a toothache.'

She worked out every last detail, she planned for every contingency — except for Ovruch's bullet . . .

Paskevich took the cloth and the documents. 'So we're a family. Père Vladislav Savik with his devoted offspring, Piotr and Raissa.' He hunched over in the posture of a man who has spent a lifetime hauling weights on his back. Raising a hand, he quavered in peasant accents: 'Well, my children, let us begin our journey with a father's blessing.'

The doctor opened the door, looking into the moonlight in both directions. 'Safe,' he said. 'So this is farewell.'

Marya's skin was pebbly with goose-pimples as she accepted another loss. She was parting from Golder. Golder who had risked everything to steal food and drugs for her in Military Hospital No. 5. Golder who had gone against his every conviction to obtain travel passes to Tobolsk for her and Stephan. Golder who had once again shelved his political beliefs to aid in Paskevich's rescue.

Golder who by now was surely anathema to his comrades in the Jewish Socialist Bund. Taking his hand, she said shakily: 'There's no way to say what I feel, but thank you, Pavel, thank you for everything.'

'We will meet in a happier future,' he replied, shaking her hand ceremoniously. His smile, though, was yearning and infinitely sad. He and she both knew that this was goodbye.

The full moon was up, silverplating rooftops and bare branches. The garden walls cast shadows like long, velvety black prayer-rugs. They hugged the darkness, moving stealthily in Indian file, Stephan a few steps ahead of Marya, with Paskevich bringing up the rear. At a sudden burst of sound they froze. An untuned piano began playing with skill and verve.

The music gave a sense of normality. Paskevich shifted into the moonlight to examine the travel passes. Thick boots planted apart, head back, he made the porters' rags appear a post-revolutionary style of general's uniform.

'The Finnish border, yes,' he said drily. 'Hardly original; but, under the circumstances, why be trailblazers?'

Marya, perceiving the remark as a mocking attack on Golder, felt obliged to attack Paskevich in return — no matter how irrationally she went about it. 'Finland,' she snapped. 'Ovruch'll be expecting us there. He said that the Monarchists were all rushing for the Finnish borders. He said Stephan and the other liberals would soon be following.'

The moonlight shadowed Stephan's frown. 'You never mentioned that.'

'Well, my pet, you've convinced me. Finland's a mistake. The Crimea . . . Yes, why not? It's Odessa and a boat across the Black Sea for me.'

'Us,' Stephan said.

'I'm deeply grateful, of course, for your concern, Strakhov. But you've done your bit.'

'I gave my word,' Stephan said, 'to see you safely to Switzerland.'

'At last, a man of principle.' Paskevich bowed. 'You've obliged me to respond in kind. So let me forewarn you, Strakhov, accompanying me is a mistake on your part. Marya's my wife. I intend to keep her as my wife.'

'I'd prefer to be buried alive,' Marya said.

'Interesting choice, that.'

'The minute we arrive in Zurich,' Stephan said in a taut voice, 'we'll leave you.'

Marya clamped her icy hands inside her pockets.

After that they no longer kept to the shadows. The two men strode well apart, Marya, swaddled in her two sets of clothing, trotting between them. They passed a long fence lined with tattered Bolshevik posters.

'What about Klazkha?' she asked.

Stephan sighed. 'She's dead.'

'I know that. I just went a bit crazy back there. But she has no people. Who'll arrange the funeral?'

Rather than voicing his conviction that the Cheka were at this minute dissolving Klazkha's body in the lime-pit behind the squat yellow police building in Gorokhavaya Street, Stephan said: 'The Women's Internationale idolized her. They'll see she's buried decently.'

Marya wiped her knuckles across her tears. 'I still don't understand. Why didn't Ovruch shoot one of us? Why her?'

'I don't pretend to understand the new ascendancy,' Paskevich said, 'but is it conceivable that he viewed your girl as a traitress?'

Accepting the validity of the question, Marya didn't respond.

They passed nobody in the mews.

At a wide avenue they halted. Two men were staggering along singing a revolutionary ditty. Across the street, a burned-out mansion was surrounded by tree-stumps. After the drunken singing had faded, Paskevich said: 'That's old Gurovich's place. The gardens were his pride and joy. You idealists uncorked quite a genie in the Bolsheviks.'

'Baiting me is a waste of time,' Stephan said in a cold voice. 'Marya, I've been thinking. The journey to the Crimea's long and dangerous.'

'What do you suggest as an alternative,

Strakhov? That we leave my wife in St Petersburg while your oversized friend scours the city for her?'

'No. You're right, of course.' Stephan fixed his gaze on the house. 'But if we don't stop sniping at one another, we'll get her killed before we're halfway to Odessa.'

'And now you're correct,' Paskevich said with a bow. 'If you'll curb your nobility of soul, I'll do my utmost to keep my wit less personal.'

Marya's hands tensed with the urge to strangle him.

Paskevich's teeth shone briefly in the moonlight. 'I'm sorry, my dear,' he said, 'but you're in for a long trek to Tsarskoe Selo.'

'The new name's Detskoye Selo,' she said. 'And the town's been nationalized under the jurisdiction of the Petrograd Soviet. So, if you're hoping to get some of your possessions, there's not a chance.'

'Thank you for the information,' he said blandly. 'It happens that the nearest railway station is in — what was that you just called Tsarskoe Selo?'

Chapter Forty-five

The tulle-thin clouds to the east were vivid pink with dawn as the three travellers trudged into Tsarskoe Selo. The once-immaculate summer retreats of the aristocracy had taken on a rundown appearance under the weight of their numerous tenants, some of whom seemed intent on destruction. A shabby worker blew on his hands as he emerged into the cold morning and joined the men already outside in whittling at the porch's delicate carving. At the next palace three thin children were kicking down a segment of low ornamental fencing: most of the fence already lay on the gravel. A woman heaved a stained mattress through the remains of a magnificently glazed window. Paskevich, who had tied on Klazkha's kerchief and bent his back as if he had spent a lifetime humping heavy burdens, slowed as they reached his 'cottage'. Twin queues curled towards the pair of latrines that now defaced the rose garden, and the right gate sagged drunkenly because one of the immense brass hinges had been stolen.

'This is dangerous, and there's no point,' Stephan said in a low voice. 'Everything was taken months ago.'

In response, Paskevich pushed at the left gate, which creaked open. 'Enough dawdling, you two,' he quavered loudly. 'Step lively for a change.'

'Keep your voice down,' Stephan muttered.

But already the gatehouse door had opened. Looping her arm through Stephan's, Marya trilled: 'Go ahead, Papa dear. Brother and I'll wait here for you.'

'Just because the pair of you learned your letters doesn't mean you can pull the wool over my eyes.' Paskevich cast a tortoise-like glance at the loitering sentries across the street. 'I know that Piotr's got in mind a card game with those soldiers. And Almighty God alone can judge, my girl, what it is *you* want with them.'

An elderly woman with huge pillow-like breasts had emerged from the gatehouse. 'How wise you are, old comrade. These young people today, they go in search of trouble. Myself, I'd keep a sharp eye on a pretty girl like yours, and on that handsome boy as well.'

'If my rotted tooth wasn't a torment, I'd give the pair of them a thrashing. I'm not too old for that. Lounge around with the soldiers indeed! Why do they suppose I brought them here if not to dig their Aunt Polia's vegetable garden?'

'Vegetable garden?' The woman clasped a hand between her over-ample breasts. 'I don't have any vegetable garden.'

'Neither do I — not yet.' Paskevich gave a cunning wink. 'But spring's almost here, so the commissar'll be assigning us our plots any minute. In the meantime, these useless children can do a bit of work. Are you in charge of the shovels, my fine-bosomed darling?'

The woman preened at the compliment before she said sourly: 'The latrine committee hogs the shovels.'

Paskevich argued with the hatchet-faced chairwoman of the latrine committee until she reluctantly agreed to lend them two battered short-handled spades. Paskevich led Marya and Stephan through the untended grounds. Near the burned-out ruins of the Chinese pagoda, he set them digging. Marya hacked, but the earth was still frozen and her efforts were largely futile. Stephan succeeded in turning a few clods. Men and women wandered over, offering advice on how to plough up the 'vegetable plot'.

Paskevich held a hand over his kerchiefed jaw. 'If this tooth wasn't poisoning my system, I'd pitch in. Comrades, help a sick man. Pitch in, and the job'll be finished in no time.'

The hefty cross-eyed Siberian was the first to drift away. As Paskevich continued to cajole, the other spectators followed him.

Alone with Marya and Stephan, Paskevich moved to the south-west corner of the pagoda foundations, taking three long strides forward. 'Here,' he ordered. 'Dig here.'

Frost scattered as Stephan slammed the shovel into the hard ground. Marya dug where he'd broken the soil. They had been sweating in the cold morning air for nearly an hour when her shovel clanged against metal. Paskevich stood behind them, hiding them from view from the house, turning occasionally to make sure nobody was watching as Stephan cleared earth from the top of a black strongbox.

As Paskevich kneeled to raise the lid, Marya gasped. Before her gleamed the jewellery that he'd bestowed on her each night of her brief tenure as his countess. Gold set with barbarically large sapphires, emeralds, rubies, diamonds, coiled ropes of immense glowing pearls! Marya's initial burst of pleasure at seeing her possessions gave way to a sour taste in her throat. She was trying to estimate how many men would be alive with their families today if these cold baubles had been sold to purchase medical supplies for Military Hospital No. 5. She neglected to include the voracious pilfering of the matron and the chief surgeon in her calculations.

Paskevich was rapidly shovelling the gaudy heap into her nurse's cape.

'You'll see. Comrade Lenin has set us on the right path.' The stout flour-skinned man who was crammed against Stephan gave his droning lecture above the clack of wheels so everyone in the compartment could hear. 'The Romanovs ground us down for three hundred years; they bled us dry with their extravagances, and slaughtered us in their imperialist wars. I do not complain about a few shortages here and there. The people have taken charge —'

'Enough jabbering, professor,' interrupted the flat-nosed sailor. 'Who gives a shit about the views of the likes of you, professor? We're trying to sleep in here, professor!' The sailor growled his repetitive 'professors'.

Like a prodded anemone, the pasty-faced orator withdrew into his own flesh. Professors, like lawyers, doctors and merchants, were *burzhui,* part of the bourgeoisie, and, as such, targets for mob violence.

Hail drummed on windows, wheels rattled, ungreased axles grated as the travellers jammed into the compartment fell silent.

How sour it has turned out, the Revolution, Stephan thought. His sigh came from deep within his chest. Yet paradoxically he had not lost his hopes for justice in Russia. A violent upheaval of the people had thrown off the Autocracy. The Bolsheviks, who had grabbed power illegally, would be cast aside, too.

I ought to be agitating against Lenin, he thought. *I should be doing something now.*

Stephan's eyes were drawn down with fatigue, but he couldn't doze. Instead, he yearned for the impossible power to turn back the calendar. Given a second chance, he would never have given that blind promise to Nicholas Romanov. He shifted cautiously, so as not to disturb Marya, who slept with her head on his shoulder, then glanced across the narrow aisle at Paskevich.

In spite of the pauper's clothing, he somehow retained his dignity. However much Stephan despised Paskevich for his inbred sense of superiority and his reactionary politics, he knew he loathed the count more for the mockery in those dark little eyes, which were now shut, and for the cleverness below that disguising kerchief. Though Marya had chosen to sit with him, and slept with her head jiggling trustfully against his shoulder, his jealousy was increasing with every hour, like plague bacilli multiplying and spreading through his blood vessels.

By now the other passengers were all dozing, chins upraised or sagging on to chests.

Suddenly the train whistle shrilled.

Marya awoke with a start.

Stephan turned his head on the damaged plush. 'No need to worry. We've come to a station, that's all.'

'Remember Eydkunin?'

'How could I forget?'

The compartment door slid open. A narrow woman sidled inside. Hail melted, flowing with raindrops off her slick English-style mackintosh to the stained carpeting. The plopping could be heard as she turned her bulging eyes on each of the passengers. A peculiar whinny came from the stout man who had praised Communism.

'Comrades.' The woman paused, scanning them again. 'Comrades, for your own safety the train must be inspected. You are to wait on the platform.'

'The platform? Are you making some sort of joke?' asked the flat-nosed sailor. 'Out there it's like a cow pissing gallstones.'

'Orders from Petrograd Soviet,' the official said in a higher, more nasal tone. 'And hand me your documents as you go. They'll be stamped and returned when you reboard.'

Paskevich extended a sheaf made out for Vladislav Savik, his son Piotr and unmarried daughter Raissa.

The woman's bulging gaze remained fixed on the hunched old porter with the filthy rag hiding most of his face before turning her attention to the young woman who seemed obese under her sheepskin coat and the tall student who wore a naval jacket. After a long pause, she asked: 'So the three of you are a family?'

'I won a scholarship to university years ago,' Stephan said to explain the disparities in their appearance.

'And your sister's unmarried?'

'Her sweetheart was killed in Bloody Nicholas's war. He died in Galicia.'

'Come, Piotr. Enough bragging. Do what the lady — the comrade — tells us.' Paskevich gripped Marya's trembling arm as if to support himself.

The hailswept station consisted of the platform, a small stone building and an already crowded narrow shelter. Travellers pouring from more remote carriages were dashing towards the shelter. Paskevich, still gripping Marya, used his free elbow to push their way against the oncoming surge.

Marya balked, peering around. 'Wait for Stephan.'

'Keep moving,' Paskevich hissed. 'Our fish-eyed comrade's on to something.'

'Then, why didn't she detain us?'

A slope-shouldered man who might have been a clerk halted, panting, to rest his suitcase on the platform. Paskevich smoothly scooped up the valise by its handle, continuing to tug Marya through the oncoming mob. At the edge of the high platform, he tightened his grip on her waist. 'Hang on,' he said. Plunging down, he took her with him. The packed cinders jarred her ankles. Then he was trotting away from the station, pulling her with him.

'Where are you going?' She was gasping at the hail dashing in her face and at keeping up with him.

'Away.'

'We have no papers. We're in the middle of nowhere.'

'An excellent place for us to be, nowhere.'

'You want to lose Stephan, that's all it is!' Marya swivelled her head. She spotted Stephan almost immediately. A half-head taller than the crush of passengers, he was peering around the platform.

'Stephan,' she called. 'Stephan!'

'Keep quiet!' Paskevich was dragging her now.

But Stephan was racing after them.

The hubbub surrounding the train faded

594

into the racket of the hail. The hard-packed sand ended. They were at a hedge of brambles. Paskevich went first, but nevertheless thorns caught her sheepskin coat and she had to wriggle and wrench her way through. Engulfed by hail and blackness, the three moved more slowly across rolling ploughed land. Marya held her layered skirts high, struggling at every step with the clay-like mud that sucked at her boots. Both men gripped her arms.

'Do you have the least idea where we're going?' Stephan asked.

'None,' Paskevich responded. 'All I know is we'd have been arrested if we'd stayed at the station.'

'Oh?' Stephan said. 'Then, why did they empty out the train?'

'As a suggestion, to weed out the threesomes travelling together. Strakhov, suspend that wondrous belief in humanity for a minute. That oversize peasant has sounded the tocsins —' Paskevich broke off, halting. 'Did you hear something?'

Immediately ahead the hail was less resonant.

'I think we're coming to some woods,' Marya said.

'Yes,' Paskevich replied impatiently. 'I meant behind us.'

Marya listened. The faraway high-pitched sound might have been the wind. Then several blurred circles pierced the night.

'Flashlights,' Stephan said grimly.

'Our best chance is to hide in Marya's woods,' Paskevich retorted. 'Let's hope she's discovered a good-size stand.'

The field ended abruptly, and they were surrounded by trees. The hail clattered against the uppermost branches, which kept the pine-needles underfoot more or less dry. At first they felt their way slowly, carefully and as silently as possible through the blackness, halting every few steps to listen for pursuers. As their pupils adjusted, vague shapes became visible. They went more rapidly, Stephan holding aside branches, Paskevich using his free hand to grasp Marya's waist when they came to thickly enlaced roots.

Paskevich handed Stephan the valise and carried Marya across a swollen rivulet.

On the far bank, Stephan said: 'I think I saw something a bit upstream.'

His steps crackled on the pine needles, fading then returning. 'It's a deserted hut.'

The interior reeked of the sickly odour that Marya had learned in hospitals to associate with putrefying flesh. Paskevich managed to strike a match, and she let out a sigh of relief. From hooks attached to the low rafter beams dangled a dozen or so hares, their furry grey heads lolling on skinned bodies.

'A poacher's lair,' Paskevich said. 'If he returns, we'll need to deal with him.'

That unremitting self-assurance of Paskevich's! Marya, drenched, winded and exhausted, was surprised by the force of her outrage. 'I never knew you to steal before.'

'My pet, you must learn the new vernacular. That bag's been nationalized; these rabbits and firewood are the property of the people.'

Stephan was already rolling firewood across the dirt floor to a cinder-filled pit. Paskevich showed neat skill in placing pine cones and needles between the wood; but, even so, the thick damp logs required much blowing before a small blaze glowered sullenly. The piny smoke was veneered with aromas of drying wool and roasting rabbit.

When they had wolfed the rare flesh, Paskevich opened the suitcase.

He surveyed the neatly packed clothes, which had kept remarkably dry. 'It was too heavy for those few rags.'

'Nationalized things do weigh you down,' Marya retorted.

Paskevich was systematically fingering the wet leather. Suddenly the bottom of the bag sagged, revealing a narrow space. He drew out a clump of underwear that swaddled a Mauser with ammunition-clips.

Marya was still irritated. 'Hooray for us. Now we're equipped to fight the Red armies.'

'I'd pit you against them every time.' Paskevich chuckled. 'But you'll need some sleep first.'

Stephan reached for the pistol. Flames swayed and smoke swirled as he pushed open the crude plank door.

'Where are you going?' she cried. 'Stephan, it's not safe outside.'

'My military experience is none too recent,' Paskevich said. 'But, to the best of my recollection, men never stood watch inside.'

'I'll be right here . . .' The door shut as if Stephan were cutting off the unsaid words, *If you need me.*

Marya stripped off her many-layered wet clothing and put on the hairy dressing-gown that was packed in the suitcase. She stretched out by the firepit. Every sound was magnified. Hail on pine branches, the continuous drip from leaks in the roof, the occasional loud pop of damp burning logs. Paskevich's breathing, slow and regular.

She couldn't hear Stephan, but she pictured him on the other side of the crude door as he gripped the German handgun that was his sole protection.

Her auditory concentration wavered, and she wept softly for Klazkha. Then she found herself comparing her travelling companions.

Paskevich's behaviour was no different from what it had always been. He took the same zest as ever in needling her; he protected her in the infuriatingly authoritarian way that, even when she knew his decisions to be irreproachable, transformed her into a stubborn child. Danger, foul weather, the porter's rags, even the presence of his rival, seemed part of an amusing game to him.

Stephan, on the other hand, in Paskevich's presence was changed entirely. He had been passionately independent to the point of being aloof. The Democratic Reform Party, she saw now, had remained a minor force in the Provisional Government because of Stephan's inability to compromise his high moral standards. To reach every decision, he consulted his own conscience, neither asking nor accepting advice. Even in the Army he hadn't rated highly on following orders. Yet now he'd allowed Paskevich to take command. In Tsarskoe Selo he'd dug in the rose garden and, once the treasure had been retrieved, had left the travel plans to Paskevich. He could have a hot temper, yet when Paskevich questioned him about the Revolution he disregarded the heavily veiled sarcasm and gave thoughtful answers. It was Marya, churning like an angry sea at each jab, who sprang to the defence of his principles.

At a loud crack, she jerked to a sitting position, her heart hammering.

Sparks were flying in an upward constellation. She relaxed. A log had burned through and fallen. She stretched out again. Why was Stephan so edgily contained? Why did he obey Paskevich? Why didn't he behave more possessively towards her? Had he so much as touched her since they'd left that stable?

She jerked again as Paskevich spoke.

'In many ways he's a real Romanov. Blood will out,' he said as if he had been eavesdropping on her thoughts. 'He and Nicholas are quite a bit alike, you know. Both bottle up their anger, and they're stubborn. Of course, this one's far more intense and creative, and has double the intellectual power. Yet he shares Nicholas's *naïveté* about human behaviour.'

'Whereas you Paskeviches are crafty and clever.'

'Aren't we just?' Paskevich chuckled, then his tone changed back to rumination. 'Nicholas's benevolent instincts are fixed on his family. Strakhov's the reverse. He's out to benefit humanity and doesn't get bogged down with specific individuals. A pity he wasn't born a tsar.'

'What sort of nonsense are you talking? Stephan cares about people — cares too much. And you know as well as I do that he spent his life fighting to end the Autocracy.'

'At this point in time, my dear, he's *en route* to turning White.'

'That is a joke, isn't it?'

'You don't consider him a Bolshevik, do you?'

'Of course not. But he despises the concept of superior birth.'

'He's not a boy any more. He's old enough to have learned that, no matter how thoroughly you sweep the farmyard, when the straw settles there's a pecking order.'

'You were raised to trample on others!' she snapped. 'How could you understand anybody who believes in helping the people?'

'I've noticed that those intent on benefiting "the people" are the most likely to disregard those closest to them. The great humanitarians, including our honoured Leo Tolstoy, were either tyrants to their families or neglectful.'

'You're jealous of his talent and decency and the courage of his convictions.'

Paskevich was rising to his feet. He, too, had changed into clothes found in the purloined suitcase. The reasonably new railway worker's uniform was a vast improvement over the dun-coloured smock. He'd rolled up the trousers, and wore a heavy sweater under the jacket, which strained across his shoulders and barrel chest, refusing to button. From Marya's prone position, with the smoke coiling, he appeared a Neibelung, mythically squat and strong.

'You're right about one thing, my dear,' he said quietly. 'I *am* jealous. Not of his so-called talent or his befuddled politics, but on a far more personal level.'

At first light, when they left the hut, hail no longer sounded on the branches. The forest was not as dense as it had seemed in the darkness, but a misty fog coiling around the tree trunks made it seem a ghostly place. The solitude was disturbed only once, when a startled deer blundered into the undergrowth.

They had changed their appearance as much as possible. Paskevich had kept on

601

the railway worker's clothes. Marya had put on the damp nurse's uniform. Stephan, too tall for any of the stolen things, buttoned up his sailor-coat, discarding his student's cap in favour of a leather motor-cyclist's hat. Tight-fitting with earflaps, it covered most of his face, making his eyes appear a darker, more intense blue, and showing the whitish line around his tautly closed lips.

They walked southwards all morning, and then trees abruptly gave way to cleared land.

Above them curved the immense white sky, a milky bowl with the sun melting through like a pat of butter. Ahead, stretching as far as the eye could see, was an oddly striped mosaic of farmland: the long fields that had been left fallow were bearded with wintry weeds while the tilled wet earth shone like black oil. In the distance families ploughed or sowed.

'So lovely and peaceful,' Marya sighed. 'Who'd guess there'd been a war and two revolutions?'

As they picked their way along the muddy path, Paskevich explained to Marya about strip farming. The long, narrow fields, he said, were an unfortunate legacy. In the days of serfdom, fields had been divided down the middle, enabling the serfs to simultaneously cultivate crops for their own households and their masters'; after the Emancipation Edict in 1861, most landowners sold their land, so a peasant could end up with strips at a great distance from each other.

They reached a fork in the road. The sign-post leaned at an odd angle. It was impossible to tell which way the arrows pointed.

'Don't worry about it,' Stephan said when Marya tried to make out the worn lettering. 'They're two villages that've grown into one town. Maly-Iupatovsk.'

'Strakhov, you gave no inkling of your expertise in local geography. Tell me, does this Maly-Iupatovsk have a railway station?'

'It serves the St Petersburg-Crimea line.'

Chapter Forty-six

Maly and Iupatovsk had merged at the bottom of a valley; and, as if to prevent jealousy between them, the turreted government building had been built at the centre of the declivity.

The travel commissar couldn't have been thirty; however, his missing upper teeth sank his mouth into his jaw, giving him the appearance of an ancient. Surveying the nice little bit of a nurse, the tall fellow in the concealing leather cap and the man in shabby railway attire, he immediately saw them for what they were. Their posture, their assured tread — everything about them shrieked Class Enemy. Anticipation warmed the commissar's chest. Lounging at his desk, he left them to stand.

The older man, short, ugly, yet somehow intimidating, stepped closer, leaning on the desk in a negligent way that made it appear that he, rather than the commissar, was in charge. Giving names which were presumably false, he didn't bother to disguise his educated accent.

'Our train was attacked by a band of Whites,' he said. 'Comrade, they gathered up all the passengers' identification documents and travel passes to make a bonfire.'

The commissar, who had heard nothing about Whites capturing a train, allowed the statement to pass unchallenged. With a wave, he indicated a bench to the tall man and nicely rounded sister. He and the bald 'railway worker' understood each other, and what point was there in delaying negotiations? 'This is Maly-Iupatovsk,' he said. 'Either you have papers or you're a spy.'

'That's why we've reported directly to the bureau, Comrade. To obtain new documents.'

'Absolutely the right thing to do, Comrade. All I need now is proof that the three of you are who you say you are.'

'Proof? What kind of proof could we have? Those damn Monarchists burned our papers and stole everything — almost.' Paskevich glanced over at Marya and Stephan, who perched stiffly on the pine bench, the valise between them hidden by Marya's cape. He went on in a low voice: 'During the Galician campaign my niece saved a Cossack officer from death, and his mother showed her gratitude. The girl keeps it pinned inside her apron, so those White bastards never saw it.'

The large fist opened to show a bar pin that Marya had worn on the throat of her delicate summer frocks. The Fabergé enamel-ware was far more valuable than the diamonds, but the commissar noticed only the gems. His toothless upper lip folded over the lower, an expression of raw cupidity, and for several seconds there was only the ticking of the wall-clock.

'Those stones look small. Jewellery's not worth much any more anyway, with all the exploiters selling what's the property of the people,' he said finally. 'Well, let me see it.'

Paskevich closed his large fingers over the brooch. 'The three of us're on our way to her father, my older brother. He's dying. In Odessa.'

'Hmm, Odessa. The Black Sea? A long journey. What else did your niece manage to hide? Sometimes women have a gold ring . . .'

Leaning across the scarred desk, Paskevich whispered: 'She got a pretty little necklace from her dead sweetheart, and when we started out she gave it to me for safekeeping. If you want the truth, I'm sick and tired of being asked if I still have the damn thing.'

'Where is it?'

Paskevich reached under his shirt, surreptitiously drawing out a choker. Each of the hammered gold pansies was centred with a cluster of tiny garnets.

'No diamonds,' the commissar said in a disgusted tone.

'Real garnets, though, and solid gold.'

Stephan breathed through his nose to dull his incipient nausea. Corruption sickened him in an actual physical manner; he was ashamed of having so strong an aversion, yet couldn't control it. *If this is what you have to go through to get papers, I'm a hopeless case,* he thought.

After staring another few moments, the commissar accepted that the brooch and the necklace in the big hand were the final offer. 'Let me see what can be done about replacing those papers,' he said.

The three passed the morning in a squalidly dirty hall with other supplicants and Red Guards smoking foul-odoured wartime cigarettes. Paskevich held the valise on his lap — he seldom relinquished it. Inside the false bottom were stored the jewels and the Mauser.

At a little after twelve a deep-voiced woman boomed out their current pseudonyms. Hurrying them up two flights of stairs to a dark attic, she stuck her head under a black cloth to snap their photographs. They returned to the hall. Daylight was fading when they were ordered back to the toothless commissar's office. Paskevich set the necklace and brooch on the desk, the commissar slid documents across the surface. 'Now, get out of Maly-Iupatovsk,' he growled. 'There's always room in our jails to squeeze in three more bodies.'

When they were in the misty twilight Marya's pent-up anxiety burst like a blister. Turning on Paskevich, she hissed: 'Dead sweetheart! Dying brother! You've become quite the expert at bribery!'

'Become? You know how to hurt a man. What sort of business do you imagine I was conducting at your Friday Night soirées?' His grin showed maliciously in the dusk. 'My pet, the Bolshevik government is like any other. A bit of grease turns the wheels.'

At the station, the ticket windows were boarded over and carried handwritten signs.

A RECEIPT FROM THE
STATION-MASTER
and travel passes
are required
to buy all tickets.
Apply within.

The station-master's warm tobacco-scented office was rimmed with messy heaps of books. Marking his place in a slim volume, he looked at them through his pince-nez.

'Iskra?' he said, blinking. 'Can that be Iskra under the motorcyclist hat?'

Marya felt as if spiders were crawling down her back before she noticed that the bubble-cheeked face was deferential.

'You don't recognize me?' the station-master continued. 'Well, why should you? Before the war — must be a good five or six years ago — you gave a private lecture at my brother-in-law's house. As you can see' — he waved at the heaped books — 'literature is my God. Pushkin! Turgenev! Tolstoy! Iskra! I can still remember how you hypnotized us all with your description of how Russian life would be when fairness and liberty were ours. You expressed every one of my own yearnings and hopes. *Days of Freedom* became my bible. And your poetry. How I've devoured your poetry! Magnificent, truly magnificent. What depictions of humanity, such truth, tender grace and exquisite beauty.'

Paskevich interjected: 'So even Bolsheviks get starry-eyed?'

'I'm no Bolshevik, but I have a wife, two children, old parents. Then there's my brother's family. We'd starve, all of us, if I lost my position. So I'm forced to play Red.' The station-master fingered the indentations where tsarist gold braid had been cut from his jacket, and added slyly: 'I recognize you, too, Count Paskevich.'

'What a curse an elephant's memory must be nowadays,' Paskevich said. The blandly spoken remark had the afterbite that had reduced decades of *chinovniks* to babbling subservience.

The station-master of Maly-Iupatovsk was no exception. Clasping his hands, he mumbled: 'I once had the honour of overseeing the uncoupling of your Excellency's private car; but I would never tell a soul that you're here now, Excellency. Never.' He glanced around at his slovenly library. 'I despise the Bolsheviks. Lenin writes so badly it hurts the teeth, and the rest of them are illiterates. Can't run a railway or lead an army. But, of course, you're aware that seven out of ten officers in the Red Army also served under the tsar. Here in Maly-Iupatovsk, they were recruited by force. I myself saw them rounded up while their families were herded into a big detention centre beyond the old market-place. Imagine! Keeping families as hostages is the way they ensure their officers' loyalty!' He tapped his cigarette, and ash sprinkled on the desk instead of in the ashtray. 'In this district they've burned down the homes of the nobility. And this past month they've arrested anyone who was ever active in a political party. That's the reason why, if any liberal comes in here, no matter the personal risk, I manage to find him space on the train.'

'What inspiringly selfless generosity!'

The station-master, lacking in humour, heard no sarcasm in Paskevich's compliment. 'I do my best, given the circumstances.' He bowed in Stephan's direction, adding: 'I pray for the just and open Russian future that you prophesied.'

Stephan, who reddened at the fulsome praise, asked crisply: 'What news have you heard?'

'Rumours, just the usual rumours. White forces joining with the Czechs. The grand dukes organizing armies to rescue the tsar. American forces landing in Vladivostok —'

'They have?' Marya interrupted.

'*On dit*; it could be hearsay, it could be true. The one fact I know for absolute certain is that something big is going on in the north.'

'What makes you so sure?' Paskevich asked.

'The telegraph office is in this building. The Reds've cut all the cable lines to Murmansk.'

Stephan looked bewildered. 'Why would they cut their own wires?'

'It seems strange to me,' the station-master responded.

'Only one reason I can think of,' Paskevich said. 'The Allies have landed troops there. The last thing Lenin would want spread around is that an army's in Russia to put down Bolshevism.'

'Let's hope that's the situation!' The station-master beamed. 'Half a dozen of my friends have left to join Wrangels or Denikin or one of the other White generals. I'd have gone with them like that' — he snapped his tobacco-yellowed fingers — 'if I weren't encumbered. Mark my words, before 1918 is over the Provisional Government will be back in power.'

'I live in hope of that halcyon day,' Paskevich said drily. 'In the meantime, we need to be on the next train to Odessa.'

Earlier, in the privacy of the only available room in Maly-Iupatovsk's inn, he had nudged open the false bottom of the grip to remove a ruby ring. Marya, calculating this as his moment to proffer the bribe, watched the large muscular hands. Instead of covertly displaying the ring, though, Paskevich didn't move.

The station-master, adulation glowing on his podgy face, was staring at Stephan. 'I can't believe it. Iskra. Stephan Strakhov, the

611

founder of the Democratic Reform Party —
here in my office!'

Stephan's throat reddened.

'The three of you will be on the next train
to Odessa!' The station-master clapped his
hands. A wizened old waiter appeared. After
a few minutes the ancient tottered back with
chipped glasses surrounding a pottery jug
of vodka and a plate arranged with thinly
sliced black bread, a thimble of sour cream,
rounds of cucumber pickle and the ubiqui-
tous bony little *vobla.*

The old man held out the tray first to
Paskevich. 'Excellency,' he said with a deep
bow.

After toasts were drunk and the *zakouska*
devoured, the station-master sighed. 'My
deepest regrets, but there are no reserved
places on this train. You'll need to wait on
the platform.'

A night mist hung over the crowded platform. The mass of veterans returning home
was swollen by peasants who had sought
work in the factories of Poland, Finland,
Estonia, Latvia and Lithuania — territories
ceded to the faltering Germans by the Treaty
of Brest-Litovsk. Now the Russians were
being forced to return to their shrunken
country.

A foul smell rose from the packed cinders
of the tracks, where shadowy figures squatted.

'If the Revolution's equalized nothing else,
it's equalized bodily functions,' Paskevich

said. 'I better find that old waiter and give him a few roubles for boiled water.'

'The station-master', Marya said, 'would be delighted to help you.'

'Being of a cynical cast, I prefer to deal with those who act out of self-interest rather than fawning admiration. You two try to arrange for seats. Here, take this.' He slipped the ruby ring into Marya's palm.

As he left, Marya took off her glove and shoved on the ring. 'That bit about the station-master, hinting he's untrustworthy just because he praised you!' Forgetting the mass of humanity around her, she spoke angrily. The nurse's uniform had already drawn curious glances, and more heads were turning in their direction. 'He's enjoying every minute of this whole miserable journey! It's made him even more contemptuous of everybody else!'

Stephan laid a finger over his lips.

She continued in a no less furious whisper. 'And you stay so calm!'

'Calm? I'm fighting down the urge to batter him.'

'Me, I feel obliged to bring him down a peg. God, how I wish I were a thousand miles from him!'

'Do you?'

She was summoning a response when a yellow light shone through the mist. Swaying back and forth on the other side of the track, the blurry arc was a signal. Several of the more substantial-appearing travellers were already picking their way over the cinders to a waiting wagon.

'Stephan, that drover's taking passengers. Why don't we go? Just the two of us. Your friend said the Murmansk telegraph lines were cut. That means in the north they haven't heard a word about us. Nobody will be on the look out. We'll be able to find our way to the trans-Siberian railroad. Maybe there really *are* American soldiers in Vladivostok, like the station-master said. And if there are not — well, in a port you can always find freighters. We'll get across the Pacific. Boris is in America; you have no idea how I miss him. Stephan darling, you'll absolutely adore San Francisco. You'll write magazine stories, I'll work in a hospital . . .' Her voice faded as three men boarded the wagon.

'Marya —'

'If we don't hurry, there won't be any room!' She clutched the thick wad of bills in her cape pocket — Paskevich had exchanged a marcasite watch for paper money. 'We can pay. And there's the ring for later. Stephan, what a perfect opportunity.'

Since they had left that burned-down palace in St Petersburg, Stephan had been adrift in amorphous dreams of the two of them inhabiting some peaceful landscape. Marya was gazing up at him with eyes that held the fire and promise of opals. That soft upper lip rose. Her parted mouth was red and moist. In this moment he saw the future stretching ahead: they would be free as the birds in the blessedly warm, citrus scented sunshine of California. *Why not?* he thought.

Then a skinny boy brushed by, undoing his pants as he rushed towards the track. Stephan returned to reality.

Pressing Marya away, he sighed. 'It's impossible.'

'Because of your promise? Klazkha died rescuing Paskevich. Isn't that enough? Besides, you know we're a drag on him; he's far more likely to get out of Russia without us.'

Stephan sighed. 'Try to understand. Nicholas didn't come to me. I went to him. I pledged myself to do whatever he asked.'

'Darling, just the two of us,' she coaxed. 'Think how wonderful it would be.'

'I can't go back on my word. I wouldn't be able to live with myself.'

One of the reasons she had fallen for Stephan was his tenacious integrity. But she, too, was stubborn. 'The point is that your Nicholas is desperate for money. If you're worried that Paskevich won't carry it through in Zurich, believe me, he will. That's how he is: he has a peculiar, warped code.' She whispered in a yet lower murmur: 'They're looking for two men and a woman travelling together. Don't you see? There's every reason in the world for us to separate.'

'Every reason. Except honour.'

Marya's shoulders slumped. There was no

point in further argument. The cart was jammed with passengers sitting on their baggage.

A short burly-shouldered railwayman was striding across the tracks. He and the carter bent their heads together as a spiralling fog briefly obscured them. When the cart was visible again, the carter was gesturing vehemently to some of his passengers, ejecting them.

'A minor change of plans.' Paskevich was below them on the track. 'We'll board the Odessa Express a few stops down the line. We're leaving in that cart this minute.' He reached up to help her from the platform — a husbandly gesture.

As their hands joined Stephan looked away.

Chapter Forty-seven

In the compartment everything had been ransacked except for the metallic map showing the Ukrainian section of the Odessa line. Kremenchug was printed in pink, the shade indicating cities of between fifty thousand and a hundred thousand inhabitants.

At Kremenchug station, a grandiose structure with a soaring arched roof that trapped engine smoke and a flock of sparrows, all passengers were ordered to get off with their baggage. To counteract the travellers' angry shouts, a woman railway official cheerfully bawled through a megaphone: 'Attention! Attention! Glorious news from the Kremenchug Soviet. All passengers are being transferred to the Odessa Express, which arrives in a few hours. Attention! Attention . . . !'

The new arrivals staked out places amid those already stranded there. Paskevich, however, took advantage of his railway uniform, striking up a conversation with a ticket-collector who told him the Odessa 'Express' wasn't scheduled for two days — and nowadays one could count on a far longer wait.

'An old schoolfriend of mine, Lenko, lives here,' Stephan said. 'Lenko'll know about food and lodgings.'

It was agreed that, while he went off in

search of his friend, Paskevich and Marya would rest on a bench in the station square.

Alter being packed in with so many un-washed bodies, Marya took deep appreciative breaths of the fresh spring air. They were far south of Petrograd, and already the slim birches inset into the paving of the square were full of greenery.

The surrounding buildings — town hall, shops, theatre and opera house — remained impressive despite broken windows and bullet scars. At the tram lines, the majority of the women had on citified hats and coats, and the men's shoes were cleanly polished leather. A number of men had the long beards, wide-brimmed hats and long gaberdines of orthodox Jewry.

'A lot of Jews in Kremenchug,' Paskevich said. 'This was part of the Pale of Settlement.'

'Golder told me that the Pale stretched all the way from the Baltic to the Black Sea — it was the only part of the Russian Empire where Jews were permitted to live.'

'Did he mention that even within the Pale they were restricted to specific villages and towns, which naturally became predominantly Jewish? Like Kremenchug. Before the Revolution, the areas were a ferment of culture — and manufacturing. I often pointed out to Nicholas that allowing the Jews to spread out would leaven our stodgy black bread. I also told him he ought to do more to stop the anti-Semitism; the Ukrainian pogroms were a major stumbling-block in our negotiations for foreign loans. He and Alexandra were far too devout to hear such anathema.'

They were sitting near what had been an immense equestrian bronze of a tsar or maybe a general; it was impossible to tell the subject because all that remained were four gigantic hoofs. The limestone plinth, which was intact, cast a rectangle of shade squarely on to the news-kiosk. Strutting lavender pigeons didn't take wing as Paskevich strolled over to buy *Pravda*, the only daily available. Returning to Marya, he handed her the front page.

COMMISSAR V.I. OVRUCH FOILS WHITE PLOT

Commissar Ovruch was in the line of fire when he gallantly thwarted a White Guard attempt to rescue a tsarist cabinet minister.

Commissar Ovruch spotted armed counter-revolutionaries hidden in the crowd that had gathered as the arch-imperialist Count Ivan Paskevich was transported from a Petrograd prison. Paskevich, who had held numerous advisory posts to the ex-tsar, was *en route* to face a tribunal for his numerous crimes against the people when the scheme was thwarted. Alerting the police, Commissar Ovruch personally took charge of the struggle, taking the band into custody. By then, unfortunately, the White Guardists had slain one woman and injured several more bystanders.

Paskevich was immediately removed to a prison of tightest security, where he is currently being held. The tribunal has been delayed while the Central Executive Committee examines recently captured documents that implicate the ex-minister in a conspiracy to wrest the tyrant Romanov from lawful detention. All materials will be published in the near future.

'Did you ever see such a pack of lies?' Marya cried.

Paskevich was using the edge of the other sheet to wipe dark smudges of printers' ink from his fingers. 'What it tells me is that your big oaf is hunting us down.'

'He's got men sifting through these millions of refugees for us? Oh, come on!'

'I'm convinced of it.' Paskevich crumpled the paper. 'Admittedly, though, my knowledge of our gallant commissar is all hearsay while yours is first hand.'

'I thought I understood him, but I don't.' Marya sighed. 'Why did he shoot Klazkha instead of you? Or me?' *After all, I'm the one who rejected his proposition to go to Moscow as his mistress; I refused to 'educate' American masses.* 'We're "class enemies", she was a worker. Why her?'

'Haven't we already chewed that one to the bone? In his eyes, she betrayed them; and the closer a traitor is, the greater the killing instinct,' Paskevich's mouth went down wryly. 'But don't give in to gloom, my pet. Rest assured we're on his list.'

'It's been eight days since they lost us, and there's no sign of them.'

'Frankly, throwing us off the train was a favour. Too many people in Maly-Iupatovsk know who we are.'

'Are you still harping on the station-master? Just because he admires Stephan?'

'Ah, well, that's how I am: jealous to the core.' Paskevich rested his arms on the back of the bench, lounging back with the air of being master of all Kremenchug. 'How are you enjoying our holiday?'

'Enjoy?' She gave a shudder. 'God, those trains! The lavatories!'

'I meant, does it please you being jousted over by your spouse, an arch-imperialist with high talents for bribery, and your lover, that "truly magnificent" poet who towers above Pushkin? Tell me, is it merely wishful thinking, or is there a lack of communication between you and our noble revolutionary?'

'How should we behave, with you along?'

'The husband's presence does make hopping into an adulterous bed a trifle awkward. But beware of other impediments. Especially watch out for those windmills.'

'Windmills?'

'Strakhov has been tilting at them all his life. First the Autocracy. Now the Reds. But surely at this point you've noticed that he's forever riding off and leaving you, my poor charming Dulcinea, in the dust?'

'Just because he's not all talk and no action —'

'Get up casually!' Paskevich interrupted in a low harsh growl. 'Act as though you're going over to buy another paper. Then duck behind the plinth.'

'What on earth —'

'Two Cheka agents are watching us. *Go!*'

As she rose, she spotted a pair of men in the station's shadowy portico. Wearing fedoras and high-necked Russian shirts under their suit jackets, inconspicuous attire in Kremenchug, they lounged against the tiled wall chatting. As a family group streamed through the entry, one of the pair glanced casually towards the bench. They must have been recruited from the Okhrana's most skilled operatives. How had Paskevich, lounging on a bench facing into the square, spotted them? She stood, touching a sleeve of his corduroy jacket as if for a brief goodbye. Her thighs were like lead as she moved towards the kiosk.

When she was ten feet away, the first shot cracked out.

Pigeons took flight with a mighty rustling of wings. Instinctively, Marya flung herself towards the marble base. The kiosk vendor shoved beside her, and then a young man with a wailing child on his shoulders. Within seconds a dozen or so sweating, gasping people were squashed together. An unseen woman screamed, her agonized cry soaring above rushing footsteps and shouts.

Then, silence.

As suddenly as the pigeons had wheeled into the sky, the little crowd behind the plinth was racing across the square away from the station. Marya peeped around the marble.

Five bodies sprawled near the station's grandiose entry arches. One corpse was a Cheka agent. He lay face-down, blood draining from his head towards his fedora which lay a few feet away. His partner was also horizontal, but in a military position, shoulders raised, left hand under right wrist as he took aim. Paskevich pounded towards her. Encumbered by the valise, he gripped the Mauser.

The Chekist fired.

Paskevich staggered.

Regaining his balance, he pivoted, the revolver to his hip. The two shots rang out simultaneously. The Chekist's smoking revolver clattered on stone. His shoulders sagged to the pavement as his head turned in profile, the impossible angle of figures depicted in ancient Egyptian tombs.

'Come on!' Paskevich shouted, thrusting the Mauser under his belt. 'Hurry!'

As Marya charged across the square at his side, he extended the stolen valise. Taking the bag, a question fluttered: Why was he handing it to her? He'd never permitted her, his countess, to carry anything. The weight slowed her, but he was moving sluggishly, too. They reached the theatre.

'Inside,' he muttered.

Faded posters with Hebrew lettering jumped around her as she bounded up the steps ahead of him. She knew the two carved doors would be locked, yet she rattled the nearest one, pushing and banging, as frantic as a trapped bird. Paskevich bent almost double, lunging forward, hitting the wood with his right shoulder. The door burst open. He staggered inside, and she followed, pulling the door shut.

They were in a narrow foyer. The stage must have been dark for some time. Dust lay thick on the black-and-white marble floor, and powdered the green baize covering the doors to the auditorium.

Holding her hand over her racing heart, she wondered how Stephan would find them in here. Where was he? Had he, too, been watched? Followed?

With a raucous grunt, Paskevich sank on to a banquette.

Marya saw a splotch like a dark enamelled order on the left shoulder of the railway jacket.

Kneeling in front of him, she eased back the corduroy. The left side of his heavy cardigan was crimson.

'Just a flesh wound,' he muttered.

Golder had emphasized how important it was to reassure the wounded.

'Yes, that's all. This will stop the bleeding.' With steady fingers, she unbuttoned the sweater and drew up the sodden flannel shirt and underwear.

The bullet had entered several inches below his thickly muscled, dark-haired shoulder. From the spurting blood, she knew a major artery had been pierced. Again the words of her medical mentor flashed. *Always make certain that whatever goes near an open wound is sterile.* Every piece of clothing in the valise was grimy. She'd read somewhere that saliva was the most primitive disinfectant. Rapidly licking the heel of her palm, she pressed it against the slippery wound with her full strength.

Paskevich stared at her as if to gain strength from the eye contact. *Don't die, don't die,* she thought. *Don't die, don't . . .*

His heartbeats throbbed against her palm. The bleeding continued unabated. After what seemed like an hour, but in reality was no more than a minute, she shifted her dripping hand to press three fingers hard in the hollow between his collarbone and the musculature above the first rib.

By the time the bleeding had stopped, Paskevich was shivering violently and sweat stood out on his yellowish pallor.

Shock, she diagnosed. Easing him on to the banquette, she covered him with her

625

cape, piling on Stephan's naval jacket, her shawl, the heavy skirt.

'Strakhov,' he mumbled.

Stephan.

She had forgotten him entirely. Maybe he'd been shot, too. Or maybe captured and was now being 'interrogated'. A wave of dizziness overcame her. She bit the inner flesh of her cheek.

'Find Strakhov . . .'

It was what her every instinct cried out to do, but she said: 'I can't leave you.'

'Tuck the revolver in your cape . . . We need a hiding-place . . . Find him . . .' Paskevich's voice faded to a thread.

After a moment, she slid the cape from under the heaped clothes, arranging the folds so that the splotches of blood were reasonably well hidden. Gingerly lifting the Mauser, she gave a hysterical titter. *Talk about finding a needle in a haystack! I don't know Kremenchug and I haven't a clue which direction Stephan took once he left the square.*

Chapter Forty-eight

By a stroke of luck, Stephan had found Lenko in the second place he'd looked: a gathering-spot that Lenko had often mentioned, the Bear Café. For privacy, they had come here to the dark stairwell where the odours of rotting potatoes and turnips mingled with the reek of a blocked lavatory. They had known each other from boyhood: Lenko's father, a noted Ukrainian sculptor, had joined the Moscow School of Painting as a colleague of Professor Strakhov's. The entire family had been ardent Ukrainian separatists, but that hadn't interfered with Lenko's becoming one of the first members of the Democratic Reform Party. In those days, he had been a stout teenager with thick wheat-coloured hair and a wide cheerful smile. His hair had receded, and he'd lost a tremendous amount of weight. His thin face had deep lines of embitterment between the nose and the mouth that gave him the look of an ageing tubercular. In a low impassioned voice he sketched in the local situation.

'When we Ukrainians proclaimed ourselves a free and independent state, I was deliriously happy; we all were. Ever since it's been hell. Sheer hell. The Rada can't govern, and the peace treaty they signed with the Germans and Austrians is criminal! To let them just march in! Oh, the Germans play cat-and-mouse with us, pretending Ukraine is an independent country under that tsar-lover Skoropadsky. The bastard can't even speak Ukrainian — but German requisition officers take every ear of grain, every last scrap of hemp, meat and hides to ship back to the *Vaterland.* What little the Kaiser leaves, Skoropadsky and his crew of bourgeois merchants and landowners keep. It goes without saying that workers have flocked to the Bolshies. And the nobility's White. I'm over-simplifying, you understand. There are at least sixty political factions, not to mention supporters of Makhno and his anarchists and assorted bandit chiefs.'

'Are the Reds divided?'

'Lenin sends organizers from Moscow to make sure there are no splinter groups. The Bolsheviks are unified, and so are the Germans,' Lenko said bitterly. 'Everything else in Ukraine is in total combustion. Cities and land change hands, sometimes daily. At the moment, as you can see, Kremenchug's Red. And, believe you me, the Commissar of Supply's far tougher than the Germans: if the Bolshies suspect that one kulak is holding out on them, they burn the entire village.'

'God . . .'

'I'm getting to the worst. The Reds've been merrily shooting everyone suspected of any political activity, past, present or future. If you don't embrace Marxism like a drowning man, you're shot. No arrest, no trial, just a bullet. "Weeding out of counter-revolutionaries", they call it. Is it any wonder nobody organizes against them?' Lenko's gestures had become more and more agitated until he appeared to be fanning away the fetid odours rather than underscoring his points. 'The Bolsheviks have a history of using terror, so why didn't we see this coming? No wonder the Democratic Reform is withering —' He broke off. A one-legged man came through the door to the café, clicking on his crutches to the noisome lavatory. Stephan and Lenko nattered about some shared boyhood prank until they were alone again.

'So our membership's down?' Stephan asked.

'Disintegrated. There's a dozen of us. We have to do *something,* otherwise it'll be too late. Strakhov, the situation here's critical.'

'What I'd give to open another soup-kitchen! All these begging children with bloated bellies! I passed an old man stretched out on the pavement. He was dead. An old man, lying there, and everyone walked by. Nobody paid any attention. If only we could feed the hungry one meal a day!'

'When the wolf gnaws the belly, a bowl of soup can lure back the membership, eh?'

'Political coercion with food? I couldn't do that, not to starving people.'

'Harken to the voice of the incorruptible one.'

'Is it wrong to have principles?' Stephan asked coldly.

Lenko scratched a fleabite on his cheek. 'You say you came through Maly-Iupatovsk? So that lard-arsed station-master knew you were on the train?'

'We didn't board until we were a few stations down the line.'

'But arrived here. What lucky star do you live under?'

Stephan blanched. 'He's a Red agent?'

'He's a genius at sniffing out disguises; he acts as a truffle pig for whoever's in charge of Maly-Iupatovsk. So for the moment, yes, he's a Red agent.'

'My . . . friends . . . they're at the station, waiting for me. Lenko, is there a safe place here in Kremenchug for a few nights? We can pay — pay well.'

Lenko's eyes narrowed, a speculative look, and after a moment he said: 'The Bear's run by a Jewish Socialist. Levitz. You know how terrible the conditions have always been for them in Ukraine. Well, it's far worse now. The Reds say Jews're all capitalists, the Ukrainian Whites say Jews're all ravening Marxists, the patriots call them German spies, and the priests keep on with their usual Christ-killer sermons. That's the one thing Ukrainians are united on: tormenting and killing Jews. Our national pastime. Levitz has no reason to love any of us. But I've been a friend. Once during a pogrom I hid him and his family in my father's studio. Let me see what I can do.'

Lenko left through a rear door. Stephan thought of Marya, exposed in the station square. He kneaded his shoulder impatiently until Lenko returned.

'It wasn't easy,' Lenko said. 'I told him you'd pay however much he asked for the room; but, even so, he wasn't convinced until I gave my personal guarantee that you were safe.'

'Thank you,' Stephan said stiffly. He'd forgotten this less pleasing aspect of Lenko's personality: his favours were given like loans, to be repaid at a later time.

The Bear lay in the heart of old Kremenchug. Generations of landlords had added storeys to the narrow tenements until the buildings leaned towards each other like aged mourners after a funeral. The meandering alleys that never saw sunlight were crowded with beggars. Men in ragged uniforms — legless or armless veterans — stared mutely at their collection-cups, but the ragged children tugged at every passer-by. Stephan, who had already given away what little money he had, felt an uncaring monster by the time he reached one of the broad new avenues that led to the station. These thoroughfares were relatively empty. A few customers hurried furtively into shops whose windows were boarded over.

Coming within sight of the station, he halted. The big square was completely deserted: no pedestrians, no tramlines — even the kiosk was closed. There was not a sign of Paskevich or Marya.

Lenko's words about the Maly-Iupatovsk station-master ringing in his ears, Stephan stood paralysed with indecision. Should he search the streets and alleys? Kremenchug was large. Maybe they'd gone back on to a platform and attempted to hide amid the travellers? No. Giving the devil his due, Paskevich was keenly shrewd: he'd realize they'd be sitting ducks inside the station.

Stephan's palms were wet as he threaded along the side-streets. He was halted by workers setting up a barrier. Red Guards were drawing their revolvers as they trotted up the steps of nearby houses.

'Stephan!'

Marya wasn't running, but her arms pumped like a runner's as she propelled herself towards him.

'Oh, thank God, I found you!' she breathed. 'Something terrible's happened.'

Back in the theatre foyer, Paskevich lay shivering. Marya took his pulse. The beat was slow.

Drawing Stephan away, she whispered: 'He's in a bad way. We can't move him.'

Paskevich must have heard her. 'Be looking for us everywhere around the station . . .' he whispered.

She returned to bend over him. 'Stephan's found a room,' she reassured him. 'We'll work out how to get you there.'

'As soon as it gets dark . . .' he muttered.

'Yes, then Stephan can bring a doctor here —'

'Can't stay here . . .'

'Then, we'll need a taxi or a cart —'

'No. Under my own steam.'

'You can't even sit —'

'Pretend I'm drunk. You'll help me.'

At dusk, he was still shivering, yet he shoved off the blankets, insisting they haul him to his feet.

He was hoarsely mumbling ribald lyrics to the tune of 'Volga Boatman' as they emerged from the theatre. Stephan and Marya linked their arms around his waist, propping him up. Adjusting to his erratic pace, they staggered along unlit streets where they attracted no attention, even on the block where a search was being conducted. Bread might be a luxury in Kremenchug, but illegally distilled *samogen* was plentiful: though it was barely evening, men, and women, too, already were reeling out of buildings or slumped stuporously against walls.

By the time they'd hauled Paskevich up the staircase to the room above the Bear, he was shivering so violently that the bed shook. His skin was clammy.

'Shock,' Marya said.

Stephan didn't need to be told. Shock had killed many of the wounded in his command before they reached the field hospitals. He helped Marya raise Paskevich's legs with the pillows, then ran to ask Levitz for more blankets. Paskevich's teeth continued to clatter.

'That bullet's going to kill him,' Marya said in a low voice. 'You'll have to find a doctor.'

Stephan nodded.

'First, I need some salt and baking soda. Plenty of boiled water. Oh, and some clean rags!'

Stephan took the stairs three at a time. He was astonished by his desperation to save Paskevich, the landowner, the man who typified the worst inequities of the Autocracy, the all-powerful noble who had corrupted Marya then locked her in a tomb. Paskevich, his rival.

Stephan clenched his molars while Mrs Levitz, thick-hipped and placid, methodically provided what he wanted.

Marya stirred the soda and salt into a glass of water. Lifting Paskevich's head, she spooned the liquid between his blue lips. His teeth clicked against the pot-metal spoon. 'Drink it all,' she said, then whispered to Stephan: 'His pulse is faster and weaker. We'll have to get him to a hospital.'

'No hospitals,' Paskevich muttered.

'The bullet must come out,' she retorted calmly.

Beads of sweat broke out on the pallid skin. 'Don't trust anybody . . .' It was an order.

'He's right,' Stephan said grimly. 'I'd better talk to Lenko. He'll know a safe doctor.'

After Stephan had left, Marya dipped a clean rag in boiled water, easing the glue of blood that bound underwear to hairy skin and raw flesh — an ordeal that routinely wrung screams from the most stoical. Rapid movements of Paskevich's squeezed-shut eyelids were the only sign of his agony. Before she had finished rebandaging his chest, he'd lapsed into a coma.

'There were only two politically reliable doctors, and Lenko says they've both disappeared.'

Marya's long sigh wavered. Military Hospital No. 5 had been a hell-hole, true, and when she'd nursed Stephan she'd been frantic, but Golder had been there. Golder, a quiet bulwark against death. With Paskevich, all responsibility rested in her unskilled hands.

She dragged the chair closer to the bed.

As a hint of purplish dawn suffused the window, she unwound her careful bandaging. Tilting her ear close to the puffed, inflamed wound, she touched a fingertip to the angry redness. She heard a tiny crackling. The sound she most dreaded.

'Stephan?'

Stephan, asleep in the chair, raised his head and blinked. 'I meant to take a turn watching him,' he said apologetically.

She beckoned him into the corridor. 'As soon as the light's good enough,' she whispered, 'I'm taking out the bullet.'

'You?' He peered at her. 'Marya, you've told me you've only performed minor surgery.'

'There's no choice. It's gas gangrene.'

'The red death . . .' This was the enlisted men's name for gas gangrene. 'What do you want me to do?'

'Find some surgical tools.'

'That's asking for the moon.'

'Then, sharpen the razor.' A razor case had been packed in the valise. 'Find a large steel needle, strong thread, tweezers, scissors. Get disinfectant. Pay whatever you have to for an opiate: morphine, laudanum — or anything that'll knock him out. And ask down in the café for more clean rags and their biggest pot filled with boiling water.'

Stephan was bending over the valise to open the hidden compartment as Marya sponged Paskevich's face.

That eternal morning while she waited for Stephan to return!

The buzzing of the horseflies, the unintelligible cadences in the street below. Paskevich's face, which seemed to be hollowing and greying as she watched, his hoarse breathing. The fears that Stephan had been imprisoned or even shot.

At the tap on the door and his whispered, 'Marya, open up,' she went limp with relief.

Stephan carried an earthenware jug. 'There were no opiates of any kind, so I bought vodka. And not a drop of disinfectant to be found. This is the best I could do.' He reached in his pocket for a hardened cracked lump of carbolic soap.

He held a tumbler of illicit vodka to Paskevich's mouth while Marya rolled up her sleeves. First she soaped her arms, then her wrists, then her hands and fingernails. The soap was a sliver when she finally shook off the water.

Stephan lugged in a huge cast-iron pot, setting it on the floor. Marya kneeled to thrust the blade of the razor in the still-bubbling water, flinching yet holding steady while the steam reddened her hand. She sterilized the tweezers and threaded the needle the same way.

Paskevich, unfortunately, had a huge tolerance for alcohol: the *samogen* had little effect on him. As she cleaned his wound with boiled water and the soap, he bit his lip until blood oozed.

'Something to bite on,' he muttered. She put the cork from the *samogen* jug between his teeth.

For a full minute she stood over him with her eyes squeezed tightly shut. She was summoning her knowledge of anatomy, she was visualizing Golder's assured movements as he operated on bullet wounds, she was telling herself she could do it.

Opening her eyes, she said to Stephan: 'Hold him down. Keep the wound still, no matter what.'

With a steady hand, she brought down the blade.

The bullet lay on a cloth. Paskevich was alive — inert, white, breathing with a raucous rattle, but alive. Below the bandages, the gangrenous flesh was gone and the wound was joined with eighteen large black knots that resembled butterfly antennae.

Rinsing the blood from her hands until the water in the bowl turned the colour of rust, Marya grew increasingly elated. 'It's surprising how well he's doing.'

Stephan didn't respond. He couldn't. He was too shaken, too bewildered at his own emotions. Holding the twitching, heaving body as he'd assisted in the makeshift operation had brought him and Paskevich into a strange communion. As Paskevich's face contorted in agony and strange animal grunts came from around the cork, Stephan's envy and loathing had melted away. He'd found himself imagining, maybe a little too poetically, that he and Paskevich were gazing at each other from opposite sides of that dark river whose name was death.

'We did it, Stephan, we did it!' Marya laughed light-headedly. 'Dr Alexiev and her male nurse.'

'What if you'd nicked the artery?'

'What if the moon were green cheese?'

'You don't have surgical tools.' He was irritated by her light-heartedness. 'You've never performed a major operation.'

Suddenly Marya clamped her hand over her mouth, running from the room and down the stairs. In the foul lavatory, she vomited in a long projectile spew.

He could have died. He still can die. Any minute he can die.

Chapter Forty-nine

When Marya took into consideration Paskevich's age, the often fatal shock of an operation without anaesthesia, her blundering surgery, she worked out that before he was able to travel he would need a minimum of two months in bed and a couple more to regain his strength.

Say five months, then.

Far too long to stay here.

The shoot-out at the station had convinced her that there was more than a grain of truth in Paskevich's *idée fixe* that Ovruch's tentacles were reaching out through the turmoil of Russia and Ukraine: a Cheka had been organized in Kremenchug. What was to prevent Levitz or his family or even a client of the café from informing on them? And, if nobody told, Levitz himself, a Socialist, might easily be arrested. Would everyone in the Bear and rooms above be hauled in, too? Besides, rumours flew that Makhno was gathering forces under his black flag of Anarchism with plans to occupy Kremenchug. If the gossip were true, they would be trapped in the middle of a bloody siege. She gnawed her lip and tended Paskevich as best she could with her limited supplies.

To her surprise and gratification, though, the wound healed as cleanly as any of Dr Golder's surgical incisions on young men.

Within five days her difficult patient insisted on feeding himself. By the end of the week he asked for the razor and shaved himself. Within two weeks he was sitting in the chair for several hours. True, he got out of bed with agonizing slowness and turned grey as he manoeuvered to the seat, but after his first time he refused to take her helping hand.

Stephan left early in the morning, returning to sleep.

To her questions about how he spent his time, he invariably responded: 'With Lenko.'

'At his place?'

'Generally.'

'Why not meet here at the Bear?'

'Stop worrying about me, darling.'

It was just as well he wasn't around, she told herself. Being cooped up together in the sick-room would only fuel the antagonism between the two men, thus inhibiting Paskevich's recuperation.

Her nerve-ends prickled all the time Stephan was gone.

Nobody was loitering near the Bear Café. Housewives shoved fistfuls of newly printed Ukrainian currency into street-traders' hands, hurrying away with rotted vegetables and unidentifiable meat cradled against their bodies. A gang of stick-figure children bolted off with scraps of refuse. The wretchedly painted war widows who generally solicited outside the café hadn't shown

641

up. And neither had the veteran, a cheerful legless stump who stationed himself there to beg.

It had been as empty yesterday.

'Blame it on Moscow,' Lenko had said, explaining that, according to his sources, Lenin had just made a pronouncement that random violence was a weapon of Revolution. Ukrainian Marxists, always far less 'soft' than their Russian counterparts, had taken his words to heart. Unprovoked gunfire rang out in the streets. Young Jewish-looking women had been dragged into hallways and gang-raped.

Stephan strode rapidly in the direction of Lenko's place. Turning the corner of newly named Liberation Street, he was surprised to see the clothes-sellers at their usual station, their secondhand merchandise hung on window-ledges or spread on the pavement. Old uniforms, many from the previous century, had been arranged across a flat wagon whose sway-backed dun horse stood docile in the traces. A female customer was paying for a naval officer's uniform while a younger girl was trying on a faded Don Cossack skirted coat.

Buyers and sellers alike pressed against the wall as an open coupé swerved around the corner. The passengers didn't need their crimson armbands to identify themselves: in Kremenchug, only Red Guards had access to motorized vehicles. The car rammed into the side of the wagon. As merchandise flopped on to the pavement, drunken laughter erupted from the back seat. The driver, though, was red-faced and cursing. Swivelling the machine-gun mounted on the window, he fired at the horse. Under the onslaught of bullets, the animal toppled. The white-bearded merchant, wailing something in Yiddish, ran to his dying animal. Bullets hailed on to the old man. Amid raucous cheers, he fell across his horse's twitching rump.

By now buyers and sellers alike had melted away. Stephan, though, was too angry for logic. Recalling that Jews always covered their heads, he darted forward to replace the fur-brimmed hat. The top of the skull had been sheared off like an egg, exposing the convoluted, greyish-yellow brain matter. As Stephan lowered the fur hat over this senselessly stilled accumulation of a lifetime's hopes, aspirations and knowledge, he could hear the car backing out and the braying laughter.

He was still quivering with outrage as he recounted the incident to Lenko.

'What animals!' Lenko said. They were sipping palely tinged tea in his room, which was on the fourth floor overlooking the wharfs along the swift-flowing grey Dnieper. The docks and the river were singularly quiet. 'But you can see now, can't you, that Ukraine'll be hell if the Reds stay. And the Whites are just as vicious.' He paused. 'This is our golden opportunity.'

'For what?'

'How can you ask? The people hate what's going on; they want nothing more than a decent socialist-democratic government, a government like we would give them. But it's not going to spring into existence. We have to work — gather the moderates together, get public support.' Lenko rubbed a finger on the glass. 'Given any more thought to your relief-kitchen idea?'

'That's not going to get rid of Moscow — or the Whites.'

'I agree. Lenin and Skoropadsky and Petliura, Denikin and Wrangels won't run and hide at the sight of a soupbowl. But meals will let the people know the Democratic Reform is on their side.'

'There's no food available.'

'For a price there is. Our kulaks are marvellously ingenious at hiding their crops. The problem is they insist on being paid in gold or jewels.' Shrewd lines cut deep into Lenko's thin face. 'Lewitz showed me those earrings you gave him for the room. Nice emeralds. Very fine workmanship.'

'They weren't mine,' Stephan said.

'Come on, I never thought you loaded your pockets with gemstones.' Lenko continued to watch him. 'You have access to more like them, don't you?'

Stephan, at the window, grimaced down at the swollen river. He was being manipulated; and, as always, manipulation galled him. 'You still expect your favours to be repaid, don't you?'

'Stop me if I'm wrong,' Lenko said angrily, 'but aren't you the one who originally suggested food distribution?'

Stephan rarely stopped brooding about a relief-kitchen, yet the manner in which Lenko had dragged it into the conversation roused his darkest obstinacy. ' "Bread makes a convincing political argument" — isn't that how you put it?'

'Oh, for Christ's sake, I'm not some greasy opportunist you just met; we've been friends since we were boys. We're on the same side! Yes, a soup-kitchen's expedient. What's so wrong with that? If the moderates like us don't step in, Ukraine will be pulverized by the Reds, Whites, Greens until the oppression of the tsars will seem like the golden age.'

After a pause, Stephan said quietly: 'The jewellery's not mine to give.'

'Strakhov, forget the political angle! I'm sorry I brought fucking politics into it! It's just that Ukraine and this entire broken-up Empire have *become* politics. There aren't human beings any more, just political pawns.'

'It's still not mine,' Stephan said quietly.

'Then, think of all you've seen here. Your old Jew dying for no reason at all. The beggars, the starving children, the women who can't suckle their babies, the people toppling in their tracks. Now ask yourself a question. Which do you give a higher priority? Saving human lives or keeping that highly touted conscience of yours all spick and span?'

'Have you heard the old Buddhist proverb, my dear?' Paskevich asked. 'Once you save a man's life, he becomes your responsibility.'

'When — if — we reach Zurich, you're no longer our responsibility. We're leaving you there.'

Two and a half weeks after the impromptu surgery, Marya and Paskevich were at the window finishing their midday meal. Because his arm was in a sling, he wore the corduroy jacket over that shoulder, which gave him a jaunty look. His bowl was already empty: having regained his appetite, he'd hungrily spooned up the potato soup — potatoes and watery turnips were the only items available on the Bear's stained pre-revolutionary menu-cards.

'Has it slipped your mind that you're my wife?'

'That's what divorce is for.'

'Divorce? Myself, I've had three remarkably unpleasant matrimonial experiences but never considered fleeing the field.'

'Why would you? You took mistresses and slept with any woman who tickled your fancy. Stephan has a sense of honour.'

'Where does he leave it when he's with you? Outside the bedroom door with his boots? Does he get them shone together?'

'Oh, very clever,' she said. 'And, as for our marriage, you've admitted you trapped me into it.'

'The psychiatric doctors say that we permit ourselves to be trapped into acting out our hidden desires.'

'You're unbearable!'

The truth was that, except when Paskevich's jibes were directed at Stephan, she relished their bickering disputes. His snapping repartee brought invigoration to the stale air in the bedroom.

'Where does Strakhov go all the time?' he asked.

'He's with his friend.'

'Lenko. Isn't that the name? Lenko . . . It has a familiar ring. Yes, now I remember. This Lenko was a double-threat revolutionary. Belonged to some outlawed Ukrainian separatist party as well as to Strakhov's group.'

'What were you, an Okhrana agent?'

'Stop fretting, my pet. It's no surprise to you that I had access to Strakhov's dossier. So he's been spending his days and evenings with a fellow-radical?'

'I don't see what difference it makes.'

'But, then, you've always been remarkably blind about our magnificent poet.' He glanced around the room. 'By the way, where do you keep the valise?'

'In the wardrobe. Why? Are you planning to use the gun on him for being with a friend?'

Paskevich didn't respond. He was pushing heavily to his feet and opening the narrow, raw pine wardrobe. The jaw muscles near his ears clenched as he lifted the small valise on to the bed. Sitting, he drew several breaths before he fingered the hidden catch.

The compartment was empty.

Marya couldn't control her gasp.

'You didn't know he'd taken everything, did you?'

'He's storing the pieces in a safer place,' she explained airily. 'We've been exchanging them for the room and food, the bandages . . .'

'You still have most of the jewellery, haven't you?' she asked Stephan. She was out of breath. Unwilling to stage a confrontation in Paskevich's presence, she had watched for Stephan from the window, then run downstairs to meet him outside the café.

He reddened. The flush didn't fade, and his mouth was bracketed with twin pale curves as he replied: 'No, I don't.'

'What happened? Did the Levitzes blackmail you?'

'Since the earrings he's refused to take another piece.'

'Where did everything go, then?'

Instead of answering, Stephan nodded his head towards an inert bundle of rags in a doorway. 'A human being's starving to death right in front of our eyes. Marya, think of the misery all around us. Is it fair to hoard so much wealth for ourselves?'

The emotional depth in his voice resonated inside her chest.

'It's terribly wrong,' she said softly.

'Lenko has the jewellery at his place. We're opening a relief unit. Right now we're arranging for food deliveries. The peasants around here squeeze us for every dribble — not that I blame them. If the Reds discover any kulak selling privately, his entire family's shot in front of him, then he's hanged.'

'What would happen to you?' she asked in alarm.

'The Communists don't concern themselves with the buyers.'

'And the gun?'

'Exchanged for the cooking-vats,' he said. 'Marya, how can we be selfish?'

'I'm glad of what you've done. You should've told me before. It's made me feel human again.'

Paskevich lounged fully dressed on the bed as Marya blurted out the story of the relief unit.

'I can only bow in admiration,' he said when she finished. 'Strakhov can convince you that black is white and betrayal is altruism.'

'It's exactly how I wanted my jewellery used.'

'Actually, the jewels were mine — but let it pass. You, my pet, have always been a creature of impulse and doubtless haven't considered the ramifications. Strakhov should have. He didn't rescue me from Trotsky's trial for the pleasure of my company. And this journey's not a holiday jaunt. If he'd at least left us the pistol . . . But I suppose a scrupulous man like him makes his *beaux gestes* without limitations. The crux is that he's reduced our already slim odds at releasing the Romanovs' funds. Or does he have some high-minded plan to get us to Switzerland without bribery?'

As usual, Paskevich's sarcasm was irritatingly on the mark. Marya busied herself with folding the boiled strips of cloth that she used for bandaging.

'And the pity is,' Paskevich continued after a few seconds, 'for all the good his charity'll do, he might as well have thrown the baubles in the cesspool.'

'I know it's nothing to you, but a few yards from here there's a man — or maybe it's a woman — too weak with hunger to move.'

'And a bowl or two of soup probably would keep the poor devil breathing a few more days, is that it?' he said. 'My pet, in my lifetime I've seen enough dying to know that a quick death is a merciful death.'

'You've always been callous,' she snapped. 'And your dressing needs to be changed.'

'Like the subject?' he asked with a malicious grin. 'Marya, tell me, is he so noble of spirit that he's not the least jealous of the hours you and I spend alone together in this bedroom?'

'He knows you're nothing to me.'

'Oh?' Paskevich reached out with his good arm. Clean rags scattered as he tumbled her on top of him. Crushing her buttocks against him, he kissed her hard on the mouth. Her lips parted; the kiss became all tongue and teeth. As they kissed on the narrow bed it seemed to her that her life had made a full circle since that brutal first night in the Crimson Palace. Now, ten years later, she understood only vaguely the power, carnal and otherwise, to which she continued to succumb. Paskevich rolled over so that she was below him, his good hand yanking up her skirt. She could feel his erection. It had been months. Trembling, aroused, she thought: *Stephan.*

She slammed her hand into his bandaged shoulder, and as he inhaled sharply, releasing her, she jumped from the bed. 'You're despicable.'

His face was white with pain, yet he raised an eyebrow. 'The question, my pet, is whether you prefer an honourable lover who shares his generosity with the masses or a despicable, highly sexed husband who puts you above all else.'

Chapter Fifty

St Vladimir accepted the Christian faith from Byzantium in 988. This titbit of Ukrainian history had become Marya's internal drummer today: she repeated the phrase mindlessly as she trudged. The newspapers she'd padded inside her worn boots had clumped under the left instep, but by now she was as numb to the discomfort as she was to the callused-over blisters on her toes or to the fields around her.

It was three weeks since Paskevich had announced that he was recovered enough to travel. Of course, she had argued; but the street violence had escalated, and Stephan was out there arranging for the relief kitchen. And — who knew? — maybe the new local Cheka, which Levitz reported was now headed by a Moscow commissar, had orders to track them down. So she had packed, and the trio had left the Bear Café before the drizzly dawn of the following day.

With nothing to barter for train tickets or steamer passages, they travelled on foot. The most direct way south to Odessa was the old post-road, along which the mail had once been carried by carriage or troika. It was also their obvious route. Paskevich, with his obsession that Ovruch had spies everywhere looking for them, insisted that they take these muddy meandering tracks that beaded villages together.

The Ukrainian peasantry, who viewed all things Russian with sullen distrust, would have slammed doors in their faces if it weren't for Marya's uniform. They bestowed the same reverence on her grubby headgear as they did on the Virgin Mary's gilded halo: this one, too, could perform miraculous healings. Each time the threesome neared a whitewashed village, she was approached. 'Sister, you're needed.' 'Sister, please come.' 'Sister, my man has a terrible fever.' No matter how weary Marya was, she went to the thatched *izbas,* where she lanced boils, sewed up wounds, delivered reluctant babies. Once she had even sawn off a gangrenous foot. In return for medical services, she, Stephan and Paskevich were invited to share meals of young potatoes and onions, loaves of chewy bread, the home-distilled brandy, which was astonishingly potent. In the one-room huts, they slept beside the huge clay stoves amid the patients and their families.

Quite a few nights, however, they had foraged for berries and green apples, sleeping in the open because the nearest village had either been torched or was crowded with troops.

Ukraine bubbled with large and small warfare.

At this moment, Marya couldn't believe that there was fighting anywhere, much less nearby. The air smelled of the green sprouting wheat that furred the tar-black fields; the low rolling hills to the east lay serene and quiet, marbled by the blue shade of clouds. Southwards, several miles ahead of them, sunlight gleamed on a gold cross; but otherwise the settlement was concealed by a daisy-strewn hillock.

What landscape could be more serene?

Yet less than three hours earlier they had entered a hamlet to find absolute stillness, as if a great wind had swept through and carried off all the inhabitants. Women and children often toiled alongside the men in the fields, but generally there were a few toddlers and old folk stirring about. They had found the entire population in the square. Maybe a hundred or so bodies of all sizes had sprawled around the water-pump. A few swollen-bellied dogs had growled, but the carrion birds had continued to feed. From the lack of decomposition and odour, the villagers had been shot within the last few hours.

Marya wiggled her shoulders, attempting physically to shrug off the memory.

'Wait here,' Paskevich said.

They had come to a footpath leading eastwards between two long, narrow fields.

'What's wrong?' Stephan asked.

'After that last village, a bit of scouting is in order, don't you agree?'

Watching Paskevich stride up the slight slope, Marya reflected that the Russian high nobility must have bones as hard as diamond. What other explanation could there be for that erect vigour after her untrained surgery, a too-brief convalescence and this relentlessly punishing journey?

Stephan, who carried the valise strung over his back like a rucksack, had untied the knots and was setting the bag on the damp grasses that edged the road. 'Sit down a while,' he said.

'How thoughtful,' she said. 'I'm more than ready for a rest.'

Unlike Paskevich, who stropped the razor and shaved latherless every other morning, Stephan had grown a beard which he kept neatly trimmed. The small beard and dark sunburn made a perfect foil for his vivid blue eyes. Marya visualized him with a narrow gold circle around his black hair, a medieval knight. 'Hopefully he'll find there's no trouble ahead there,' she said.

'Is there any part of what was Russia that's not fighting?' As he spoke, a baffled melancholy came into his eyes. Lately, she'd seen the expression more and more often.

'Ah, Stephan, don't take it personally.' She moved as if to comfort him.

His cool expression made her drop her arms. Why, in the infrequent times they were alone, did Stephan keep this distance between them?

'What's wrong?' she asked.

'How can you ask?'

'None of this is your fault,' she said, sighing. 'I meant between us.'

'I don't understand.'

'You're so . . . I don't know . . . *remote.* You're not blaming yourself that we're walking, are you?'

'In answer to the first question, I'd give the rest of my life to throw you on the ground this minute and make love to you. God, we can't touch or say a few words alone. He's always there.'

'Telling us what to do, making every decision —'

'He's always right,' Stephan said abruptly. 'To answer your second question, how could I not feel rotten?'

'Walking's nothing — less than nothing when you think of . . .' she shuddered. 'Whoever did it, how could they even kill the babies?'

'The Four Horsemen are abroad in Russia,' Stephan said. 'Marya, I wish I'd never gone to Tobolsk. Then you wouldn't be here at all. And you wouldn't be seeing any of this, you wouldn't be slogging through the mud all day and nursing villagers all night, if I hadn't given away your jewellery.'

'You can't think I care about that? I'm *glad* we had it to give. I'd have done exactly the same thing.' She stopped, gazing thoughtfully as a disturbed nightingale swooped from a thicket. Nightingales, she'd learned, were a symbol of the Ukraine: at night the villagers would stand outside their cottages listening to the birdsong with the same rapt attention that concert-goers give inspired musicians.

'Would you?' Stephan asked.

'I'd have only given my third,' she admitted. 'Paskevich was still in very bad shape, so I'd have saved his share. And I'd have asked you first.'

'Those people were starving. Starving.'

She felt tears welling. 'You're better than I am.'

'Don't cry, darling. It wasn't altruism. I just couldn't bear to see that misery.'

Paskevich was striding back downhill. 'A town — probably the regional centre. There are Red flags blowing everywhere. Well, now we know who sang the executioner's song this morning.' He pointed his large hand at the narrow footpath. 'I'm sorry, my dear, but we'll need to circle around.'

Marya got to her feet. The rest had stiffened her. It took a mile or so for her muscles to loosen again.

The winds died down, and the still air pulsated with susurrations of locusts, cicadas, mosquitoes, bees, huge green grasshoppers. The fields gave way to rocks that thrust out of the earth like the remains of immense palaeolithic creatures. Marya stooped to pick one of the blue wild flowers that flourished in every crevice. As they trudged upwards the path dwindled into animal tracks. The sun was high in the immense cloudless sky. Marya lifted the nurse's veil to wipe sweat from her neck.

She was thirsty, but there was nothing to drink: they hadn't filled the leather bottles at the destroyed village.

The hill tumbled into a ravine. Birches poked up through the tumbled shale, casting welcome shade. Hearing rushing water, she heaved a sigh of gratitude.

'That stream must feed into the Dnieper,' Paskevich said.

Three enormous flat-topped boulders dammed off a clear little pool. Kneeling, Marya cupped her hands to drink until her thirst was slaked, then she shook her hair free of its restraint and tugged off her boots, leaning back on her hands to watch Stephan as he waded into the stream to refill the leather flasks. Paskevich was watching her, but she didn't realize it.

They picnicked on goat's cheese and wheat bread, the gifts of the farmer's wife whom Marya had successfully delivered of a son two nights earlier. The desultory luncheon-talk centred around whether they had travelled far enough east from the Red forces to turn south again. These tactical debates about their route were the only form of communication between Stephan and Paskevich. Stephan offered his opinions with a concise formality that brought a glimmer of amusement to Paskevich's eyes.

'Why can't we cut south along the stream-bed?' Marya interjected.

'Mountain goats would have no difficulty

with that, but we —' Paskevich broke off in mid-sentence.

Pebbles were clattering down the ravine.

They swivelled around.

Four men were already halfway down the steep incline. Until now they had approached in complete silence, and their sudden materialization made them seem more frightening than their appearance, which was terrifying enough. They held their rifles at waist-level, the classic position of advancing infantry, and they wore tattered earth-coloured clothing splotched with dark stains. Each had a bright crimson rag knotted high on his right sleeve.

Paskevich cursed under his breath, reaching for the smooth rounded stones he'd gathered earlier — he always kept a few in his pockets. He and Stephan rose slowly to their feet. Marya instinctively used animal camouflage, remaining still. Idiotic. She was clearly visible to everyone in this ravine.

The man in front was badly scarred: the carapace of bright lumpy red covering the left side of his face and the tiny slick mushroom of an ear seemed like a mask, the kind of mask that witchdoctors use in ritual dances to strike fear into their primitive spectators. At a nod from him, the others spread out on the rockfall, converging from different angles on the picnickers.

A few feet away, the scarred leader came

to a halt, and the others followed suit.

At the top of the ravine, dark and immense against the blue sky, stood a khaki-uniformed figure.

Chapter Fifty-one

Ovruch.

She'd had recurring nightmares about him since he'd shot Klazkha, and for this reason at first sight Ovruch appeared to be a bulky phantom summoned from the netherworld of her imagination.

Agitated larks burst out of the birches as he stamped down the incline, his boat-like boots dislodging the shale. He wore no insignia — he needed no sign to denote his rank. His clean tailored uniform, the enamelled red stars adorning his collar and peaked cap were unnecessary, too. He was set apart from and above the others by his bearing. Ovruch, unlike Paskevich, didn't hold himself imperiously erect; in fact his immense shoulders were curved inwards as he shambled down the incline. But he had taken on the near-visible emanations of power. He was one of the new ruling class.

Paskevich watched the commissar with a faint smile, as if anticipating a trick from a performing bear. Everyone else in the ravine, especially Marya watching hypnotized from her perch on the rock, felt dwarfed in his presence.

'Ovruch,' Stephan said, his low voice charged with disbelief.

'Why're you surprised, Comrade?' Ovruch

responded. 'You must have known I'd catch up with you.'

He halted close enough for Marya to see the sweat beading his forehead and luxuriant moustache, and to smell his pungent odours of leather, fresh perspiration, wine and tobacco. He looked down on her with benign eyes. The calm gaze was more terrifying than if he'd brandished his revolver.

Her thoughts raced. The terrain made flight impossible — they were like goldfish in a bowl. It was pointless to consider physical force when they were unarmed, outnumbered.

The fate they had fled these past months had finally caught up with them.

Her head felt wobbly, her spine crumpled, as though the strength of her body were being sucked into the stone. Yet sitting like this made her even more vulnerable. With shaky arms and legs, she pushed up on to her bare feet.

'Well, little one,' Ovruch said. 'Here you are bedraggled in a Ukrainian gully. How different things would have been if you'd followed the party.'

Don't let him see you're terrified, she told herself. 'How *is* life in Moscow nowadays?' she asked. Her voice sounded high and breathless to her. 'Have the Red Guard managed to put down the riots yet?'

'I see you've lost none of your spirit,' he retorted mildly. 'And Strakhov, after all that *burzhui* intellectual talk about abolishing privilege, what are you doing? Rescuing the worst of the oppressors.'

Stephan said nothing. Paskevich, though, responded with a small mocking bow.

I must keep talking, Marya thought. *Distract him. But what's the good of distracting him? It's just putting off the inevitable.* 'And you?' she said. 'What happened to those speeches about the rule of the people?'

'For the first time in Russia's thousand-year history, the land belongs to those who toil on it.'

'A majority of those toilers appear to be in active rebellion against your new Utopia,' Paskevich said. As he spoke, Marya wondered fleetingly if he'd tacitly agreed with her unformulated plan of talking, or if his response emerged from his natural bravado in the face of danger.

'Pah! After centuries yoked by bloodsuckers like you, then eight months of fiddling talk from the Provisional Government, a few disturbances are to be expected from the slow-witted folk in the countryside. We Communists have our programme of action.'

'So you have,' Paskevich said drily. 'We saw an example this morning.'

'That village! Pah! Profiteers, every last one of those kulaks. Hiding wheat again. They were warned. Our cities are starving, and they hide their crops!' He paused. 'The wrongs of private enterprise will die only when all the class enemies are re-educated.'

'Klazkha was a worker, a Bolshevik,' Marya said. 'Why kill her?'

'She abused her power — and she had too much power. The Women's Internationale, pah. Those women had to be brought back into the party fold.'

'Klazkha helped you when you needed help the most,' Marya said. 'And you murdered her!'

Ovruch gave her a slow patient look. 'We can't go by the old morality any more,' he said. 'Those so-called virtues were invented to crush the masses.'

'What about friendship?' Marya asked. 'What about loyalty?'

'The success of Communism is the supreme law,' Ovruch said. 'And, little one, as for loyalties, who rescued you from the Trubetskoi Bastion?' His glance at Paskevich showed that the question wasn't to remind her of an obligation but rather to divide the three.

As he looked away, she was suddenly aware that his brown eyes had held hers since he'd come down the ravine. And she realized that the Red Guards were staring at her, looking her up and down from her bare feet to the top of her head. From her naked ankles to her tumbled curls, and back down to the slender ankles. She had a swift, pictorially clear memory: three days after they'd left Kremenchug, they'd come upon a recently dead female body sprawled beside a roadside shrine, shapeless felt boots and lumpy padded jacket in place, full skirts pulled up around her blood-caked white thighs. *Don't think*, she told herself. *Keep talking.*

'Why didn't you just get rid of us all then and there in Petrograd?' she asked in a squeak.

Ovruch gave her a warm compassionate nod, as if he were on her side, not an enemy, but a teacher. 'You and Strakhov had been whisked away by the women.'

'And you were going to spare me?' Paskevich said.

'You're to be tried in a public court. Comrade Trotsky will prosecute. After that, you'll be executed.'

'If the sentence is already passed, why go through the trial mumbo-jumbo?'

'How else will the masses learn the truth about the crimes against the people that you performed for your Romanov master?'

'I trust Comrade Trotsky doesn't practise law using that kind of jargon,' Paskevich said. 'I'd hate to have my big moment drowned out by snoring.'

Ovruch, still looking at Marya, spat in the pool.

'And Stephan and me?' she asked. 'What'll happen to us?'

The Red Guards were staring at her and grinning. Their scarred leader guffawed.

Ovruch's smile was unexpected. Under the moustache, the strong teeth were astonishingly white and straight. 'Strakhov deluded the masses with empty promises of equality and fraternity,' Ovruch said. 'The comrades here are fed up with lies.'

In the charged moment of silence, she couldn't speak. Her mouth was dry, her throat too tight for speech.

'And you, little one,' Ovruch said, 'over and over again you've proved yourself an enemy of the people; but maybe there's a chance that my comrades can re-educate you.'

She understood how a rabbit feels in the presence of a fox. Poised for flight and too terrified to move, unable to look away from the danger even.

He reached for his holster. Was he going to kill Stephan first, or make him and Paskevich watch her being raped? As if drawing the Mauser were a signal that she was fair game, the others lowered their rifles, staring at her as if she were in fact that rabbit, their helpless prey. Their bast boots moved in unison.

At that instant, she was aware of a blur of motion. A flash of memory lifted her back to a St Petersburg cemetery, a small coffin, a black crow winged by Paskevich's unerringly hurled stone.

Ovruch staggered backwards.

Simultaneously, the birch boughs trembled in agitation. Larks again burst upwards. Marya at first didn't realize that the prolonged roar that had disturbed the flock was uttered by human vocal cords.

The battle-cry that had carried Russian officers over the tops of trenches and into the direct line of enemy fire now launched Stephan at the scarred Red Guard leader. 'Aghhhhh . . .'

Taken by surprise, he dropped his rifle. Stephan's hands encircled the burn-scarred neck in a throttle-hold. His savagery was sparked by the looks on those four faces as they had approached Marya. The fury that mottled his face, though, had been incubating within him for the three weeks that he'd been trudging through Ukraine, moving across that peaceful rural landscape with its outcroppings of horror. He slammed the back of the skull against the rock.

'Stephan!' Marya screamed. 'To your left!'

Releasing the limp body, Stephan whirled, parrying his arm like a fencing sword. His new opponent's rifle fell. It clattered down the boulder, splashing into the pool. Stephan raised his thigh. As his knee connected with softness, he felt a triumphant sense that he'd struck the root of Marya's danger. He heard a prolonged howl of pain. The injured man clutched himself, straddling wide-legged up the ravine.

The oldest of the Red Guard, a short leathery peasant, fell on to his back, knocked cold by another slung stone.

Paskevich, eyes narrowed with ruthless concentration, weighted a stone in his palm. 'If you want to remain intact,' he said to the last standing Red Guard, a slack-jawed adolescent who held his rifle uncertainly, 'put that down. Take off your ammunition-belt. Then get the hell out of here.'

Gasping loudly, the youth obeyed. As he clambered upwards, his boots slipped and he used his hands for momentum.

Paskevich retrieved Ovruch's Mauser, casually raising it. Two shots echoed through the ravine. The stooped-over boy flung out his arms like a swimmer using the breast stroke. Then he dropped. Almost simultaneously the straddling man, who had almost reached the top of the incline, tottered backwards and fell. The body rolled over several times, arms, legs and head flopping, before coming to a rest.

Moving to the stunned victims of his stone-throwing, Paskevich's expression was faintly quizzical. He shot first one then the other.

Ovruch stirred, slowly moving his head from side to side.

'He's all yours, Strakhov,' Paskevich said. And with the same half-mocking politeness with which he'd offered his Friday Nights guests the silver humidor, he extended the German handgun by its butt end to Stephan.

Stephan's murderous frenzy had evaporated. In this fraction of a moment he saw the iridescent gleam of a dragonfly, saw blood oozing like a thin crimson viper down a crevice in the grey rock, saw the precarious angle of a ragged corpse. He inhaled the familiar odours of the battlefield: acrid gunpowder, hot metal and bowels voided. He felt the sun's rays on his forehead, felt the rivulet's cooling spray on his neck.

He saw the large German handgun with its cross-hatched stock.

Then time returned to its usual beat. He was aware of his own laboured, percussive breathing, the uneven rock beneath his worn soles; aware of Paskevich's lifted quizzical eyebrow. Marya was watching them.

Ovruch groaned. A maroon graze was swelling above his right eye. Dazed, he struggled to lift his shoulders, and the tailored uniform was pulled awry to reveal the high neck of a lavishly embroidered blouse.

Ovruch. The burly twelve-year-old sent to a Siberian prison-camp for defending his father. The bright peasant boy whom Lenin had tugged from illiteracy and steeped in Marxism. Ovruch the disciple. Ovruch the crusader who slaughtered under the sacred red banner of the proletariat.

The enormous torso slumped, and Ovruch fell back, groaning.

The weakness struck a chord within Stephan. Ovruch the old comrade-in-arms who'd also spent years evading the tsarist secret police. Ovruch the engineer of Marya's freedom. *Less than two minutes ago,* Stephan thought, *he was ready to stand guard while she was gang-raped, then shoot her.*

He did kill Klazkha.

He would have killed me.

And how much of the blood of Stephan's old Provisional Government comrades — those deluders of the masses — stained the huge lax hands?

Vengeance is Mine, saith the Lord.

And, even if it were otherwise, how could he, Stephan Strakhov, that staunch believer in fair play and justice, consider shooting a helpless man?

He shook his head. 'I can't do it.'

'A minute ago the hulking butcher would've let those vermin at Marya, and forced us to watch.'

'We were friends of a sort.'

'What a saintly disposition you have,' Paskevich said. 'You do understand, though, that if we leave him here alive he'll track us to our graves?'

Stephan thrust his clenched grazed fists into his pockets and turned away. Blood had stained the pool to the colour of diluted Crimean wine.

Stephan anticipated Paskevich's shot. Yet, even so, at the deafening crack he whirled around.

With stupefaction so profound that it felt like a blow to the pit of his belly, he saw Marya staggering back at the recoil, the heavy Mauser dropping from both small hands.

Chapter Fifty-two

Regaining her balance, Marya looked down at Ovruch. His coarse brown hair lay flat on his massive forehead; his open round eyes had not yet become flattened and opaque but gleamed with life.

The lower part of his face was a hollow pulp of bloody meat interspersed with white scraps of bone. A fragment of moustache still attached to the skin had landed on the red star adorning his collar.

A moment ago she'd grabbed the heavy weapon from Paskevich's extended hand, aiming downwards in one swift unpremeditated motion. An impulse she could no more fight than the torrential force of waters can refuse to break a cracking dam. There were a thousand reasons to execute him; yet, pulling the trigger, she'd thought as clearly as if she'd spoken aloud: *Klazkha, this is for you.* Now, gazing into the scoured wreckage of a face, she fought back the urge to vomit. Klazkha was gone, and retribution meant less than nothing. *He rescued me, he was once a friend,* she thought. *And I've killed him.*

She sank to her knees, closing the staring round eyes.

'Forget those lugubrious regrets, my dear. If you hadn't pulled the trigger, I would have. Not that killing helpless peasants is any more to my taste than Strakhov's, but there was no choice. It was obvious what they intended for you, wasn't it?'

With a violent thrust, she got to her feet and stumbled to the nearest birch tree. Trembling and shaking, she clutched the trunk. Paskevich was right. Why indulge herself in tricked-up elegiac remorse? Ovruch would have eventually caught them and consigned them to their predetermined fates.

'You did good work,' Paskevich said.

Shuddering, she glanced at Stephan, hoping he would add his own absolving words.

But Stephan averted his gaze. 'Let's get started on burying them,' he said.

'Bury them? Strakhov, do you have canine ancestry? There's no other explanation for this obsessive urge you have to bury bones.' Paskevich's observation was reasonable. Stephan had suggested that they stop to dig graves for bodies they came upon — although, to be fair, this morning he hadn't said that a mass interment was in order.

'If we don't, they'll be found,' Stephan said. 'And then the hunt will be on for us.'

'No doubt somebody will come upon them sooner or later. But who's going to connect the bodies to us? And, if it should cross anyone's mind, he'll keep his thoughts to himself. Wouldn't it be — what's that new phrase? — *counter-revolutionary defeatism* to say the great Commissar Ovruch and his entire group were done in by a woman, a wounded man and a *burzhui* intellectual?' Paskevich looked around at the corpses. 'Myself,' he said drily, 'I see a brutal ambush by hordes of partisans or Whites, or whatever.'

Marya left the tree and retrieved her boots. It seemed like a lifetime ago that she'd taken them off. Pressing the newspaper inside flatter, she said: 'Stephan's right. We have to bury them. If they're found, the Red Guard leader in that village will keep right on following the instruction from Moscow to track us down.'

'Do you really believe the local Bolshevik big shot gives a damn about Moscow? He probably doesn't even know where Moscow is. But let's be generous and assume he's literate. He'll weep a few crocodile tears on paper about the mighty commissar's demise. He'll report that he's continuing to hunt us down mercilessly. He'll file his despatch. Then he'll be convinced he's done his duty. It won't matter what Moscow orders; he'll get back to his own problems and blank us from his mind.'

COMMISSAR OVRUCH SLAIN

Yesterday in Ukraine, Commissar Ovruch was ambushed in a dastardly attack by a large Monarchist force . . .

Marya found the tattered *Pravda* on the riverboat.

673

She and Stephan were leaning against the cabin of an overcrowded asthmatic vessel that plied the Dnieper. Paskevich had traded the four Red Guard rifles for three deck-spaces. Now he was below searching out a card game — a skilled and lucky gambler, his winnings paid for their meals.

Handing the paper to Stephan, she said: 'Ivan the Terrible strikes again.' A phrase she had murmured to Boris in San Francisco whenever their illustrious visitor had mockingly shattered yet another of the parental Alexievs' pretensions. 'He was right.' She swatted at the cloud of mosquitoes.

Stephan continued scanning the column. ' "Brutal massacre . . ." So much for me being a pacifist,' he said ruefully.

'You should be decorated with a chestful of medals identical to your Cross of Saint George.' She paused, forcing herself to broach her shooting Ovruch — a subject upon which Stephan had not once commented, either for or against. 'Me, I went berserk. Not a rational thought in my head. All I could see was him aiming at Klazkha. And I wanted him dead, too.'

'You were terrified,' he said in a low voice. 'You were upset by the village.'

His exoneration was falsely grounded, and she should have said so. Instead, she watched the willow trees slipping by on the deserted riverbank.

At the end of a mosquito-plagued week, they docked at a noisy wharf in Donetsk.

This time Paskevich elbowed his way to an open lorry. Within five minutes he no longer had Ovruch's Mauser and they were climbing aboard the lorry with a Siberian family, three adolescent mercenaries and a pair of superannuated over-scented camp-followers.

On the road to Odessa, the driver and his passengers slept grouped around the lorry. Twice they defended it from bandits. The men foraged together, the women cooked.

This together with the lack of privacy forged a camaraderie.

Stephan was congenial, but in a withdrawn way.

Paskevich's eyes glinted maliciously as he skewered their companions, who took no offence — indeed, appeared proud to be worthy of his roasting. During the attacks they obeyed his commands.

Marya, who wore her peasant clothes on the dusty journey, sewed up the wound when the oldest mercenary's arm was sliced from shoulder to elbow by a bandit's bayonet. Thereafter she was the mascot of the journey.

Odessa marks the ultimate end of the steppes, lying on a plateau that overlooks the Black Sea. On the June morning that the lorry let them off at the top of a shallow cliff, each wavelet had become a bronze plate whose shimmering metal reflected the sun. The ocean's brilliance tormented the eye.

Marya raised a shielding hand. Below the

surface, she could make out the debris of one of the two huge breakwaters. A few anchored vessels bobbed as gently as dead fish within the ruined carcasses of the port's five harbours.

On the riverboat and the lorry there had been enough talk of the battles for Odessa as well as the French fleet's bombardment, yet by some mental legerdemain she had been envisaging cliffs lacy with bougain-villaea, elegant villas, a promenade where naval officers escorted ladies in huge prewar hats — scenes shown on the tinted post-cards Boris had sent Lally. The shells of villas and ruined gardens, the artillery-pits shocked her as they made their way down to a wharf. This week the Reds had control, and a limp red flag flew on the dock. Across the remaining wall of a warehouse was painted: 'By order of the Odessa Central Soviet, all vessels beyond harbour limits will be scuttled.'

They bought sardines fried in stale oil and ate at the rickety table. A wiry fisherman with chestnut-tanned skin approached them. After a long look at Marya's peasant skirt, he introduced himself as the lorry-driver's cousin.

'My name's Golovine, like his. But he said the woman was a nurse.'

'I am,' Marya said.

'So where's your nurse's rig-out?'

'I can't imagine how that is any of your concern,' Paskevich said.

'No insult intended.' Golovine looked around. The cook's rowing boat was fifty feet away; otherwise there was nobody else nearby. He sat at a chair and leaned across the table, whispering: 'What's this about the three of you looking for passage?'

'Go beyond the harbour?' Paskevich asked in mock horror. 'Why, Comrade, that's against the Central Soviet's orders.'

Golovine chopped with the flat of his hand, a quietening gesture. 'My cousin told me you were quite the joker,' he muttered. 'Well?'

'Why don't you just say what's on your mind?' Paskevich said.

'I'm sailing with a man whose wife's dropping her first foal. To get her a midwife, he's willing to pay for three of you. Do you want to be aboard?'

'Yes,' Marya said.

'Then, Sister, wear your uniform.'

Late that night, the fishing smack slid from a nearby inlet, Golovine steering while his two rough-looking fishermen hoisted the musty sail. The passengers leaned against the rail together.

They exchanged first names. The prospective father, a newly minted millionaire from Kiev, was Feliks. Feliks was soon boasting about the fortune he'd paid Golovine for passage to Varna on the Bulgarian coast. 'As you can see, my Ilka's due, so I doubled the payment providing he had a midwife aboard.

Sister here's earning her keep, and it's only because of her I'm paying for the two of you.'

Marya could feel Stephan's arm tense.

Paskevich laughed. 'An impoverished ancestor of mine restored our family's fortunes as a gigolo, but I confess it's a career I never expected. The fact is Marya's been supporting her two men for some weeks now.'

Constellations swayed above the outline of the sail, and Stephan's clenched voice came out of the darkness. 'Any news from Russia?'

'Nothing important.'

'Feliks dearest,' the pregnant Ilka cooed, 'what about the Ural Bolsheviks moving our dear emperor and his family to Ekaterinburg?'

'A rumour. And what's the difference where they're cooped up? It's not as if we're all singing "God Bless the Tsar" any more.'

Feliks bragged about his remarkable acumen in picking his charter. Kiev landlubber though he was, he'd unerringly chosen the best man for the job. The boast was true. Golovine had fished the Russian, Romanian and Bulgarian coasts since early boyhood: he knew the currents and inlets — and, seemingly, every fisherman. Hiding his boat in deserted coves each morning, he found shelter of some kind for his passengers. They were provided with blankets, and often Ilka had a bed; they were sustained by endless fish stews. He navigated by the stars. Twice they slipped by Turkish warships, and once they rocked in the luminous wake of a French convoy.

On a windy moonlit night Ilka went into labour. Marya had already scrubbed the deckhouse. No amount of carbolic, alas, could lessen the overpowering reek of fish. The cabin gyrated, and poor Ilka was a bad sailor. With each pain, her nausea increased. Mercifully, she had the pelvis of a whale: her delivery was uncomplicated and rapid for a first child. As dawn pink bannered the sky Marya was sponging seawater on a squirming, complaining boy.

She carried him screaming to his father.

By now Feliks was swaggeringly drunk on Scotch whisky he'd kept for the occasion. Folding back the lacy wool to show the baby's genitals, Feliks proclaimed: 'Like father like son. What a fine lusty lad I've sired! Here is my gratitude to the charming midwife.' He fumbled in his waistcoat pocket for a bag of clinking coins, dropping it. Paskevich stuck out a boot to prevent the heavy purse from sliding overboard.

The coins were gold.

Feliks, like his wife and son, had to be carried through the surf to the beach that morning.

At dusk when they sailed, he was red-eyed but sober.

'Where's my purse?' he growled at Marya.

'You paid the Sister,' Paskevich said. 'I shouldn't want to get the idea you're reneging.' He glanced from the makeshift bed on deck where Ilka nursed the infant to the dark sea with its eerily phosphorescent waves.

'Never,' Feliks said stoutly. 'A fine son like mine is worth every rouble.'

Chapter Fifty-three

'How can you call Switzerland boring? All this magnificent food!'

'The Swiss have the knack of neutrality. No dash, no flair, no foolish aptitude for excitement like us Russians.'

Marya used her pastry fork to scrape up the last of the creamy éclair. 'Mm. Can we afford that Napoleon?'

'A confession, my pet: we haven't a sou.' He shrugged. 'In case you haven't noticed, travel's expensive nowadays.' By the time Golovine's smack had finally tied up at a Varna dock, factions within the Bulgarian High Command and Cabinet were agitating for a separate peace with the Allies, a dissension that throttled the country. The civilian railway no longer functioned. Paskevich had slipped enough gold coins into uniform pockets, and they were permitted to board a military train.

'There's nothing left?' Marya asked.

'I can't pay for . . .' With a negligent wave of his narrow brown cigarette Paskevich indicated the coffee set and half-empty platter of cream cakes between them. 'So what's the difference? Go ahead, indulge your sweet tooth.'

It was too late for lunch, too early for tea: theirs was the only occupied table on the sunny terrace of the Locarno café. The waitress, after bringing their order, had stamped back to the kitchen, the painted wooden *zoccoli* on her feet clacking out her disapproval.

Paskevich's filthy trousers were torn at the knees; and Marya, whose uniform had split across the bodice during Ilka's delivery, had changed to the Russian peasant skirt and stained woollen blouse that Klazkha had provided. Stephan, equally disreputable, had just gone inside to read the newspapers racked neatly on wooden spines.

'Maybe I shouldn't, then,' Marya said as she replaced the tongs. She looked around.

The peace of the surrounding wooded green hills flowed like a benison on Locarno. A party of stout holidaymakers were walking sedately down the incline towards the lake while two chatting women came uphill carrying baskets laden with fruit and vegetables. A small boy clung to the handle of the large perambulator wheeled by a uniformed nursemaid. An electric tram passed, the bell chiming a silvery note. Lecarno, so far as Marya was concerned, would have been heaven — if it weren't for one flaw.

The white stucco establishment across the street.

It was the one building in the tight-shouldered row that lacked flower-spilling window-boxes. On the door was fixed a highly polished brass plaque: 'First Bank of Zurich. Lecarno Offices.'

Behind those stucco walls, the grey-haired

branch manager was supposedly wiring the bank's president, Herr Eichorn, in Zurich.

'Let's hope he's sending the telegram,' Marya said. 'You couldn't show him a passport — or any other identification. Why should he bother to send the wire?'

Lighting a fresh cigarette, Paskevich inhaled. 'I don't have a doubt that he was certain we're imposters. But he has a flunkey mentality, and I carried off the interview with enough aplomb to give him pause. Don't worry your head. He'll contact Eichorn.'

She stared at the building. 'If he *does,* how long will it take for a reply?'

'I wouldn't hold my breath. Bankers everywhere take themselves with the utmost seriousness, and Swiss bankers in particular worship a prudent deity. Eichorn's not going to commit himself for a day or so.' Tapping ash from his cigarette, he lounged back. 'Myself I'm in no rush to get to Zurich.'

'You have a personal account there, don't you?'

'Nothing of importance, but here in the capitalist world money's easy enough to acquire.' He shrugged dismissively and took another puff. 'My dear, haven't you told me often enough that the instant we reach Zurich, you're returning to Russia?'

'Wild horses couldn't drag me back.' She gave a shudder.

'You've given every indication that you

were set on hitching your wagon to Strak-hov's star.'

'Stephan's never going back. Never! What he saw was too devastating. Or were you enjoying yourself too much to notice what was going on?'

'I'm a Russian, my dear,' he said sombrely. 'Each time I saw an example of the Bolshevik Terror or the peasants' vandalism or the destruction of an army — Red, Green, White, you pick the colour — I was ready to strangle somebody. Strakhov was angry, too, but his anger was self-directed. With each horror he felt guiltier.'

'He feels awful,' she said. 'But why, Paskevich? Why?'

'An odd question to ask about a man who spent his life fomenting this Revolution.'

'He wanted justice for everyone. Time after time he put himself in danger — you know he did — and all he wanted in return was some kind of fairness in the country. Why should he blame himself when things didn't turn out the way he'd hoped?'

'That's a realist's question, my dear. Strak-hov's a romantic. Worse, he's an idealist. The destruction lacerated him personally. Now, we realists, we enjoyed our world's excesses and after the deluge feel no respon-sibility.'

Marya swallowed and bent her head. Much as she disliked being ranged along-side Paskevich rather than beside Stephan, honesty forced her to admit that, however much she had tried to alleviate the subsequent human anguish, until this moment she had never once equated the wreckage of an empire with the hedonistic extravagances practised in her Fourstatskaia Street flat.

At the sound of the café door, she turned. Stephan had emerged. Clutching a newspaper against his chest, he groped with his free hand for a wrought-iron chairback to support himself. His mouth was contorted with pain.

Beset with remembrances of a nursing-school lecture on ruptured coronary arteries, Marya darted across the flagstones. 'What is it, darling? What's wrong?'

Stephan blinked as if a stranger were accosting him and sank into the chair. She rested two fingers on his wrist. In her panic she couldn't find the pulse.

'They've done it,' he said heavily. 'They've done the unspeakable.'

Paskevich took the paper, smoothing where Stephan's hand had crumpled. He had the ability to read a page with a single glance. He sighed heavily. 'Exactly what I've been anticipating.'

'What does it say?' Marya was loosening Stephan's collar. 'Read it to me.'

Paskevich's clever ugly face was pale and drawn into lines of grief yet his cadence was ironic as he read: ' "At the first session of the Central Executive Committee elected by the Fifth Congress of the Councils a message was made public. The message was sent by direct wire from the Ural Regional Council and worded as follows: 'Recently Ekaterinburg, the capital of the Red Ural, was seriously threatened by the approach of the Czecho-Slovak bands. At the same time a counter-revolutionary conspiracy was discovered, having for its object the wresting of the tyrant Romanov from the Council's authority by armed force. In view of these events, the Presidium of the Ural Regional Council decided to shoot the ex-Tsar, Nicholas Romanov.' " '

Decided to shoot . . . Nicholas Romanov . . .

Marya's eyes filled with involuntary tears. She was visualizing the throng of jewel-armoured nobility sinking into reverent bows and curtsies as their spry, trimly bearded emperor — and putative master — escorted the broad white cloud who was Paskevich's third bride to the altar of the Khazan Cathedral.

The tsar shot?

Had Nicholas, like Louis XVI, been executed in front of a jeering crowd? Had he faced a public firing squad? Or had the regicide been carried out in a secret place? Did the Ekaterinburg Soviet force his wife and children to witness the murder?

Paskevich had continued to read. ' ". . . decision was carried out on July the sixteenth. The wife and son of Romanov have been sent to a place of security." Then there's the usual rubbish. Nicholas was going to be tried by a Moscow tribunal for his crimes, and so forth. Papers incriminating him will soon be made public, and et cetera.'

He dropped the newspaper on the table. A breeze ruffled the page. Stephan steadied it with a shaking hand.

'Strakhov, don't reproach yourself. If you must cast accusations, blame fate.'

Marya glanced sharply at Paskevich. Not that it was out of character for him to comfort Stephan — he often indulged in random magnanimous gestures — but why choose fate, a concept he normally classified with Tarot decks, Ouija boards and gypsy fortune-tellers?

Paskevich caught her look. 'Blame karma, blame destiny,' he said. 'Or whatever you wish to call the malevolent force that thrust Nicholas into the role of tsar. Believe me — — and I knew him extremely well — he lacked the ruthlessness, the authority, the guile and cruelty needed to govern Russia. And, to make matters worse, he was henpecked. Strakhov, you were not your brother's keeper. His wife was. What a catastrophic mistake he made in his choice. That poor, sad, interfering woman! She was his keeper.' Paskevich grasped Stephan's tensed shoulder.

Stephan shrugged off the large hand. His eyes were a chilling blue. 'She and the rest of the family', he said, 'will need that account in Zurich more than ever.'

That night, Stephan lay fully dressed in the narrow, scrupulously clean bedroom overlooking Lake Maggiore. How Paskevich, ragged and penniless, had procured the three rooms at the height of the holiday season Stephan had no idea, yet in some obscure way admired. At this minute, though, Paskevich was far from his thoughts.

The tears oozing down his cheeks weren't easing his pain and they weren't for the slain Nicholas Romanov. Stephan wept for his own youth: those sweet innocent years when he had dreamed and written of a better world, the years before he'd read Irena's letter and understood that his rebellion against the Autocracy meant that he was forever locked in dubious battle with his reigning half-brother.

The air in the clean little room seemed without oxygen, smothering, and he struggled to draw every breath.

At a soft hushed sound, he lifted his head. Was that rain? The sky had been clear at sunset, but rain-clouds moved swiftly in the Alps. Going to the window, he pulled aside the net curtains. Misty droplets ran down the panes, casting an Impressionist halo around the ornamental lamp-posts that lined the lakeside promenade.

A small rain, he thought. *A cleansing rain.*

His calf boots, bought second-hand from a cart in Bucharest, had already been polished and returned. He glanced across the hall. Marya's down-at-the-heel but dainty black shoes, also bought in Bucharest, waited. He knew he could tap on that closed door and she would comfort him with soothing words and her body. He knew just as surely that he needed to get through this particular night by himself.

He padded down to the empty foyer, sitting on the bench to tie his bootlaces.

The needle-fine drizzle, though not cold, was penetrating. Trudging through pools of yellow light on the deserted promenade, he felt the weight of his wet clothing. *Heavy as a shroud,* he thought.

The paper had reported that Alexandra with the heir had been moved to a 'place of security', but there had been no mention made of the grand duchesses. An oversight? Were Olga, Tatyana, Marie and Anastasia with their mother and younger brother? Where were they, that pretty Imperial foursome who before the February Revolution had been photographed together in co-ordinated pastels and pearls so often that it was impossible to grant them each a separate identity?

'My nieces.' He spoke out loud, and the words sounded so alien that he might have spoken them in Urdu. 'My nieces . . . what's happened to them?'

They won't be as heavily guarded as Alexandra and the heir . . . He frowned.

A place of security.

Where was this place, and from whom was it secure?

Was escape possible?

In the distance, a woman was trotting along the promenade. Until she raised her arm, waving, he didn't realize that it was Marya. He had exorcized the horror of Ovruch's destroyed face but he couldn't eradicate the memory of Marya staggering back from the Mauser's recoil: he still wasn't sure if he admired or was revolted by her ability to kill their enemy.

'I've been so worried.' Her voice was thin and rushed. 'I dreamed of — I had this terrible dream. And I needed to make sure you were all right. But your boots were gone, and you didn't answer when I knocked.' She gripped his arm as if to assure herself of his corporeal reality. 'Stephan, it was as if the nightmare had come true.'

'Poor darling.'

She took a long, shuddering breath as if to calm herself. 'Hysterical over dreams! God, what a madwoman!'

In the vestibule, he put both arms around her waist — an embrace that was an apology for his absence.

She pressed closer. 'Come to my room?' she whispered.

His brain was lined with photographs and portraits of the half-brother he'd never met, and would never meet. 'Another time, darling.'

'We haven't been . . . together . . . since Petrograd.'

'Maybe tomorrow,' he said, resting his cheek on her hair.

Yet what she said was true, they hadn't made love in months, and he was aroused. He kept his arm around her as they climbed the staircase, and at her door he showered kisses on her cool forehead, her cheeks; then kissed her lips, arching her backwards as their breathing quickened. The lavatory door up the hall opened, and a portly man in a bathrobe emerged. Flushing deeply, Marya drew Stephan into the room.

Soon their clothing, wet and dry, was strewn all over the rug. He was already in bed when she bent to roll down her stockings. How could he have forgotten the unconscious grace and sensuous curves of the small body?

She felt his gaze, and turned to give him a slow hot smile.

Afterwards, when she slept, he peered into the darkness, as if with enough tenacity he would be able to see through the barbarity and chaos to his half-brother's daughters, to his nieces.

He'd learn more about them, hopefully, when he reached Zurich.

Chapter Fifty-four

They left the Zurich station, merging with the window-shoppers along the sunlit Bahnhofstrasse. Marya couldn't take her eyes from the displays: after the ravages of war, the merchandise seemed nothing short of miraculous. Here, lush pelts awaited transformation into coats; there, bolts of cashmere and Chinese silk tempted the eye. The confectioner's shop displayed a pyramid of satin-ribboned chocolate-boxes. Brightly painted square tins lay on their sides to show every shade of tea leaf. Brown sacks artfully spilled coffee beans. Porcelain figurines. Gold watches. Cuckoo clocks. Hints of buttery delights wafted from *pâtisseries*. Fragrance and colour exploded around the flower-girl at the corner.

Across the street, a window showed a silk-draped dummy. Paskevich halted. In his pocket was most of the two thousand francs that the Locarno branch had advanced. 'As I recall, my dear, Madame sells off the peg. Take whatever looks halfway decent. Strakhov and I will be across the street at that tailor's.'

'I don't need anything,' Stephan retorted.

At the same moment, Marya said: 'This outfit's fine.'

Then they both flushed.

Paskevich's unpleasant smile indicated

692

that this mutual embarrassment at taking his money proved what he already knew: they had spent the last few nights in the same bed. Glancing pointedly at Marya's stained peasant blouse, he said: 'My dear, charming as you always are, that outfit's not quite, if you follow my meaning, the thing Eichorn will expect my wife to wear. And, Strakhov, let me assure you that Zurich bankers give short shrift to prospective clients in frayed jackets.'

Marya selected the least expensive dress available, coarse ecru linen that was far too large. The *vendeuse,* a Frenchwoman, cinched in the waist with a wide belt from the shop's selection of locally made raffia items. Tucking a nosegay of cloth lilacs into a straw hat, she stepped back to survey her frugal customer. Touching her thumb and forefinger to a delicate kiss, she said: 'Madame is perfection.'

Stephan also bought the cheapest available garments, a check suit with narrow lapels and narrow trousers. Looking in the mirror propped in a corner, he saw a stranger, a riverboat gambler with a long sun-browned face and hollow smudges instead of eyes.

Paskevich selected the finest linen shirts and underwear while the tailor, sitting cross-legged on his table, shortened the trousers and let out the shoulders of the best lounge suit available in the establishment. 'Not Savile Row,' Paskevich said.

'But it's good enough for Eichorn.'

The cloistered hush of places dedicated to the preservation of capital prevailed at the First Bank of Zurich. A rosy-cheeked messenger-boy greeted them in low-spoken English, a language he hadn't yet mastered. 'Herr Eichorn is requesting I bring the gentleman and his friends to a privacy.'

He led them past the busy cashiers' windows, down a broad flight of marble steps to an electrically lit basement corridor, ushering them into a windowless conference room.

'If you are so kind as to wait.'

Looking around at the stern bearded bankers gazing from portraits and photographs, Paskevich murmured: 'Abandon all hope, ye who enter here. We're being intimidated — an excellent ploy.'

Within a minute, the boy returned. 'Herr Eichorn is sending his utmost apologies; he was not expecting you so early. He is begging your indulgence for five minutes.'

'The delay — another meritorious technique.' Paskevich took one of the massive dark chairs that surrounded the immense circular table, stretching out his short legs and lounging back. 'I'm confused as to what to do when the funds are released.'

'The secret account, you mean?' Marya asked.

'That's why we've come all this way, my dear.'

'Something you've never explained,' she snapped back, 'is how you plan to get the money to Siberia.'

'There are Russian couriers here who would have done anything for their tsar, abdicated or not,' he said. 'But Nicholas is dead.'

'Alexandra and the children need it,' Stephan said. 'More desperately than ever.'

'I gather, then, that you're convinced they're still among the living?'

'The empress and the heir were moved,' Marya said, responding for Stephan. 'It was in every paper.'

'And, of course, being printed makes it true,' Paskevich said. 'It did strike me as odd, though, that the girls weren't mentioned.'

'A lapse in the original communiqué,' Stephan said.

'Is that your opinion, or wishful thinking?'

With a rapid glance at Stephan's drawn expression, Marya turned on Paskevich. 'The Communists aren't all brilliant like you. Some of them can't read or write, much less report the news accurately.'

'Not to mention honestly,' Paskevich said.

'Must you always be so cynical?' Marya snapped.

Paskevich flicked an imaginary thread from his new trousers. 'The boy, Alexandra, the girls — could there be more splendid symbols? Properly used, any one of them could consolidate every shade of opposition to Marxism. From what you've seen of Lenin-the-humanitarian, would you say he'd permit human rallying-banners like them to survive?'

'Where's all this pessimism leading?' Marya asked. 'That *you* should keep the cash?'

'Let me confess that the idea hadn't occurred to me. However, it certainly is excellent. What a go-getting Yankee you are, my dear.' He chuckled. 'Myself, I was suggesting that if Strakhov and I are of the same school of thought, that the Romanovs are dead, then the assets should be thought of in a different light.'

Stephan gazed down at the table.

'What do you mean?' Marya asked.

'Myself, I rather visualized arming the anti-Bolshevik forces.'

'We just walk into a shop on the Bahnhofstrasse and say, "I'll take three dozen tanks"?' Marya asked.

'That's more or less the idea. Not here in neutral Switzerland, of course. However, every army has its share of dishonest supply officers, and now even the honourable men can justify a larceny with the comforting thought that the war's grinding to an end and they'll only be selling tomorrow's surplus. I dare say that in the Balkans German artillery goes at astonishingly low prices.'

'Before you came here to open the account you told me that it was solely for the tsar's immediate family.'

'Ah, but I have access. And, if the Romanov family's been slaughtered, what better use to which to put Romanov gold than to avenge Romanov blood?'

Each time Paskevich repeated *Romanov,* a muscle in Stephan's jaw twitched.

'Now I see what you're doing!' Marya jumped up from her chair. 'You're manipulating Stephan back into Russia!'

'I?' Paskevich turned to Stephan. 'Did you need any cues?'

Stephan's finger was tracing the grain of the tabletop. 'I'd already made up my mind to deliver the funds to them personally.'

'We're talking about several million,' Paskevich said. 'Bullion's impossible. And jewels are being devalued by the amount being exchanged for food. However, I dare say the finest diamonds, emeralds and rubies are still in demand.'

'My conclusion, too,' Stephan said.

'What about America? What about your writing?' Marya asked in a low voice. *What about marriage and growing old together? What about us? What about me?*

Stephan raised his head, looking at her. 'I can't get what we saw out of my mind.'

'Horrible, it was horrible,' Marya said. 'And I'm sure the empress, the grand duchesses and the heir are alive. But if they aren't . . .?'

'Then, as Count Paskevich just said, the money must go to buy arms.'

'For whom?' she demanded. 'The Greens? The Whites? Denikin or Kolchak or Wrangels? This new Ukrainian leader, Petliura?'

'The trick is,' Stephan said, 'to unite them.'

Paskevich nodded. 'One cohesive army should have an excellent chance.'

Marya wheeled around at Paskevich. 'And what about you? Will you go back?'

'I? No.'

'At the Kresky you told me you'd fought for Russia and you'd never leave.'

'A heroic speech, wasn't it?' Paskevich drawled the question, but his eyes were vigilant as he searched her face.

At a discreet tap, she turned expectantly to the door.

Herr Eichorn's thin silver hair, plastered across his flat skull, didn't match his beetling black eyebrows and the dark walrus-bristled moustache sprouting above his plump red lips.

He gave Paskevich one quick look and sucked in his considerable girth. 'Count Paskevich.' He bowed respectfully. 'The greatest of pleasures to see you again.'

Paskevich acknowledged him with a careless nod. 'My dear, may I present Herr Eichorn? Herr Eichorn, Countess Paskevich.'

Furious at the wifely appellation, Marya tensed her fingers as the Swiss banker raised her hand to the vicinity of his moustache and mimed a kiss. On being introduced to Stephan, the banker quickly took in the cheap suit and turned back to Paskevich.

'Please accept my heartfelt regrets about

that delay in Locarno, Count Paskevich. An over-zealous branch manager. In his defence, though, I must say that imposters are flooding in from Russia. Anarchists, Bolsheviks — a bad lot. And you should hear them. Shouting demands for funds that are not rightly theirs.'

'I extend apologies on behalf of my countrymen.'

'Caution is a banker's responsibility,' Eichorn said with a fawning smile. 'Just tell me what size draft you require, Excellency, and the bank will be delighted to accommodate immediately.'

'Naturally,' Paskevich said. 'My business here today, however, concerns account number three four one seven.'

Eichorn's smile faded. 'Thirty-four seventeen? Count Paskevich, I take it you haven't had an opportunity to see the newspapers in the last few days?'

'Alas, I have read them.'

'Then, you understand the problem. Our accounts are all highly confidential. And thirty-four seventeen is delicate in the extreme. So it would be best if we continued our discussion in my private office.' His soft belly shook as he forced a cough. 'If Countess Paskevich and Mr Strakhov would excuse us . . . ?'

'My wife has my complete confidence,' Paskevich said. 'And Mr Strakhov was close to his Imperial Majesty. Remarkably close.'

Stephan's expression was set.

Paskevich stared at Eichorn. Eichorn stared back. He looked away first, picking up a small silver bell. At the tinkle, the rosy-cheeked assistant opened the door. Herr Eichorn nodded, and the youth took the wooden chair in the corner, propping a notepad on his thigh. His pencil sped as he jotted down the conversation in shorthand.

After a few opening pleasantries, Eichorn began his stalling tactics. 'The bank has a fiduciary responsibility to the empress and the Imperial Family. You surely understand that, Count Paskevich. For any withdrawal we require a signed request from each of them.'

'That's an impossibility, and you know it,' Stephan snapped.

'It's the only way we have of preventing the withdrawal from falling into the wrong hands.'

'The account is being closed,' Paskevich said.

'Closed?' the Swiss banker echoed.

'I am entitled to do so,' Paskevich said.

Again Eichorn tugged at his moustache, gazing around the windowless walls as if soliciting guidance from the bearded visages of dead bankers. 'With deepest respect, Count,' he said finally, 'I must study the documents to make sure that is the way the account was opened.'

'A ridiculous waste of your time,' Paskevich said. 'But go ahead. I'll expect the letter of credit to be ready this afternoon.'

Eichorn's red mouth tightened. 'Count Paskevich, in caring for other people's assets we bankers carry the heaviest of burdens. We therefore conform stringently to regulations.' Lacing his plump white fingers, he continued with coaxing tact: 'Surely you understand that withdrawing a deposit of such magnitude requires caution? We have a minimum waiting period of a month.'

It took Paskevich nearly a quarter of an hour to overcome Swiss caution.

'I can't promise,' Eichorn said, 'but possibly my partners will agree that five business days are adequate to ensure safety.'

'Have the letter of credit made out to Mr Strakhov,' Paskevich said.

The banker's eyes widened. 'Mr Strakhov?'

'You heard correctly. And now, if you'll be so kind, summon a taxi to take us to our hotel.'

The head porter at the Baur au Lac, accustomed to the finest baggage, tensed his nostrils at the travel-worn, cheaply made valise which was taken to Paskevich's suite. The pink cardboard box that contained Marya's peasant clothes was borne solemnly to her rooms while she remained downstairs.

She sent a cable to New York. Because of the war, hours, even days, might pass before it got through; and she had little hope that Boris was still at the Waldorf Astoria Hotel. But where else did she have a glimmer of a chance to contact him?

Marya and Stephan took a stroll after dinner. The night-time view of Lake Zurich was partially obscured by the huge trees of the hotel park. The fresh scent of recently mown grass perfuming the darkness was overpowered by the strong odour of cigars as two guests sauntered by, speaking in some Germanic language.

After their footsteps had faded, she asked: 'Stephan, don't you see how clever Paskevich has been?'

'It's not him, Marya, it's me. I've thought constantly about going back.'

'But you promised —'

'And, I swear, at the beginning, in Tobolsk, I intended to follow Nicholas's request and see the money on its way. And I planned to stay here only as long as it took to make plans for us to get to the States. But what we saw — oh God, what we saw! Kremenchug. Those villages where the Reds, Whites or Ukrainians had stolen every grain, even next year's seed. The hatred, the pogroms, the massacres. Can you block out those bodies in the square?'

'Never,' she sighed. 'But you'll only be sucked into the horrors.'

'I can try to help the heir and Alexandra — if they're still alive. But, Marya, I'm convinced the girls can be rescued.'

'Maybe it's true, what Paskevich said.'

'I can't let myself believe that.'

'You've said yourself that he's always right.'

'They're alive,' Stephan said doggedly. 'And I can help them.'

Their shoes crunched on gravel for a dozen or so steps.

'All right, maybe the unthinkable has happened,' he said with a sigh. 'Marya, isn't it my obligation to make sure the money's used properly?'

'You mean to fight the Reds?'

'The country's crying out to be united against them.' Stephan's voice rang with the fervour that had drawn her to him. Recalling the grey day on the English Channel, she reached up, her fingers caressing his cheek.

'It's not there,' she said in surprise.

'What, darling?'

'The scar.'

'Remember that bad sunburn I got in Ukraine? I suppose it happened when the skin kept peeling.'

'I'm going back to Russia with you,' she said.

'That's insane. Think of the dangers.'

'I'm a nurse. I held my own on the way here, didn't I?'

'Stop talking like this.' He put a restraining hand on her wrist. 'When it's over, I'll come to America.'

'We're not getting separated again,' she said. 'Ever.'

Chapter Fifty-five

Marya jerked out of another of her nightmares.

Consciously she couldn't recall any of the horrors, but the memory lingered in her muscles. Sunshine poured through a crack between the heavy brocade curtains, and she unclenched her fingers, reminding herself that she was safe in a bosomy Swiss bed.

What had awakened her was a light tapping at the hall door.

Assuming a valet or chambermaid had brought her a breakfast tray, she drew the sheet up over her shoulders, calling out: 'Entrez.'

Paskevich stepped inside. 'Even in secure reliable Zurich, my dear, never leave your room unlocked.'

Her face grew warm. When Stephan had left the previous night, she'd been too drowsy to get up to bolt the door. 'I thought it was breakfast.'

'Breakfast? It's high noon,' he said. 'After we lunch we'll make another trip to the Bahnhofstrasse. I'm tired of that dress of yours.'

'Aren't we going to the bank to prod Herr Eichorn?'

'Strakhov and I have concluded our business with the gentleman.'

'The two of you?' She tried to remember

whether during the long months of their journey they had ever been alone together. 'It's all handled? So quickly?'

'Eichorn's not a glacier; he can move with remarkable speed when it comes to keeping the francs in his establishment. I pointed out that since Strakhov would need a reputable bank it was far simpler not to close the account, but merely to change the signatories.' Paskevich's teeth gleamed in the shadows. 'There's irony for you. One of Tsar Alexander's by-blows now has the Romanov nest egg.'

'Stephan will hand everything over to the family,' she said.

Paskevich's sigh, dredged from deep within his chest, filled the shadowy gloom. 'Much as I hate to think about it, they're beyond needing money.'

'That's not true.'

'Marya, none of the armies, whatever flag they happen to fly, blinks at the massacre of women and children. So why would the Bolsheviks, with their penchant for terror, suddenly grow fastidious about killing off one paltry family — a family who could endanger them?'

His logic, as always, was unassailable, yet she said: 'They're alive.' *They have to be alive.* 'Did Stephan mention I'll be going back with him?'

Gloom swathed the room, and Paskevich stood too far from the bed for her to make out his expression. 'Tantalizing a subject as you are,' he said, 'we're both gentlemen. Neither of us referred to you.'

'We settled it together,' she lied. Stephan had continued to argue that it would be suicidal for her — Countess Paskevich — to return to Russia. She had persisted with hotter and hotter stubbornness, finally crying: 'Why can't you be man enough to admit that you don't want me with you?' In a low defeated voice he had acquiesced: 'All right, we'll go together.' She was recalling that vanquished tone as she added: 'And, whatever you think about the Romanovs' chances, we're going to Siberia to find them.'

'Are you? Then, here's a bit of advice. Rise and shine.' The words were excessively silken. 'This afternoon's your one chance to stock up on whatever you'll need on the jaunt. You're taking the train tomorrow.'

'Tomorrow? He told you that?'

'Not at all. I made a flash deduction from his and Eichorn's detailed conferences about railway timetables to Bulgaria.'

'And you don't mind if I go?'

'To answer one question with another: if I did care, could I prevent it?'

'No, never!'

'That sounded a mite over-assertive. Perhaps you're considering that I'm your husband? In Russia under the Autocracy, that meant legal power over your mind and body. But that world's vanished under the waves like Atlantis. Ergo you're free.'

'Is this another of your traps?'

'From my point of view you'll always be my wife. Reason, however, forces me to accept that even under my so-called sovereignty you never kept away from handsome fervent poets.' Paskevich had stepped closer to the bed. She could see him clearly. The flesh around his eyes and mouth sagged, and the webbed lines showed. He looked as mortally ill as after her unskilled surgery.

'Are you all right?' she asked.

'It's been a long-drawn-out journey,' he said. The neutral flatness of his tone made the remark enigmatic. Was he referring to their travels or using a metaphor for a relationship that had lasted her entire lifetime? 'If I were of a generous heart, I'd wish you well. But, since I am what I am, let me reiterate that you don't have a clue about Strakhov's feelings for you. Not the foggiest.'

'He loves me.'

'I've become convinced you're right, my dear. But have you ever asked yourself what amount and quality of passion he is capable of investing in you?'

'That's an ugly question.'

'Tell me something, then. The minute we left Russia, why wasn't he planning a life with you? Discussing ways for the two of you to get to America? Why did he insist on accompanying me every step of the way here to Zurich? And please don't remind me about keeping his famous vow to the late Nicholas. If you'd been willing to come with *me*, I'd have snatched you away, whirled you as far from him as I could, and then done everything in my power to clear him from your mind. I'd have said to hell with the Romanovs and their bank accounts.'

'Paskevich, he's better than we are.'

'And there you've put a finger on the crux of it. He is better. Inflexibly better — "I could not love thee, dear, so much, loved I not honour more", and so on. My pet, you have two rivals: his sense of honour and his altruism.'

'I wouldn't feel like this about him if he were different.'

'But we're not talking about *you*, are we? *He's* the one under discussion. And you refuse to listen to the obvious.' Paskevich looked even more weary.

'Oh, Paskevich, I never meant it to be like this for you . . .'

'Spare me your pity. I abhor pity. As you surely know by now, I've never been adept at granting it, and in my life I've never thrown myself on the clemency of others.'

His tone of hauteur touched her yet more, reminding her of that brave little boy. She pushed herself up on her elbow. The sheet fell back, revealing her breasts. She yanked up the eiderdown.

Noting the gesture, Paskevich inclined his head in a brusque nod of farewell.

'I really am sorry,' she said. 'I care for you, but —'

The door closed. He was gone.

708

Chapter Fifty-six

Late the following morning, Marya was hastily winding three pairs of grey winter stockings into balls. She pressed the first ball into a corner of the already full steamer trunk; but, no matter how she squeezed, the woolly mass refused to fit. Below the deceptive softness of blankets she'd wedged bars of carbolic and, below these, Sandoz opiates and disinfectants, quinine pills, cases of aspirin, and at the bottom a thick protective layer of rolled bandages. She'd forced herself to be methodical, repacking the trunk twice to squeeze this much in. She frowned impatiently at the stockings.

Stephan had gone downstairs with his baggage ten minutes ago, and she'd promised to follow immediately. She could hear the footsteps of the thick-necked porter as he paced in the hall.

Blowing back a wisp of hair and wiping the perspiration from her forehead, she unwound the stockings and aligned them over the blanket. Her eye told her that the lid would never shut. She glanced at the new calf suitcase, which was already closed — she'd needed to sit on it so that Stephan could fasten the straps. Inside were gleaming surgical instruments and pipettes for draining wounds — the pipettes, being friable, were wrapped inside her bulky underwear, winter uniforms, extra aprons.

The previous afternoon and earlier this morning, Stephan and she had been on a frenzied shopping spree. He had run from jeweller to jeweller pricing and buying the finest gemstones, while she had darted in and out of druggists, uniform shops, haberdasheries: the Baur au Lac's house physician had fulfilled his promise to secure the surgical tools.

'Madame?' The hall porter edged inside. 'It's very late.'

She pushed to her feet. Smoothing back her hair, she said: 'I'm having a terrible time with this trunk. Would you be an angel?'

With a dubious expression, he rested a knee on the lid, pressing down. A gap remained. He pushed with both hands, his back arching, his shoulder muscles bunching. Snorting an exhalation, he snapped the central brass lock home.

Being able to pack her warm stockings seemed the best of omens. 'You're a miracle-worker!' she cried.

The porter locked the trunk, handed her the key, and swiftly loaded her baggage on to his cart, trundling away. She didn't waste time closing the door after him but hurried around flinging open drawers to make sure she hadn't left anything. Running into the immense bathroom, she dashed cold water on her perspiring face.

Over the running tap, she heard footsteps.

Paskevich, she thought.

She hadn't seen him since the previous morning, and in this moment hope surged that he'd come to wish her godspeed. During the frantic hours of preparations, she'd kept recalling their farewell. How inadequate that brusque nod was for what they'd been to each other. Yet she hadn't been able to bring herself to knock on his door. He would, she knew, have responded to an overture with caustic mockery or aristocratic hauteur.

'Madame?' A high childish voice.

Groping for the towel, she wiped her eyes and saw with disappointment so keen that it was almost pain that her visitor was a diminutive messenger-boy.

'A thousand pardons for the intrusion, your Excellency,' he piped, extending a salver with a telegram. The name 'Countess Paskevich' showed in the Cellophane window.

She tore open the envelope.

DEAREST MARYA WE THANK GOD YOU ARE ALIVE STOP AM RECUPERATING OR WOULD VISIT STATE DEPARTMENT IN WASHINGTON TO FACILITATE YOUR RETURN STOP LET US KNOW IF YOU NEED MONEY FOR PASSAGE STOP IMMEDIATE REPLY URGENT LOVE BORIS

'We? Us?' Marya whispered. Then her eyes flooded with tears of joy. These ribbons of

711

pasted-on print were a chain linking her to her brother!

Gripping the yellow telegram paper, she ran to the lift but was too impatient to wait for its creaking ascent. She flew down the wide staircase and past the concierge's desk, circling the three men who stood writing at the tall desk beside the telegraph office.

The dignified white-haired doorman took off his cap as she burst out of the door. Her trunk and suitcase were already roped on the back of the hotel carriage.

'I was about to send up for you,' Stephan said. 'We're set to leave.'

Exuberantly waving the cable, she cried: 'It's from Boris!'

'That's wonderful,' he said. 'Jump in.'

'I have to answer.'

'Now?'

'Right away.'

'We're already late.'

'It won't take any time at all.' As she said this she thought of the men waiting at the telegraph desk. 'Maybe a minute or two.'

Stephan grabbed her arm, halting her as she started back up the steps. 'The train goes at twelve. That's less than thirty minutes.'

'I'll just say I got his message, that's all —'

'Swiss trains are on the dot —'

'Darling, Boris is ill —'

'— and there's only one connection a week to Bulgaria.'

'He's been frantic about me. He'll be worried to death if he doesn't get an answer.'

'I've a contact in Sofia.'

'Please, please try to understand. We're talking about my brother, my only close relative.'

'Herr Eichorn sent a message to a Bulgarian officer.' Stephan spoke softly and rapidly. 'He's high up in the intelligence division. He'll know what happened in Ekaterinburg.'

'It's my brother.'

'We'll never make another contact like this.'

'I just can't leave Boris dangling. I'm all the family he has.'

'In a week it might be too late.'

They were standing so close that each could feel the warmth of the other's breath, yet they might have been shouting from opposite sides of the Atlantic.

Stephan could neither see nor hear Marya. Instead he saw a starving beggar, saw a fallen student with raspberries of blood in the snow around him, saw the newspaper column announcing the execution of Nicholas Romanov. His ears were filled with the caw of vultures, the snarling of dogs around corpses in a village square. Where in this post-revolutionary landscape were his icons, compassion and justice?

A breeze stirred Marya's straw hat, and she reached up to hold the brim. A blue vein at her temple pulsed with frightening vitality, and every beat shouted, *Boris, Boris, Boris.*

Stephan saw the finest of lines at the corners of those pleading unique eyes, saw that the roundness had been chiselled from her face to reveal her cheekbones. The vibrant gregarious Californian girl he had fallen for ten years ago had been transformed into a magnificent woman.

I still love her. She still loves me.

But the decade had matured Stephan, too. He was accepting that nowhere did the implacable contrast between them show more than in their differing ways of love.

Marya strewed warmth and nurturing affection with both small hands; she was willingly laying her life on the line to be with him in Russia. Her love was unstinting, intense — and personal. She could never give herself to a cause.

And he? What he felt for her remained a fixed compass-point of his existence. Yet his heart was hostage to abstract ideals. The obligations he had shouldered in Zurich weighed heavily on him. *I can't miss that train. The truth is it's for the best if she doesn't come — she'll slow me down.* Once he would have condemned himself for having ice instead of a heart, but he no longer wasted time on self-recriminations. He had accepted that his greatest lack and his highest virtue were identical: he could place duty, obligations and, yes, the greater good ahead of all personal desires.

Marya watched Stephan's face take on an expression of asceticism. He also looked cornered. This was how he'd looked in Kremenchug's old quarter when he admitted taking the jewellery to start a famine-relief station. *How can we be selfish?* he had asked then.

Did he consider love selfish?

Coldness ran up her arms, prickling on the skin of her shoulders. What was it that Paskevich had said? *You have two rivals: his sense of honour and his altruism.* Yes, matched up against the misery, the horror, the destruction they'd witnessed, of course a man like Stephan must believe that what he felt for her was trivially selfish.

The fluttering straw hat cast mercurial shadows across her suddenly lifeless expression. 'You go ahead,' she said.

'What about you?'

'I'll have the concierge telephone for a motor taxi,' she said.

'Marya, are you sure?'

'I'll be there before you have the baggage on the train.' Her forced little smile was a last-ditch entreaty. *Tell me you refuse to let the carriage leave without me. Tell me you'll wait while I send the cable. Tell me I mean more to you than anything on this earth. Tell me that you love me as much as I love you,* that hungry smile pleaded.

He touched her cheek with his lips. She felt the light pressure, the warmth of his sigh. 'Then, for the time being, *dasvidan'ye,*' he said.

He hauled himself into the carriage. The doorman slammed the door. Rubber wheels crunched on gravel.

Stephan's shoulder muscles trembled with the effort of facing forward. *I'm Orpheus,* he thought. But Orpheus had looked back, and Stephan Strakhov didn't. Not once. He knew that, if he took one glance back, his conscience would be blinded by the radiant embodiment of his joy and happiness. He would tap on the glass and order the carriage to return to Marya.

He was stronger than Orpheus — or was he weaker?

As he moved further and further from the hotel, the clipping hoofs and the hush of rubberized wheels were repeating *Goodbye, auf wiedersehen, adieu, dasvidan'ye . . . via con dios . . .*

Farewell . . .

Marya wept the afternoon away.

Not until the dinner-gong chimed did her wrenching sobs subside, but tears continued trickling down the sides of her face. Her throat was raw, her ribs ached. The thought of food made her retch. And, indeed, while the maid turned down the bed, Marya retreated to the bathroom, throwing up what little breakfast remained in her stomach.

A part of her had gone with Stephan, and

the loss would never heal. It was more than an amputation. Her emotional ties to him were in the marrow of her bones, and would remain there even when she was an old, old woman and her skeleton had shrunk and turned brittle.

At the moment, the pain overwhelmed her. Fully dressed, she lay on the bed yearning for nepenthe. Finally accepting that sleep and its oblivion wouldn't come, she decided to get some air. Smoothing her rumpled white cotton frock, running her fingers over her hair, she went downstairs. It was after three, and the brightly lit public rooms were deserted. She found a rear door that was open.

Without thinking, she followed the same route through the dark grounds that she'd taken with Stephan. She saw nobody until the path converged with three others at a fountain.

A male figure stood smoking with one foot on the rim of the fountain. Though his back was to her, it was unmistakably Paskevich.

She halted, hoping that he wouldn't turn or, if he did, that he wouldn't spot anyone in this dark curve of the path.

But he sensed her presence. Coming towards her, he said: 'I didn't expect to find another insomniac tonight.'

'I'll give up the rooms tomorrow.' Her voice rasped from the weeping, and she coughed. 'Today.'

'Didn't Strakhov feel like a pre-dawn stroll?'

'He's not here.'

'Oh?'

'There was an urgent telegram that I needed to answer right away.' She coughed again, feeling the movement in her sore ribcage. 'He went on ahead; he was worried about missing the train.'

'Swiss trains are notoriously punctual.' He dropped his cigarette, stubbing it out with a gleaming toe. His small narrow ankle-boots appeared handmade, and she wondered apathetically whether the Swiss cobbler, like Paskevich's other tradespeople, had worked all night to speed delivery and thus accommodate his demanding customer. 'Did you arrive at the station too late?' he asked.

'I never went.' To her surprise she went on to voice what had been crowding her mind all afternoon and evening. 'He didn't want me.'

'He *told* you that?'

'No.' She sighed. 'But I realized that was what he wanted . . .'

'Now will the scales fall from my eyes,' he said.

'It's the same as the jewels in Kremenchug. He gives everything he has and everything he is. He has no pettiness, he acts for the highest goals.' Opening her unhappiness to Paskevich, of all people, might be self-flagellating but it was cathartic. 'I'd hold him back. I'm not in the least altruistic.'

'My dear, stop putting yourself down. Saints are saints because they can't abide the everyday rubbing and grating of human relationships.'

'He's not a saint. He's an eagle; he soars by himself.'

After a moment, Paskevich asked: 'What about that telegram? Who sent it?'

'Boris. I'd wired him, and he answered — he's still at the Waldorf. The cable said "we".'

'We?' Paskevich tilted his head. 'Unless our feckless boy's taken to using the royal plural, he's found a wife.'

'I thought the same thing.'

'Shall we cable and find out?'

'The office is closed.'

'We'll rouse the teletypist, then.'

She hadn't intended to go anywhere with him. During the long tear-swept hours since the carriage had pulled through the pillared gateposts, she had heaped blame for her misery on Paskevich. He had known exactly what he was doing when he'd signed over the Romanov account to Stephan.

Noting her hesitation, Paskevich crooked his arm.

He was like the fountain statue, a figure in the landscape. He had always been there. Long before she was born, he with his incalculable wealth, his power, his wit and intelligence, his ancient name, had beglamoured his kinsman, that poor inept exile, Fedor Alexiev. And, because of this, her childhood was indelibly imprinted by Ivan the Terrible. He had swept her, Boris and Aunt Chatty to opulence in a decadent empire where he had cosseted her, abused her, maybe fathered her child. He had wreaked a terrible vengeance on her infidelity, then made her his countess . . .

And now, although his wealth was minimal and his worldly power diminished, his title anathema in his own land, he retained the paradoxical blend of personality and character that made him an irresistible force.

She took his arm.

'My dear,' he said, briefly resting his free hand on hers.

The implications of possession shivered through her. Yet, for the first time since the carriage with the hotel's emblem had pulled away, she drew a breath that didn't hurt. As a breeze rustled through the pruned shrubs and trees, they walked side-by-side towards the flaring gasoliers that lit the hotel terrace.

Epilogue

A problem in the translation of one of my novels took me to Russia in 1995. I was kept busy at the publisher's office on the Nevsky Prospekt. Petrograd/Leningrad was once again St Petersburg and, as my grandmother had said, a most beautiful city. By now, though, I was middle-aged and cynical enough to doubt everything else she'd told me. Russian émigrés have a rich tradition of spinning myths, legends and outright fibs about past glories. All I could swear to is that Grandmother, like me, was born and raised in San Francisco, had lived ten years in Russia, emerging in 1918 with her husband, my Paskevich grandfather, who with a smallish Swiss nest-egg promptly amassed a considerable fortune in war surplus — he had the Midas touch. My father, born a year after their flight from Russia, was their only child. She was widowed at fifty: moneyed, lively and still pretty, she attracted a great many suitors. She never remarried.

On my final afternoon in St Petersburg, the translator liberated me.

I took a guided tour of the city. The sun shone with impartial warmth on Stalin-architecture apartment-blocks and tsarist palaces: while others on the bus clicked their cameras, I attempted to relate the location to Grandmother's stories. I sat bolt upright when we halted in front of the Museum of the People's Heritage. The immense eighteenth-century building facing the Neva had recently been painted wine-red, and there was a triangular pediment whose marble was so leprous with battle scars that the subject-matter remained a mystery.

'Catherine the Great built this palace to reward the loyalty of her able adviser Count Grigori Paskevich,' our guide called out. 'This way, please.'

I was right on her heels as we trooped up the branched staircase. She led us into an opulently furnished room.

'And this', she announced shrilly, 'is an exact replica of the last Count Paskevich's study. It was damaged by German artillery-fire in the Great Patriotic War but has been perfectly restored.'

The study bore no resemblance to what had been described to me. This furniture was all brocade and spindly gold; not a comfortable chair in sight. The one small étagère held books.

'I'd heard that the count kept his miniature collection in here,' I ventured.

The guide, like guides all over the world, bristled at this intrusion into her territory. 'Every piece is precisely as it was,' she snapped. 'Highly authentic. We have photographs. This way, please.'

As the others trooped out, I lingered. Why should I — a novelist after all — be disappointed that my grandmother had beguiled me with fiction? Was it a criminal offence to fabricate a deathless love-affair with a man younger and more handsome than her husband? I wandered over to the bookcase. I can't read Cyrillic script; however, it was immediately apparent to me that a fair number of the volumes were new. A very young man had joined me, and I pointed out the anachronism in my rudimentary Russian.

After ascertaining that I was an American tourist, he replied in excellent English: 'A nice collection, though. Very representative of that period. Let's see. Tolstoy, Chekhov, Bunin, Gorky, Mayakovsky — are they familiar in the States?'

'Tolstoy's considered a genius, the greatest of novelists. Chekhov's read and performed. So's Gorky, but only on college campuses. The others . . .' I shrugged helplessly. 'I've heard their names, that's all.'

'Ah.' He turned to me, his eyes glowing. 'See this one here? It's by the finest poet of the twentieth century. What a life he led! A Revolutionary exiled by the tsar, fought with the Whites then spent years in a Siberian Gulag. Someone with a sense of humour must have put the book in here, though. The rumour is that he was the countess's lover — you'll be interested to know that she was from your San Francisco.'

My knees felt wobbly. 'You're talking about Stephan Strakhov?'

'Strakhov's known in America? I'd always believed the exquisite music of his language was untranslatable.'

'Is that *Days of Freedom?*'

The young man looked even more impressed. 'Yes, Strakhov's only novel.' He declaimed in Russian too histrionically for me to follow.

I didn't rejoin the group. Instead I invited my new friend back to the Europa Hotel, where we had a marvellous lunch — a meal he admitted would cost him six months' salary. That afternoon I stayed in my room remembering, wondering, pondering about my grandmother's life. When I returned to the lobby, there was a package for me. A tattered book without binding. The note said: 'I am taking the liberty of repaying your hospitality with Strakhov's most enduring work.'

The tour bus was pulling up. I showed my gift to the guide. 'Oh, that's not an original,' she sniffed. 'Strakhov's writing wasn't published at all in the Stalinist era, and his books were confiscated. But we Russians do esteem artistic excellence, so people gathered to recite his works from memory. His later poetry was all printed illegally. Imagine, there were people who risked jail and worse to print his words. What you've got there is just another of those pirate editions of the *Marya Cycle*.'

'The *Marya Cycle?*' I repeated.

'Young people are forever quoting from it, but as far as I'm concerned the poems are excessively romantic.'

Early the following morning, before the airport bus came, I returned to the Crimson Palace. When the guard strolled out of sight, I slid my gift in the étagère among the other undying works of Russian literature. Doubtless I'm excessively romantic, too, but I'm positive it's where Stephan and my grandmother both would have wanted the *Marya Cycle* to be.

St Petersburg 1995

We hope you have enjoyed this Large Print book. Other G.K. Hall & Co. or Chivers Press Large Print books are available at your library or directly from the publishers.

For more information about current and upcoming titles, please call or write, without obligation, to:

G.K. Hall & Co.
P.O. Box 159
Thorndike, Maine 04986
USA
Tel. (800) 223-2336

OR

Chivers Press Limited
Windsor Bridge Road
Bath BA2 3AX
England
Tel. (0225) 335336

All our Large Print titles are designed for easy reading, and all our books are made to last.